Praise for

'Evocative, compelling and p[...]
suspense, riveting action and a plot as tricksy as a dare-devil
free-climb' – **Philippa East, author of CWA Dagger-
shortlisted *Little White Lies***

'A high octane, no holds barred thriller. I couldn't turn the
pages fast enough!' – **Barbara Copperthwaite, bestselling
author of *The Darkest Lies***

'With complex characters battling their demons in the
bleakest circumstances, *On The Edge* brings the dark side
of Cornwall to life in this atmospheric thriller. A true page
turner with unexpected twists' – **Sophie Flynn, author of
*All My Lies***

'*On The Edge* is an outstanding debut. With distinctive
characters, an intriguing plot and an enticing blend of action
and atmosphere, it is a truly gripping read' – **Sarah Clarke,
author of *A Mother Never Lies***

'Jenifry Shaw is smart, impulsive, bull-headed, and too daring
for her own good. She might be a bit of a mess, but she never,
ever backs down from a fight. In short, she's the girl you want
at your side when stuff hits the fan and a fantastic character
to anchor a new mystery series' – **Heather Young, author of
The Lost Girls and *The Distant Dead***

'An exceptional debut. Skilfully written, tightly plotted and
compulsive reading. Highly recommended' – **Maddie Please,
author of *The Summer of Second Chances* and
*The Year of New Adventures***

On The Edge

...pulse pounding, with cliff-edge

ON THE EDGE

JANE JESMOND

VERVE BOOKS

First published in 2021 by Verve Books,
an imprint of The Crime and Mystery Club Ltd.
Harpenden, UK

vervebooks.co.uk
@verve_books

ISBN
978-0-85730-816-0 (Paperback)
978-0-85730-817-7 (Ebook)

2 4 6 8 10 9 7 5 3 1

Typeset in 11.4 on 15pt Garamond MT Pro
by Avocet Typeset, Bideford, Devon, EX39 2BP
Printed and bound in Great Britain by
Clays Ltd, Elcograf S.p.A.

For my darling dad, Alastair Shufflebotham

PROLOGUE

A long the road from my family home in Cornwall, the lighthouse at St Matthew's Point dominates the landscape. As a child I used to lie in bed and watch its great beam sweep the night in unending, unhurried circles and feel safe. During the day, it seems asleep. In winter, it is a solitary brooding tower; even in summer, its peace appears untouched by the tourists who cluster round its windswept base or pay a pound to climb the 163 steps to the viewing platform and stare out over the sea. Most of the time, I remember it as the visitors see it, stately and still, gleaming white against blue skies and the grey-green of the wind-whipped grass.

Yet sometimes, even now, dreams of the lighthouse as it was on that Friday night, my first night back in Cornwall for months, disturb my sleep. The dream is always the same. A storm of wind and rain batters the coast. The tapering white form of the lighthouse appears in the distance, stark and motionless against the turbulent backdrop of dark clouds and darker seas tearing shreds out of each other. Its shaft of light shoots out into the night and circles, steady and constant, despite the blasts of the gale.

In my dream the lighthouse comes closer and closer as though a wave of rushing wind carries me towards it. A blotch appears, dark against the white walls. At first it's a shadow that dances from side to side as the beam passes overhead; then it becomes a figure. A person, dangling off the viewing platform that encircles the top of the lighthouse beneath the lantern. Clad in dark clothes that gleam with wetness, a thin rope looped in a figure of eight under its arms and over one of the stone blocks that give the lighthouse the look of a medieval castle. The wind dashes the figure against the wall and shakes the stream of water that falls like a cord from its bare feet.

Closer still and a face with tight-shut eyes appears. A young woman. The skin of her eyelids and around her mouth twitches and trembles. She is lost in some fantasy sparked to life by the drugs crackling through her veins while all the time the rope thins and frays. And even in my dream, I know I must wake her before it's too late, before the rope breaks and she falls to the ground.

Except I can't. Because this is a dream and the young woman is Jenifry Shaw. She's me. The figure hanging from the lighthouse is me.

One

Another night in rehab. A Thursday night and my eight week anniversary. It was much like all the other nights – sleepless and long. I'd done fifty-six days of rehab. Fifty-six days of talking, talking, talking. Of sitting in meetings: group therapy, yoga classes, 'Preparing to Change' sessions, counselling. Meetings meant people, and I'd never liked being around too many of them. At least not without drugs making everything blur. Eight weeks of breathing stale air passed through the lungs of too many people. It was long enough. Surely it was. I wanted to get out.

I was free to leave at any moment. All voluntary patients were. And I'd gone into this willingly, scared witless by what I'd become and trying to recompense by shelling out vast sums of money for help.

I paced around my room, my hands tying knots in a length of string I'd found in the bottom of one of the drawers: bowline, double figure 8, clove hitch and so on, over and over again. I couldn't sleep. The room was too small. Too hot. It smelt of disinfectant overlaying vomit and the window lock prevented it from opening more than a couple of inches. Someone cried out. Not for the first time. The night was often punctuated by people howling for the things they desired. Hidden longings set free by the dark. I made a snap decision. It was time to go. I packed my bag and went downstairs, told the duty staff I was leaving. Told them I was fine. Told them I'd recovered.

They wanted a chance to discuss it with me first and wore me down with smooth torrents of words asking me to wait for the morning until I gave in and trailed back to my room, painted yellow to look cheerful and with random framed prints of birds pinned to the walls. It still felt like a cell.

Which was what I deserved, after all.

I rested my head on the windowsill and stared up at the night sky, feeling the narrow shaft of air cool my skin. And I thought. I thought about the drugs. I thought I was over them. I was sure I was over them. Somewhere in among the endless talk about addictive behaviour and triggers, I'd grasped enough to understand they were only a substitute for something I couldn't have.

And that was climbing.

Free climbing. The clue's in the name. Free climbers rope up to save ourselves if we fall. We don't use the rope to climb. We use nothing but our bodies to get up the face. Nothing but us and the rock. Sometimes working in harmony. Sometimes fighting each other.

That was all over, though. I'd never climb again. I'd promised my brother Kit and I kept the promise. But I hadn't promised to stop thinking about it.

I shut my eyes and remembered the smell of the rock in the Verdon Gorge. It changed during the day. In the morning it was sour and damp but by midday the sun had warmed it to a harsh grittiness overlaid with sharp spikes of lavender and thyme. The climb was called Luna Bong. We got there early, before the sun dried the rock. Fingers slip on damp edges so we waited for the heat and while we waited I stared up, scouring the rock for holds and feeling the movements in my body. Grid, my ex-boyfriend, loved that climb and we must have done it twenty times, so it's imprinted on me. Muscle memory.

In the cell-like room, I shut out everything else and turned my attention to the cliff. Let myself feel the heat bouncing off the rock and hear the cicadas rattling in the scrub. It soothed me. And as my body remembered itself moving up the rock face, I finally fell asleep.

In the morning, still desperate to escape, I thought of grabbing my bags and running. I knew I was fine. But the staff would never believe me. The words to bridge the gulf between us didn't exist. Feeling restless and tense, I waited to see my counsellor, watching a line of other patients shuffle into a morning meditation class, and checked my phone. And saw the mail from Kit. It wasn't recent. They take your phone away in rehab. It's voluntary, of course, but everybody hands it over. And, actually they're right. It is a distraction. They give it back to you from time to time to check for anything urgent, though. I went to delete the mail like I'd deleted all Kit's texts recently, but a stray memory from our childhood caught my thoughts and stopped me. It had been a meditation class, too. Something Ma thought would be good for us to do, like collecting herbs by moonlight or dying T-shirts with crushed flowers.

We'd spent the first session sitting cross-legged in the crowded front room of a friend's cottage. Thin carpets covered the stone flags but their chill rose through and numbed my bottom as we concentrated on the breath slipping in and out through our nostrils. It wasn't difficult, if a little dull. We then moved on to observing the sensations in different parts of our body. Observing only.

I observed my toes, cramped at the end of trainers that were too small. The whisper of cold air passing over a graze on my wrist.

And the muscles in my legs, twitching up and down the length of them, unable to be still for so long.

I couldn't help it, I had to obey my legs. So I leapt up and ran out of the room, out of the back door, past a woman stirring something that smelled fragrant and strange, into the garden and over the stone wall at the end, barking my knee on the top. Not that I cared. It was a small price to pay for the bouncy grass of the moor and the prickle of heather against my shins and the feeling of air in my face.

Kit ran after me and we lay on the ground and laughed together. And I knew he understood.

Ma didn't take us again.

I opened Kit's mail.

Dear Jen, it started. Nothing peculiar in that, except I didn't think Kit had ever been so formal. When we worked together, the mails had been cursory. *Plan attached, please review.* That kind of thing. Otherwise it was always, *Hi.* So the *Dear Jen* worried me. The rest of the message showed how right my feeling was.

Dear Jen

I've tried to call but I never get you. You don't answer your mobile and the office say you're not there. I hope you're not avoiding me.

Sofija says you haven't been in touch with her either.

Will you come down and see us? Please, Jen. Something's come up. We need your help. We really need your help. We'd like to see you anyway. It'll be easier to explain face to face, so don't ring up and demand to know what's going on. Text me when you're coming.

Kit

No mention of the row we'd had seven months ago. No mention of the promise he bludgeoned out of me. Although 'promise'

12

is a weak word for what Kit forced me to give, out of my mind with guilt after Grid's accident and battered by all Kit's fury and accusations that had the nasty sting of truth. I'd sworn I'd never climb again, then screamed at him to fuck right out of my life. And I hadn't seen or spoken to him since. Or Sofija. Or Ma.

No contact until now. But he was my brother and he needed me. He had a problem and he thought I could solve it. It was the perfect excuse to leave. And anyway, after weeks of gritting my teeth and gratefully nodding at the carefully chosen words of the counsellors helping me, it felt wonderful to be the rescuer. Plus, Kit was in Cornwall and Cornwall was full of air, great gusts of it blown in from the sea, scouring the land and imbuing it with a salty tang.

I left rehab, feeling like an escaped prisoner. *Family crisis*, I told them. *Got to go*, I said firmly. And, with less conviction in my voice, *I'll come back and finish*. They weren't keen for me to leave. They didn't think I was ready. They thought I was still 'in denial'. I was sure they were wrong.

It felt good to be out. It felt good to be driving. To be on the move. To be doing something again. And to be alone. My car, my lovely red Aston, ate up the miles even though I stuck to the speed limit. Most of the time anyway – there were moments when the motorway was clear and a song I loved came on the radio and then I sped up and sang along.

My mood wasn't quite so upbeat after Exeter as the signs for Cornwall started flashing by. I wondered what Kit's problem might be and the thought of what could be waiting for me was as depressing as the deepening grey of the clouds brooding overhead. As I crossed the Tamar, the heavy sky lowered and squeezed the colour out of the rolling hills and farmland that lined the road

13

and instead of lifting my heart, Cornwall, moody creature that she was, showed me her sullen and bitter face. My doubts grew. My driving slowed. Was this yet another of the impulsive escapades that littered my past? The closer I got to Craighston village and Tregonna, my old family home, the twitchier I became.

I pulled off at a service station in the end and called Kit. No answer. No answer from Sofija, his wife, either. I thought of calling the Tregonna landline but Ma might answer. I was sure Kit's problem was to do with her so probably best to avoid speaking to her for the moment. She had an uncanny way of getting me to commit to things I didn't want to.

Staying at the hotel was a spur of the moment idea. I got to Craighston and hesitated. Tregonna was only a mile or two away, up the steep road that led out of the other side of the village and past the lighthouse at the top, but I couldn't face my family yet. Couldn't face the explanations of why I'd been away so long. Couldn't deal with the aftermath of Kit's fury in the carpark. Besides, none of them knew I was on my way so they weren't expecting me. I made a quick decision and pulled into the car park round the back of The Seagull, as it was now called. In my day it had been The Smuggler's Arms, then The Craighston Inn and, for a few short seasons, The Piskie's Revenge. It was Craighston's only hotel, slap bang in the middle of the village, owned by a series of incomers who arrived full of dreams and left worn out a few seasons later.

Reception, drab in the damp weather and needing the chatter of families on holiday to bring it to life, was empty. Voices came from a room behind the desk and when I pinged the bell, a sour-faced woman with iron-grey curls stuck her head round the door and looked at me accusingly.

'Are you open?' I asked.

'Yes.'

'Could I have a room? Just for the night.'

She sighed but she came out. 'Of course.' She was about as welcoming as the weather.

'Your name?'

'Jen Shaw.'

She didn't react. My name meant nothing to her. She tapped it into the computer, asked me for my card and gave me a key – the old-fashioned kind attached to a brass rectangle with the number punched into it. Heavy enough to stop guests taking it with them by mistake. She pointed down a corridor whose uncarpeted floor showed a few splotches of fresh paint then thought better of it.

'I'll take you to your room. They've finished decorating but I'm not sure if they've put the room numbers back on the doors.'

I trailed after her, wondering why anyone would have chosen to use that particular shade of yellowish beige paint and hoping its smell hadn't penetrated my room. When she pushed the door open and I walked in, I realised it hadn't. Or maybe it was smothered by the overwhelmingly musty odour. I pulled back the curtains, flung the window open and found myself staring out into the car park. Fab. The rooms on the second floor had a view over the rooftops of the squat buildings around the hotel, all huddled together against the winds that regularly tore in from the sea despite Craighston nestling in a little creek. From up there you could see the sea and the cliff path rising through the village and, if you stuck your head out, the tall white figure of the lighthouse on the point, an exclamation mark against the wild skies. I thought of asking if I could change rooms but this one looked clean, if a little too full of Cornish knick-knacks for my taste – china piskies and fishing boats and the obligatory framed picture of smugglers hauling barrels off a boat in a small cove. Besides, it was only for one night.

'No kettle?' I asked.

'The electrics can't cope if everyone turns them on at once,' she said shortly.

I thought about asking how many people were currently staying here but decided it wasn't worth it. She must have seen the irritation pass across my face.

'I've got a spare one in the flat. I'll bring it down later,' she said. 'Sorry, we're a bit at sixes and sevens with the redecoration. I'm Vivian Waring. Reception isn't manned off-season but you can call me on my mobile if you need anything.'

'I might go out for a bit of fresh air,' I said. Anything to escape the damp smell and unlock the knots of tension in my neck.

'Well, be careful. There's a storm on the way and it will be dark in an hour or so.' She handed me a card. 'Key code,' she said. 'For the front door.' And with that she turned and left me. I glanced at it. 2468. Very original.

Craighston out of season. About as cheerful as my mood. I chucked my bag on the bed and sat down. For the first time in a long while I had nothing to do, nowhere to go, no one to see, no meetings to sit through. It should have been a moment of peace. Instead all the old longings crawled into the emptiness and scratched their way into my blood.

And then… my memory dissolved into shreds and tatters: the tufts of the bedcover under my fingers… my hand closing a drawer… the raucous screams of seagulls wheeling overhead… then rain… nothing but rain.

Then… nothing. The stream of my consciousness stopped. Dead. As if a surgeon had sliced the memories out of my mind leaving nothing but a few flickering images and echoes behind.

Two

A nd then... something.
I woke.

Through the spiralling confusion in my brain, I knew I was awake. Everything was sharp and clear and real.

Not a dream.

But unbelievable. An undecipherable maelstrom of sound and motion and sensation. Brightness above me jerked my head back and turned the water falling over my eyes into glittering beads.

Rain.

I was outside.

And noise.

A confusion of wind, crashing waves and rain drumming a hard surface.

A storm.

Then pain, as a blast of wind hurled me against a white wall. The shock knocked the breath out of me and blew the mists of unconsciousness away.

Where am I?

A wall in front of me; white and smooth. But not in a climbing gym. There were no grips and no route markers.

The wind battered me again. Spun me round. Giddying my brain.

I need to get out of here.

I forced my thoughts to grip onto the here and now, and looked up. The wall ended against the dark sky. Then the blinding beam of light stabbed through the dark again and passed over my head. And disappeared.

I know what this is.

And I knew where I was. On the lighthouse along the coast from Tregonna. St Matthew's lighthouse. Hanging from the viewing platform that jutted out below the lantern room, my knees against its bottom edge and my feet threshing the wild but empty air.

How…?

My brain screamed.

No time to panic.

I looked down. Through my feet, the concrete circle at the base of the lighthouse lay on the wind-lashed grass of the headland. I'd seen it so many times before from the safety of the viewing platform, leaning over its wall and staring down at the same grey circle, resting like a raft on waves of grass. A tiny raft far below, waiting to smash my body when I fell.

Not falling. You're not falling.

Something held me up. Something under my arms dug pain into my flesh. I lifted my hand to touch it. A rope.

The beam circled overhead again and a glimmer echoed off the clouds onto the white wall. The rope was sash cord. Very old sash cord, hairy with loose strands that had broken or worn through.

The rope gave. A matter of millimetres. Even less. But I felt the drop in my bones.

My eyes scanned the wall above. The top of the parapet gleamed briefly as the beam passed overhead again. Not far to climb. But the surface was smooth. Super-smooth. No holds. No edges. No cracks. Nothing. I've climbed cliffs you'd think were impossible. Flat sheets of granite, smooth to the eye as butter sliced by a hot

18

knife. Nature loves imperfection, though and there's always a ridge or an edge in the rock your fingers and feet can use to swarm up the face. Even if you can't see it, you can feel it. But the lighthouse was man-made, its surface grainy, gravelly, slippery in the wet.

The rope dropped again. A micro millimetre. A whisper of a movement but enough to tingle the sweat pores in my palms and sharpen my breathing, as if a hundred blades cut through my body and sliced through the confusion. Sliced through it and let it fall away. I felt alive, like I only ever do when I'm climbing. Even coke can't compare to it. I laughed. Fuck the rain. Fuck the cold. It was just me and the wall.

I ran my hands over the surface: up, down, side to side, seeking a fault or a crack I could widen.

Slow. Too slow.

As if my hands and brain were disconnected. I forced them to keep moving. All I needed was a hole big enough to jam a fingertip in. Inch by inch, my fingers searched, over and over again, but there was nothing.

Except the rope.

Use the rope.

It slipped again.

The moment when the rope would snap hurtled towards me and fear fired my sluggish neurones. I grabbed the rope and pulled myself up the lighthouse. Hand over hand, inch by inch, until my feet hit the bottom of the viewing platform and I flattened them against its side and pushed. Thrust out and up, forcing the grit into the flesh of my soles and toes. Dragged my body up the parapet, hauling on the rope's fraying strands. Suddenly the rope came alive, twitching as its strands snapped and unravelled.

Shit.

I hurled an arm over the top of the parapet, gave a last kick, heaved myself up and over and tumbled onto the rough, wooden floor of the viewing balcony.

Adrenalin shook my limbs as I rolled onto my back. The sky was stormy black. *There should be stars*, I thought. *There should be fireworks. There should be great, roaring bursts of rockets to celebrate this moment.* Only the lighthouse beam travelled across the sky in its majestic orbit. I counted the length of its circuits as my breathing calmed. And then there was nothing but a slow fall into blackness as my consciousness drained away once more.

I woke again to cold and pain. My head and nose hurt along with the flesh under my arms and round my back where the cord had bitten. I made myself move to the doorway round the far side of the viewing platform, where the tower gave me some protection from the wind coming off the sea, wrapped myself in a tarpaulin that was lying there and tried to think as rivulets of rain gathered in its cracks and creases and ran in streams onto the wooden floor.

I huddled in the doorway for a while waiting for something to make sense. It could have been a few minutes. It could have been a lot longer. Time became elastic so some minutes stuck to me and held on for an age and when they let go the minutes waiting behind them shot past in a blur. And when I finally thought to try the door handle, it opened and I tumbled inside.

The quiet of the musty interior, out of reach of the storm, calmed my shaky brain. I brushed the worst of the water off my face, noticing my hand did what I wanted without hesitating. The strange disconnect between body and brain was passing.

Shit. Drugs. It must be. What have I taken? How the fuck did I get here?

The last thing I remembered clearly was the hotel room. How had I ended up two miles along the coast, hanging off the lighthouse? God knows I'd come to in some strange places before. Crept out of strangers' houses as the first lightening of dawn dimmed the street lamps; been woken by cleaning ladies hammering on the door of the toilet cubicle in whichever bar we'd ended up in the night before. Come to, leaning against the closed grille of the tube station and, once, propped in someone's doorway with a faint memory of an angry taxi driver. The memories were always vague. And lost in the glittering blur of bars and drinks and mirrors dusted with the last few grains no one had yet taken. Saving them for a last gum smear before heading out into the night. But I always had some memory of how I'd ended up where I was. Nothing like this utter blankness.

Pain in my hands dragged me back to the here and now, where I crouched in the dim and quiet of the lighthouse stairs. I'd dug my fingers into the crumbling wooden floor and driven splinters into the grazed and battered flesh. Cold seeped into my bones. I'd think about all this later. Now I needed to get back to the hotel.

I felt for my phone with some idea of calling a friend or a cab but I didn't have it with me. Had I left it in the hotel, charging up on the bedside table? Not that it mattered. I was in Cornwall, not London. And in an area that was quieter than quiet. I looked at my watch. It was a few minutes before one o'clock. No chance. If you wanted a taxi here, you booked it the day before. As for friends, they'd all left Cornwall. At least the ones you could call at one in the morning when you needed help. Which left my family: Kit, Sofija and, I supposed, Ma – and even if I'd had a phone I wouldn't call them. Two years ago, I'd have called Kit straightaway. A few months ago, I might still have called him. But not now. No way.

Tregonna was closer than the hotel but I couldn't let Kit see me wrecked like this. He'd be furious and I couldn't bear that. I just couldn't bear any more of that. I'd get back to the hotel by myself.

I stood up and started down the steps. The door at the bottom of the lighthouse was open, swinging and banging in the storm. I went out and onto the coast road.

Three

It's a a mile or so from the lighthouse back to Craighston village. Fifteen or twenty minutes tops. Unless you have bare, sore feet and torrents of rain drumming on your head. I almost gave up on the tarpaulin, not sure if the barricade it gave me against the rain was worth the struggle to hold it tight against the wind. It might be easier to dump it and walk free. But then the rain would beat against my head again. Its noise was already starting to eat away at my brain and cut my thoughts into pieces.

Keep walking. Get to the hotel. Keep walking.

Ahead, the road ran past one of the great lumps of granite that litter this part of the coast. The lighthouse beam lit up the clouds behind it and, for a moment, the rock's outline was sharp and harsh.

The beam circled away and the rock became less distinct. More of a dark hole looming over the road than a thing of any substance. Its shape shifted slowly. A trick of the night, I thought. But the closer I got, the more the granite became a living thing, a great bear maybe, moving its weight from leg to leg as it readied to rear up and snatch me with a great clawed paw. My feet slowed and my heart thumped. I forced myself on. It was only a rock. There were no bears in Cornwall.

Keep walking. One foot in front of the other.

It was a drug dream. A phantasm called into life by the cells in

23

my brain flailing in paranoia as the chemicals ebbed to nothing. But knowing that didn't help. The bear waited for me. Any minute now, it would lean forward and amble towards me. I'd smell its damp fur and the faint rust of blood and my skin would feel the heat of its body before it lashed and raked me with its claws.

A light came from behind me and lengthened my shadow out onto the road. It lit the cracked and folded surface of the rock and chased the vision of the bear away. A wave of spray washed over my legs and feet as a car sped by. The shock of it made me stumble and fall onto the scrubby grass at the side of the road. I'd heard nothing. The rain on the tarpaulin and the battering of the wind blocked out everything else. When I struggled back up, the car had stopped a few yards ahead. Its driver must have seen me. It reversed and something about its slow creep unnerved me. Fear, hot and raw, poured acid through my veins, blanking out everything but the glistening car rolling noiselessly back towards me.

My hands met a thick branch in the short grass, enmeshed in strands of bramble. I ripped the spiky tendrils away, not caring that the thorns tore my fingers. I gripped the stick and waited.

The car stopped on the opposite side of the road from where I stood. It was a bit battered. Lines of rust curled along its dents. A river of shiny tarmac separated us. Rain ran down the windows and obscured the figure inside. A dark grey blob of a face turned to stare at me and the window rolled down. The stick dug into my palm. A man. I waited for him to put his head out of the window. The stick waited. He said something but it was lost in the storm.

A little rational thought sneaked into my brain. *A Good Samaritan*, it said. *He wants to help.* The man leaned back into the driver's seat and the dashboard light of the car caught his face. It was not the face of a Good Samaritan. His eyebrows hooded his eyes, making black holes. His face was a mask. I willed him to leave but he leaned out of the window.

'Go away,' I screamed. 'Leave me alone.'

His voice carried through the storm. 'You need a lift.'

It was not a question but I shook my head.

'You need a lift,' he said again and opened the door. 'Where are you going to? There's not much nearby.' Fear pressed my hands tighter round the stick and lifted it a couple of inches. 'Let me give you a lift. You're wet through. You can't stay out in this storm.'

I stepped back and pushed one hand towards him with the palm flat, like a policeman directing traffic. He hesitated and I grabbed at the last shreds of control, holding the fear tight inside me as I turned and staggered away onto the path.

The car started up. I heard it through the drum of the rain because every cell in my ears was straining backwards. The urge to whirl round and smash the car whipped my blood to a froth but I held on to myself. Drugs, it was the drugs doing this to me. I was sure. And I stumbled towards the great rock, reached it then ran behind a low boulder split off from the main bulk.

I looked back. The car hadn't moved. I lifted my hands to shade my eyes against the glare of the headlights; he turned them off. I could see him now, leaning forward and staring at me through the back and forth of the wipers. We stayed like that for an age. Gazing at each other, until the lighthouse beam went overhead once more and dragged my eyes upwards. When I looked back he was getting out of the car. Its inside light shone briefly and my eyes took a snapshot. He was the wrong shape for a climber. Too square. But powerful in a contained sort of way. A good man to have at the belaying end of the rope.

He unfurled an umbrella. Gaudy, striped, promoting some sporting event, it looked all wrong in the battering wind and rain of the storm but its incongruity calmed me. The noise of the blood whacking against my ears lessened.

'I can't leave you here like this,' he shouted. The rain was slowing and lightening. It would stop soon and all of a sudden, like a baby's tears. He took a step towards me and I slipped sideways and further round the rock. 'I won't hurt you.' He sounded pissed off. Monumentally pissed off. He muttered something I didn't catch. 'I'm Nick,' he called. 'Nick Crawford. I live up beyond the fields.' He jerked the umbrella inland to where a smaller road ran high up but parallel to the coast road, linking a straggle of cottages and small farms.

'Go away.' I tried to shout but my words had no force and I wondered if he'd even heard them.

He did nothing for a moment and then went to the boot of the car. I thought about disappearing into the night but the path to the village was right by the road at this point and the cliffs fell sharply away on the other side. No hope of escaping once I left the rock. He came back round and I saw he'd put on a creased yellow oilskin.

'Can you drive?'

The words took a while to make sense. I nodded.

'Take the car then. I can walk from here.'

He gestured to the door and half-bowed like the doorman of a fancy hotel showing me the way. The rain stopped. He put out a hand from under the umbrella and laughed.

'It'll be a lovely night now, you'll see. It's always like this. One minute rain, the next clear, the next… well, you never know. Look, the car's running. Get in it and go…' He closed the umbrella and shook it. 'Where are you going to?'

I found my voice. 'The hotel in Craighston. The Seagull.'

'OK I'll call round tomorrow morning and pick it up. You can

26

leave the keys at reception if you don't want to see me.' He laughed and I found myself wanting to laugh with him. He was as crazy as I was.

He started to walk away, then turned. 'What's your name? It would help to know.'

'Jen Shaw.'

'Jen Shaw. Short and sweet. Goodnight, Jen Shaw. Safe journey home.'

He walked away and I fixed my eyes on his back, watching in case he made a sudden turn and raced back, but, as the distance between us grew, he became less and less distinct until all I could make out were the luminous strips on his jacket bobbing up and down like two demented caterpillars dancing against the black.

Nick Crawford. Not a name I knew. Not a local name. And he didn't look or sound local. He must be an incomer. A recent one. I would have remembered if I'd met him before.

The sky was clearing. Only a few wisps of cloud remained and they were scudding inland, fleeing the wind coming off the sea. The dampness on my face was drying and I tasted the salt of the wind on my lips. It was chilly. The great beam of light passed overhead once again and ignited cold sparks in the sky. I shivered. No sign of Nick Crawford. He must have turned off the road to climb up to his house.

With the passing of the rain a kind of peace settled in my brain.

I peered into the car. The seats were battered and the interior grey with age but it was clean. And probably warm. The thought of heat drove everything else out of my mind and I opened the door and got in.

I turned the heating to full and locked all the doors. The glorious warmth drove the chill from my body in violent shakes. I didn't care. They would pass. My feet hurt as the feeling came back

27

but not enough to stop waves of drowsiness engulfing me. It was awesome. Like swimming in hot soup. My thoughts left my body and went wherever they go when I sleep, and I passed out.

I don't know how long I was out for. Long enough for the steering wheel to make a dent in my face and the dribble from my mouth to crust in a vampire drool. The car stuttered and rumbled again. I opened my eyes and saw a face looking in at me through the windscreen. Shock tingled through my veins and I screamed. The face vanished. I flicked the headlights on full and they caught a figure disappearing round the back of the rock. I thought they had a torch but it was difficult to tell in my half-asleep state. The car was locked. But there could be another key. Probably in Nick Crawford's house. Hanging on a hook by the back door or in a bowl on a shelf in the hall. That was where it would be. Nothing to stop him picking it up and coming back down to the car. Or giving it to the grey figure I'd just seen.

I forced myself to be reasonable. It was probably an insomniac like Ma taking advantage of the break in the weather to get some fresh air. Or someone from the fishing boats heading home and curious as to why a car was parked and running on the headland road. So I focussed on the controls of the car, released the handbrake and, careful of my bruised and grazed feet, drove off. I made it back to the hotel safely, although tremors and stray thoughts snatched at my concentration.

The clock in reception showed half past five and there was no one around. I panicked for a moment in front of the door to my room. I had nothing with me. No coat. No bag. Nothing but the tarp. So no key. The brass door handle slipped and rattled in my shaky hands – then opened. I fumbled the clothes off my body and turned the shower on full, letting the hot water sluice the mud and dried blood off my skin. My head hurt and when I put my hand up to check it, I found a large bump covered by a tangle of blood-matted hair. Another injury to add to the tally of cuts and grazes. I let the water run gently over my head. It flowed pink through my hands, with a few flecks of solid blue. I wondered what they were. Bits of tarpaulin maybe? The wobbles were severe now, as well as the tiredness. I patted myself dry and, for the first time, thought back to the evening before. Or tried to. Tried very hard. But nothing came. And I don't mean the kind of jumble of images those druggy nights often left behind. The grating edges of words and laughter you chase but can't quite grasp. No, this was a total blank. Rien. Nada. Nothing. As if my memory had stepped off a cliff.

One minute I'd been sitting on the bed, the next, the wind and rain were battering me against the lighthouse wall. Panic started to flood my head. The air in my room thinned and my lungs snatched at what was left. An anxiety attack, I told myself. Common when coming down. Breathe slowly. Distract yourself. Watch TV. Make a hot drink. Whatever works for you. None of it worked for me.

So I thought again of the climb up Luna Bong. I'd leave everything else till tomorrow. Maybe then my scrambled brain would have found the missing hours. With the memory of the rock beneath my fingers soothing me, I went to bed and fell asleep as the last few metres of the climb dissolved into the blue sky.

Four

I woke up, lying flat on my back, with my hands clawing the sheets for holds on the slippery walls of the lighthouse. Grey light peered round the edges of the thick curtains. I knew where I was. The hotel. Safe. In bed.

For a moment I thought the lighthouse had been a dream.

I dreamed a lot in rehab. Everybody does. It's a way of escaping. Some dreamed of their childhoods, most dreamed of their drugs, but I dreamed of climbing. So I thought it was another of those dreams until I got out of bed and winced as my grazed and bruised feet hit the floor. Until I went into the bathroom and saw the clothes and the tarpaulin lying in muddy dampness on the floor. Questions raged through my brain. *What had I done? Why had I been at the lighthouse?*

A knock on the door interrupted my whirling thoughts. *Shit.* I shut the bathroom door on the filthy clothes and tarpaulin. The knock again.

It was the woman who'd checked me in last night.

'Ms Shaw?'

Her name came back to me – Vivian – and with it, a tremble of relief. My brain was working better.

'Yes.'

'There's a man in reception, asking for you. A Mr Crawford. Says you've got his car keys?' She raised an enquiring eyebrow.

The second part of the night came back to me. The road. The car. The man. The umbrella. Him leaving me his car. Somehow that seemed even more unreal than the rest of it. He was here for his keys though, so it had happened.

I couldn't find them. They weren't on the bedside table. They weren't among my wet clothes. I hunted among the ornaments cluttering the surfaces. All the time, Vivien stood at the entrance and watched me. With her tightly curled hair, tweed skirt and look of irritated patience, she reminded me of my friends' mothers and it was doubly hard to think while she was there. A glint caught my eye and I saw the keys poking out from the empty teacup and saucer on the little table by the door. When I handed them to her she waited for a moment as though expecting something more.

'Tell him thanks, will you? And…' And what? Dribs and drabs of how I'd behaved to him last night floated into my mind. Shit, I'd been off my head. There was nothing, absolutely nothing I could ask her to say to him that would explain or excuse. 'Just thanks.' I shut the door and sat on the bed.

Time to think about last night. Drugs? It had to be. Nothing else explained it. But how? And why? I needed to think. That's what they'd told me to do. In case of a relapse. They don't like to talk about it. Not when you're a new and shiny recovered addict. But it doesn't take much to work out it happens. I only had to look at the people in rehab with me. Not many first-timers there.

Process the relapse, they'd told me. *Work through it. Identify the motivating factors. And, above all, don't be overcome by guilt and shame.* Guilt and shame – ha!

I was pissed off. Deeply pissed off. With myself? Yes, I guess. *Analyse the feeling, Jen. Stay with it. It's a guide.* Pissed off. Angry, if you like. Super-bloody-angry. Because I thought I had it nailed. Yup. In my heart of hearts all that time at the centre, I had thought I wasn't a proper addict. I thought I could have stopped by myself, without the therapy and the strategies. They were just an insurance policy.

So I was wrong. The creature in my head had only been asleep, waiting for something to poke it awake so it could snake its fine tentacles through me again and grip me tight. One day out of rehab, one bloody day, and I'd relapsed. Because whatever had happened last night, one thing was certain: drugs had been involved.

One big problem, though. I had no idea what had woken the beast. I still couldn't remember a thing between getting to the hotel and waking up on the lighthouse. The big rift in my memories was still there. And without a few hints I couldn't see how to stop it happening again. For the first time I wondered if I might have gone too far and done my brain in for good. My palms sweated and I clenched my fingers into fists. No good for climbing, but good for fighting. And fighting was what I needed to do because the old longings were reaching out to me.

I needed tea. A hot cup of tea that I could wrap my fingers round and sip, feeling it chase the fluttering panic out of my stomach. I forced myself to focus on the tea. It would have to be very hot. That went without saying. And in a big mug. One made of thin china that clinked with a musical note when my teeth hit it. Fragrant Darjeeling or maybe an infusion. Camomile, with its grassy smell. Or mint – that made me remember camping in the hills outside Marrakech and sipping the tea the guides made at the end of the day, its faint scent of sweetness and mint cutting through the harsh grit of sand and wind. I concentrated on the memory and the feeling of softness that had swept through my body as the day's heat subsided into dusk.

I mustn't think of the things I wanted even more. Things I knew I couldn't have. Like a quick hit of weed to soothe the sourness in my head. Or some Valium to calm the itch beneath my skin. Or even a swift breath of coke to make the inside of my head sparkle. Every time my mind started to consider them, I turned it back to the tea.

A shadowy image came into my brain. Me sitting on the bed last night, not long after I arrived, feeling the tufty counterpane rub against the tips of my fingers. I'd wanted something then. Something to soften the spikes in my mind. The longing for it had etched a trail in the debris of my memories. Had I given in to the urge? Gone out into the night? I forced my brain to relive the last clear moments but nothing of what I'd done afterwards came back to me.

I went down to breakfast in the hotel bar. Drank tea and ignored Vivian's curious glances, which was difficult as I was the only person there.

The bar looked familiar in the way all bars do. Had I been here last night? I liked bars. I liked the warm sparkle of lights reflected in bottles and the clinking noise of glasses and money. Maybe I'd come here. Maybe I'd met someone. An old friend from way back. Maybe the evening had developed into something else.

'Some hot water?' Vivian's voice broke into my thoughts.

'Thanks.'

I wanted to ask her about last night but it was hard to find a question that didn't sound stupid. Quite tricky to ask someone 'Do you know what I did last night?'

'Did you get badly caught in the storm?' she asked. I stared at her stupidly. 'Lucky for you Mr Crawford was passing. I did try and warn you there was bad weather on its way when you said you were going out.'

'Going out?' I said, pouncing on her words. 'Yesterday evening?'

'Yes. But you went anyway. I guess you got caught in it.'

I nodded. A vague memory of wanting fresh air came back.

'I thought you might miss the worst but obviously not.'

'Do you know what time I went out? I didn't have my watch and I wondered… um.' What the fuck could I be wondering? Nothing came to mind. It didn't seem to bother her, though.

'Oh, I couldn't say. You arrived around four-thirty. So sometime after that. Maybe five-ish.'

I had no memory of it but I was sure she was right. It was another strategy they'd suggested in rehab. *If you're desperate for a hit, go for a walk. A brisk walk.* Exercise wakens your endorphins, the hormones that make you feel happy naturally – the ones that cocaine shuts down.

No point sitting here any longer hoping for memories to return. Forget the convenient scenario of friends turning up in the hotel bar. It was off season. The bar wouldn't have been open. I'd gone for a walk. I didn't have a clue what had happened next but, fuck it, I was going to find out.

Kit came back into my thoughts. Shit. I should go to Tregonna. Find out what lay behind his plea for help. I'd put it off long enough. But I hesitated. My head wasn't right. My brain still stuttered and trains of thought evaporated before I'd reached the end of them. I'd go back to the lighthouse, I thought. That was the thing to do. Maybe something there would pierce the mist and help me remember. Besides, it was on the way to Tregonna. I could go there afterwards.

It was dark grey outside. A dour sort of day. The kind that glares at you over its cup of coffee in the morning, willing you to leave it alone. A hangover from last night's storm, which instead of clearing the air had left it full of weariness. And my feet hurt. Shit, my feet hurt. I'd lost my old suede boots last night, with the soft lining that bagged and stretched in every direction. Instead I was wearing trainers, which were new and stiff and rubbed my cut and grazed skin.

I slipped out the back way to the hotel car park, praying my car would be there. Worried I'd driven it last night and left it somewhere unremembered. Thankfully it was still in the corner by the gate, red and shiny and parked slightly askew. My lovely car. Again it hit me how kind Nick Crawford had been. I'd never let anyone drive my car and certainly not a half-crazed waif in a storm. He was awesomely nice. Or just mad.

I drove slowly down the main street – if you could call it that. Two pubs. The hotel. Three shops selling tourist tat and a small convenience-store-cum-post-office. Not even a takeaway any more. It had been driven out of business when the takeaways in the nearest town started delivering. Whatever I'd taken last night, I must have got it here. It didn't seem very likely. Only the pubs would have been open. And probably only one of them – the older one that catered for the sullen men who stomped in for a drink and a grunt at each other most nights. The other one shut early once the holiday season was over. A half pint of cider, a packet of crisps and a grumble about the Parish Council was the most you'd get on an average winter night in Craighston.

The lighthouse reared up at me as I drove round the last corner. A huge chess piece on a grey slope and in the dark light it looked as flat and fantastical as an illustration in a child's storybook. I shivered.

I stopped in the little car park along the cliff from the lighthouse and pressed my knuckles into my temples as though they might stick my broken memories back together. Nothing came. Even when I walked over to the lighthouse, last night remained as blank as its hard white walls. A few paces away, something brown and soft caught my eye. A small rabbit, huddling in a scrape?

No, my boot. One of them. Sodden now from all the rain.

I stared up at the ramparts circling the top of the viewing platform. The boot must have come off as I hung above. I hunted all around the base but the other was nowhere to be seen.

Someone had shut the lighthouse door. Or what remained of it. It was little more than a few planks hanging at an angle off the top hinge. There was a hole where the lock had been, its edges showing splinters of fresh wood under the peeling blue paint. Someone had broken in. It wouldn't have been hard. The wood was rotten. It had needed renewing for ages, except why bother when it only led to the inside of an empty lighthouse? The door that accessed the lantern room and the lamp mechanism was steel and triple-locked.

I stared at the door for a while. The 'someone' who had broken it down might well be me. Shit. Would I have done that? I realised I might have. It grated over the doorstep as I dragged it towards me, then shot open, hit my toes and startled a couple of gulls that were stabbing the grass for worms. They flew off with angry shrieks and the man mopping the red quarry tiles inside looked over his shoulder.

'Ah,' he said. 'You're back home, are you?'

He went back to his cleaning, moving the mop across the floor with the care of a painter stroking his brush over a blank canvas. I bent over and massaged my toes.

'Gregory,' I said.

He turned around to face me, leaning on the mop and I was shocked at the change. He'd always seemed old but the years since I'd last seen him had collapsed his body into a hunch so his head was like a tortoise's poking out from his curved shoulders.

'I've got that one's pair,' he said, nodding at the boot in my hands.

36

Even his voice was a croak of what it had once been.

I looked for the Jack Russell that was always at his feet. An annoying little dog that wouldn't play with us when Pa visited Gregory in his bare stone cottage. It was cramped and dark so Kit and I stayed outside but Gregory liked it. He'd been lighthouse keeper for years until automation made him redundant and Pa said it made him prefer small spaces.

'Where's Pip?' I asked.

Gregory ignored me and shuffled the bucket onto a patch of damp floor. The stairs, as far up as I could see, bore traces of water.

'You've not mopped all the way up?'

'Ay. All the way down, you might say. What'd be the point of mopping all the way up? You'd have to wait on top 'till it dried. Could be a long time in this weather.'

He painstakingly cleaned the last few square feet and poured the water down a grating outside the door. It splashed onto his boots, leaving dark marks where the sole was peeling away from the leather.

'Dirty today,' he said and I looked at the sky. 'Not the weather, the floor.' He pointed down the drain. 'Some buggers broke in last night. Left mud everywhere. Police are on their way.'

'Oh.'

'Oh.' He echoed my careful tone. 'Oh, indeed. Would be just like you and that brother of yours.'

'I'm grown up now, Gregory. And Kit… wouldn't.' The last of the water slid down the drain with a faint gurgle and I remembered why I'd come. 'Can I go up? Is it open?' He looked at my trainers. 'They're clean. I won't dirty your floors.'

I didn't run up like I remembered doing as a child. Racing Kit to see who could get to the top first. My muscles wouldn't move fast enough and I had to stop for breath on the second landing. I brushed the damp fringe from out of my eyes and wondered at how unfit I was. Seven months without climbing, eight weeks sitting in rehab and last night's efforts had turned my legs to jelly.

At the top, I leaned over the edge and waited for the shaking behind my knees to go. Gregory's cottage was below me on the opposite side of the lighthouse from the broken door, tucked up to it as though sheltering beneath its bulk. I watched Gregory trudge back and forth returning the mop, bucket and other cleaning paraphernalia to his cottage. If I'd fallen the night before, I would have landed in front of his window and he would have had more than a bit of mud to clean up this morning. I shuddered and looked around to see if anything might help me remember. The viewing platform was small, only half a circle in fact. The other half was walled off and used to access the lantern room above, where the working bits of the lighthouse were housed.

It wasn't hard to identify the block that I'd hung from. A few strands of cord had caught in the stone and I stroked them as though they might transfer their memories to me.

Think, Jen, think. Travel back in time from huddling under the tarpaulin, to finding it, to the desperate lunge up and over the wall. Remember hanging there. Watch the girl wake up. What had she done before? How had she got there? Where had she been?

I squeezed my brain tight as though I could force the gap in my memories to reveal its secrets, but it was a wall of obsidian. Black volcanic glass, reflecting images of before and after, but impenetrable. My thoughts slid and bounced off it.

Two cars arrived in the car park by the road. One was a police car. *Shit.* I should have questioned Gregory before I came up here.

They parked either side of my car, so no chance of slipping

away unnoticed. *Double shit.* I looked round for any evidence of my presence last night. I really didn't want to be arrested for breaking in. In between the wall and the tiled map for the tourists showing the names of the rocks and islands out at sea, I caught sight of the frayed and torn cord. I stuffed it in my pocket and pulled all its remnants off the wall, rolled them into a ball between my thumb and forefinger and shoved it in my pocket too. Nothing else broke the grey of the stone, apart from a few flecks of blue paint. I guessed they'd come from the broken door. I guessed they were the same as the ones in my hair and clothes. I guessed I'd broken the door down. It was a depressing thought.

When I came down, Gregory was waiting, sitting on the bench outside. I sat beside him and waved away the smoke of his roll-up.

'Not stopped yet?' I said.

'Ay. I know.' He wrinkled his lips round the thin roll and sucked. 'Mebbe next year.'

'Sure. Make it your New Year's resolution.'

He grunted.

'You see anything last night then?' I asked quickly.

'No.'

'Nothing?'

'No. I saw nothing.'

We sat in silence, apart from the noise of Gregory sipping the smoke of his cigarette. The sound of car doors slamming travelled from the car park. The police would be here in a minute. I tried once more.

'You slept through the storm, then?'

'Didn't say that.'

I waited.

'Didn't see anything,' he said. 'But I was awake. Bloody seagull wailing. Woke me up. Thought it was someone screaming until I saw there was a storm coming in. Couldn't sleep after that. Sat up and listened to the radio.'

I thought about it. Had I screamed? It was possible. Anything was possible.

'It was definitely seagulls, was it? Not…'

'Kids, you mean? Larking about? No. Anyway I came out and looked up. There was nobody on the lighthouse that I could see. The rain had started and the gulls were coming off the sea.'

I knew what he meant about the seagulls. When there was a big storm coming they swooped and looped along the cliffs, calling a warning before they dived off to shelter inland. Gregory's words stirred something in my brain. Seagulls. It was a memory, sure, but from when? I'd watched the seagulls circling so many times. They were part of my childhood. So it could be a memory from then. Or it could be a memory from last night.

Footsteps crunched on the gravel path. The police. I leant back and tried to look relaxed. I was Jen Shaw, visiting an old family friend. Not a druggie nutter one day out of rehab with a police record for trespass and vandalism. Jen Shaw, daughter of Morwenna Hammett, famous author, and Charlie Shaw, equally famous mountaineer. Local heroes. Although the shine might have worn off since Ma stopped paying her bills and Pa left and never came back.

Five

It wasn't the police. Nick Crawford crunched down the gravel path towards us and spoke to Gregory. I felt a bit sick.

'He's ringing Trinity House to see if they want to send someone down,' he said.

Shit. He was talking about the police. He must have come with them. I stayed where I was, half hidden by Gregory, trying to think myself invisible. Something told me it wouldn't be a great idea for the police to know I'd been wandering the coast road last night. I'd recognised Nick instantly, but then I'd studied his face hard last night. With luck he wouldn't recognise me. It had been dark and I'd been wrapped in the tarpaulin during most of our strange encounter.

'Ay. They'll want to know but there's no sign of a break-in to the lantern room.'

'Have you got the key for it?' Nick asked.

Gregory pursed his lips.

'No,' he said. 'I don't have the key. Trinity House, see, they don't want me poking around up there. I know that lantern better than anybody but they'd rather send out one of their technicians all the way from Plymouth if there's a problem.'

'Hello,' Nick said, glancing at me. His voice was neutral. 'I see Gregory has given you the mystery boot.'

'No, Mr Crawford, I didn't give it to her. She found the other one.'

'It's Nick, Gregory. Not Mr Crawford. And who is she? You might introduce us.'

Everything about him was light and pleasant. I was almost sure he hadn't recognised me.

'Oh ay. Forgot. She went away before you came here. This is Jenifry Hammett.'

For a moment, I thought about letting it go but I'd have to give my real name if the police asked me.

'It's not Hammett, it's Shaw. You know that, Gregory.' And to Nick Crawford, 'Hammett is my mother's name. My father's is Shaw. Everybody here knows my mother. They forget I have a father too. And Jenifry's a bit of a mouthful. Most people call me Jen.'

Nick's expression didn't change but I felt his gaze intensify as if someone had turned a bright light onto me while I waited to see what he'd do.

'Jenifry.' He said the syllables one by one. 'It's a very pretty name. Pleased to meet you. So your brother is the Kit Hammett who's renovating Tregonna?'

'Yes. He uses my mother's name. It's complicated.'

'I can see that. You do seem quite a complicated person, Jen Shaw.'

I couldn't read him. Not his face. Nor his body. His hands – the things that give most people away – were still and relaxed by his side. I told myself to watch out. He was a little bit too in control of himself but at least he hadn't said anything in front of Gregory.'

'How about you, Mr Crawford?' I said with as much calmness as I could dredge up. 'What brings you to our little community?'

'Call me Nick,' he said. 'No one calls me Mr Crawford. And, anyway, I feel like I know you already.'

42

The corner of his mouth twitched as he spoke. Amusement? I thought so. I hoped so. His words were a gauntlet he'd thrown down, lying between us, tempting me to play. Despite everything, I felt my lips curve in an answering smile. Playing with Mr Crawford would be fun. No doubt about that. A whisper of curiosity about him distracted me from the worry he might give me away.

More feet on the gravel and this time it was the policeman. As the uniform approached I realised I knew him. Knew him very well. *Shit, double shit and super double shit.* Talan Rashleigh. The boy with the whitest of white blond hair at school. Kit's friend, Talan. And my first boyfriend. My boyfriend for a long time. Two years and eight months, to be exact. He'd seen me through the crappiest period of my life. Well, the crappiest period until now. I was fourteen when Kit went to university and Pa left on another expedition. It took me a while to realise he wasn't coming back. I don't remember how long. I only remember the emptiness in Tregonna when it was just me and Ma trying to be a family. By the time I was fifteen I was desperate to get away. Talan was my escape. Crammed into a little cottage, his parents were lovely to me, and Talan, with his love of the countryside, his exploring, his shooting and his walking, had half-filled the gap left by Kit. I repaid Talan for all of his kindness and patience and love by leaving as soon as I was eighteen, when Kit asked me to come to London to help him set up Skyhooks, his specialist rigging company. I hadn't seen Talan since.

'Talan,' I called out straightaway, walking towards him, letting him recognise me before he reached the others. I owed him that at the very least.

He was startled. I could tell from the falter in his purposeful trudge and the sudden flattening of his features. His face never had much colour and I remember him burning on the mildest of sunny days. He said it was because he came from a long line of miners who never saw the sun. Now he'd seen me his cheeks were tinted pink, though the skin around his mouth was white as if the blood had been pressed out of it.

I babbled to cover the moment.

'Talan! How lovely to see you. And you're a policeman here, now. When did that happen? How's your mother? And Kelly?'

Talan didn't call his sister Kelly. Like me, she had a Cornish name she'd adapted when she moved to London, but right now I couldn't for the life of me remember what it was.

'Fancy running into you today,' I babbled on. 'I was on my way to see Kit and Sofija. And Ma, of course. Have you seen them recently?'

I sounded like the kind of gushy girl I hate but it gave Talan time to get hold of himself and as I stumbled on, he lifted a hand to stop me.

'I was just speaking to Kit,' he said. 'He's in the village but he said he'd call in to see if Gregory needs a hand. He didn't say you were coming down.' And then he smiled. 'Mum went to live near her sister in Padstow and Kelynen has come home. It's nice to see you, Jen.' And he walked past me to the others.

I considered my options. Make my excuses and leave before Kit got here? It was hardly the ideal setting for a family reunion. Except Talan would be sure to tell him he'd seen me and that would be worse. Better to stay and tough it out. Stay calm and not let Kit provoke me into anger. Although I wasn't feeling very tough or calm. Yet, if I went, I'd never find out what Gregory and Nick were going to tell Talan about last night.

I stumbled after Talan, wincing as the loose stones slapped the sore patches on my feet. They were discussing the door when I joined them, their shoulders hunched against the breeze.

'It wouldn't have taken much to break it. The wood's rotten.' This was Nick.

'Ay. It's needed replacing for years.'

Talan peered inside. 'You've washed the floor, Gregory.'

'It was dirty.'

Talan sighed. 'Have you polished the handrail too?' The bite of his words surprised me.

'You wouldn't have got anything useful from it,' Nick said. 'Think how many visitors there've been.'

'Never mind. Did you find anything?'

'The boot,' Nick said. 'He found the boot.' He pointed to the boot in my arms.

'No, she found that one. Outside, wasn't it, Jenifry?' Gregory opened the chest at the bottom of the steps and brought out my other boot. 'I found this one inside. Up on the viewing platform.'

Now I understood what Gregory had been going on about earlier. All that talk about pairs. My brain was mush, I thought. How had I managed to lose one boot on the platform floor? Luckily no one knew they were mine because I could really do without being arrested for breaking and entering.

Talan held out his hand for the boot.

'Small, isn't it? Maybe youngsters?' he said.

They all looked down at their feet except me.

'What happened exactly?' I asked.

'Someone broke into the lighthouse last night. Smashed the bottom door and left the top one unbolted. Mud everywhere but it was a foul night. Whoever it was left their boots behind,' Nick said. And he looked at my feet. Had he noticed they were bare last night?

'How strange,' I said. 'Why would anyone break in? There's

45

nothing to steal, is there?' I forced myself to meet Nick's eyes, but they were as hard and smooth as marble and I couldn't penetrate his look.

'It's not the first time you've reported a break-in, Gregory,' Talan said.

'Me?' Gregory looked surprised. 'I've never done such a thing.'

'Not a break-in exactly. But people on the viewing platform.'

'Oh that. It was nothing. A mistake. It's not easy to see what's up there. Not when the beam's shining in your eyes.'

Nick and Talan looked at him. Exasperation appeared on Talan's face; I still couldn't read Nick's expression.

'Not what you said at the time, Gregory,' Talan continued. 'We had a patrol car going past the lighthouse every hour for a few nights because of your report.'

'Really?' I said. 'Wasn't that a bit excessive? For a few kids having a bit of fun.'

Talan turned to me and I nearly laughed. He looked like a caricature of a policeman. Sort of ponderous and self-important.

'A couple of bodies washed up near here around the same time, so we were taking reports of anything strange very seriously. Not that we don't always take every report very seriously. Especially a report of unauthorised people in a dangerous building.'

He gave me a meaningful look which I tried to make sense of, but couldn't. Then, clearly thinking he'd put me in my place, turned back to Gregory.

'My tarp,' Gregory said.

'Pardon?' Nick said.

'Stole my tarp, they did. It was over the map thing up there. The buggers took it. And the bit of rope I used to tie it on.'

'A blue tarpaulin?' Nick asked.

I looked at the low ceiling of clouds and the wind-tossed grasses

46

and the cuts on my hands and thought of the tarpaulin, too big to leave in the hotel bathroom and stuffed in the boot of my car.

'Ay, blue.'

'That rings a bell. Where have I seen a blue tarpaulin recently?'

I gave him a quick glance and he raised his eyebrows at me.

Talan interrupted.

'It's a common colour for a tarpaulin, Mr Crawford. I don't imagine they broke in to take it. Sounds like some local kids taking the mick. But you were right to phone us. The lighthouse is still important for local shipping.'

'Still?' I said.

'GPS,' Talan said. 'Most people use GPS.'

Gregory muttered something sour under his breath.

'I'll take a quick look upstairs, though.'

'It doesn't look as if the door to the lantern room has been messed with,' Nick said. 'Gregory and I checked it before I came to the station.'

'Ay.'

'I'll make sure, and someone from Trinity House'll be along later too. They'll have to check inside.' He filled his lungs and took hold of the stair rail, then turned to Nick. 'Was it you or Gregory who discovered the break-in?'

'Gregory.'

Talan waited. He waited for Nick Crawford to explain what he'd been doing at the lighthouse. It was a policeman's tactic. *How funny. Talan is a proper policeman.* For a short moment I thought Nick wasn't going to answer. Then he narrowed his eyes and spoke.

'I was out early this morning,' he said. 'Went for a run in the car to get some bread in Craighston.' I snatched a quick look at him but he was focussed on Talan. 'And on my way back, I stopped at the lighthouse. For a quick walk. And to call in on Gregory.

He'd just found the door broken so we had a look round together and then I went to the station. It seemed a bit over the top to call 999.'

'What did you find?'

'Nothing really. The boot, like we said, and the stairs were wet and muddy. The door had been splintered round the lock, but it wouldn't have taken much to do it.'

I was sure Nick had put two and two together and realised the strange woman he'd met the night before had come from the lighthouse.

'Do you often stop by the lighthouse?'

The suspicion in Talan's voice surprised me. I knew Nick Crawford hadn't told him everything but I couldn't see why Talan doubted him.

'Ay, he does.' This was Gregory.

'Gregory makes a good cup of morning tea.' Nick added.

It was enough for Talan and he started up the stairs. He was not as fit as he could be, I noticed, and he took his time.

We waited in silence. Each of us, I thought, wanted one of the others to leave. I wanted Nick to go, so I could finish questioning Gregory. Nick, I guessed, wanted Gregory to go so he could question me. And Gregory? I didn't know. Symmetry would suggest he wanted me to go, but actually I thought he wanted all of us to go and leave him in peace. By the time Talan came down, the silence between us had solidified.

'Doesn't look as though they tried to get into the lantern room. Did you see or hear anything last night, Gregory?'

'Nope.'

'Nothing whatsoever? You didn't hear them breaking the door down?'

'Nope.'

'The door's the other side of the lighthouse from the cottage,' Nick said. 'And the walls are thick.'

'And you, Mr Crawford, did you see anything unusual? Maybe you were out and about getting some fresh air last night.'

I held my rib cage still, waiting for his answer.

'No,' Nick replied. 'Not a thing. But then I didn't go out. Who would if they didn't have to? In a storm like that?'

I breathed.

'Jen?'

I stared at Talan and I realised I was being asked to account for myself too. *Shit. I'd have to lie, too.*

'No, nothing, Talan. Knew nothing about it. I popped by this morning to see Gregory. On my way home.'

'You drove up from London overnight?'

'No, I drove up yesterday. But I stayed at The Seagull. Tired, you know. And I couldn't get hold of Kit.'

Talan switched his weight from one foot to the other and back again. He wanted to leave but something was keeping him there.

'Walk with me to the car, Jen,' he said in the end. 'And tell me what you've been up to. It's been a long time.'

The path was too narrow to walk side by side so I trailed after him, trying to put a spring into my step although my muscles ached. We stopped at his car. He cleared his throat.

'Jen, this is awkward –'

I interrupted him. 'I know and I'm sorry. I should have kept in touch. I always meant to call… or write.' I skirted round the memory of all the times he'd called and I hadn't answered. 'It was a bad time. You know. It wasn't you. It was everything about here.'

He dismissed my words with short wave of his hand.

'Not that, Jen. Water under the bridge. Although I was relieved when Kelynen met up with you in London. Told me how happy you were working at Kit's company. But that's not what I meant. No. What are you doing here in Craighston? Kit didn't tell me you were coming when I saw him this morning.'

'It was a spur of the moment thing. You know how I am.'

'You're not here for any other reason than to see the family? Don't get me wrong, I'm glad you're here, finally. It's been tough for Kit trying to sort out the mess your mother's made of Tregonna. I think you could have made more of an effort to help.' I was speechless. Talan had it so wrong. 'Family's important, Jen. And I know Kit needs you at Tregonna. So it worries me that you stayed in The Seagull last night. Were you really coming to see Kit?'

Now he'd lost me. What other reason could there be?

'You hadn't come to go climbing?' he asked.

He had all my attention now.

'Climbing all sorts of things,' he continued. 'Cliffs and such-like of course, but also quarries and mine towers. And perhaps, now, lighthouses...'

He knew, I thought. *He knew about the Game.*

Time went backwards. A ribbon of images unfurled in my head. Snapshots of different moments of different climbs. Dawn light on the sea cliffs at Cribba Head. A clump of pink flowering thrift clinging to a cleft on the face above Bodrigan. Turning three hundred and sixty degrees on top of a granite spire near Land's End and seeing nothing but sea and sky all the way round. I couldn't speak. I could only stare at Talan and open my eyes wide to hold in the tears.

There were four of us. Grid, Vince, Ricky and me. We took it in turns to decide where to go, but it was mainly Cornwall as Vince and Ricky lived in Plymouth. There was nothing much to the

Game, really. Just climbing. One person chose the place and the others had to climb it. No matter what. No matter how. At first, the one who chose the climb checked it out, but later, as we grew more reckless, we went up stuff none of us knew anything about. Picked at random. *Pure climbing*, we called it. As if not knowing there was a way up made it somehow better.

I'll let you into a secret.

It did.

There's nothing like it. The first tingle of anticipation as you stand at the bottom of something completely unknown. Your palms moisten and the thoughts spill out of your mind, leaving it empty and waiting for your eyes and ears and skin to tell it about the rock. And every sense is keener. Every little thing is more real than normal. The tiny catch in Vince's breathing as he stares up the face is louder and the colours and shapes are stronger and sharper, like a picture that's just snapped into focus. Up we went. We always reached the top. Sometimes it would be easy and then I'd feel cheated. Secretly. And despite all the high-fiving and fist-bumping, we all felt the same. Something was missing if you didn't experience just once that heart-pounding, adrenalin rinse when your feet slipped on the tiny ledge you were balancing on, when the next hold needed an awkward leap above a sheer drop or when the edge you'd grasped splintered beneath your fingers. There's nothing like it and nothing like afterwards when the adrenalin drains out of your body and a kind of calm purrs through in its place. That was what the Game was all about. That feeling.

And nothing else came close.

At first, it was cliffs and mountain faces and quarries. The mine towers and other man-made ruins came later and I regret them. Even at the time they didn't satisfy me. They're dead stone. They don't work with you. Or against you. No fight in them. Bricks held in crumbling mortar, and the only excitement is not knowing whether they'll hold or not.

The last time we played the Game, seven months ago, the bricks didn't hold. A warmish, humid day that had brought the biting insects out in force, distracting us from the climb, which was tedious anyway. Another old mine tower. Just a crawl up a brick wall, sandy and slippery. Dull. Until Grid fell. Or rather the top part of the wall fell, taking Grid with it and all the equipment he'd carefully placed to secure the rope. The force of his fall would have ripped me off the old windowsill I was sitting astride but the belay attached to an old iron bar held.

At first.

Inexorably but smoothly Grid's weight bent the bar outwards until it gave way with a quiet crack and clattered after Grid, leaving me holding him. Inch by inch, my knees lost their grip on the stone. My muscles screamed as his weight hauled my legs over the rough granite.

I cut the rope. I had to. It was the logical, rational action. It's something all climbers think about and hope will never happen to them, but we all know what we have to do. If I hadn't cut it, I'd have fallen too. And taken the others with me.

I'll never forget the climb down, wondering with each new hold whether the wall would collapse and, all the while, the noise of Grid screaming down below. Only the drugs turned off my waking nightmares of those moments.

'No, Talan,' I said now, in the windy car park, with the memories crowding my thoughts making it hard to get the words out. 'No. I haven't been climbing things.'

I couldn't tell if he believed me.

'Be careful, Jen. I won't mention you in the report, but be careful.'

He opened the car door, pulling it against the wind.

'Be careful?'

'Yes.'

I was being careful. Very careful. Careful not to give myself away because I didn't know what he meant.

'It wasn't me, Talan.' He let the door go and it slammed shut. 'I don't climb any more.' Then, because he still looked doubtful, I said. 'Something happened and Kit made me promise.'

Talan smiled.

'Kit told me you'd promised to stop climbing and I'm glad. You frightened me. But, don't forget, you still have the caution. It's on your record and if anyone finds out you were here they might put two and two together. It probably wouldn't amount to anything, but you don't know. This is a lighthouse. A functioning lighthouse. Not an old ruin in the back of beyond. They'll take it seriously and with a caution on your record you'd be looking at a prison sentence, probably not long and probably suspended, but you don't want that, Jen. You really don't want that.'

Caution. So Talan knew about the caution and the accident. Of course he did. It had happened nearby. The local police had given me a caution and he was one of them. He was also my brother's friend. And a good person, an upholder of the law. Talan the responsible and mature.

One unimportant mystery was solved. Talan must have been the person who told Kit about Grid's accident. I'd wondered from time to time how he'd known. Talan had been the reason Kit came to find me at the hospital and screamed at me while I was desperate to get to Grid.

We hadn't been able to move Grid on our own. It was clear when we got to the bottom. The ankle joint of his left leg had splintered and pierced the skin and his foot hung from it. It swayed when we tried to lift him. We needed specialist equipment and paramedics and when they came, they brought the police. Vince and Ricky slipped away. I told them to. We knew there was going to be trouble but I couldn't leave Grid.

I'd admitted everything to the police. It was the quickest way out of the police station and to the hospital. They'd taken Grid into theatre but I didn't know if he was going to come out with both feet still attached to his body and I had to be with him when he woke up, whatever the outcome. And while I was being interviewed, Talan had been calling Kit.

Talan patted my arm and I gave him a little wave as he got into his car and drove away from the lighthouse. I stood watching his car disappear for a while. It meant I could keep my back to the others as I waited for the panicky feeling that thinking about Grid's accident always stirred up to subside. I'd talked about his fall time after time in rehab but reliving it never failed to strip the strength from my bones. The counsellors said that was good. That I needed to feel the loss and grief. I knew they thought that running away from it was what drove me into taking drugs. They were probably right. No, I was sure they were right, although sometimes it seemed as though I'd been running away from something else. Something that was still chasing after me.

I traipsed back to Gregory and Nick. My legs were still wobbly and all the rest of me ached or stung.

'… And the metal eyelet in one of the corners is missing. Rusted right away, although it shouldn't.'

Nick smiled at me. *You shouldn't*, I thought. *You don't know how close you came to having your head smashed in last night. You don't know what a messed up… mess I am.*

'Tied on with a bit of cord, it was. That's gone missing, too.'

'This?' Nick said. He reached into his coat pocket and brought out a handful of frayed sash cord. 'I found it. On the ground.'

I felt in my pocket. My piece was still there. Without thinking, I pulled it out.

'Snap,' he said. But they weren't identical. His half had a knot in it. I took it from him and stared at it. My stomach lurched and I forced myself to breathe lightly and rapidly to control the nausea.

'Ms Shaw,' Nick said. 'I'll say goodbye for now. I live in what was Simon Mullins's place, or so I'm told. I'm sure you know it?'

I forced my mind away from the rope, nodded and tried to smile. I wanted him to know I was grateful to him. For helping me. For keeping quiet in front of Talan and Gregory. Something flitted across his face in response.

'Pop in some time,' he continued. 'I'll show you my furniture.'

'Furniture?'

'Yes, I make it. Along with more run of the mill carpentry. I made some doors for your brother.' He pulled a card out of his back pocket and handed it to me. For a brief moment our fingers met. A fleeting touch of warmth on my chilled skin. I would have liked to look at his hands, to have grabbed one and turned it over. You can tell a lot from hands.

'And you can show me your car,' he continued. 'I assume the flashy beast in the car park is yours. I like Astons. Maybe you'd let me take it for a spin. If you trust me.'

It was impossible to tell if there was a threat in his words or amusement. His face was a blank too. Smooth as the slick slabs in Yosemite, squeezed out of the earth and polished by the slow passage of glaciers, it gave nothing away. I like a mystery and a challenge, and Mr Nick Crawford was certainly both of those.

Once he had left, I turned to Gregory.

'When did Nick Crawford arrive in Craighston?' I asked. 'He's not one of the normal no-hoper outsiders.'

But Gregory, gazing out to sea hadn't heard me. I thought he didn't listen much any more. The inner current of his thoughts preoccupied him and the rest of us were rocks in the river he bumped up against from time to time.

'Well?' I said.

'Crawford? A while back,' he said vaguely, and started hobbling back to his cottage.

I drove back to the hotel. I couldn't face Kit. Not yet. And I couldn't stay at the lighthouse. I needed somewhere quiet and impersonal to check what I'd seen was right. When I reached the car park, I picked up the knotted cord Nick had given me from the passenger seat on which I'd flung it, and examined it. It matched with the half that had been in my pocket, as I knew it would. The edge of the stone on the lighthouse must have cut some of the threads and the rest had snapped. I ran it through my hands like a nun with her rosary, slowing over the knot. The sickness I'd felt when I first saw it returned. I hadn't tied that knot. I'd never have tied that knot. A reef knot. My fingers traced its flat interlocking semi-circles. It's an attractive knot in its neatness and simplicity. But yank too hard on one side of it and it slips through itself and comes undone. I never used it. Someone else had tied that knot. Someone else had been with me last night at the lighthouse. I tried to think what it meant but I couldn't. Ideas flickered in my head but vanished as soon as I reached for them. Nothing made sense. A shiver crawled over my skin and I made a decision. I was going to grab some sleep, then go back to London. Back to rehab. I'd ring Kit and tell him where I was. Explain why I couldn't come to see him. Force him to tell me what the problem was.

I thrust the rope out of sight under the car seat and looked up.
Shit.

Sofija, Kit's wife, was in the hotel. In what must be the office behind Reception. The day was grim and dark and the light was on so I could see her clearly. Arguing, I thought, with someone I couldn't see. Vivian? Her hands clenched in fists and the long black plait of her hair rose and fell with the rhythm of her words.

I slipped out of the car and closed the door softly, bent double and scuttled behind the van I was parked beside. Could I get in through the back door without her seeing me? Now was absolutely not the time for us to meet.

I peered round the back of the van. A quick dash across the tarmac and I'd be out of view of the window. I put the hood of my jacket up and prepared to run when strong hands gripped my shoulders from behind and dug themselves into the gaps between my bones. I gasped.

Six

Fright shut my brain down and my body took over. It threw my weight back onto my assailant and at the last moment, just before I collapsed against him, I kicked back onto his knee. He yelped, swore and released me. I spun round.

It was Kit. Bent over and clutching his knee.

'What the hell did you do that for?' he said.

'What did you expect me to do? Next time try approaching from the front and saying "Hi Jen",' I snapped back, anger and surprise unravelling all my determination to stay calm when we met.

I made my breathing slow down. Kit straightened himself. My brother. Tall and stringy. It annoyed me he had Pa's inches and I had Ma's lack of them. He had Pa's authority too. Mainly because of his hawkish nose and a certain confidence in his physicality that when you knew him well you learned was nothing more than that. Kit's body was sure, his movements calculated and exact, but his mental gifts were confined to the laws of physics and engineering. Outside of that he was lost. And in the months since I'd last seen him, he'd developed a stoop in his shoulders and a way of looking at the ground rather than straight ahead that was new, along with the bitterness tightening his lips.

What had happened to us? We'd always been different people but, despite the four-year age gap, there'd been a bond between us, forged by our chaotic childhood and erratic parents.

Pa was often absent, away on a climbing expedition or in London meeting sponsors and raising money, and when he was at home, he was rarely alone, bringing fellow mountaineers with him. Eager voices and laughter echoed through the house as they shared experiences and planned future expeditions. Kit and I would hang around and wait for those rare occasions when Pa would have time to teach us to climb or take us on night-time jaunts over the moors, dumping us somewhere with a map and a compass and instructing us to find our way back to the road.

Ma wasn't much better. Her awareness of us rose and fell like the tide. Sometimes she'd spend days with us, fishing for crabs in the rock pools below Tregonna or making costumes to celebrate the winter and summer solstices; other times she'd be absorbed in one of her many passions and spend hours alone making candles or taking long walks along the sea shore. If one of her sailing friends appeared we wouldn't see her for days. Even when she was around, she was never very concerned about clean clothes and regular meal times.

Kits and I were happy, though, and in our parents' absence, we looked out for each other. But our lives were very different to those of our friends and I think it was that realisation which held Kit and I so tightly together. No one else had a childhood like ours, so no one else understood the magic of those golden days when we roamed free through the grounds of Tregonna and the surrounding countryside.

Now, in the hotel car park, my brother shoved his hands into his pockets and tried to get his anger under control. His face, thinner than I remembered, calmed except for the occasional spark twitching the stretched skin round his eyes.

'I thought I recognised your car,' Kit said. 'If you want to sneak around, you shouldn't drive such a conspicuous one.'

'I'm not sneaking around.' I was angry too, but I made a better effort than Kit to control it. 'I'm on my way to you.'

He gave me a look like he didn't believe me and rubbed his knee again. I *had* been on the point of leaving without seeing him but I pushed the thought away.

'Well,' I said, 'this is a great place for a family reunion.'

'Yes. So it is. Another car park. Another occasion when you've come to Cornwall without telling us you're here. We must stop meeting like this.'

I didn't want to discuss the fight that had torn us apart. I didn't want to discuss why I'd stayed at the hotel. I didn't want to think about how Kit and I had ended up like this. I didn't even particularly want to find out why Kit needed my help. Not now. But if I walked away I had a feeling the damage between us would be irreparable.

'Kit. I'm here to see you. It's not how it looks.'

He acted as though he hadn't heard me. I felt my teeth grind, top against bottom.

'For fuck's sake, Kit. You've dragged me all this way with your mysterious mail. I'm freezing and I'm tired. Let's go inside and talk.'

'No.'

'You want to talk here?'

'No.'

'Well, what the fuck do you want to do?'

The hotel door slammed and Sofija marched into the car park. When she recognised me, she hesitated for a second before looking over to Kit.

'Well?' he said.

She shook her head.

Sofija was thin, I thought. Terribly thin. She'd never been fat but there used to be a sturdiness about her. Some sense of the Bulgarian farmers her family came from, although they'd long since abandoned farming and become bank clerks and shop assistants. Now she looked as though the slightest touch would break her.

'Not even a few days?' Kit asked.

'No, Kit. They've heard the rumours. You can't blame them. They won't wait for their money.' She turned to me. 'Hello, Jen. Are you the hotel's mystery guest, then? The one who went out last night and came back in someone else's car? Dripping wet?'

Only her pronunciation of 'dripping' gave her away. The hint of a guttural roll on the R and the falling tone of the vowel. Otherwise she sounded as English as I was. She looked me up and down and I saw a flicker of something in her still, dark eyes, a twitch in the muscles round her mouth as though she was holding something back. Was she angry with me too? But she stretched her lips into a smile.

'Talan just passed by and told me you were back,' Kit said.

I knew he would. I bet he'd gone and found Kit. I wondered what else he'd said.

'Let's go home,' I said.

They looked at each other.

'It's cold,' I said.

'We can't talk at Tregonna,' Sofija said.

I sighed. 'OK. So, Kit, why did you want to see me?'

Kit didn't look at me but he didn't look at Sofija either, and I wondered if it would be easier for him to talk to me alone. Neither of them answered my question.

The strain of the last twenty-four hours caught up with me.

'Could we do something, please. Go somewhere. Or have you both lost the ability to move?'

'Wow,' Kit said. 'What's got into you? No, don't bother to explain. I'm sorry, I thought you'd want to help. Or are you still pissed off with me because...'

His voice trailed away and we stared at each other like two cats preparing to fight, bodies tensed, silent anger threatening to spike out. Kit made the first move.

'Because I told you a few home truths.' He spat it out as though it was a poison pellet he'd just discovered in his mouth.

'Please, Kit...' This was Sofija.

'And it's no surprise to find you here. Breaking into lighthouses now, are you? I should have realised you –'

Sofija cut him off.

'Don't, Kit. Leave it be,' she said.

But he couldn't.

We once had a cat that got knocked over by a car and put back together, but afterwards, no matter how much it hurt, the cat licked and bit and pawed away at the stitches until it opened the wounds again. Kit was like that, I thought. We could have been back in the hospital car park. Kit hurled the same accusations as he had after Grid's accident. I was a thrill-seeker, he said. An adrenalin junkie. Not a real climber. No! A hooligan. Flawed. And now I'd broken into the lighthouse. I couldn't be trusted. And on and on. Clearly Talan had shared all his suspicions with Kit.

But it wasn't quite the same. Sofija was there for a start, her hands fiddling with the end of her plaited hair as she watched anger shred her husband apart. And the other big difference was in me. Kit's anger didn't provoke me to rage.

Seven months ago, shocked by Grid's fall, I'd been so glad to see Kit arrive at the hospital. My big brother. The person I could always count on, even if we'd already started to drift apart. I thought he'd come to comfort and support me. Instead, he'd been raging and the shock of it had made me react with fury in turn.

Most of what he said was fair enough. I'd betrayed all the climbing principles Pa hammered into us as children. People died doing what I'd done. A couple of weeks before I went into rehab, two of my free climbing heroes had been killed in separate accidents on easy pitches. Then a young lad had lost his legs train-surfing on the Paris Metro. It felt as though life was paying us back for the glorious insolence of our youth.

So now, I let his rage break over me and pass. Even when he told me I didn't deserve to call myself a Shaw. Although the irony of the accusation from Kit – the one who'd changed his name – stung.

Sofija stopped him in the end, seizing his face in her hands and forcing him to listen to her.

'Rosa,' she said. 'Not in front of Rosa. Please, Kit.' She waved at Kit's Land Rover, parked sideways under the hotel. Rosa, strapped into a booster seat, stared out at us through the back window. Her breath had clouded the glass and she'd wiped a hole so she could watch her father fall apart.

Kit was falling apart. It was too much. I turned and ran away.

Seven

I raced through the village and up and along the coastal path until I reached a high point where the cliff beneath me fell straight in a stark line down to the sea, uncluttered by the shards and blocks of rock that normally impede its way. Although the wind had dropped to almost nothing, the sea still smacked great waves against the cliff base. I stopped and stared out to the blurred line of the horizon where grey sea met grey sky.

And I thought about Grid. Not about the accident. Not here and now, with Kit's bitter words echoing in my ears and the vestiges of last night's drugs running through my blood. Instead I thought about how much I missed him. About how he was one of the few people who understood about me and Kit. One of the few people I could have talked to.

One particular climb hammered at my thoughts. A summer night in London. The weather perfect. A light breeze to cool the sweat of our palms.

And a crane.

And Grid saying. *A crane? Shall we?*

And the blood rushing faster through my body as I smiled.

Breaking into a site is simpler than you'd think. There's often a gap in the fencing or a loose upright left by the workmen to make coming and going easier. And then up the crane. Not climbing. No need to work out a route. No need to look for the next handhold. More like a pianist's fingers rippling an arpeggio up the keyboard.

At the top, we sat side-by-side, legs swinging free. The rungs of the crane were small beneath us and I felt as though I was sitting in the bowl of someone's upturned hands raised high above them. Grid rolled a slip of a cigarette and we talked about work. Grid often talked about work. He was like Kit in that respect. He loved thinking aloud about ways to solve problems with projects we were working on. I didn't, but I didn't mind up here. He smiled and I thought how odd it looked. His face was bony and often expressionless as if the closeness of his skin and bone left little room for movement. He used his hands to colour and punctuate his words. It was only a small smile, made even smaller by the pointiness of his chin. I wondered if at some point during his adolescence he'd looked long and hard at his reflection and given up on his face. I smiled back. I liked him just the way he was. Faces weren't everything.

'You going to the end?' he asked.

'Yup.'

'Get me a picture, then.' He passed me his phone.

I held the bar that ran along the top of the triangular arm and walked sideways until I reached its end. Away from the centre structure and its crosspieces, the space cleared around me. Then I sat astride, wedged my feet under the rungs and stretched my arms into the cool night air. I took my time. Like a child nibbling a piece of cake to make it last. I shut my eyes.

No noise except the occasional buzz of a motorbike and the clang of Grid's steelies against metal as he moved around behind me. The little sounds anchored me. I held onto them and let the rest of me drift. The feeling started as it always did with a prickling in my hands, as though the skin was dissolving, evaporating into the night and letting the coolness flow into my blood. It spread. I floated.

I opened my eyes. The night and the lights robbed the city of its personality. Only the newest buildings with their distinctive shapes held their identity. The rest was squares and lines. A star cloth cityscape. I loved it. My eyes traced the lines of streetlights and followed the tower block windows up and down.

Then I climbed inside the boom and lay face down surveying the ground below. I thought this must be how hawks felt, their wings wide and hovering on the updraft. And for a while I let myself be a hovering bird cradled in the air, scanning the earth for small movements that revealed where the little creatures hid. A flap of plastic caught my eye and I imagined plummeting down to snatch it before swooping back into the sky again. I imagined diving through the sharp, clean air, untethered from the ground. Soaking it in through my skin and rinsing all the staleness and stress away.

I forced myself back to the now, sitting on a bit of rock amidst the dark green bumps of thrift, staring out at the sea. But the memory of feeling like a bird had awoken another. As faint and transparent as a shred of printed voile, it fluttered through my mind, so insubstantial that I was scared to breathe in case it blew away. It was a memory of air rushing through my hair, streaming it out behind me. I let it take on form and colour. I was sure it was a memory from last night.

But even as I relived it I knew it couldn't be real. Because I remembered flying. Flying through the night, buffeted by the wind and the rain but exulting in it. I knew it wasn't a real memory. Of course it wasn't. But my body didn't. It thought it flew. It thought it soared through the storm clouds above the lighthouse. Diving through the light and chasing seagulls. It thought magic lashed through my blood and bones and hurled me into the sky. It remembered each banking turn and roller coaster drop and lift. It remembered the shockwaves of bliss as I surfed the wind.

I knew what it was. Drugs make you dream. The chemicals search through your mind and find the things you want most of all and they bring them to life. Sometime in all the chaos of last night, that had happened to me. I'd dreamed I was flying high above the world. The drugs had prised open my head and let the ghosts out.

I wanted to cry. I'd messed up so badly. I knew that. Knew I had a lot to sort out. But how could I do it if my brain was zapped? I wrapped my arms around myself and stared out to sea, counting my breathing, in and out, and fighting to calm the roiling inside me. It sort of worked. I got back to a kind of dreariness as dull as the cliffs and sky around me and the dark grey sea. No point trying to remember anything else while the dream of flying lurked on the edge of my consciousness, desperate to spring back into life.

The little birds that live in the brambles and hawthorn bushes along the cliffs started to sing. I didn't know why. Some change in the air that I couldn't feel. Maybe it was a little warmer. I walked on until I reached a small path that split off the main track and curled down through the rocks and clumps of wild thyme to a tiny beach at low tide. I swam from it as a child and afterwards clambered over the granite to explore the pools where strange mixes of sealife lived in forced closeness, caught together for a few hours until the tide swept them free again. A few tiny shrimps clustered at one end of a narrow strip of water avoiding the wriggling tentacles of a sea anemone. Or a crab desperately burrowing into a thin layer of sand at the bottom of a shallow pool to hide from the heat of the sun.

I loved that cove. I'd spent hours lost in its rock pool worlds. I was a rowdy child, always moving, and the cove was the only place I remembered being still and quiet. I went down the path to where it opened out into a ledge cut into the cliff a long time ago by the farmers of the fields above, looking for a safe place to hoist seaweed up from the rocks to fertilise their soil. They'd bolted an iron ring into the granite of the ledge and Kit and I used to tie a rope to it to lower ourselves down to the beach.

The iron ring was still at the edge, fixed as solidly into ground as it always had been, and a rope hung from it. Beside it was a small plaque on a stand that displayed a picture of men and donkeys hauling great bags of seaweed up from below alongside an explanation of the importance of seaweed as a fertiliser which included a broad hint at the end that the system might also have been used for bringing in contraband. Despite everything, I laughed. The tourist board loved Cornwall's smuggling history. They never missed an opportunity to mention it.

The tide was out and the rock pools were uncovered, although a host of seagulls hopped over the rocks and screeched at each other. I thought about going down but the path was slippery and narrow. Besides, I ought to go and find Kit and Sofija – it was what I had come down to do and I couldn't leave things as they were between Kit and me.

Except it was pleasant here. With the clean smell of the sea and the noise of the swell sucking and rattling against the sand, dragging the grains up and down and leaving fingers of foam. It drowned out the raucous cries of seagulls, gathered in a cluster at one side of the cove, pecking wildly at something caught in a shallow pool. I threw a stone and they half rose in the air, fluttering and squawking, long enough for me to see the blood specks staining their white plumage.

Seagulls are scavengers. The sharks of the air. They peck out the eyes of baby seals so they can't find their mothers and starve.

An easy meal. I hated them. I collected several stones and threw them one after the other until the seagulls flew for the safety of the cliff.

I looked at what they'd left behind. Dark and gleaming, like a seal, its body wedged against the rocks, the waves crashing and pulling against its lower half. But not shaped like a seal. Shaped like a cross with a thick upright and a spindly crosspiece. Just like the top half of a body. A human body. Lying face down and arms akimbo.

I made for the path, screaming at the returning seagulls, then saw the rope still attached to the iron ring. I don't remember climbing down. I remember standing on the beach, kicking sand and waving my arms at the birds, and knowing my fears hadn't lied. It was a body. The skin of its hands and the back of its neck were greenish-black and blistered. I couldn't touch it. I couldn't move it. The skin looked ready to peel off and fall into my hands.

'Jen.' A voice called from above. 'What is it?'

Kit looked down at me from the ledge above.

'It's dead,' I said.

'A seal?'

'A body. A person. I think. No, I'm sure.'

He came down at speed and ran over to me, bent over the body and reached out a hand to touch the folds of its navy-blue jacket.

'Don't, Kit,' I said. 'I don't think we should disturb it.'

'Just wanted to see if it was anybody I recognised.'

'No, Kit. Don't turn it over. Please. Leave it be.'

He straightened, put out an arm and drew me to him. The waxed cloth of his jacket was cold against my cheek but he smelled of my childhood. The sharp and musty scent of old coats dried too slowly. And mud. And bits of bark and moss.

'It's definitely dead, isn't it?' I asked.

'Yes. Washed up last night in the storm and beached.' He nodded towards the holes on the back of its neck. 'Gulls have had a go already.'

'I know. I caught them at it.'

'I'll call Talan. Tell him where it is.'

'We can't leave it. The seagulls will come back.'

'OK, but turn around and stop staring at it.'

He walked back and forward along the sand as he spoke to Talan and I watched him, waving my hands behind me from time to time to discourage any bolder gulls. He must have come looking for me, I thought. Followed me along the cliff path. I was glad.

'Talan's organising people to come and pick it up but they might be a while. He said for you to go to Freda Mullins' cottage. You know which one that is? Just back along the path a way.'

I nodded.

'Get a tarp or something to cover the body and bring it back.' He gave me a little shove. 'Go on. I'll wait here and keep the birds away.'

'Were you coming to find me?'

'Yes. Sofija told me to say sorry,' he said. 'She told me I was a fool.'

'She's right.'

He smiled. 'I'm sorry.' And then his voice cracked and his smile collapsed. 'Go on. We'll talk later.'

I left him and ran back to the cottage, one of the older stone-built ones whose garden stretched down to the coastal path. Washing hung on a line. Sheets, it looked like. White with large pink blotches, probably flowers but faded from years of use.

A woman was sitting down on the low wall that marked the boundary between the cottage garden and the path. She lifted a hand and waved at me. So I waved back. Beside her I could just make out a bundle of blue. Probably a tarpaulin. Someone – Talan – must have rung to warn them.

'Jen?' she called as I came close enough to hear. 'Talan called me.'

I stared at her, willing my brain to come up with a name or an identity, raking through my childhood friends.

'Jen?' she said. She wiped her hands on the folds of her black dress and reached one out to me. The nails were bitten but the gesture was graceful. And then I recognised her.

'Kelly. Oh, my God. Kelly! What the… What are you doing here?'

It was her hair that threw me. I suppose you'd have called it blonde but it wasn't. It was the colour of catkins. Pale yellow with a hint of green. And hanging as tumbled and streaky as they did after a storm.

'Your hair – last time I saw you it was black,' I said. 'And long.'

Kelly, the dancer. Talan's sister. He'd said she was back in the village but I hadn't registered it. Three years younger than me, she'd danced out of school when I was ten, talent-spotted by an outreach programme for the Royal Ballet School, and disappeared to Richmond. Kelly whom Kit and I had seen from time to time in London, but only at night. Kelly who danced every evening and then went clubbing and slept all day. Kelly of the city. Always indoors, lit up on a dark stage in a sculpted array of dancers or glittering in a heaving mass on the dancefloor of whatever club was the flavour of the moment. She didn't belong in this cottage, sitting outside by the sea.

She shrugged. 'I've taken a break,' she said. 'From dancing. My hair was only black for dancing. Its real colour was never right.'

Now that I looked closely I saw the darker tips straggling round her ears.

71

'A forced break from dancing,' she said and lifted the hem of her skirt and gestured towards a knee wrapped in an elastic bandage. 'Some ligament thing. It happens to a lot of us.'

'I'm sorry.' And as the meaning of her words sank in, I truly was.

Another shrug. But there was something about the precision of the placement of her shoulders that spoke of a lie. She cared more than she wanted me to know.

'It doesn't stop me from doing normal things. Just dancing,' she said and handed me the tarpaulin. 'Talan said to protect the body and then come back here to wait. He'll get someone out as quick as he can.'

My feet were hurting again so I walked back, clutching the tarpaulin. The tide had ebbed further and the body's legs were now uncovered. Kit was scraping a trench in the sand around them and he'd collected a heap of stones. I threw the tarp down to him and gave him Talan's message. He shrugged.

'Hope he's not going to be too long because the tide will turn soon,' I said.

'I think Talan, of all people, knows about the tides.'

He threw the tarp over the body and buried its edges in the sand where he could, using the stones to weigh down the parts that lay on the rocks, then climbed up the cliff and joined me on the ledge. He untied the rope and looked at it thoughtfully.

'You taking it away?' I said.

'It shouldn't have been left there. It's an encouragement to kids to use it.'

'Like us, you mean? Kids like we were?'

But he didn't reply. We watched the gulls investigate the tarp. I didn't think it would keep them off for long.

Eight

'You OK?' Kelly asked.

We sat on the low wall at the back of the cottage and watched Kit and the police head back to the cove. Kelly smoked a thin rollup; its bitter smell mingled with the saltiness in the air.

'I think so. It didn't seem very real.'

She waited and I wondered if she was hoping for a description.

'I didn't look closely, though,' I added.

'Probably not from round here anyway. Talan says bodies can float for hundreds of miles in the sea.'

I didn't want to think about it any more.

'What are you doing here?' I said. 'I mean, back in Craighston?'

I remembered her saying time and time again that she would never come back. Her eyes flicked away from me and I knew she was remembering the same conversations.

'I had no choice. No money. No work. Last of my pitiful savings finally ran out a couple of weeks ago. So I came back. Living with Talan was the only option. That and finding a job here. I thought looking after Freda would be easy.' She mimicked the tones of someone older and patronising. '"It's just spending the night with an elderly lady, Kelynen dear. She needs a bit of help getting in and out of bed, you know, if she's caught short in the night. And sometimes she's a bit confused when she wakes up. She's gone

73

wandering off in her nightie a few times. We just need someone to keep an eye on her. Poor old dear.'" She pulled a stray piece of tobacco out of her mouth. 'Poor old dear, indeed. She sits in her chair all day and dozes on and off, like she is now. Not even the police at the door woke her. So she isn't a bit tired at night. I'm up and down like a fucking yoyo and mostly it's because she fancies a chat and hasn't a clue what time it is.'

She clamped her mouth shut as though she'd revealed more than she meant to. We looked round the cottage's back garden. If you could call it a garden. Grass and rocks and a few plants, but all low. Nothing high could withstand the wind from the sea.

'I met Talan this morning,' I said to break the quiet. 'He looked good. I never saw him as a policeman, though.'

'What did you see him as then, Jen?' There was an edge to her voice that I remembered of old. A bite to her words. 'What did you think he was going to do when you upped sticks and left without so much as a backward glance? You're good at that, aren't you? Leading people on and then disappearing.'

'Hey, Kelly. Look who's talking? I don't remember you hanging around much. Coming back in the holidays. Spending quality time with Talan.'

'I am now,' she said and laughed. A mocking laugh that jarred. 'Back and spending quality time with my brother. Who'd have thought it? Me and Talan. Chalk and cheese.' She laughed again and stretched her arms out and touched me on the shoulders in a kind of stylised embrace. I thought she looked wrung out, thin and somehow empty. She'd lost muscle, like I had – and for the same reasons, I supposed. No exercise. No point trying to keep muscle tone when you know you can't do the only thing you want it for. I guessed her injury might be a permanent thing.

I also guessed she didn't want to talk about it. I could understand that. Talking about it doesn't always help. No matter what all the therapists and counsellors say. Sometimes you have to grit your teeth, put your head down and battle on because nothing but time is going to get you over the next ridge. I thought Kelly was doing the best she could and I forgave the acid in her voice.

'And what about you, Jen?' she asked. 'Have you come back to spend quality time with your brother?'

'I suppose you could say that. Not for long, though. I got here yesterday and…' I decided not to say that I couldn't wait to leave.

'Yeah, I know. Freda and I saw you last night.'

My body jerked. I couldn't stop it. I grabbed the top of the stone wall. Kelly was staring at me with eyes narrowed.

'Last night?'

'Yeah. I saw Talan at lunch today. He told me about the lighthouse and seeing you there. He thought it might be you who broke in. You and some friends, maybe. Told me you'd sworn you had nothing to do with it. That you never left The Seagull last night. So I didn't let on I'd seen you yesterday evening, on the cliff path. Why should I care if you wanted a bit of fun in this arse end of a place? Not my idea of a good time, though: breaking into a lighthouse. But hey, whatever floats your boat. You were always a bit strange like that.' She paused and shot me a quick look. 'Do you still do that urban thing? What did you call it? Urban something. Urban exploring?'

'Urbex? Place hacking?' I said. A little bug crawled out of the wall and onto my finger. I shook it off. 'No.'

'Oh.' She raised her eyebrows like she wasn't sure she believed me. It killed me that no one ever believed I'd stopped.

'Was I, like… OK? Last night when you saw me?' I asked.

Kelly fixed me with another of her blank looks, then her eyes focussed into hard points and a smile curled her lips.

'You're kidding me. You're absolutely kidding me. You'd taken some shit.'

'What makes you think that?'

'You slay me, Jen. You come home and the first thing you do is get high and break into the lighthouse. Only you. Only you could do that. I salute you. I thought you were your mother, you know. I've seen her a few times, dancing along the headlands at dusk.'

'Dancing?'

'Yeah.' She went over to her washing and smacked the heavy sheets as though forcing the water out of them.

'I was dancing?'

'No. You were head-down and going fast. As though the devil was on your heels. But a storm was coming. I thought it was your mother rushing home.'

'Maybe it was.'

She shook her head and her hair whipped round in tight circles. I wondered if its strange bruise-like colour was because she'd tried to remove the black dye. 'It was you, Jen,' she said. 'Your mother's hair is longer and she doesn't wear jeans. If I'd known you were here I'd have recognised you straightaway…'

I made a swift decision. I wasn't going to get any further without telling Kelly part of the truth.

'I guess it was me. But the thing is, I don't remember a lot of it. You know how it messes with your head sometimes.' And I was sure Kelly did know. I'd mixed with a big crowd in London. Lots of different groups of people. Friends from work. Friends who went to the same pubs and clubs. Friends from home who'd moved to London like Kelly: Josie, who worked at reception at Skyhooks; Seb the journalist; and Pete, who'd surprised us all by becoming a surgeon at Kings. Plus all my different groups of climbing friends: the purists, the urban explorers, the parkour nutters who run over roofs and jump between buildings. And these groups weren't entirely separate. Imagine a huge and complex Venn diagram with multiple overlaps. Surprising overlaps. Many of my work friends did some sort of climbing as well. And Kit sometimes employed a couple of friends from home. Kelly belonged to the friends from Cornwall group but often mixed with my climbing friends, too, because some of them went to the same gym as her dancing friends. The circles were fluid.

When I started partying after Grid's accident, I couldn't bear to spend much time with people who knew us well. So I drifted towards friends on the outer edges of these circles. The ones who took stuff. And, as if they saw where I was going, they passed me on to their friends and, before I knew it, my friend centre had shifted a little. I discovered surprising overlaps, even then. Most of my madder climbing friends smoked and some of them dabbled in other drugs. On second thoughts, maybe that isn't too surprising. So I came across them from time to time. And Kelly. I was sure Kelly had been around. I'd seen her occasionally, strangely expressionless in the blur of laughing faces.

'It really messed with my head,' I said again. She smiled a long, slow smile and nodded. 'So I can't remember a lot of it,' I continued.

'Well, you were fine when we saw you.' She stubbed the dark brown remnant of her cigarette against the wall.

'And I didn't stop?'

'You didn't see us. I was smoking outside the back door and Freda was standing inside wittering at me.'

'What time was it?'

She stared back at the cottage and its low back door, trying, I thought, to fit me into her timeline.

'Just after six, I guess. I do nights. I'm only here this afternoon because Freda's neighbour is away. She normally gives her lunch. But I started at six yesterday. One of the family pops in when I'm due to arrive.' She paused. 'To check up on me, I think, although they always say they've come to see Freda. Still, I generally go outside when they arrive. Have a ciggie and hang the washing out or bring it in. There's always washing because dear old Freda won't wear her incontinence pads and she doesn't always wake up in time, does she? It's a fucking nightmare trying to keep up with the washing.'

She reached in her pocket and pulled out a tin of tobacco and papers and a few already-rolled cigarettes and offered me one. I shook my head. One of the few vices I'd managed to avoid. Kelly lit hers, turning away from the wind. I wondered what else I could ask her. I'd arrived at the hotel at around four-thirty. She'd seen me walking towards the lighthouse at around six. It all fitted in.

'So I didn't stop? I didn't talk to you?'

'No.'

'You're sure?'

'Jesus, Jen. Do you think I'd forget? I haven't seen you for months. I'd remember if we stopped for a chat yesterday. It would be the highlight of my bloody day. Chatting to someone with half a brain.' She sighed and blew a cloud of smoke in front of her, spat and fished another piece of tobacco from her mouth. 'So you don't remember if the body was there last night?'

I stared at her. 'Surely it came in on the morning tide?' Thoughts hammered in my head. Beating faster and faster. I looked out to sea so Kelly wouldn't see the panic I was feeling. Someone had been with me last night. I knew that. Had they fallen? The washed-up body… What did it mean?

The sound of a door slamming broke the silence. Kelly jerked her head around. 'Shit,' she muttered.

Freda had a walking frame but it didn't slow her down. She lurched towards us at speed. I caught Kelly's arm and tugged gently.

'So there's nothing else you can tell me? Nothing else you remember?'

She pulled her arm away and shook her head as Freda joined us.

'Jenifry Hammett,' she said. 'Kelynen told me you were home. You get more like your mother everyday.'

I could have replied that my surname was Shaw but there was no point. She wedged her walker against the wall and settled her weight onto it. I knew I'd be stuck here for a while unless I was prepared to be very rude. And I wasn't. Poor old Freda was delighted to see me.

'How is your mother, Jenifry?'

'Fine.'

'She must be pleased to have Kit home?'

I nodded.

'Nice for her to have her granddaughter as well. What's her name? Isolde, isn't it?'

'Rosa. Isolde is her second name.'

'Nothing like children in the house to keep you young.'

I suspected that Ma didn't see it like that. Freda wittered on about all the people in the village with grandchildren while Kelly squeezed the excess water from the base of the sheets. Her face was expressionless as though she'd long given up trying to show an interest.

'Shouldn't you be bringing the sheets in, Kelynen dear?' Freda asked.

'Hardly worth it. They're wet through still. No one hung them out this morning.'

'Oh,' Freda's flow of words faltered. 'Was I supposed to do that?'

'No, no. It was… Never mind Freda, it doesn't matter.'

Kelly took a last drag from her cig and ground it into a stone to join the other dark brown remnants.

'I'm cold now, Kelynen. I want to go back in.'

'Go on, then. I'll be in in a tick.'

'We should bring the washing in.' She turned to me. 'Goodbye, er…'

'Jen,' I said.

'Oh yes, Jen.'

'Morwenna's daughter,' I said. 'Kit's sister.'

'Yes, I know. Tell her… What did I want to tell Morwenna, Kelynen?'

'I don't know, Freda.'

'What were we talking about? Do you remember?'

I shook my head.

'What's for dinner, Kelynen?'

'You've had your… Never mind. We'll have fish, shall we? A nice piece of fish. You go on in and I'll serve it up. Go on. And then it'll be time for a rest. You must be tired out after everything you've done today.'

'Oh yes dear. I'm very tired. But I sleep well when Kelynen's here, don't I? Like a baby?'

'Yes, Freda, you do. Just like a baby.'

Freda started her stagger back to the cottage, the walker clattering on the path and dislodging wedges of moss. We both watched her.

'Is she always like this?'

'Most of the time. One minute, she's right on the ball and the next she's somewhere in the past. I think she sort of knows but she doesn't think it matters. She doesn't care if you're Jen or if you're your mother. Anyway, I prefer it when she's in the past. She rambles on for hours and I just have to nod from time to time. Sometimes I listen to music while she's rabbiting on. She can't tell. I'll have to go in. She'll start trying to cook or something.' She sighed and her finger picked at a bit of loose skin on her lip.

Freda turned and called as she reached the cottage. 'Kelynen,' she said. 'There's someone at the door. I forgot to say. Someone's knocking.'

Nine

Sofija was at the door of Freda's cottage. She looked at me over Kelly's shoulder, the skin over the planes of her face pulled flat by her tightly plaited hair. She tried to smile.

Rosa stood by her, her arms around her mother's leg as she peered up at us. The breath caught in my throat. She had grown. Of course she had. It was months since I'd seen her. But the change was bigger than that. The last vestiges of babyhood had left her and she'd become a little girl.

I dropped down to Rosa's height, calling her name with my arms stretched out but she didn't move.

'Rosa, it's your Aunty Jen,' Sofija said. 'Remember? Aunty Jen. She took you to the park. With the ducks? And the swings? You remember playing on the swings. Going higher and higher? Say hello to her.'

She tried to prise Rosa's hands off her legs.

'It doesn't matter,' I said. 'Give her time.'

'She's forgotten you. Seven months is a long time for a three-year-old.'

She bent and whispered something in Rosa's ear but Rosa shook her head and clung tighter to Sofija's leg. I'd been away too long. I should never have stayed away. I smiled at Sofija and Rosa and gave the little girl a wave. She released her grip on Sofija's knee enough to give me a wave back and I felt my eyes prickle. But I was pleased.

I hoped she'd remembered the swings and screaming 'more' as she sailed higher and higher into the sky. And I was pleased because these were real feelings. Not the rush of coke-induced chemicals. No. Real feelings. Blurry and confused, running into each other like the colours on a child's over-wet painting.

'We won't come in, Kelynen,' Sofija said. 'I'm here to pick Jen up. Kit called me. He's up where the path meets the road.'

Where I'd met Nick last night, I thought. Of course, it was much easier to take the body that way.

We walked in silence to the Land Rover and I waited while Sofija strapped Rosa into her seat.

'Is this all right?' she asked in the end. 'Kit said things were OK now. Between you?'

'Yes.'

'He shouldn't have said what he did, but it's not you. It's everything. Give us a chance and he'll explain.'

She gave me a worried look over her shoulder as she clipped the belts of Rosa's seat into place and I wondered if she had made Kit write to me for help. I had never known if being married and having a child had changed Kit or if it was Sofija herself. She seemed reserved but I often had the feeling she called the shots in her own quiet way.

Kit was waiting by the side of the road, not far from the big rock that I'd feared might be a bear on Friday night. Last night. Was it only last night? Less than twenty-four hours ago. He scrambled into the back next to Rosa and blew on his hands.

'Put the heating up, Sofi, will you. I got a bit wet helping them.'

'Have they gone?' I asked.

'Yes.'

'What did they say?'

'Not much.' He jerked his head towards Rosa. 'Not much that I can repeat.'

'Did they say how long it had been in the water?' I had to know.

'Two, maybe three weeks.'

Relief surged through my veins. 'Sure?' I asked.

'You saw the state of it, Jen. Besides, they had a doctor with them. To certify, you know. They have to, even if they're sure. She said two or three weeks. Any longer and, er, things start to fall off.'

Sofija pulled a face but I felt better. It was a coincidence. That was all. I knew someone else had been with me last night. On the viewing platform of the lighthouse with me. Someone who'd tied the knot in the cord because I would never have done it. But the body was a coincidence and nothing to do with me. Suddenly I felt very tired and hungry.

'So where to now?' Sofija said. 'I need to get Rosa home for her tea.'

'Why can't we go back to Tregonna and talk?' I asked.

'Ma's there.'

'Is she the problem, Kit? Is it Ma?

Silence.

'What's going on, Kit? Why did you want me to come down?' I asked and waited.

He looked at the back of my seat as though he might find the words there.

'Where have you been, Jen?' he said in the end. 'I know you're mad at me but… it's been a terrible few months.'

I thought of the calls from him I hadn't answered. The texts he'd sent I hadn't read. The birthday card from Rosa with the scarf that I never acknowledged. Guilt opened a hole in my stomach.

If I was honest though, the estrangement had started long, long before our fight. We'd started to drift when Kit married Sofija and

Rosa had arrived. He'd stopped climbing shortly after. It was only natural, I'd told myself, when increasingly work was the only place I saw him on his own. I loved work anyway. I loved Skyhooks. Working with Kit on building it up to become the UK's go-to rigging company had been like returning to the days when we ran wild together at Tregonna, Kit with a new idea every day and me following in his wake. Our bread and butter work was rigging for events but we also worked on films. Coming up with ways to manage stunts safely or to get cameramen into difficult places: hanging from the undersides of bridges or slung between two buildings and, once, following climbers up the rock faces at the Kalymnos Festival in Greece. So when Kit had announced, out of the blue, that he'd had an offer for the company and he wanted to accept it, I'd been shocked. I tried to change his mind but I couldn't explain what Skyhooks meant to me. How it had been my escape from the misery and dreariness of Tregonna and Cornwall. He said he was bored. That he wanted a challenge. That the buyers wanted one of us to stay on anyway and he'd prefer it was me. So nothing would change except I'd have a lot of money.

He was wrong on every count – except the money, I guess. Skyhooks without Kit was a drag. The new owners quickly imposed stricter Health and Safety protocols and operating procedures. Even Grid, normally the most easy-going of people, had started to mutter about them.

Then, eighteen months ago, when Ma's debts had grown too big even for her to pretend they were irrelevant, she'd asked us for help. So Kit and Sofija went down to Tregonna to prepare her for the inevitable sale of the house.

The phone call had come a couple of weeks later. Kit's voice had been flat like the surface of a millpond hiding the power of the underwater currents. His calmness unnerved me. Would I get one of the local estate agents round to value his flat? He and Sofija had had a brilliant idea. He couldn't think why he hadn't come up with it before. There he was, with all the money from the sale of Skyhooks and, by the terms of the sale agreement, not permitted to work in the same industry for two years. It had come to him all in a flash. He was going to sort Tregonna out once and for all. Put an end to all the piecemeal repairs and get the place completely sorted. Then he and Sofija were going to open it as a year-round learning and conference centre. Ma had loads of friends who ran meditation retreats and art courses and that sort of stuff. And he could organise adventure holidays and outdoor pursuits. Walking holidays. There was nowhere more beautiful than this part of Cornwall, was there? He could even offer it as a centre for people planning expeditions. It would be like the old times when Tregonna was full of Pa and his colleagues arranging the early group tours up Everest and planning to conquer unclimbed routes in Nepal and Pakistan.

What could I say? Kit, I thought, had things leftover from childhood that tied him to Tregonna and Cornwall. Things to do with his memories of the days before Pa left. I'd told him to leave Tregonna alone. Tried to explain Tregonna was no longer the golden place of our childhood, that the romantic myths Ma had spun about the Hammett's ancestral home were just that – myths. But, even then, I'd known there was no point. Tregonna had him in its claws.

He and Sofija sold up and moved with baby Rosa to Cornwall. I stayed in London. I left them to get on with renovating Tregonna. Bored and restless, I started playing the Game with Grid, Vince and Ricky and I never even told Kit when I sped past Craighston on my way to whatever spectacular climb one of us had chosen. It was the beginning of my mad time and we slipped further away from each other until the drifting apart culminated in a total breach after Grid's accident, when Kit hurled insults at me outside the hospital.

'Let's get out of the car.' Sofija said. 'We won't be long, *skupa moya*,' she gave Rosa a biscuit.

We got out and stood where the rock protected us from the worst of the wind. Dusk wasn't far away, I realised. The grey light was fading into dark.

'Kit?' I said.

'We're in a bit of a mess,' he said in the end.

I blocked out Sofija's presence and waited for Kit to explain the problem and the solution. Kit only dealt in solutions. Plans and solutions. He was a much better climber than I was in that way. He could look at a rock face and plan the route up. When we were young I used to climb for Kit. He'd teach me the route then set me at the slope like a hunter sending his dog after a rabbit. The thrill for him was in the planning. That was where Kit fought and conquered his climb and I guessed that was why he'd been able to walk away from climbing without regret.

'For God's sake, Kit. Tell her.' Sofija's voice shredded the air. 'If you won't, I will.' She turned to me. 'It's your mother. She's conned us.' Kit opened his mouth. 'Yes, she has, Kit. It's a con. A complete con. You just don't see it.'

Kit's face emptied and he leaned back into the rock.

'It's not that simple, Sofija.'

'Yes, it is. She's taken all our money to sort Tregonna out. Every penny we had. She's ruined us.' Sofija's voice rose slowly in pitch. 'And now she wants us out. Now we're finally finished, she wants to see the back of us.'

'We aren't quite finished. There's still...' Kit stopped, as though he could see it was pointless continuing. His eyes were fixed on

Sofija and his expression was hopeless, as though her rage was more than he could take.

'Kit?' I said, but before he could speak, Sofija continued.

'Kit'll say it's not true. He'll say I'm imagining things. But it is true that she won't lift a finger to help us. Isn't it, Kit? Even though we're drowning in debt. Even though our cheques bounce and I have to beg the hotel for time to pay for some catering equipment we bought off them. Even though Kit won't answer the phone in case it's someone we owe money to.' Sofija clenched her fists and pushed them into her thighs, then slowly relaxed them. 'Whatever,' she said. 'You tell Jen your own way. I don't see what she can do anyway. I can't leave Rosa alone in the car any longer and I'm due at the hospice. You two sort it out.'

And with that she got into the car and drove away. I'd never seen Sofija lose her composure before. I darted a quick look at Kit but he was staring into the distance, his mouth set in a tight line.

'Hospice?' I said as the car disappeared.

'Yes. The one in St Austell. Nursing Assistant. She does a couple of shifts a week. Bit of a waste of her talents but there's not much work around. It helps anyway.'

'And Rosa?'

'Ma looks after her if I can't. It's the only thing she does do. Let's walk into Craighston. We can go to the pub. I need to move.'

We tramped down the road to the village without talking. Both lost in our thoughts. As we got to the outskirts, lights were coming on in the houses and it looked almost welcoming. But I wasn't fooled. There was nothing for me behind those glowing windows, except more of the same old, same old shit. No one ever did anything except get up, go to some boring job that was probably tiring and draining, come home, clean, eat and grunt at each other. Their only escape was gossip and speculation or endless harking back to the glory days of Cornwall, when it was a land apart with its own language and identity and a love/hate relationship with the sea that surrounded it and provided food and jobs. The sea defined Cornishmen. It soaked into them. It belonged to them. They fought the excise men to use it as they chose, refusing to pay taxes on the contraband they smuggled over its waters. Why should they? The sea was theirs in the same way that an Englishman's back garden belonged to him.

Except, of course, it was a load of rubbish. And I'd got sick of it. Sick of the romanticism that tied them to the past. *Four and twenty ponies trotting through the dark*. And all that sort of crap. I hated that poem.

There was no one in the pub. Kit had to call before the barman emerged from a back room, wiping his mouth on the back of his hand and bringing the smell of salty, greasy chips with him.

'Half of bitter and...' Kit looked at me.

'A tomato juice and some crisps. Three packets, please.'

We sat in a corner and Kit told the barman to go back to his meal. We'd call if we wanted anything. I took a mouthful of the juice and opened my first packet of crisps. Cheese and onion. I devoured them while Kit sipped his beer and scratched at the grease spots on the table.

'It *is* money, Kit, isn't it?'

And suddenly Kit looked swallowed up and defeated.

'Yes. It's money.' He sighed a big gusty breath. 'We haven't got any money left. In fact, we've got less than none. We owe money to everybody.'

He sank back into the high-backed bench.

'But how?' I said.

'Jen, you have no idea what it's like renovating a house the size of Tregonna. You think you've got it covered: quotes for everything, allowances for extras. Then you discover that there are things you didn't know needed doing. Drains and pointing. Access for people in wheelchairs. Landscaping the gardens. And the further in you get, the more horrors you discover in the house. And then Ma orders stuff without you knowing, or changes things. And Sofija changes other things and then that, in turn, affects other things and on and on and the total spirals and spirals ever upwards until you don't dare look. And then you don't have time to look because everybody needs you to decide something. And then one day there's no money left and the bills keep on coming in. And Sofija —'

He broke off and bit the inside of his mouth. I wondered if it was Sofija's stress even more than the money that had brought him so low. I thought about the money and started on the second packet of crisps. We'd sold Skyhooks for close to £800,000. A third to me and two-thirds to Kit, which was more than fair. It was his baby and relied on his sort of expertise. I'd ended up with just shy of £200,000 after lawyers' bills and taxes and stuff. Kit must have had twice that. I'd paid off some of my mortgage. It was the only sensible thing I'd done. I'd bought my car and taken a lot of holidays. None of which were particularly sensible. I'd frittered most of the rest away on partying. On cocaine and partying, if I was going to be brutally honest. The last of it had paid for the weeks in rehab. It wasn't cheap. So I could understand how Kit's money had disappeared. Mine had seemed like a fortune at first but it had slipped away as fast as water going down a plughole.

'All of it?' I couldn't stop myself asking. Kit nodded. 'The money from your flat too?' He looked down. I took that as a yes.

'No one has spent any money on the house for years, you know, Jen. Just buying it took every penny Pa had. And it was falling apart then. So everything needed doing. When I still had grand ideas, I spoke to an architect and he quoted me a thousand pounds per square metre to renovate it. Well I laughed at him. And sacked him. I thought it was bound to be cheaper than that. But you know, he wasn't far wrong.'

The pub was chilly. The radiator nearest me was lukewarm at best.

'I wrote to Pa.' The words jerked out of him. 'But I haven't heard from him. He's away until the New Year.'

Pa was somewhere in South America with one of the firms that run climbing expeditions for wealthy people. It had to be bad for Kit to think of asking him for help. Things between them had been tricky for years. Kit had changed his name to Hammett. My relationship with Pa was non-existent, but I couldn't be bothered to change mine.

'So can you lend me some money?' he said. 'I hate to ask. Absolutely hate it. But there's nothing else I can do. I can't see any other way out.'

He smiled an odd sort of smile. Almost like a child handing over the last sweet in a packet.

'Of course,' I said.

'You don't know how much. Wait until you know how much.'

The figure would have shocked me into silence if he hadn't warned me. He needed £80,000 and he needed it straightaway.

'Of course,' I said. Nothing mattered except bringing the old Kit back. The one who laughed with me. The one who understood how I felt without me having to explain. My mind reeled. How could I get money? Sell the flat? Too slow. But I could borrow against it. Still too slow. I would have to sell it anyway. Couldn't afford it now I was unemployed.

The car. I'd sell the car. My beautiful Aston.

'Of course,' I said again.

He looked unsatisfied. I had agreed too quickly. Leaped into it, he would have said.

'After all, Kit, I've only got money because of you.'

'Not true. You worked for it as much as I did.'

He gulped his beer and wiped the froth from his mouth.

'And then I need you to help me with Ma.' The words tumbled out of him in a rush. 'I need her to sell the land on the other side of the road and give me the money.'

Years ago, the county council had wanted to eliminate a dangerous bend on the coast road and the owners of Tregonna at the time – a school, I think – had been more than happy to sell them a strip of land that cut through the estate.

As soon as she was mistress of Tregonna, Ma conducted a campaign to get the road returned to its original route and, as she put it, mend the gash ripped through the land. It was, of course, impossible. The county council solicitors had ensured the sale of the land was properly conducted and the things Ma considered important – reuniting the trees that once were part of the same forest and keeping the estate how it looked on early maps of the property – were meaningless as reasons to reroute the road. But it had festered with her ever since and I knew Kit didn't stand a chance.

'Is the land worth anything?'

'Since they decided to build along that side of the road, yes. A small, no, a large fortune.'

'Build? Does Ma know?'

'Yes.'

'You've got no chance then, Kit. She won't want to sell it anyway. But sell it so someone can build on hallowed Tregonna land … Forget it. Look, you don't have to pay me back any money. I'll give it to you.'

He sighed. 'The £80,000 is to stave off the immediate threats. It's a drop in the ocean compared to what we owe.'

I couldn't bring myself to ask how much. He gave in first and named a sum that took my breath away.

'You owe that much!'

'Not all of it. But I need the rest to get the place finished. We can't open without all sorts of approvals. Health and Safety. Fire precautions. Disabled access. It goes on and on.'

He stumbled through what I thought was a sort of prepared speech. How when the money started to run out, he'd thought the bank would lend him some. But they wouldn't. Instead they'd shut down the overdraft facility he'd negotiated. They didn't think his business plan would work. He was bitter about that. Couldn't see why they wouldn't understand he was a successful entrepreneur. He'd started one company from scratch and sold it at a massive profit. He could do the same again. But as he spoke I understood why they'd turned him down. Tregonna would never be able to pay back the vast sums he'd invested in it.

'Why not walk away from it?' I said to Kit in the chilly pub as I opened my last packet of crisps and his hands, the hands I remembered deftly and firmly tying knots and hauling rope, shook.

'Last I knew, you can't walk away from your debts.'

'Well, Ma'll have to sell Tregonna.'

'You don't understand, Jen. The debts are mine. The house is Ma's. If we went to court we might win something but we might not. And it would cost a fortune. And, anyway, I can't take Ma to court. No. The only solution is to get her to sell that bit of land. If you talk to her about it, I think she'll come round. It's the logical solution.'

So I said I would.

Obviously.

Although Ma had never been one for logical solutions.

'But not right now, Kit. I need to think about how to speak to her. You know how difficult she is.'

'OK, but when? You're not going to go back to London?'

'No. I'll go back to the hotel.'

'Why did you stay there, Jen? Why didn't you come to Tregonna?'

I couldn't tell him I'd had second thoughts about seeing him so I spun some half-truths.

'I couldn't get hold of you. Your phones were turned off and I didn't want to turn up out of the blue. I'll stay at the hotel tonight and come over tomorrow.'

I was desperate not to go to Tregonna and drown in the floods of tension that seemed to have engulfed my family. I wanted some time to myself to think about last night and what, if anything, I'd learned at the lighthouse.

'We were in Plymouth,' Kit said.

'What?'

'Yesterday afternoon. That's why you couldn't speak to us. And our phones were switched off.'

'Oh.'

Kit leaned over and put his hand over mine.

'We went to Seb's grave yesterday. Mark asked us if we wanted to go.'

'Seb's grave!' Horror washed through me. Surely he didn't mean my friend Seb from school, the same Seb who'd been one of my closer friends in London until Grid's accident.

'Seb Vingoe? Seb the journalist? That Seb?'

Kit nodded.

'Seb's dead?'

'Didn't you know? How could you not know? Where have you been, Jen?'

'It doesn't matter. I'll tell you. But later. Tell me about Seb. How did he die?'

'A stupid accident. Parkour. Free running. He slipped and fell, leaping between two buildings. Broke his neck. Never stood a chance.'

I thought of Seb. Dark and intense. With the black hair and skinny frame of a typical Cornishman. He'd have looked like one of those taciturn little miners in the old photographs at the museum in St Blazey when he grew old. If he'd grown old. But Seb hadn't been destined for mining tin and no one could call him taciturn; he mined words and shaped them into poetry and stories. Flitting from subject to subject according to his passion of the moment. One summer it had been Cornish legends and we'd sat round illicit campfires on the beach at night with Seb, his face changing shape in its flames, as he entranced us with stories where men were turned into stone and demons seized lone travellers in the night. Another time he'd fallen in love with astronomy, persuaded his mother to buy him a telescope and spent all summer sleeping during the day and staring at the night skies before he lost interest and flung himself into something else.

'I remember him talking about parkour,' I said. 'I thought it was for something he was writing. But I didn't know he did it. Not Seb. Not free running. It's not his sort of thing… When did it happen?'

'A few weeks ago.'

Seb had died while I was in rehab and I hadn't known. Somewhere among all the emails, texts and voicemails there'd been when I turned my phone back on there must have been one telling me about it, but there'd been so many I'd only opened Kit's.

'And the funeral?'

'We didn't go. No one went. His parents didn't want anyone there except family. His mother – you can imagine how she was.

Just family, she said. No friends. No lovers, past or present. She especially didn't want anyone there who had anything to do with climbing and free running. She blamed us all for not stopping him.'

We both stared at our drinks and I thought, this time, at least, no one could say it was my fault. Not like with Grid. But I understood Seb's mother. Seb's passions had been cerebral. His love had been words. They poured out of him in an unending stream of anecdotes, opinions, arguments and banter. He was never dull, always full of life. But he wasn't sporty or physically active in the least. He was always the first to hail a taxi, to prefer the nearest pub, or to duck out of a proposed walk with an excuse about a deadline.

'How's Mark?' I said. 'He's Seb's only brother, isn't he?'

A ripple of emotion passed over Kit's face. 'Not good,' he said. 'Mark's not good. But he thought we should have the chance to say goodbye to Seb. Just a few of us. The ones who knew Seb before he left Cornwall. Old school friends mainly, who wanted to say goodbye quietly. None of the nutters from London. No one Seb went free running with. We all went and said a few things about Seb or read one of his poems. By his grave. That's why you couldn't get hold of us.'

'Seb would have liked that.'

'Mmm.'

Seb was dead. I felt the fact of it reach into my core and twist it into a different shape. I hadn't seen much of him since Grid's accident and, if I was honest, not for a few months before that, when I was unhappy about Kit disappearing from my life and all my spare time was taken up with climbing. But he was a friend, a childhood friend and he'd never pour out the details of his latest obsession to me again. A wave of depression gripped me.

Everything was so awful. Kit. Seb. And me. I supposed it was time to grow up. Time to say goodbye to excitement. Time to think about the future and become sensible. Except I wasn't sure if I could. Not while the hole in my memory of last night held so many secrets.

I dragged myself back to the present and my brother sitting opposite, his restless fingers picking at the thick varnish on the arms of the bench.

'OK,' he said. 'You go back to The Seagull, Jen. And come over tomorrow. We'll go out and leave the place clear for you to talk to Ma.' He patted my shoulder. I tried not to wince. 'You are OK, aren't you?'

This was my chance to talk. An invitation really. Except, looking at Kit's shut-in face, I didn't think he would want to know. So I told him everything was fine and we left the pub and walked off in separate directions – me back to the hotel and him along the road past the lighthouse and back to Tregonna.

I didn't go into the hotel, though. It was only seven o'clock. Although I was shattered, seeing Kit in such a state had unsettled me. I wasn't ready for sleep just yet and the crisps had calmed my hunger.

Nick Crawford. He'd hovered at the edge of my mind all afternoon. Unfinished business. I owed him an explanation to keep him quiet and now I wondered if he had seen something, someone, anything that would help me pierce the black of last night.

Ten

I didn't think I had any memories of Simon Mullins's cottage, but as I stopped the car outside I remembered playing there with his great niece, Debbie – a thin curly-haired little girl who always wore woolly tights and skirts in winter, even out to play, while the rest of us wore jeans or sweatpants. We'd played at house in the tumbledown barns at the side of the cottage. None of the walls were more than a child's knee height but you could see where the different rooms had been.

The outbuilding was no longer tumbledown, however. Its stone walls had been rebuilt on three sides and the gable end filled in with huge doors. A white van was parked outside and I recognised Nick's battered car next to it. The cottage was in darkness, but lights shone through a half-open door at the side of the outbuilding and a noise of hammering came from inside.

I went round to the side door and called. A warm and spicy scent drifted out into the night as it opened. Nick Crawford stood there. The light behind his head glinted off the sawdust spattering his hair and the shadows lent a dark hue to his skin.

'Ah,' he said. 'Ms Jenifry Shaw. I thought you might come round. How nice.'

His voice was amused on the surface yet underneath I felt a tension. Maybe it was the pitch black and the quiet of the night but there was a jumpiness about him, as if he was charged with static that needed only a touch for it to crackle out.

Or maybe I was putting my own mood on to him.

I realised I was staring at him just as he was staring at me. There was silence broken only by rapid breathing. We sounded as though we'd both been running. Awkwardness took my eyes from his face and I said the first thing that came into my head.

'Can I have a look? I used to play here when I was a child.'

His eyes flicked into the building before he answered.

'Sure. There's not much to see, though. The furniture is mostly packed in my van. I'm taking it to London tomorrow.'

'Ah. I thought you suggested I came round to have a look at it.'

He gave me a smile like we both knew there'd been more to his invitation than furniture and I couldn't help smiling back.

Another long pause.

Nick broke it. 'Come in anyway. Not much call for handmade furniture here, you see. I sell it through shops in London and Bristol or people order it off my website.'

The scent inside the barn was strong. I picked up a shaved curl from the floor and sniffed it.

'Sandalwood?' I asked.

'Cedar. The smell is intense when you sand it or plane it.'

He stood facing me across his workbench which was empty apart from a few scattered pieces of wood. Behind him, on the whitewashed walls, hung saws and clamps and tools I couldn't put a name to. I swivelled round. His workshop was white, bright and very clean. Something about it felt all wrong. The momentary spark of pleasure I'd felt at seeing him died and depression bogged me down again. I was in a weird mood. It was time to do what I'd come to do and go.

'I've got Gregory's tarp in my car,' I said. 'Do you think you could get it back to him without mentioning me?' Surprise opened his eyes wide and he looked hard at me. Clearly he'd guessed it had been me on the lighthouse last night, but he hadn't expected me to admit it. 'And thank you for last night,' I said. 'You were very kind.'

'So,' he said. 'You're full of surprises, Jenifry Shaw.'

'I wish you wouldn't call me that.'

'It's your name. I suppose your mother chose Jenifry. A Cornish name. And Shaw from your father. The famous Charlie Shaw.'

'Is he? Famous still, I mean?' The comment was meant to be throw-away. A step in the dance between me and Nick. But it came out tinged with a bitterness I didn't understand.

'I think so. Mountaineer and adventurer, Charlie Shaw? People down here still talk about him. You must have inherited his adventure lust?'

'You guessed then.'

'That it was you in the lighthouse? Yes. What exactly were you doing there?'

My story was full of holes but it was the best I could do.

'I didn't break in. I was out for a walk and saw the door was smashed. So I went in and when I was up the top I heard someone on one of the lower floors. I don't know if they followed me in or what. But it spooked me. I hid up there for ages until I was sure they'd gone. Then I tripped and fell down the stairs while I was racing to get away. Knocked myself out. I was in a bit of a state when you stopped.'

His eyes sharpened. Although he said nothing, the empty white room with its harsh lighting boring into my head made me feel as if I was in an interrogation chamber. Maybe I should have told him the truth but I couldn't quite trust him. Something hid behind his easy exterior and it both intrigued and disturbed me.

I ploughed on. 'I wondered maybe if you'd seen anybody else around. Before you found me, I mean. Or after, I suppose. Because if you had… it must have been them who actually broke in.'

Bit by bit his face shut down while I spoke. His eyes lost their warmth and shifted away onto the wall behind me. His lips settled into a perfectly horizontal line. He didn't believe me. Nothing else could explain the coldness invading his face. My voice died away to nothing like the last gurgles of bathwater going down the plughole.

'I didn't see anyone,' he said. 'Apart from you.'

He was going to say something more but the noise of a car driving up and stopping outside took his attention away. Doors slammed and the sound of voices slipped in through the door. Low male voices. Nick's head lifted and his shoulders tensed like a dog catching the first sense of an intruder.

'Will you excuse me for a moment? I know who this is and it won't take long.'

He shut the door behind him, cutting the sound of voices off and leaving me in the empty workshop. My hands were still outstretched, frozen mid-gesture, he'd left so quickly.

That hadn't worked. All I'd done was to make him suspicious of me. What the fuck. When he came back I'd tell him the truth. If he'd been going to shop me to the police, he would have already. A hint of unquiet niggled me, but I ignored it and looked around the studio instead. There were no windows so I couldn't even sneak a look to see who his mystery callers were.

The room was empty apart from his workbench and a long, narrow sideboard. I went over and ran my hands over it. Made of two contrasting woods, a dense, ruddy one for the frame and a lighter and grainier wood for the doors and panels, the sides had a slight curve that broke up its square-ness and made the two woods flow into each other. It was beautiful and elegant, and not a bit like Nick Crawford.

The darker wood must be the cedar that scented the workshop. I traced its shape around the side panel and winced when my fingers caught on a raised edge. It wasn't quite as beautifully put together as I'd thought. The join where the side panel was fixed to the cedar frame had snagged the tips of my fingers, still sore from digging into the stone last night.

I knelt down. The panel wasn't lined up with the frame. I tapped it and it sank into the frame even more, leaving a proud edge all the way round. *Shit. Maybe I could push it back out from inside?* But when I opened the doors I saw the inside was lined with more cedar. I'd just have to confess when he came back.

The lining was smooth with an oily gleam and smelled even more strongly of aromatic wood. I wondered if he'd rubbed cedar oil into it. I sniffed my fingers, but if the spice had impregnated them, I couldn't smell it.

There was a faint trace of powder on the fingers of my right hand. I looked at the dresser again and saw where it trickled out of a corner of the uneven join. Too fine to be sawdust and too white, like icing sugar. I rubbed it between my thumb and forefinger. Was it the grains of some product used for filling wood that had dried and crumbled when I dislodged the panel? I thought not. It would have a greasier feel. This was dry and felt like tiny sharp crystals on my skin. The air in the room throbbed in time with the circular motion of my fingers and I felt dizzy. My mouth was dry but my palms were damp and heat beaded my forehead and the skin above my top lip. I knew this feeling.

It was the moment of anticipation. The moment of holding back. When the first line of the night glittered before you. The moment before you bent and inhaled and let the drug tear through your body into the deepest corners of your head.

I looked at the powder again. Was that what my body was trying to tell me? There was a sink in one corner and I crossed over to it, ready to wash whatever the powder was off my hand, then stopped. There was only one way to be sure.

I lifted the fingers to my mouth and bared my teeth ready to rub the powder into my gums. In the mirror above the sink, a face snarled at me with the same expression I'd seen so many times on other people's faces as their shaking fingers rubbed every last grain into the bony flesh above their teeth. They were like the stray cats down at the harbour pulling each scrap of flesh from the fish carcasses, their eyes flashing threats and fright at the same time. This time the face was mine and its expression of longing shocked me.

But there was only one way to be sure...

I didn't rub the powder into my gums. Instead, I touched my fingers with the tip of my tongue. A sour taste. Dried lemons. And then the faintest of tingling. A sparkling breath that made my tongue curl.

I was right. My body hadn't lied. It had known straightaway, recognising the scent and feel like you recognise the touch and smell of a lover even with your eyes shut.

I grabbed the tap, turned it on full and plunged my hands into the jet of water, gasping at its coldness, like icy needles on my skin. I rinsed away the sweat, swilled water round my mouth and spat.

There was only one cupboard in the workshop, its shelves full of an array of bottles of glue and stain, tins of varnish and paint, stacks of sandpaper, clean brushes and a couple in use that were wrapped in cling film – and stuff in bags and plastic pots. Stuff that felt like powder when I squeezed it or shook it. Some of it was whitish. I hunted through for a bag that had already been opened but they were all sealed. I thought about tearing a little corner off but there were so many. Most of them must be filler or abrasive grit or whatever the packaging claimed they were but I couldn't open them all to check. I made a swift decision, tore off a length of cling film, grabbed a brush and knelt down by the sideboard. The brush was the smallest there was but still too big to sweep the minute amount of powder into the cling film lining my other hand. Louder voices cut through the silence, followed by the noise of car doors slamming. *Shit*. They were leaving, whoever they were. I had no time.

I gave it one last go. Leaned my elbow against the loose side panel pushing it in so that more powder trickled out, praying the panel wouldn't fall in completely and spill whatever hid behind all over the floor. I was mad. I knew I was. But I had to know if it was cocaine.

The door started to open. I brushed the powder into the cling film, screwed it up and shoved it into my pocket. A brief skid of my feet over the white floor scattered the traces and by the time Nick came back in I was standing by the sink, rinsing my hands and face and trying to calm the ragged gasps of breath that sounded thunderous in the quiet.

'Are you OK?'

My eyes raked the studio. It was fine. Nothing to give me away. Except the deep shadow round the panel in the sideboard. He must have been fitting it when I arrived and shoved it into place. Would he remember how it had looked?

'Are you OK?' he asked again.

I took the towel from beside the sink and patted my face.

'Fine. The tap came on stronger than I expected. I was thirsty.'

In between pats, I stole glances at his face, trying to make sense of what I'd discovered. His surface expression was pleasant. Maybe a bit set about the mouth. But giving nothing away. It was a chameleon's exterior, and not to be trusted.

His voice cut over my thoughts.

'If you're thirsty, would you like a tea or a coffee? Or I've got beer in the cottage.'

He was a dealer. No one would hide cocaine in furniture like he had done if it was purely for personal use. I fingered the crushed cling film package in my pocket.

'No, thanks. The water was fine. Just what I needed.'

'A glass of wine?'

'No, really, no. I'd best get back.'

All the time, running underneath my words, threads of anger tugged at me. I'd liked him and he'd turned out to be bad.

'The sideboard's lovely,' I said.

'Thanks.'

'I love the different wood.'

'It's nice, isn't it? Cedar and oak.'

I walked over to it and stroked the top, watching to see how he reacted.

Not a twitch or a shift gave his thoughts away and a prickle of fear scurried over my skin. He was too cool. Far too cool. Time to go. Through the door the night looked like velvet. Folds of soft black velvet I could wrap myself in and hide.

The silence had gone on a long time.

'Really lovely,' I repeated. 'But now I must go. Thanks again.'

My voice sounded brittle and false and it hit each surface of his bright, white room and rebounded. I stumbled past him through the open door, muttering something, and into my car. Slammed the door and thanked the god of automobile technology for keyless ignition. I was clumsy with the accelerator and the car roared wildly, breaking the quiet of the night. I wrenched the gearstick into reverse, pulled away, my eyes fixed on his dark figure soaking up the light in the open doorway, and, with a snatch of the wheel, headed out onto the road.

The night was thick and low with cloud and through the windscreen my headlights flattened everything so I seemed to drive through a strange grey painting of trees and hedges. From time to time, headlights appeared in my mirror and followed me, until they turned off into the lanes that ran over the moors to the main road to St Austell and beyond, and I was alone again.

Nick Crawford was a dealer. Or at least that was what it looked like. A retired policeman came into rehab one evening to talk to us about dealers. He said there was a glamour associated with drugs, particularly cocaine. People saw it as something for the young and rich. Exciting. His job, he said, was to show us the reality behind the glamour. And he did. It was an hour of awfulness. Of gang wars. Of children used as drug runners. Of violence and killing. Photo after photo of dead bodies. Each with their own tragic story. And every time, he told us, every time we snorted a line, we were helping it continue. We were as bad as the thugs who grew rich from the trade.

I parked at the hotel and put the car keys in my pocket. My fingers met the little packet again. I pulled it out and turned it over and over. About half a gram, I estimated. I was probably right. It was a skill I'd acquired. The ability to weigh cocaine by sight.

The heat of the car and my body had warmed it through and it felt soft against my skin. I was sure it was cocaine but I needed to check. That was why I'd taken it, although I didn't have a clue how to find out. I wanted to know what Nick Crawford was up to.

But maybe I'd had another reason.

It called to me, you see.

Just one last night, it said. *Then never again. It's been a dreadful twenty-four hours. Give yourself a break. Breathe in the sparkling crystals and let*

them explode pleasure along your nerves. Just this once. Once doesn't matter.
You stopped before. You can stop again.

It lied. I knew it lied.

And I gripped onto that thought tighter than I'd ever held onto any ledge on a slippery rock face. Clamped my concentration onto it and chucked the package into the glove compartment, locked the car and went to my room.

Eleven

Next morning, I parked my car at the top of the drive leading down to Tregonna and walked to the house through the woods that shelter it from the road. Bruises were still appearing all over my body although my brain felt clearer today. Thoughts stayed in my head longer, letting me follow them through. Cocaine was their principal subject. The cocaine I'd taken from Nick Crawford's workshop, the little white package still locked in the glove compartment. Still intact. It was a small victory. Whereas the other cocaine that dominated my thoughts, the cocaine I must have taken on Friday night, marked a big defeat.

Where had I got it? Had I come across someone in one of the houses along the headland? Most of the people I knew from school had stayed here, as tied to the place as Ma was. Maybe I'd had a few drinks with one of them to take the edge off the tiredness, ignoring the warnings they'd given in rehab. A few drinks and your inhibitions dissolve. You feel better. Not quite great but not bad. And you remember what would make you feel really great.

Cocaine.

But suddenly I wasn't so sure.

Coke blurs your life together so that the bars and clubs, the nights of laughing faces and glittering lights, shrill chatter and pounding music, melt into one party. But it doesn't leave great holes in your memory like I had. As my feet crunched through pine needles and old leaves, I realised something else was much more likely. Something I would have thought of straightaway if my brain hadn't been so jangled.

Roofies. Rohypnol. The amnesia drug.

I remembered how my body had felt when I tried to climb up the lighthouse. How it seemed to move in slow motion as though the air around it was thick and muddy. And I thought of people I'd seen on roofies. They took it if the coke was making them edgy. It slowed them down. Made them loose. Some went to sleep but with their eyes open, watching what was going on but not interacting. And afterwards they remembered nothing. Roofies made much more sense than cocaine.

Except I'd never have taken it. Not willingly. I hated what it did to people. The zombie-like stares and the empty eyes. I'd never have done it.

What did it mean?

Only one thing I could think of. Someone had given it to me. Slipped it into a drink? The same someone who had been with me on the lighthouse? Who'd tied the knot in the cord? But why?

There was one obvious reason. The one everybody associated with Roofies. *Roofies – the date rape drug.* A roaring sound like waves crashing against the shingle filled my ears and I felt sick.

No.

Please, no.

I sat down on a pine tree that had fallen and been left where it'd landed and drew in long slow breaths of air filled with the smell of crumbling leaves and fungus. I couldn't think about Friday night now.

I moved on to Ma instead and the thought of her calmed me. She loved this forest. She claimed Jack Hammett, who built Tregonna in the early seventeen hundreds, bought the surrounding land to save the forest from being destroyed. And maybe it was true. Certainly, all the hills nearby had been stripped and the timber sent to Plymouth to build ships for whatever war England was fighting at the time. Pa muttered that Jack was waiting for the market to top out so he could make a second fortune after smuggling had given him his first.

Jack's portrait hung in the hall. A young man against a dark background, wearing black clothes which made his thin face and the white band round his neck stand out. He was glancing to his right, as though something had distracted him as he posed and the painter had captured that precise moment. People say the eyes in a portrait follow you round a room but it was not the case with Jack. As you moved around the hall, his gaze always shifted away from you.

I stood up and walked to the edge of the woods and gazed down at Tregonna, my childhood home. It was the setting that made it special. Cradled between the woods and the first rise of land after the coastal cliffs, yet close enough to the sea to feel its freshness. The house itself was ugly. Jack Hammett had wanted value for his money and for him size was everything. Tregonna was a plain oblong of four storeys and the fourth storey had been paid for by sacrificing every element of style and design. There were no pillars, no grand entrance and the windows were different sizes and unaligned as if their positions had been decided by someone inside each room with no thought as to how the exterior would look.

Horrid lump. If only Pa had never bought it back. Everything had been devoted to keeping it going. Ma's royalties and the bits and pieces she earned from appearances at festivals. Every penny that Pa earned from climbing and public speaking and sponsorships. And now it had eaten Kit.

Everything told me this talk with Ma would turn out badly. Standing at the point where the woods gave way to the sloping lawn leading to the house, with tiredness draining my energy and the background buzz of my brain fretting away at the hole in my memories and fraying the edges of my focus, something shifted inside me and a crack opened. Kit was wrong. My once sure-sighted, think-of-everything brother had made a mistake. Ma didn't deal in logical solutions. His plan wasn't going to work.

I hesitated, but, in the end, I had no choice. So with absolutely no idea what I was going to say to her, I stepped out onto the grass and went down to Tregonna, the apple of Ma's eye, to fight with her on Kit's behalf.

Ma's hair had undergone a subtle shift from golden blonde with light grey streaks to predominantly grey with flashes of its old colour. It looked messy. A reviewer once said she resembled a Pre-Raphaelite painting with her long, tumbling curls and delicate chin. Much to Pa's amusement. Since then she'd cultivated the resemblance, changing her Indian-inspired prints and heavy jewellery for loose pale clothes. Once her hair started to lose its curl and thickness, she dried it in tight plaits so it sprang away from her face when brushed.

She embraced me with a whiff of patchouli and incense sticks – some habits die hard. She didn't appear in the least surprised to see me.

'Jenifry. Gregory told me you were here. You've lost weight. It suits you.'

She pinched my cheek and I gritted my teeth. *Kit*, I thought, *keep focussed on Kit and his problems*. But I couldn't resist the tiniest of digs.

'Still in this room, I see.'

Ma had two rooms that opened onto each other on the side of Tregonna that looked out to sea. Two of the grandest rooms on the first floor but choked with stuff. She'd built herself a nest out of the choicest bits of furniture and ornaments Tregonna possessed and now she fluttered around the remaining space like a shabby sparrow.

'Aren't you going to change rooms? It can't be convenient for Kit and Sofija, having you in the midst of the guest rooms.'

She waved her arms around in a flurry of movement, jangling the slender bangles on her wrists.

'Of course, I am. Not yet, though. The timing isn't right. My consciousness is changing, moving into a new state. It's a painful thing. Birthing a new person. It's better I stay in this room. The forces are balanced here.'

'A new person?'

'Yes, darling Jenifry. You see before you a new woman. One who moves now with the waning moon. Her time of walking with the full moon is passed.'

The muscles in my shoulders tightened but I forced them to relax. Letting her annoy me with her wafty hippy speak wasn't going to solve Kit's problem.

'I hardly recognised the house, Ma. It's wonderful what Kit and Sofija have achieved. And you, of course.'

And it was. I'd had a quick look round before following Ma up to her room. Everywhere was fresh and clean. New paint on new plaster. Woodwork and floors stripped back and polished. Beneath it, the structure of the house had been renewed too. The damp had been dealt with. The defective wiring, the dodgy plumbing, the rot. All gone. And when I'd peeped round the door into the old stables, I'd seen the metal doors of a lift and beyond them the gleaming stainless steel of a professional kitchen.

'So Tregonna too is ready for the next generation and several after that by the look of it,' I said. 'Isn't it wonderful?'

She turned away and gazed out to sea but her fingers caressed the battered copper of an old ship's light.

'You can't feel it either, can you?' Her voice was husky.

'Feel what?'

'The spirit of Tregonna weeping.'

'What?' I could hear the years of pent-up irritation vibrating in my voice. This kind of comment was why I avoided having serious conversations with Ma.

'Kit's torn the soul out of the place.'

'What utter crap!'

She turned towards me, the hint of a smile curving her lips and ran her fingers over the carved wooden chest by her bed. The dust rose in a trail behind her hand and somehow made me feel better.

'Did Kit ask you to speak to me? He always used to send you to do his dirty work. And you always did. Like a faithful little dog.'

I made a supreme effort and pushed the irritation back down.

'You know he's in deep trouble, don't you? A complete financial mess?'

'I never asked him to spend so much money, Jenifry. I just needed to pay a couple of bills, but he came along and gutted the place.'

'But Ma, it was falling down round you.'

'He's poured money into it. Smothered its spirit with... with luxury.'

In a way, she had a point.

'Maybe he has got a bit carried away. But he was only trying to do his best for Tregonna, and for you.'

'No. He sees Tregonna as a building. Something he can make money out of. He doesn't understand the place like I do.'

'It *is* a building. There's nothing to understand.'

She walked back towards me, grabbed my hand before I could stop her and stared into my face.

'Not you too.' she said.

'Not me what?'

'You shouldn't need to ask.' Her fingers found a cut on the side of my palm and she turned my hand over and examined it. I winced. 'I've got a comfrey and honey salve that will help,' she said, but she stayed where she was and ran a finger along the grazes on the ends of my fingers. 'History. That's what you can't feel. Neither you nor Kit. The sense of the family and Tregonna intermingling down the centuries. I thought Kit and I were going to work together to preserve the spirit of the place. I was so excited. But all he meant was getting exact replicas of doors and finding suitable bathroom fittings.'

Her face had lit up as she spoke of Tregonna and its history. My anger drained away. Ma was bonkers. But what was new? She'd always been odd about her family heritage, laughable as it was. A dodgy but go-getting ancestor with money from dubious sources and, since then, a slow sinking into poverty through the ages until debts forced her uncle to sell the house when she was a teenager. Maybe that was why she was so obsessed by its future.

'I wish Pa had never bought it back for you,' I muttered.

'What?'

'Nothing. It was nothing.' I took a deep breath and concentrated on what I had to do. 'Kit loves Tregonna, Ma. We both do. It gave us a wonderful childhood –'

She interrupted me.

'Oh Jen, and it's all been lost.'

I had to stop her thinking that. Focus her on Kit.

'Do you remember the time Kit and I climbed in through the attic?'

I'd been eleven, maybe twelve, and Kit must have been fifteen. We'd been late coming home. Very late. I don't remember why. And Pa was home so there would be trouble.

'We should have a rope hanging from our bedroom,' I'd said. 'Then we could bypass the parents and pretend we'd been home for ages.'

Kit surveyed the higgle of windows punched out of the stone facade, his face thoughtful. I knew that look.

'Can you see a way up?' I asked.

The wide ledge outside our parents' bedroom on the first floor was a short leap from the jutting stone frame of the scullery window. From there it was an easy scuttle from window to window, a short swarm up a drainpipe and then a shuffle round a corner, using the gutter for support. The drop down from the gutter to the windowsill outside the attic playroom was the only difficult bit. I was too short and Kit had to go first and catch me as I let go and haul me in.

Ma didn't remember any of it. I could see from her face. It had been Pa who'd found it funny when we'd come downstairs acting like we'd been there for hours. He'd guessed. Of course he had, and he'd told Kit not to do it again, at least not without ropes. But it had given him an idea and later on he'd installed pulleys in the roof and we practised climbing with them.

I hunted out another memory.

'And the time we had the bonfire on the cliffs and danced round it? Do you remember?'

'Beltane. Yes.'

'And the coastguard came round and said we were distracting the shipping.'

'It was a large fire,' Ma said. She laughed.

'He was a grumpy old bastard,' I said.

'I placated him. He stayed for a drink as I remember. Mead, I think. We had some bees, didn't we?'

'Yes, Ma. We had bees until they stung that friend of Kit's and… So you see we had a wonderful childhood. And that's why Kit wanted to save Tregonna. For us all. He loves it. He wouldn't have spent all his money on it – and more – if he didn't.'

She nodded her head slowly and I crossed my fingers. Maybe there was a chance.

'I don't think he's explained properly. He's so stressed about everything. About money, really.'

'I've told him not to worry about money. You must tell him too. Worry creates its own negativity. Look at how bad things were with money last year but I didn't worry. I knew something would turn up. And then darling Kit came and saved the day. So you see there's no point worrying about money.'

Ma was like one of those infuriating games we used to get in stockings at Christmas with little silver balls that had to be rolled into tiny holes. You'd get one in but it would slip out as soon as you got another one close to a hole. I ploughed on, though.

'Ma, I know Kit's asked you this already. But please, you need to agree to sell the land. The bit over the road. We never use it. And it's a pain to maintain. It would solve everything. Pay Kit's debts and leave enough for him to market Tregonna as a holistic conference centre. You'd like that, wouldn't you?'

Clearly not. She strode from one end of the room to another, the hem of her dress swirling against the clutter of chests and small tables, while she told me exactly what she thought. Tregonna was the Hammetts' home. Always had been. Always would be. The spring where we renewed our vitality. Our harbour from the outside world. And, make no mistake, we needed every bit of the land to protect us against its creeping darkness.

I stopped her when she started on about the road cutting a gash through the heart of the place. 'What about a mortgage then? You must have hundreds of thousands of pounds of equity in the house now that it's been renovated.'

I didn't think a vast mortgage would solve Kit's problem long-term but, as the owner of Tregonna, Ma would have to take it out, so at least the debt would be transferred to her and to Tregonna. But she wasn't having any of it. In fact, the idea of a mortgage seemed to infuriate her. She clenched her hands and raised them into the air. 'Impossible. Never. But never.'

For once it was a straight answer.

'OK, OK. Calm down. But what are we going to do?'

'Something will come up.'

'Really! Like what? And while we're waiting, Kit has to carry on avoiding everyone because of all the money he owes them?'

She sat down on the bed and started combing the fringe of a shawl with her fingers.

'Come home, Jenifry,' she said.

'I'm here now, aren't I?'

'Come home and stay. With all the family together we'll find a solution. The Hammetts always have.'

It was patently obvious they hadn't and I opened my mouth to remind her of this but something about the look on her face made me stop. She was serious, deadly serious. And she had more to say.

'I can see you've been suffering. Come home and heal for a while. It's what Tregonna and this part of Cornwall does. It's a healing place. I know I'm explaining badly and I know you don't think the same way as I do about Tregonna, but please stay. I sense there is great danger for you outside.'

Her eyes were fixed on me as she spoke and her words stung a swarm of thoughts into life.

'Great danger,' she said again.

'Ma, I'm not in any danger.'

Black spots. Like flies. They buzzed round the outside of my vision and I swatted them away. Missed them and staggered.

'Jenifry. What is it? You're very pale.'

'Feel a bit dizzy. Hate arguing with you.'

She pushed me down to sit on the bed, dampened a cloth with some liquid from a glass bottle on her bedside table and started patting my forehead and the back of my neck. The cold was good. I took a few deep breaths and thought about danger. The word had roused a horde of new ideas that buzzed through my mind but wouldn't settle long enough to take shape. Was I in danger?

'Sorry, Ma. No breakfast. Stupid. It'll pass.'

I couldn't think about it. Not right now.

The hard lip of a glass knocked against my lips and teeth and I sipped. Something sweet. Too sweet but it calmed me. Ma waited. Gave me time to recover. She was always good like that. I made a great effort and got control of myself.

'Maybe I should come home,' I said. 'For a short while.'

'Everybody does in the end, you know. It's how it should be. Remember Kelynen, Talan's sister? She's come back recently.'

'I know.'

'You should go talk to her. She's suffering. She's lost so much. But being home will help.'

I didn't think that living with Talan and working for Freda was going to do much to help Kelly get over the loss of the career and passion she'd devoted years to. But, hey, I had better things to argue with Ma about. I made a last effort.

'But, Ma, I'm not staying unless we do something to sort out

Kit's finances. I couldn't take it. I couldn't be here with Kit and Sofija falling apart. I don't know how you can bear it.'

'I keep away from them. I can't let their negativity poison me.'

'Ma!'

She stood up and pointed her finger at me.

'We have to be very careful, Jenifry, because your brother has opened Tregonna up to negative forces. Very careful.'

'What! You mean when the conference centre opens? The walkers, the painters, the crystal gazers and the other visitors. Aren't some of them your friends? Besides you often have a few paying guests.'

'Not them.' Her bracelets jingled as she dismissed them with a wave of her arms. 'They'll come and go. *They'll* barely touch the heart of the place. *She* is already here. You know who I mean.'

'No, I don't.'

But I thought I did. Not that there were many options to choose between. Apart from Ma and Rosa, the only 'she' at Tregonna was Sofija. My difficult to know, difficult to warm to, sister-in-law.

Kit and Sofija's marriage had been such a cliché. A successful business owner and his Eastern European bride. That's what people thought. I knew they did because a few of them had been stupid enough to make snide comments in my hearing. I'd smacked them down sharply. Maybe over sharply because I'd felt a pang of concern myself when they'd stood, Sofija and Kit, holding hands and slightly stooped under the sloping roof of my kitchen. Both so tall. So well matched, in that way at least. And they'd told me they were getting married.

And Kit overflowed with happiness. It lit up the tiny space and made me smile back at them. So I ignored my suspicions. Reminded myself that Sofija had a job, a good job. Staff nurse at Kings College Hospital. That in a few months she'd have the right to stay in the UK anyway. Besides nothing mattered so long as she kept on making Kit feel that way. It would have been nice if she'd shone with happiness too. But the more time I spent with her, the more I realised that she never showed what she was thinking.

Ma's eyes stared into mine. I thought of pebbles. Beach pebbles. Hard and wet. Bouncing the light off so you can't see what colour they are. So Ma wouldn't see through my eyes into my mind. And I stared back at her. A faint smile curled her mouth.

I knew it was no good. She'd seen a shadow of my unease over their marriage.

'So you're not going to help, are you?' I said.

'I tried, Kit,' I said to him as we walked down through the gardens towards the sea. We'd wrapped ourselves up in coats and hats and scarfs and gone out into the fading day to get some air. 'But I don't think she'll ever agree.'

'With a bit of time she will, don't you think? I always knew she'd be dead against it at first.'

'No, Kit, she won't. Nothing's going to make her agree. You'll… We'll have to find another way.'

Kit stopped by a bed of shrubs he and Sofija had planted shortly after moving down. The winds off the sea were tough on plants and Kit touched the few leaves that still clung onto stalks and life, pockmarked with brown spots and edges seared yellow. He laid his finger on each leaf in turn as though committing it to memory while the cold forced the blood to our noses. I thrust my hands deep into the pockets of the coat I'd taken, ignoring the detritus of crumbs and old tissues left behind by previous wearers, and something metallic that felt like a nut.

'What other way?' he said.

I had no answer.

The early evening light made the ruddy orange stem of a dogwood gleam, but even it had suffered, with the last few inches of each stalk burnt black. Kit picked off each dead end. Then, without speaking, he broke off each twig and branch working down until nothing remained except the central spine. He tugged at it, forcing his foot into the earth for leverage but it clung to the hard ground and resisted him.

I thought he'd given up because he turned towards me and looked as if he was about to speak but something stopped him. Maybe I didn't control my face and my pity showed. He swung his foot back in a wide arc and bashed the dogwood with the stubby base of his boot then kicked and stamped it into the ground. Afterwards his shoulders rose and fell as each of his breaths, like empty speech bubbles, whitened the air in between us.

I spoke first.

'Never liked dogwood.' It was the wrong thing to say, but I ploughed on. 'We'll think of something, Kit.' Yes, I said that too, equally stupid as it was. And Kit's breathing shook and tore holes in its white mist. I couldn't bear to see him like that.

'Look, I've rung the garage in Plymouth. They'll buy the car off me straightaway. They might not give me eighty thousand for it but it'll be quick. They want me to bring it in the day after tomorrow.'

He turned away and his shoulders heaved in great spasms as though he was vomiting into the flowerbed.

'Listen, Kit. I'm going to sell my flat too and I'll give you the money. There won't be enough for all your debts. Not after I've paid off the mortgage. But it should settle a lot of it. And it won't take long. Not the way the market is at the moment. Then we'll find a way of sorting out the rest.'

'We?' he said.

'We,' I replied and gave in to the inevitable. I couldn't leave

Cornwall yet. 'Of course it's we. You didn't think I was going to leave you to deal with all this on your own, did you?'

Sofija called to him from the back door. 'Kit. Rosa is waiting for her bedtime story and Talan rang again.'

He stuck his hands deep in his pockets and shivered.

'Jen. Talan lent me money. Ages ago. When I thought the bank would come good and it was only a cash flow problem. I have to pay him back. Could you write him a cheque? I mean, in advance of selling the car.'

'How much?' Even I could hear the bleakness in my voice. It shrivelled Kit. 'I mean, of course. But I don't keep much in my current account. I'll have to go online and transfer some.'

'I'll have to check the exact amount. It happened three or four times. But fifteen thousand should cover it.'

'Fine.'

He hesitated.

'Go in,' I said. 'I'll come in soon. Tell Sofija what we've agreed. She looks…' But now was not the time to talk about how dreadful Sofija looked. I gave him a shove and he turned and trudged back up the path.

Kit had borrowed fifteen thousand pounds from Talan. Borrowed it without being sure he could pay it back. Something about the casual way he'd announced it made me feel sick. The old Kit, the Kit I loved, would never have done that. I began to wonder if he'd gone forever. We'd all become our opposites. Kit, the successful entrepreneur and planner extraordinaire, now cadged money as he faced bankruptcy and failure. Sofija, the imperturbable, was thin and anguished. And Pa, the mountaineer, always after new challenges, virgin peaks, thrilling in walking where no one had before, now shepherded coddled businessmen up mountains in South America. I… I didn't like to think what

I'd become. Best not to. Best to shut the lid on it all and move on. Only Ma remained unchanged. A bit madder every year but the essence of her never shifted. Maybe the important thing in life was to hold onto what you were. Ma was certainly happier than the rest of us. And if her happiness was because she ignored what everybody around her wanted or needed and looked only inwards to herself… hey, that was Ma.

I picked up some dead leaves lying in the corner of the low wall round the paved seating area. Protected from the rain by the bush overhanging the wall, they had dried and crumbled until only a lacy skeleton remained. I smoothed one over the knee of my jeans and traced the network of lines that subdivided and subdivided until they blurred into each other although I was sure, if my eyes were only sharp enough, I would find each vein had an end.

But it was a distraction from what was going on in my head. Something that made my sight blur and my fingers tremble. And when I could no longer see or touch the leaf, I screwed it tight in my hand and let the idea become words.

Danger? Was I in danger? I thought I was.

I didn't think I'd been raped. There'd have been signs. I'd have known. And anyway, why all the stuff on the lighthouse? Why bother? I wasn't going to remember anything.

Someone had tried to kill me.

It was the only thing that made sense.

The words sucked everything out of me and I was nothing but a skin bag stuffed with straw. *Someone had tried to kill me.*

Every thought path I went down led to that conclusion.

Would I have taken roofies? No. I knew what they did.

So someone must have given them to me. Slipped them into a drink.

On that headlong walk along the cliff path trying to escape the addictions that clawed at my feet, I'd met someone. Gone somewhere. Drunk something. And afterwards that someone had taken my unresisting body to the lighthouse and hung me over the edge, using a rope they knew would fail, with a knot in it I never would have tied. I thought of the frayed bits of the cord. Maybe they'd done that too. It would have been easy to rub a worn bit against the corner of a stone. Just to speed up the moment when it snapped.

And who would have questioned it? Jenifry Shaw with a long history of climbing stupid things. Jenifry Shaw, dead in a climbing accident. Such a pity. So sad for her poor family.

But who? Who the fuck would have done it? Who hated me enough to kill me?

Twelve

When the cold and my horror-filled thoughts got too much, I went back inside to the warmth. The chill passed but frenzied spasms of questions still stabbed through my mind.

Who? And why? Yes, why? Why had someone tried to kill me? Someone? But who? Who hated me enough to kill me?

Sofija and Kit were sitting at the table in the old kitchen, the only bit of Tregonna that the renovation hadn't really touched. It had been rewired but that was all. Great gouges in the battered wallpaper traced the route of the new wiring but they'd been filled in clumsily, hastily, and never redecorated.

Was I safe? Would they try again? Why, though? Why?

Sofija leaped up and rushed towards me. I felt my arms twitch as though to ward her off but she didn't notice as she flung her arms around my neck. Her shell of imperturbability had cracked wide open.

'Thank you, Jen,' she said. 'Thank you. Kit told me what you are going to do. I thought you'd turned your back on us. I am sorry.' She breathed out heavily. 'And now we will celebrate. We will eat something nice and drink. And toast the end to all our problems. Yes?'

I dragged my attention back to Sofija. All her problems? I darted a quick look at Kit over her shoulder but he wouldn't meet my eyes. What had he told her? Clearly not the whole truth.

'Do sit down. You look exhausted,' I said.

And she did. The wild gratitude had wrung her out and the release from stress had left her wobbly and soft. Kit pushed her chair towards her but Rosa called from upstairs. Sofija hurried out of the kitchen and Kit slipped into the back room where Pa used to hang the maps and plans for his expeditions and turned on the TV. I followed him. The TV flashed images of the sea and boats and wet people clinging to each other. Migrants washed up on some Mediterranean shore. Displaced. Un-homed. Their lives wrecked.

'What did you tell Sofija?' I asked.

Kit muted the TV and plucked at the frayed edges of a hole in the armchair. 'I told her wrong. In the wrong order. I told her you were selling your car and your flat to help us and she thought everything was going to be OK. You saw how she was. Ecstatic. And I just couldn't tell her the truth after that. That we'd still be in the shit.'

'Well, you'll have to put her right.'

'I will. I will. Just not tonight, please, Jen.'

We both gazed at the silent images on the screen. Then Sofia was back with Rosa in her arms.

'She heard your voice and wanted to say goodnight.' She spoke a few sentences in Bulgarian and Rosa held out her arms to me. I gave her a kiss and told her we'd look for some swings together. She smiled and burrowed her face into Sofija's body. Sofija's arms tightened around her and her face crumbled into love.

I looked away. The nakedness of it was too much. I'd got her all wrong. Poor Sofija. There must have been moments when she'd wondered if Rosa would have a roof over her head.

After she'd taken Rosa back to bed, I joined Sofija in the kitchen. She moved between sink and stove, clearing away dishes and putting water on the boil while all the time, in the background, the radio chattered away. Nothing exciting, but just interesting enough to keep my mind occupied. To stop me thinking of everybody I knew and wondering if they'd tried to kill me.

'Sorry,' Sofija said. 'I always have the radio on. I don't notice it but Kit hates it.'

'I don't mind.'

But she turned it off and came and sat at the table by me.

'We always had it on as children. The BBC World Service, you know? In English. My parents wanted us to learn English and they thought it would help. My brain absorbed it over the years. Of course they taught it in school after the Zhivkov era. But when I got here, I could understand what people were saying. Most of my Bulgarian friends couldn't.' She reached out her hand and took mine. 'I am so very grateful to you, Jen.'

'You mean the money. I'm happy to help. Kit's my brother and…'

She got up and went back to the sink and looked through the window. It wasn't a great view, the back yard: the bins, a pile of old slates in one corner all covered with slimy green from the damp.

'I know you do not understand how Kit has got himself into this mess,' she said. 'I don't think he understands himself. He had great plans. And Kit is good at plans and designs and creative solutions to big problems.' She turned round to me. 'But it is not as simple as that. You have to see them through and he isn't good at that.'

She watched my face as I thought how right she was and how odd it was that she should know this when I hadn't realised it. Kit loved a problem, loved finding a solution but after that he lost interest. At work, he passed the project on to me or another rigger and we saw it through, we made the adjustments, small and big, that had to happen when real life and the unexpected collided with a plan.

Sofija smiled suddenly. 'Nothing fancy for supper. Just pasta. But I'll open a bottle of wine. To celebrate.'

She started to chop tomatoes and onions and, with the silence, questions gnawed at my mind again, and an identity parade of potential killers followed swiftly.

'What happened to Pip?' I asked, desperate to distract myself.

'Pip?'

'Gregory's dog. He wasn't there when I was at the lighthouse. Is he dead?'

'We think so. He disappeared a few months ago. He was an old, old dog. Your mother thought Pip knew he was failing and went away to die alone so Gregory wouldn't be upset. But if that's true it had the opposite effect. Gregory hunted for him for weeks.'

'Poor Gregory.'

'They said in the village Pip might have disturbed someone. He was a very barky dog.'

'What do you mean?'

'You know. People bringing things in. What do you call it? Smuggling.' She stopped chopping and looked at me.

'You've been listening to too many old tales, Sofija.'

'No. I read it in the paper,' she said. 'Yachts at Falmouth with millions of pounds of cocaine aboard and people finding packages washed up on beaches.'

Her face was serious but I didn't answer because ideas were sparking off in my mind like fireworks on Bonfire Night. I told myself not to jump to conclusions. But what if the would-be killer wasn't someone I knew? Wasn't someone who hated me? What if I'd interrupted something? Something illicit. I tried to put a brake on my thoughts but they hurtled out of my control.

Along the cliff path from Freda's. After Kelly had seen me. Above the cove where I'd found the body that morning. The ledge with the pulley. The perfect place for landing stuff. Like the tourist board panel said. Waves of logic carried me forward and a strange scenario unfolded in my head.

Tired after the long drive and frayed with the strangeness of being out of rehab, wanting a hit of cocaine to break the darkness of her mood, Jen goes for a long walk along the cliff path.

She strides past the cottages and houses on the outskirts of the village and past Kelly smoking her rollies in the garden at the back of Freda's cottage. She doesn't see her because she's walking hard. Hard enough to exhaust herself. Hard enough to kick her body's natural chemicals back into life.

That much I knew was true. And it wouldn't have been strange for childhood memories to have enticed me down the path to the ledge.

But as Jen turns the last corner before the ledge, a gust of wind blows the sound of people calling and the rasp of a pulley towards her. Unthinkingly, she continues and sees a group of men leaning over the edge and shouting down to a boat below. They haul on ropes and a white-wrapped package lurches over the ledge. They drag it onto the rock and the torches strapped to their heads catch Jen in their beams.

No. It was day. Evening. Maybe the sun was setting but it would still have been light. It didn't matter. So what? Forget the dark. Forget the torches. It was a myth that stuff always came in at night. Far easier in the day. Especially early evening with a storm threatening. Who would be around on the cliffs to see them? No one. Except idiots like me.

129

They see Jen. They stop dead and she knows something is wrong. Her heart bangs in her chest and she turns to run up the path but, for once, she is not quick enough and hands grab her legs and force her to the ground.

I thought about the myriads of bruises that were still appearing on my legs and arms. *Had they come from fighting? From hands grappling me to the ground? And the head wound from a bang? Or had they knocked me out?*

Whatever! No point sweating about the details. Just say I'd come across something illicit. Forget the romantic image of ponies trotting through the dark. The people who brought drugs into the country weren't nice. They'd have got rid of me without thinking twice. One of them must have recognised me. Known about my reputation. The lighthouse was nearby. How easy to use it. Make it look like a drug-fuelled prank carried out by a woman who was known for that kind of escapade.

My mind went back and forth over the scenario during supper. Kit and Sofija didn't notice my long silences. None of us said much anyway. They discussed the details of an open day they were planning for next week. For local journalists and the like. And I thought. I thought about the cove and the lighthouse and I thought about Nick Crawford and our strange encounter in the middle of the night. *What had he been doing on the cliff road? Coming back from collecting his merchandise?* He had to be involved. It was too much to think that there'd be two separate drug smuggling operations in the same village.

'Tell me about Nick Crawford,' I said. 'He's recent, isn't he?'

They both stared at me, forks of rolled pasta halfway to their mouths.

'You fallen for his charms?' Sofija said. 'You'll have to join the queue.'

No surprises there. He *was* charming. With a hint of toughness. A winning combination that clearly he made use of.

'I met him at the lighthouse this morning,' I said. 'He and Gregory seemed very friendly.'

'Are they? I thought Gregory had more sense.' Kit wrinkled his nose.

'Kit. That's not nice. He's been very patient with us,' Sofija said.

'Do you owe him money, too?'

'Yes. He's a carpenter. Made some doors to replace old ones that were completely rotten.'

'He did a good job. Your mother didn't even notice they were new.'

Kit rolled his eyes and carried on eating.

'Why don't you like him?' I asked.

'Very friendly to us when he first got here,' Kit said. 'Then he started hinting he could put me in the way of some cheap furniture for Tregonna. Antiques. So long as I wasn't bothered where they'd come from. He left us alone when I said I wasn't interested. He didn't even bother to hang the doors himself. He sent one of the local joiners instead. A lot of locals don't like him. He mixes with the wrong people.'

Mixing with the wrong people. I knew what Kit meant.

'The wrong people?' Sofija said. 'What do you mean?'

'Just that,' he said. 'Dodgy people. Who skate close to the edge of the law.'

'Fishermen?' I asked.

'Yup. Among others.'

He went back to eating and Sofija chatted on about the preparations for the open day, while I thought.

Dodgy people. Dodgy fishermen. Drugs in Nick's sideboard. It all made sense. Plus he was the one person I knew had been out and about on Friday night. Not a dealer, then. A trafficker. A link in the chain that brought cocaine from South America to the streets of the big cities in Britain. Brought in by boat locally and transported from here in his furniture.

The sound of the back door opening and closing came up the passage. Ma swept through the kitchen without stopping. Kit and Sofija ignored her and carried on talking.

'I looked at the outside of Tregonna,' Sofija said. 'The windows are filthy. We must do them before the open day.'

'It's the wind from the sea,' Kit said. 'It's full of salt and leaves white marks behind.'

'You said you'd wash them,' Sofija carried on. 'Once Jen was here. You said it wouldn't take a minute then.'

Kit gave her a long, hard look.

'It won't,' he said – and to me, 'You up for it?'

I didn't know what he was talking about, then I remembered the system of pulleys that Pa had fitted into Tregonna's eaves. It meant someone – normally Kit – could harness up and clean the windows while Pa pulled and released the rope to raise and lower him.

'Are the pulleys still there?'

'Of course,' Kit said. 'You don't think I'd get rid of them.'

'I'm up for it.'

'I'll get the equipment out later. Check it over.'

We nodded at each other. For too long. It meant more to me than simply cleaning the windows. It meant the two of us working together. Almost like climbing together. And I thought it meant Kit was trying to move on.

Ma didn't eat with us. She didn't like Sofija's cooking. Or so Kit said. She'd eat later when we'd all finished. I said I was tired and went to my room, newly decorated and furnished and not a bit like it used to be. Tasteful greys and soft greens and a complete lack of the miscellaneous and battered furniture it used to house. The room was chilly. No heat came from the radiator. They'd either forgotten to turn it on or couldn't afford to. As quickly as I could, I got into bed, went online and transferred the money across to cover Talan's cheque, then explored what the internet could tell me.

Quite a lot. Newspaper stories galore.

Cocaine worth £80m seized on boat off Cornish coast. A fishing trawler.

£7m of Columbia's finest found washed up on Cornish shore. And it wasn't the only time. Five similar packages had been found in the past six months.

I also found the story about the bodies washed up along the coast that Talan had mentioned. Two bodies, three weeks ago. Perhaps the body I'd found had come off the same boat. The column hinted at smuggling. The bodies had not been identified. No one had been reported missing.

The more I read, the more likely it seemed that I'd come across something illicit on the cliffs. I'd been an unlucky witness to be got rid of. It hadn't been someone who hated me. Because, after all, no one knew I was in Cornwall. I'd just arrived. I'd told no one I was coming. Not even Kit and Sofija.

And somehow that made me feel a lot better. But I still couldn't sleep. Every creak, every rattle shook me awake.

I went downstairs, fumbling for switches in unaccustomed places, and made a cup of tea. Checked the outside doors were locked. Went back upstairs. Locked my door and wedged a chair against it, then got back into the massive bed that had replaced the old one with the lumpy mattress and scratched headboard. Still wide awake, I googled Seb.

First, I found a small paragraph in one of the dailies. A leap from a high roof to a lower one with a roll in between. A classic free running move. A moment's misjudgement. He'd crashed into a gutter, scrabbled for a grip and fallen awkwardly onto concrete below. Pronounced dead at the scene.

Then a longer article in one of the local papers. Seb had started his career there and the first part was the editor's memories of him. A fiery youngster, passionate about literature and art, believing they could change people's lives. Seb was someone, the editor believed, with a bright future. He hadn't been surprised when Seb had got a job as an arts correspondent with one of the nationals. He'd thought he was waving Seb off to fame and fortune in London. Despite the clichés, you could feel his regret at the waste of Seb's life.

I tried to remember when I'd last seen Seb. He was a thread running through the years so hard to pin down to a specific time or place. I had the impression he'd been low the last few times I'd seen him. Quieter and depressed. Some of the fire the editor talked about had gone out. The job had been a disappointment, less about the arts and more about the lives of celebrities. He'd written a book, I remembered, and it had been rejected. Countless times.

I huddled further into the duvet trying to stop the chill of the room stealing warmth from the bits of me that were uncovered. Not much of interest in the rest of the article. His funeral. A quiet affair. Private; family only. Standard words: *young life cut short*; *tragedy*; *dangerous sport*. No flowers. And a quote from his mother. 'Why didn't someone stop him? One of his friends? My Seb was never an athlete. He wasn't sporty. How did he get into jumping off roofs?'

Jumping off roofs. Something came back. One night. In a bar. Soho. The end of a film shoot and two of the stuntmen had joined us. Us – me and Josie from work. I think one of them fancied her. And Seb was there too. His office was nearby.

We'd all drunk too much because the shoot was over and none of us had to be on top form the next day. The stuntmen and I swapped stories of our exploits in a friendly way but beneath our rowdy laughter a competitive edge sharpened the talk. And somehow the banter ended with us racing up the front of the building to the roof terrace bar. It was nothing. Three storeys max and covered with ornamental details, bars on windows, ledges and drain pipes that made climbing easy.

I won. They bought more drinks and Josie traipsed up the stairs to join us. But Seb wanted to have a go. One of the stuntmen went down and helped him climb to the top. His face as he emerged over the top wall reminded me of the old Seb, his dark eyes glittering with the firelight on the beach and excitement inside him.

Was that the beginning? I hoped not. Although really, really truly it was nothing to do with me. I hadn't helped him. And I'd never suggested he should take it further.

I was cold all over now. And from Seb to Grid was a short lunge. One accident to another. Besides, Grid had been on my mind since I realised the lighthouse had been no accident. His face a recurrent one in my identity parade of murderers. It *was* my fault that Grid had been injured – injured so badly. Entirely my fault. He had every reason to feel bitter about me.

And I started to wonder again. *Did Grid hate me? Enough to hurt me? Enough to…?*

But he wouldn't. He wouldn't. I knew he wouldn't. And anyway, the same excuse held good. We hadn't spoken in months. He didn't know where I was. The thoughts whirled round my head and I gave up on sleep.

I had to know.

It took me an hour to write the nine words of the message I sent Grid and, even after I pressed send, I fretted I'd chosen the wrong ones.

Hey Grid
How's things man?
I'm at Tregonna.
Jen

I didn't expect a reply until morning but it came straightaway. Someone else was having problems sleeping.

He was fine. Living in Plymouth for now, in Vince and Ricky's flat. The London flat had been too much. Going to physiotherapy daily. Did I want to meet up? Coffee, maybe? At a café near where he was living, as public transport was still a bit of an adventure. Or I could come round to the flat.

Friendly. Even cheerful. Welcoming.

And God help me, I hesitated before replying. Jittered about whether it was a trap. In the end I said yes to the café near him the day after tomorrow. Told him Kit knew we were going to meet up. Like I always shout at those stupid dicks in the movies to do before they go off to meet the villain. Not that I thought Grid was a villain. Not at all. I was sure he wasn't. I knew he couldn't be. It was the aftermath of Friday night that was poisoning my thoughts. Leading me into paranoia.

Love Jen
Delete
Bye for now, Jen
Delete
Love
Delete

Jen

Send.

Mission accomplished. Just the rest of the night to get through.

Thirteen

Kit and I cleaned the windows in the morning and it wasn't as much fun as I'd thought it would be when I was a child watching him and Pa. The wind nipped at my damp hands, still sore from last Friday. It was tedious and it definitely wasn't climbing. It was hanging off the end of a rope and being hauled up and down by Kit. Anyone could have done it. It was washing down the glass with a very wet cloth, then swishing the water away with a rubber-bladed tool, and finally polishing with a dry cloth that rapidly became damp. I didn't have enough hands to hold everything so I was endlessly juggling stuff in and out of the bag Kit had given me to tie round my waist. And every few windows or so, he dropped me to the ground so I could rinse my cloth before hoisting me back to the top.

Below me on the overgrown and tatty lawns that rolled down to the sea, broken here and there by islands of weed-choked shrubbery and piles of stones that had once been beloved rockeries, Ma, serene and unfazed by Kit and I yelling at each other, did her yoga. I saw odd bits of it in between windows. The Cobra Pose. The Sun Salutation. Not that there was any sun.

After a couple of windows, I was ready to stop. After ten, I prayed for rain, storms, snow. Anything that meant we could finish. Because I didn't have time for this. I'd woken that morning in a rage. The confusion and weakness of the last couple of days had gone completely and, although I was tired, I was angry. Furious that someone had tried to kill me and determined to find out who it was. I just didn't have a clue how to start. I'd thought of talking to Kit but when I'd gone down to the kitchen, I knew at once that he had told Sofija that their financial problems were far from over. She'd gone back into her shell, only her white face and rigid lips giving her away as she slopped milk onto Rosa's cereal while Kit, looking sullen, coiled ropes, ready for us to wash the windows. I guess he thought it was the least he could do.

I made a few calls first and confirmed that the sale of my flat would leave Kit and Sofija around a couple of hundred thousand pounds short – the amount outstanding on my mortgage – and then we started cleaning. Both of us distracted and reluctant.

The front door opened and Rosa jumped down the steps. She saw Ma and ran over to her. Ma picked her up and swung her round, the two of them laughing. Sofija appeared on the top step and shut the front door behind her. Neither she nor Ma acknowledged the other.

'*Rosa*,' she called. '*Vreme e da otidete v Tanya. Pobŭrzaĭ.*' And then she walked to the car without looking at Ma. Rosa came running over to join her while Ma turned her back and stretched into the Warrior Pose. Sofija and Rosa got in the car and drove off. Ma waited a few seconds, rolled up her blanket and stalked into the house.

I stretched over to polish the last corner of the last attic window. My left hand slipped off the window frame I was using to steady myself and I plummeted a few feet, bashing my knees against the stone, before Kit gripped the rope hard enough to stop me falling.

'For fuck's sake, Kit,' I yelled. 'Stay with it.'

He started hoisting me back up again, his hands pulling the rope easily through the pulleys above me.

'Don't. I'm coming down. I need to rinse the effing cloth again.'

But he wasn't listening to me. A car swung round the drive from the back of the house and stopped. Talan and Kelly got out.

A brilliant idea came to me.

'Let me down, Kit.' I kicked and jerked the rope to get his attention. They all stared up at me and finally Kit fed the rope through his fists and lowered me to the ground. Talan was stuffing an envelope into his back pocket – my cheque, I thought – and speaking to Kit as my feet hit the gravel. Kelly watched me and laughed.

'Definitely been in the water for a while,' Talan was saying.

'Any idea where it came from?' Kit asked.

'Impossible to say. Bodies can travel a long way.'

'Morning, Talan,' I said. 'Morning, Kelly.'

She'd wandered over to an old birdbath and was talking to a ginger kitten playing in the tangled undergrowth beneath it. She didn't look up and for a moment she reminded me of the old Kelly. Looking as though she was waiting to drift onto the stage and make exquisite shapes, with her fingers tapping in time to the music in her head. The music only she could hear. Beautiful, aloof Kelly, half with you and half somewhere else.

I left her to the kitten and tuned back into Kit and Talan's conversation.

'You talking about the body I found?' I asked.

'Just filling Kit in. It's no one local. Nobody's been reported missing.'

'I guess there are boats in the Channel that wouldn't report problems.'

Talan turned to me. He must have been off-duty because he was wearing jeans and work boots.

'What do you mean, Jen?' This was Kit.

'Drugs,' I said avoiding his eyes. 'Smuggling. Don't tell me it doesn't happen.' I pulled some of the stuff I'd learned on the internet out of my head. 'Big ships, in the Channel, off-loading onto fast inflatables. They can land in the tiniest of coves. If one of them got into trouble, no one would report it.'

We turned as one to look out to the sea. Choppy this morning and dark grey with the tops smashed into white by the wind.

'Maybe,' Talan said. 'It's an ongoing problem.'

Kit's mobile rang. He looked at it and winced. 'I'll have to take this.'

I peered over his shoulder. It was the bank. He went indoors and I took the harness off and let it drop to the ground. Window cleaning was over for now. *Thank God*. I stuffed everything else into the bag round my waist and untied it.

'Jen,' Talan said. 'I'm glad of the chance for a word. I wanted to tell you that the lighthouse file is closed. No further action will be taken. There was no real damage done.'

'OK.'

I stuffed my hands into my sleeves to coax some warmth back into them.

'So we can let the matter drop.' He paused. 'But be careful, Jen. I'm speaking to you as a friend. An older brother, if you like.'

'It wasn't me.' I was pretty sure now this was true. 'I didn't break into the lighthouse.'

He frowned.

'Someone saw a young woman,' he said.

'What are you talking about?' Kelly's voice was sharp.

Had she told Talan something?

Talan sighed. 'Nothing.'

I looked hard at Kelly but she brushed her bruise-coloured fringe out of her face, met my gaze and gave me a tiny shake of her head.

'Not that bloody lighthouse again. It's all you talk about.' She came over. Her bad leg dragged, scraping along the gravel.

'Someone saw a young woman heading towards the lighthouse that night,' Talan continued. 'On the road heading out of the village. They remembered because the rain was tipping down by then. They wondered what she was doing.'

'The road out of the village?' I repeated. 'In the rain?'

It made no sense. I'd been out of the village well before the rain started.

'Really! Who?' Kelly said to Talan.

'One of the old boys coming out of the pub. Waiting in the doorway for a break in the rain.'

'Christ, Talan. They're all ninety-five and deaf and blind. Did they say it was Jen?'

Talan hesitated. 'No. They didn't get a close look, but they were sure it was a woman. A young woman. Who else would it be? It sounded like Jen.'

He had a point, I thought. Who else would be out and about?

'Loads of people,' Kelly said. 'The one-way system's a nightmare. People often get dropped off at the top of the high street and have to walk down. Besides, why the fuck would Jen walk out of the hotel in the rain? When she'd got a perfectly good car in the car park behind it? Huh?'

Talan looked at my car, bright red against the greens and browns of the trees, and I gave Kelly a quick, grateful smile. Now was my moment, I thought. While Kit was away.

'Talan,' I said, my thoughts speeding ahead of my words. 'I know I can trust you. I've found something. Something that really worries me.'

With their eyes following me, I walked over to my car, leant in, unlocked the glove compartment and took out my little package of

142

powder. My hand didn't even shake. And my aim was true when I tossed it to Talan.

'What is this?' he asked, turning it over in his hands.

'What do *you* think it is?'

'You know what it looks like. Where did you get it?'

I made a rapid decision. I wouldn't tell Talan about Nick Crawford. Not yet. There'd be time once I knew for sure what the powder was.

'I found it in one of the attics.' I lied.

His eyes looked up into the dark windows under the eaves, gleaming from my efforts.

'Among a pile of old paint pots,' I continued. 'Thought it was some sort of plaster but it seemed strange because it was such a tiny amount. So I removed it. Put it in the car. You know, with Rosa getting into everything now, I didn't want to leave it lying about.' I was doing well, I thought. Talan's face had creased in understanding when I'd mentioned Rosa and he'd stopped fiddling with the car keys. 'So will you take it and get rid of it for me? I don't want to put it in a bin. In case…'

'But who would have left it there?'

'Impossible to say. The place has been full of people for months.' I paused. Deliberately. Then did a little flutter of the hands as though an idea had just come to me. 'I don't suppose you could get it tested, could you? Just, if it is what we think it is, I ought to tell Kit. But I don't want to worry him if it's nothing.' I paused again, as if I was summoning up the courage to confide. 'Things are bad. You know that, don't you? Kit's got a lot of problems. We'll get out of it. We'll find a way. I'm going to sell my flat. And my car. But Kit's stressed to death. And Sofija, too. I can't give them anything else to worry about.'

He reached out a hand and patted my shoulder. Sort of brotherly-like. I resisted the urge to slap it away and smiled and thanked him.

'I didn't ask Kit for my money back,' Talan said. 'I guess you're the one who's paying?'

'I don't think Kit is comfortable owing you money,' I said. 'And it's a lot, Talan. You should have it back. It's our mess, not yours.'

We shuffled around the subject a bit longer. I was touched, though, that he was prepared to forgo such a large sum. I didn't think policemen earned a great deal. And he must be helping Kelly, too. If she had to look after Freda, she must be desperate for money.

'You won't forget to let me know about the test results,' I said.

'You staying at Tregonna then?' Kelly asked.

'Yup,' I said. She raised her eyebrows. 'Of course I am.'

'Can't be easy.'

'It's OK.'

'Talan said your mother and Sofija aren't talking. That they'd had a terrible row.'

Talan looked uncomfortable. 'That was in confidence.'

'I'm only telling Jen. Keep your hair on.'

'I'd noticed anyway,' I said. 'You could hardly miss it. It's just stress. They'll be better now things are getting sorted.' But, remembering both the look on Sofija's face after she'd learnt the sale of my flat wouldn't cover their debts and Ma's vitriolic words about her, I knew it was unlikely.

As their car went up the drive, Kelly looked back at me with a sharp expression. She guessed I'd lied about the cocaine, I thought. If I could get her on her own I'd explain.

'Off to his mine,' Kit said as he came out of the house.

'What?'

'Talan's part of a band of oddballs who are restoring the old mine at Cambervale. Trying to make it into a tourist attraction.

Although I think the others have rather lost interest.'

Memories of a pleasant but narrow and steep-sided wooded valley with a large stream came back to me. Cambervale was a long walk from Tregonna but we'd gone there from time to time. Kit and I and a group of friends. It was a long way from anywhere, in fact, and quiet. The ruins of the old mine were hidden here and there in the valley, come upon by chance and covered with ivy or with trees growing out of their walls. I remembered the ivy more than anything else. It had a bitter smell that stayed on your hands for a long time.

'I'm surprised there's anything left to restore. It was falling apart when we used to play there.'

'Did we?' Kit's face was blank, his thoughts elsewhere.

'Don't you remember? Part of it fell down one day.'

'That's the buildings. Pump houses and engine rooms. Talan's working on the underground stuff.'

I shuddered. He laughed at my face and, for a moment, he was the old Kit, before financial stress squashed the life out of him.

'It's not so bad because it's not very deep,' he went on. 'Only a scratch in the hillside. Not like the shafts at Botallack or Levant that run out under the sea for miles. Awful for the miners, always wondering if the weight of the water above might split the rock. It would only take a tiny crack and the sea would...'

His voice wavered and I looked hard at him. His hands gripped his face, leaving a gap between his fingers through which his eyes glinted. Sharp and bright. I thought he might be crying and looked away.

'I can't get over Talan being a policeman. He wanted to be a pirate when we were young,' I babbled. 'We were going to sail the seas together and live on coconuts from handy desert islands. We even started building a boat.' I gave up. 'Kit, what's happened?'

'I've got to go to the bank,' he said. 'To beg,' he added. 'Not that it'll do any good in the long run, but it might buy us a bit more time.' He took his hands from his face and picked up the harness I'd dropped.

'Did you explain –?'

He cut me off. 'I told them everything. The car. The flat. But they want all their money back and we haven't got it.' He ran the harness straps back and forward through his hands. 'I think we might have reached the end of the line.'

Despair stripped his face of colour and I couldn't look. I wanted to tell him there were worse things than going bankrupt but obviously I didn't.

'The belay's in the attic with the rest of my stuff if you want to carry on with the windows,' he said.

'Maybe later.'

Fourteen

As soon as Kit had gone I went into the house. Asking Talan to test the powder was the first step. Now for the next. It was time to find out more about the so charming Mr Crawford.

A few doubts washed through my head. *Maybe I should leave it. Maybe I should disappear. Lie low. It might be safer.* But I couldn't. I wanted to get the bastard who'd hung me over the lighthouse and left me to fall. Besides, when had I ever run away from danger?

I went back to my room, typed 'Nick Crawford' into Google and scrolled through pages of hits. He shared his name with a member of a popular boy band and a very vocal scientist in New Zealand. Even when I eliminated the two of them from my search, it was a common enough name to yield thousands of matches. More surprisingly, 'Nick Crawford carpenter' brought up nothing that related to him, not even the website address on the card he'd given me. I typed that address in instead.

It was a simple site. One of the off-the-peg ones you can adapt to your own products. There was some blurb about working closely with clients, high standards and wealth of experience, contact details and lots of pictures of furniture. Nothing about Nick Crawford. Not a hint of a biographical detail. Not even a picture. I checked again but there was definitely nothing.

He could be shy. He might think his furniture would speak for itself. Which it did. Beautiful curves and abstract shapes.

Distinctive, very distinctive. A suspicion came to me. I chose a piece. An extending dining table with a top made from walnut burr and the base a half circle of a loose grained wood I didn't recognise. It was striking and simple.

I googled 'extending dining table walnut burr' and hunted through the images. There were pages of them. But I found it in the end. And this time on the website of a bespoke furniture maker in Poole. Benjamin Edwards, he was called. I went onto his site and there it was. No doubt about it. Same table. Same picture even. One of them had stolen the picture from the other and when I looked further through Benjamin Edwards's site it was clear who the thief was. In the section called 'Workshop' there was a picture of Benjamin working on the same table. And he looked nothing like Nick. Nick Crawford was a fake. His bare workshop was a lie. Wherever he got his money, it wasn't from making furniture.

I thought back to the night of the storm. How Nick had got out of his car and walked away. Lent it to me so I could get home safely. It had seemed an act of great kindness; now it looked like an entirely different scenario.

Nick Crawford is on his way home after a night bringing the drugs to shore and transporting them to the workshop in his cottage. There have been snags. The weather, for one, although at least it meant the coastguard was unlikely to be out and about. And another was the girl who'd stumbled across the lads hauling the final package up the cliff. She saw their faces. Recognised some of them. Getting rid of her was the only solution.

They drugged her and dragged her to the lighthouse. An accident. It would look like an accident. She was the sort of girl, they said, who would have thought it fun to go to the top and watch the storm. They hung her by an old length of sash cord. It wouldn't hold for long and she'd fall and, with her history, everyone would think it had been a climbing accident.

Part of me still wanted to think he hadn't been there. That he hadn't been part of whatever they'd done to me.

He wasn't there and if he had been, he thinks he'd have come up with a better solution than the lighthouse. Bash her over the head and dump her at sea, but he understands they didn't want to go back out there with the storm scudding towards them. Besides, the disappearance of a girl as well connected as she is would make the police investigate the area and he doesn't want that. At least this way there'll be a body and an explanation.

His headlights catch something at the side of the road. Someone walking. He stops.

Had he recognised me then? Or later? It wouldn't have taken long. There couldn't have been many mad, drugged creatures wandering the cliffs in the storm.

She's not going to get in the car with him. That much is certain. And he's not going to be able to catch her. But she's off her head. Drugs and fear. If she goes to the police now, he doesn't think she'll make much sense. He doesn't think they'll believe her. Not in the state she's in. And if she goes when she's calmer, he still doesn't think they'll be convinced. They'll want to know why she didn't come straightaway. The story of being hung off the lighthouse will sound like a fantasy. He just needs to make sure the lads she recognised have a good story and an alibi. Besides, there's every chance she won't remember much.

But he is a careful man. A clever man. And he wants to keep tabs on her. And most of all, he doesn't want anyone else to come across her. Help her. Hear her story. Take her to the police. Or, if she won't trust them, call the police. So he gives her his car. If she does go to the police, they're hardly going to suspect the Good Samaritan who helped her out, are they?

And the following day he picks up his car from the hotel. He finds out she is there. Not sleeping it off in a police cell or hospital. So far so good.

He goes to the lighthouse to check nothing has been left that will give his lads away. Gregory is already there looking at the damage caused by the break-in but he hasn't found anything incriminating. Nick finds some remnants of the cord and pockets it, then has no choice but to contact the police.

I still wondered why he had gone to the station rather than calling them. Had he found something else at the lighthouse he wanted to get rid of before the police arrived?

And when he comes back, she is there, chatting to Gregory.

Me, that is. Chatting to Gregory. At ease. Perhaps a bit pale. With eyes still bearing traces of the previous night if you looked hard enough. It must have given him a shock. He must have sweated even more when Talan arrived and turned out to be an old friend of mine.

And I'd thought he was being kind when he didn't tell Talan he'd seen me the previous night. Covering for me. But the last thing he wanted was any discussion about what had happened the night before. Clever, clever Mr Crawford.

Well, maybe not so clever. Because I was on to him now and I knew exactly where to go next to find out where he'd come from.

Fifteen

Looe hadn't changed. The air smelled of fish and rang with the sound of yachts' rigging twanging in the breeze. The inevitable seagulls called overhead. I remembered the town as bathed in the permanent sunshine of childhood summers. Today it was grey with a bitter edge to the wind.

And the boats were in. My mood soared. Two pieces of luck. Getting Talan to test the powder and, now, the fishermen would be around. They were a close and closed bunch of families with boats passing from one generation to another. Chances were they'd know of illegal shipments arriving. Chances were one of them might be involved. I'd have to be careful who I spoke to.

First, I went to the Tourist Information Centre. An elegant building, grey granite and high ceilings, built for one of the fishing fleet owners in the days when there was real money in fish. It was open and Rachel Mullins was there, sitting behind the counter sorting piles of brochures. She'd run the Tourist Office for as long as I could remember. The Mullins were one of the biggest local families with a finger in every pie. Freda, who Kelly looked after, used to run their affairs and, now that she was incapable, I was fairly sure the mantle would have passed to her daughter-in-law, Rachel. The men of the family preferred it that way. They might grumble about their mothers and wives among themselves but all of them ran scared at the thought of managing their own lives.

As I came in she looked up and gave me a vague smile before returning to her brochures. She was a familiar figure with her square jaw and the hint of bulldog jowls dragging her cheeks down but clearly she hadn't recognised me.

I browsed among the postcards and fingered the key rings and purses with *Welcome to Looe* stamped on them and debated how to ask her about Nick Crawford. If only I were a police officer, or even a private detective, someone who could slam a card on the counter and get straight into the questions.

Instead, I sidled up and flicked through the brochures nearest her and when she looked up again, feigned a start of surprise and exclaimed, 'It's Rachel, isn't it? Rachel Mullins? Not sure if you remember me. Jen Shaw. My mother is Morwenna Hammett. At Tregonna. I was at school with your daughters.'

Now she recognised me. We went over how much I looked like my mother and in answer to her litany of questions, I gave a brief and untrue résumé of what I'd been up to recently and lied some more about why I was back in Cornwall. She told me what her daughters were up to: one a mother, the other working for the National Trust. Both still living nearby. How nice! So Rachel saw a great deal of the grandchildren. How lovely! No, I wasn't married. No, no one on the horizon. Yes, a brief visit home to see the renovations at Tregonna. Yes, they had been pricey. No, there was no problem. All going well. Oh with finance, you mean. Just a bit of a cash-flow thing. You know what the banks can be like.

Shit, I'd forgotten just how direct and persistent Rachel could be. She didn't like to let a subject go until she'd worried the truth out of it.

'Funny thing, though.' I cut through her flow of questions. 'It's not the first time your name has come up today. You've rented

Simon's cottage out to a carpenter who Kit used on the renovation. What was his name? Neil? No.'

Simon had been Rachel's uncle by marriage and I guessed she'd be the person dealing with the rental of his cottage.

'Nick Crawford?' she asked.

'Yes, that was it. Nick Crawford.'

Her eyes narrowed. 'What about him?'

'Oh, you know. Just stuff. He made a couple of doors for Tregonna. Expensive. But worth it.' I paused. 'I wondered…' She leaned over the counter towards me. 'Nothing. It doesn't matter. Except…' I took a deep breath. 'Do you know where he came from?'

'Why?'

'Just seemed odd. That's all. Him settling in Craighston. Most people have some connection with the area. And Kit has had a few problems with him.'

'What sort of problems?'

I settled my elbows on the counter and embellished Kit's story of Nick offering to get him antiques on the cheap and his eagerness to mix with the dodgiest of people. Hinted that Kit had bought something from him and was now worried about where it had come from. And wondered why I'd dithered so much before because Rachel was enjoying every minute of this. She let her brochures lie and listened, her face quivering with anticipation, like a dog sensing a walk was in the offing.

She told me she'd suspected something was wrong from the word go when Nick had offered to pay six months' rent in advance. In cash. Debbie, her eldest, had said she was mad to let him stay. But six months' cash was not to be sniffed at. No matter what her husband said about him. Not everybody had money to burn after making a fortune in London. This said with a sideways glance at me was, I supposed, a dig at Kit.

'And anyway he was from round here,' she went on. 'I'm sure his previous address was a local one.'

'Have you still got his old address?'

'I'll have it at home. Why?'

'I was thinking of asking around about him. Getting a bit of background. Just in case Kit's got a problem with the furniture. But keep it quiet, Rachel. I don't want anything getting back to Crawford. Did he give you any references?'

'No.'

I supposed the cash had been reference enough.

I scribbled my phone number on the margin of one of the leaflets and thought about extricating myself. The bell pinged again as the door opened. Another customer. An opportunity to escape. Rachel looked past me and said, 'Finished then?'

A fisherman, by the way he was dressed. Bald under the black woolly hat he took off and stuffed in his pocket. About Rachel's age, although it was hard to tell. The sea left its mark on all fishermen's faces, aging the young ones early but then preserving them.

'Yup,' he said.

Rachel waved a hand at me.

'You remember Jenifry. Morwenna Hammett's daughter.'

'Oh, aye.' He nodded to me. I recognised him.

'Hello, Mr Mullins. How are you?'

'It's Tom. Fine. And yourself?'

'Great. Just catching up with Rachel.'

He turned to Rachel and gave her a set of car keys. 'I'm going over to the chandlery. Don't know how long I'll be. You take the car and I'll come home in the truck.'

'Are you going to pop by and check on your mum? Or shall I?'

'I'll do it. I should be back by seven.'

Rachel turned to me. 'Tom's mum's not too good these days.'

'I saw her,' I said. 'A couple of days ago.'

'Where?' This was Rachel. A tight note in her voice. 'Where was she?'

'She gets confused,' Tom said. 'She's wandered off at night a couple of times. Needs an eye kept on her.' The last phrase was said with his eyes fixed on the counter between him and his wife.

'At her cottage. I was waiting for the police.'

'The police?' Tom's voice was sharp.

'Nothing to do with your mum. A body. My brother Kit and I found it along the shore just down from your mum's cottage.'

I told him what had happened and his face settled into deep lines.

'That's it,' he said when I'd finished. 'That's enough. She can't stay there alone.'

'She's not alone,' Rachel said. 'She's got Kelly there at nights and people pop in and out through the day.'

'Kelly's not family.'

'Your mum's happiest in her cottage. She's lived there since she married your dad. It would be too much of a change at her age.'

But Tom persisted. 'I'm not sure about Kelly.'

Rachel slapped another box of brochures on the counter and ripped the tape off it.

'Give her a chance. She's only been looking after your mum for a week or so. There are bound to be a few teething problems,' she said. 'You've got a bee in your bonnet about her. No one's good enough to look after your mum.'

'Why didn't Kelly tell us about the body? A body found close to my mother's and she doesn't think to tell us.'

'The storm washed it up,' I said. 'Talan said it could have floated for hundreds of miles. Just chance it landed near your mother's place.'

'Talan is a fool.'

The lines in Tom's face screwed tighter. Rachel gave him an impatient look.

'Don't start, Tom,' she said.

'Don't you start either, Rachel. Talan and his bunch of cronies know as much about the tides and currents here as I know about knitting.'

'You think the body may have come from round here then?' I asked. The redness of Tom's face deepened towards purple.

'Well, I don't think it floated here from Africa,' he said and turned to Rachel, leaning an arm on the counter, effectively blocking me out of the conversation. Surprise made me catch my breath. I'd never have thought he could be so rude to me. Ma counted him as an old friend, buying fish direct from him and letting him use Tregonna for his daughter's wedding reception.

'We'd only need to look after her at night, Rachel,' he said. 'There's enough folk around during the day. Can't have her wandering off at night again.'

'I need my sleep, Tom.'

I got the feeling it was an old argument. Their words lacked colour, as though it had been rinsed out of them through over-use.

'What about the time Kelly didn't turn up at all?'

'Talan rang and explained, Tom. People get ill.'

'And Mum –' He shot me a quick look and lowered his voice. 'You know she's had more accidents since Kelly's been there.'

'It happens. At her age, it won't get better.'

'But all of a sudden, like?'

'She says she sleeps well when Kelly's there. So she doesn't wake up in time. That's a good thing. Sleeping. And it's only a few sheets. You need to stop going on at her about it. It embarrasses her. She's entitled to a bit of privacy.' And with an air of having finished on a high point, Rachel gathered a pile of brochures and headed over to the shelves. 'Go on, then. You'll miss the chandlery if you don't get a move on.'

He went, slamming the door so hard behind him the bell jingled for several seconds after. I followed, waving a quick goodbye to Rachel then racing after Tom. I'd rather talk to him than any of the other fisherman. We walked together down the street towards the quay. He was silent and I wasn't sure if he was lost in his thoughts or ignoring me. But when we reached the harbour, he turned to me.

'How would you feel if it was your ma?'

'Don't know, really. Can't imagine it. I mean I can't imagine Ma not doing her own thing.'

He raised an eyebrow, turned towards his truck and wrenched the door open. Something had left a big dent in it. A long time ago by the look of the rust that had formed on its outer edge.

'Tom,' I said quickly. 'Do some of the fishermen still bring stuff in? You know. *Stuff.*'

He stopped, halfway up into the cab, one foot on the ground, the other on the foot plate, and shot his head round to glare at me.

'Why do you want to know that, Jenifry?'

'Just wondered.'

'They might. But you won't catch me saying anything about it.'

'Who?'

'What do you mean who?'

'Who brings stuff in? I know you know. Or you can at least make a good guess.'

'Why do you want to know?' he said again, but this time his voice was angry.

'I just do. I can't explain.'

He stared down at me and shook his head.

'You asking for your ma?'

'What?'

157

'Did Morwenna get you to ask me?'

'No.'

He gave a little laugh and a jerk of his head as though he didn't believe me.

'I haven't discussed it with Ma. Honest.'

I pulled my scarf tighter round my neck as he hoisted his body into the cab and dragged the door shut. He took his time, made me wait, shoulders curved against the breeze, then leaned out of the window and shot the words into my face.

'I wouldn't tell her when she asked me and I won't tell you. Whatever the two of you think you're doing, you need to stop. Things aren't like they used to be, you know. It's not about bringing in a few bits and pieces any more. It's big business and it's nasty. So you tell your ma to keep out of it.' And with that he fired up the reluctant engine and yanked the truck into gear. I watched him reverse slowly through the crates of nets and tried to keep my mouth shut. *What did he mean? What the hell was Ma up to? Surely she wasn't involved with the smugglers.*

Behind me I felt the wind start to pick up. It pasted my jeans against my legs and blew my scarf in front of me like an arrow. It was all I needed to shove me into action. I ran after Tom's truck, still manoeuvring backwards through piles of fishing equipment. I grabbed the mirror bar, leaped onto the footplate and hammered my fist on his window. He stabbed the brakes and the truck stalled. A couple of fisherman off-loading crates of fish from the boat next to us turned and stared as he rolled down the window. The words exploded out of me.

'You're not driving off and leaving me like that. If Ma's involved in something you need to tell me.'

He looked away. At the fishermen who had now stopped working and were staring at us. Shit. This was not a good place for the sharing of secrets. I turned and waved at them and stretched a smile over gritted teeth. Tom nodded. They went back to stacking crates but we both knew they were listening and glancing when they could.

'Please, Tom,' I said.

'Get in the truck.'

I did as I was told and sat in silence while he reversed off the quay and stopped by the gate. His rage had dialled down a notch and he was almost calm when he spoke.

'That body,' he said. 'It'll have come from the same boat as the others. Just taken longer to wash up. You heard about that? Two corpses, the other side of the lighthouse?'

I nodded.

'You and your Ma you don't want to get mixed up with the people who let it happen. And that's all I'm saying, Jenifry. I've got daughters and a mother who's on her own. You get me?'

He leaned across me and opened the door. His face was pale now but the lines were as deep and dark as rock crevasses in the snow. I wouldn't get anything else out of him.

My mind was racing as I clambered out of the truck. *Ma asking questions about smuggling. Was she involved?* She needed money. She was relaxed about drugs; she smoked a bit of weed herself. Or, at least, she had after Pa left. Growing it in the old greenhouse – a Victorian addition to Tregonna, with small glass panes and a curved roof, crumbling into ruin. Every spring Ma got the ladder out and filled the new holes knocked through by the winter's storms with squares of old hardboard taped to the rotting frame.

I remembered holding the ladder for her the spring after Pa and Kit left. Maybe that was when I'd realised what she was growing. Or maybe she'd told me as she stood on the ladder, her dress a patchwork of different fabrics billowing above me, like the coloured plastic round the crates on the quay beside me now, flapping in the wind.

I ran up the street and back to the car park, leapt into the Aston and raced to Tregonna. For once, I was going to get the truth out of her.

Sixteen

Ma wasn't at Tregonna. No one was. I tried her bedroom door on the off-chance but it was locked, which really pissed me off. I mean, who locks their bedroom door? In their family home? With only their family around? *People with something to hide, that's who.*

I raced around the garden and grounds but there was no sign of her and my anger grew as I paced up and down the drive, waiting for her to emerge from the woods clutching a basket of mushrooms or clamber up from the cove with her skirt and hair fluttering in the breeze, until I came to a stop by the front door and glanced up once more to check she wasn't skulking in her room. Not that Ma ever skulked.

Her bedroom window was open. Just a few inches at the bottom. Like it always was. She says she can't bear an airless room. Enough was enough. I was going to find out for myself. She'd never have given me a straight answer anyway, even if she was here.

I went straight up to the attic before I could think better of it, lashed the ropes we'd been using to clean the windows together and climbed down to her room. As I clambered over the windowsill, I knocked a jumble of crap off a table. A china tray and a rose glass dressing table set along with countless rings and earrings. *Shit.* I picked them all up but the stopper had come off one of the jars and its contents had left a streak of wet on the carpet. Fingers crossed it would dry without leaving a mark.

I put everything back, trying to fit the tray exactly into the dust-free square on the table. Then I took a deep breath and looked in her dresser and wardrobe; they only contained clothes, their scents of patchouli, sea and damp bitter against the dusty odour of the room. I told myself I was looking for some evidence of her involvement in smuggling, ignoring the little voices trying to break through my rage with her, telling me to stop.

At the back of her underwear drawer I found a small key. It was for the chest by her bed, I was sure. And I was right: the key turned easily. I lifted the chest lid a millimetre so as not to dislodge the piles of books and junk and peered in but it was too dark, so I gave up and swept all the clutter from the top onto her bed and flung the chest open all the way.

Inside, all was order and neatness. No white powder, no wads of cash, not even a packet of dried cannabis leaves. Instead, there was a pile of folders. They were beige mainly with a larger green one at the bottom. All soft and woolly with age. I didn't hesitate. I dived in.

One folder contained her passport and birth certificate. Another, her O-level certificates and school photos. And another, the contract with her publishers and her royalty statements – very small amounts in recent years but I'd guessed that. And the rest were mainly photos from the time before Tregonna when we lived in London. Baby photos of Kit and me along with drawings we'd done and bits of pebble and dead flowers and grasses – mementos from day trips and holidays.

The big green file was stuffed with her diaries and notes and sketches from the two years she spent in India where she met Pa and afterwards wrote about in her book.

I've read it. When I was eleven, I think. I wanted to see what the fuss was about because every time we met someone new, they'd say to her 'Not *the* Morwenna Hammett?' Ma would give the tinkly laugh that made Kit and I look elsewhere and then they'd say how much they'd loved her book and how it made them want to visit India. Sometimes in a hushed voice they'd ask her if it was all true. She never answered. Most of them asked her if she was writing another and that would be the end of the conversation.

I quite enjoyed her descriptions of the various jobs she did – peddling trinkets and beads from a small boat to tourists staying in houseboats on a lake in Kashmir, tea-picking in Kerala with the sisters of the roadside café owner after he threw her out, scrubbing floors as a maid in a small hotel near Delhi – but it was weird, very weird, reading about her living with a string of different men in her pursuit of understanding the culture of another country. She calls the women she works with by their real names but she gives the men titles such as the Roadside-café Owner, the Agriculture Student and, of course, the Maharajah's Son. She meets Pa about two-thirds of the way through. The Young Englishman, he's called. But you can tell it's him. A passionate climber, wandering from camp to camp in North India in search of the next peak to conquer. Who else could it be? In case you hadn't put two and two together, the publishers leaked a story about it being him when the papers were full of his historic first solo ascent of Kanchenjunga.

Ma was much coyer about sex with Pa, which was a relief. You could tell she was wild about him, though. Her accounts of waiting for him in base camps and wayside shacks and her descriptions of the savage and beautiful mountains he climbed were strung through with a curious tension, as if she understood his passion for them but also hated and feared them as rivals.

I thumbed through the file. Books and papers filled with her scribbles. Rough sketches of everyday life and a few photos. Most of them were in the book. But interspersed were drawings of

Cornwall. Some of them I recognised straightaway. Charlestown port and the cliffs below Tregonna. A few, I was sure, were of the trees in the woods above the house and there were lots showing coves and beaches and rough stone walls with wildflowers poking through the gaps.

For a story about India, Ma's book has an awful lot of Cornwall in it. It's always in the background. India is compared to it. And sometimes she slips in stories of her childhood and the holidays spent at Tregonna sailing with her Uncle Daniel, her father's childless and much older brother, until Daniel, unable to afford the upkeep, sold Tregonna and moved to the south of France.

She'd gone to India the year after her Uncle Daniel died. His will predated the sale of Tregonna and its text still left the house and the estate to her even though it had long been sold and the money spent. So, wild with the loss of the one thing she wanted passionately, she flung herself into an alien culture as if she didn't care if she drowned in it.

Of course, Ma got what she wanted in the end. And I don't mean Pa. Sure, she wanted him. Loved him. But she wanted Tregonna, too. Ma's wishes had been fulfilled, her disappointment cured, when Pa made a lot of money out of an old friend's sporting equipment company and, at a time when huge houses were out of fashion, bought Tregonna back for her.

It struck me as I looked at the contents of her chest laid out around me that there was a lot that wasn't there. Nothing personal since she moved into Tregonna. No photos. No mementoes. As if her life had stopped at that point.

There was nothing of her relationship with Pa either. No marriage certificate and certainly nothing to do with the divorce. No love letters. No letters at all. Nothing to give a glimpse into their life together and the mystery of why it fell apart.

No letters at all. That struck me as strange. Ma was always writing letters throughout my childhood. Often on blue airmail paper. And receiving them. Where were they? She wouldn't use e-mail. She shunned anything electronic, claiming it gave off poisonous waves.

There were no bank statements either.

Had she systematically thrown everything away? I looked around at the heaps of junk that had colonised the room like watchful spiders: bowls of potpourri and crystals and piles of scribbled recipes and meditation texts. It seemed unlikely.

I found everything in a box under her bed. Chucked in. The lower down you rummaged, the older the date. Bills. Mainly unpaid. Some of the money Kit had spent must have gone into sorting out the worst of Ma's debts. The bank statements were here too. I found the most recent. Ma was overdrawn but not disastrously so, and there were no payments going out for a mortgage. Great. In fact, more than great. There were no regular payments going out at all. Kit must be paying all the rates and utility bills. On the other hand, not much came in. I wondered what she lived on. Cash payments from holistic treatments, dance classes, selling candles and crystals and other New Age junk?

The rest was mainly letters – years of them. I pulled out a few handfuls. Mostly from the UK. A few from India. Some from France and Italy and several from North Africa. A lot from the same people. Ma had friends all over the world and I had memories of exotic people coming to stay from time to time. Some of them friends from her travelling days or people who'd written to her when her book first came out and who'd become friends over the intervening years.

Nothing suspicious, though. Nothing except for a gun right under the far end of her bed. A shotgun. Twelve-bore. The local gun of choice. My fingers found the catch automatically and broke it. It wasn't loaded and there were no cartridges in the wardrobe or anywhere else that I could see. I shoved it back under the bed.

The sound of footsteps coming up the stairs. I froze.

Not Ma. Please let it not be Ma.

The footsteps stopped. I looked round at the mess of Ma's life strewn on the floor and the bed. Nothing I could do about it. *Don't come in*, I prayed. *Remember something you need to do. Get distracted. Go away.*

Seconds passed. Minutes. No noise from outside. Inside, the little sounds I couldn't help making – the swallowing to ease my dry throat, the tiny ragged breaths tearing the air, the creaks as I shifted my weight from one foot to the other – seemed louder and louder.

Just as I was wondering if I'd been mistaken, or if whoever had been there had slipped away, the door handle turned and the door shifted in its frame. My eyes fixed on the tiny movement. Had I missed the moment when she unlocked it? I didn't breathe. I didn't move. There was a gentle clunk as the lock hit the frame. Whoever was outside didn't have a key.

'Kit,' I said but my voice caught in my throat. 'Kit?' I said again but I wasn't sure it was loud enough to be heard.

No answer. Nothing.

'Kit? Sofija?'

The handle slid back round. Footsteps faded into the distance. I tiptoed to the window and looked out. No cars. No one. Except the ginger kitten sitting in the shelter of the rockery and staring back up at me.

Time to tidy and get out. I felt stupid as I stuffed everything back where it had come from. Searching Ma's room had been a moment of madness. With one last glance to check I'd left the room roughly as I'd found it, I rushed to the window, clambered out and stood on the ledge, my hands holding the ropes. A flick of the knee closed the window so that its edge rested on my feet and I prepared to push off and climb down.

Some whisper of caution made me hesitate – or did I catch a glimmer of something out of place on the edge of my vision? Maybe. Or perhaps the gaze of watching eyes pierced my consciousness? Who knows… But I stopped and glanced up into the eaves.

I saw a flash of movement. Then a black object hurtled past my head and landed with a thud on the gravel two storeys down. It was the pulleys. The force of their fall yanked the ropes from my hands and pulled my body away from the window so I teetered in space. I snatched at the wall, my fingers scrabbling in the bricks and mortar for a grip while gravity grabbed at my wavering body, desperate to seize it and dash it against the ground thirty feet below.

Seventeen

My feet saved me. They hooked themselves round the underside of the window and held me upright until my hands found a hold in a broken brick. I pushed one leg back into Ma's room, forcing the window open, and sat astride the ledge. It took a while for the adrenalin to stop sparking pain in my nerve endings and for my breathing to calm. And then I felt sick. This was no accident. My hyper-efficient brother had checked the system before we started washing the windows. Besides, the seconds before the pulley fell were taking shape in my mind. I'd seen something in the eaves. A hand, I thought, snaking out, yanking the pulleys and whipping back.

I gulped the air. It was cold. But that was good. Icy air calmed the dizziness. Pushed the panic down to manageable levels. I made myself focus on the now. *Was the owner of the hand still here? Waiting?*

I shut out the exterior sounds – the ever-present rushing murmur of the sea and the fainter, sharper noises of the hedgerow birds foraging in the garden – but inside the house, the silence was thick and impenetrable.

I had two options. I could climb back into Ma's room – I couldn't unlock the door from the inside so I'd have to sit there and wait to be found but at least I'd be safe. Or, I could climb down and run the risk that someone was waiting for me below.

I heard a thud, faint from travelling along corridors and up stairs. In my head, an image of the back door slamming shut appeared. I was sure that was what I'd heard. Then the sounds of footsteps crunching through the gravel at the back of the house. *Were they leaving?* I thought so. For a moment my body sagged with relief; then it didn't. I needed to know who it was. I needed to see who was running through the woods to the road. I'd have to climb down.

I looked toward the ground.

Ma looked back up. How long had she been there? How much had she seen? I couldn't tell whether she was angry or worried or shocked. Did she know I'd been in her room?

We stared at each other for a few frozen seconds that went on forever. Then she turned and stalked off.

I grabbed the drainpipe and shimmied down, tore after her and headed her off. She stopped. Colour rose in her normally pale face and she breathed as though she'd been running.

'You've been in my room,' she said. 'You broke into my room.'

I looked behind her at the drive curling round the side of the house. No matter how fast I ran up it, I'd never catch up with my would-be killer now. *Fuck!* I turned back to Ma.

'I had good reasons,' I said.

'So?'

'So what?

'What were your reasons? Your good reasons.' She raised a finger and tapped my chest.

'I thought... I thought... Oh shit, I thought you might be smuggling drugs – cocaine, heroin.'

The rapid breaths pumping her chest in and out stopped. A nasty little part of my brain wondered whether this was due to shock that I could think that of her or horror at being found out.

'Jenifry.' She moved her hands to her face and pressed her

fingers into her forehead. 'How could you think that? I'd never do anything like that. How could you...?'

'You used to grow weed.'

'That's different.'

'Don't tell me you didn't sell some of it.'

'To friends.'

'That's what they all say.'

She took a step back and stared at me as though she didn't know me and for a moment I thought she was going to walk away again. This time, I thought, I wouldn't stop her but I'd never speak to her again. Never.

But Ma stayed where she was, looking away beyond me, out to sea. Tregonna towered behind her, blocking out the light.

'I stopped growing weed,' she said quietly, 'when they started saying it damaged adolescent brains. And it was only for a few years anyway. It got me over a bad time. I needed something. But how you go from that to thinking I was... I don't know. I don't even think I'd be very good at it.'

'You need money. And you were always up for a bit of smuggling.'

'What?'

'You used to buy stuff from the boats.'

'Wine and cigarettes. That's ancient history. How could you leap from that to thinking I'd have anything to do with serious drugs?' She bent over and tugged a handful of weeds from what had been a rose bed. Some pulled free and she scrunched them and flung them away. They scattered over the grass and rolled in the breeze.

'You've always jumped to conclusions, Jenifry. You're like your father, you know. So like your father. You don't see the people around you. You're so focussed on what you want. What you think you need. So sure you're right. And you hurt the people around you in your stampede after it. Why didn't you just ask me?'

Something exploded inside me.

'Would you have told me if I asked?' I knew I was shouting. 'I don't think so. It's your top skill, isn't it? Avoiding difficult conversations. Everything has to be sweetness and light with you. As though it's all part of some great plan the universe has for us.' Now that I'd started I couldn't stop. 'You never told me Pa had left. Not in so many words. I had to work it out for myself. When he didn't come back from that expedition to wherever it was. All those months, just you and me in Tregonna, and you never said a word. I had to ask Kit when he came home from university in the holidays.'

Her face mirrored my own anger at first, which pleased me no end. I was sick of her Zen-like quality. But, as I continued, it took on a bewildered look and when I paused for breath she turned away. I thought she was going to leave.

'Ma?' I said. 'You can't walk away now.'

'I'm not.' She sat down on the grass and patted the ground, inviting me to sit too. 'Why do you think I'm a drug smuggler? There must have been another reason. Not merely because I'm short of money. I'm always short of money.'

'Can we go in?'

'No, let's discuss it here. Then we can leave it behind us. Time and the wind and rain will clear it away.'

I sighed and sat down, although I chose a large, flat stone. The grass was damp and the earth under it sodden. Only Ma would think this was a sensible place to have a conversation.

'I don't think you're a drug smuggler.' And I didn't. Not now she was sitting in front of me, her body ramrod straight and her eyes still and calm. 'But you asked Tom Mullins which of the fishermen might bring in stuff for you and I – well, I jumped to the wrong conclusion.'

'Tom. Oh yes.' She laughed. Not her normal trill but a sad laugh overlaid with a hint of sourness. 'I remember. He was horrified. Wouldn't listen to me. Warned me off and stomped away. It must have gone deep for him to tell you. But I didn't want to smuggle drugs, Jenifry. It was a person. I wanted to get someone into this country. A very dear friend. Nahla. I've known her for a long time. She's Libyan. She and her husband are writers I met at a conference years ago. He's Libyan, too... or, was, I suppose. They should have got out before the civil war but they didn't. Nahla had elderly parents and she thought she was safe but, since Gaddafi's fall, Libya's become a terrible place, especially for a woman. Her husband's dead so she's on her own. I'd have done anything to get her out.'

I'd seen the pictures on the news. Even in rehab they'd let us watch the news.

'Did you get her out?' I asked.

'No.'

'But I'm sure there are people who could do it.'

'Oh yes. There certainly are. Gregory found out for me. People will do anything for a price.' She ran her finger across the grass. 'Do you know what the going rate for bringing an illegal, as they call them, across the Channel is?'

'No.'

'It's ten thousand pounds. And rising. Ten thousand pounds. I don't have one thousand pounds, let alone ten, and neither do her family nor her friends. Besides, we'd have to get her across the Mediterranean first. So, no, I didn't get her into the UK.'

'I haven't got any money. I've given it all to Kit.'

'I don't want your money, Jenifry. I did think, at one point, I might ask Kit but...' She stood up and brushed the grass off her dress. 'I look at that hideous new kitchen sometimes and

I feel sick, when I think of what it cost.'

I stood up, too. There was nothing I could say and we walked back to the house together.

'Where is she? Nahla, I mean.'

'I don't know.' She picked up the rope and pulley and gazed at them. 'What happened?' she asked.

I took them from her. 'I don't know,' I said, but I thought I did. The eyebolt that attached the pulley to the beam had come out. It lay thick and heavy in my hand. I brushed the last couple of wood splinters off the deep thread of its screw and wondered how that was possible.

'Did you see anyone?' I asked. 'In the woods. When you got back today?'

'No. But I came along the coast path. I went to see Gregory and walked back.'

We heard the noise of a car turning into the drive and Kit's Land Rover appeared.

'I'll go in,' Ma said and turned to climb the steps up to the front door.

'You might want to change,' I said. 'The back of your dress is very wet. Oh – and why have you got a gun under your bed?'

'It was Uncle's. I use it for pigeons.'

'You shoot pigeons?'

'Scare them off the cabbages. I don't aim at them.'

'Have you got a licence?'

'I don't use it for shooting at anything.'

'You still need a licence. You must get one.' I thought again. A shotgun could decapitate a person, blow a hole through their chest, amputate a limb. 'No, get rid of it. Give it to Talan. He goes shooting – or he used to.'

'I don't want anyone using it for killing things.'

I remembered outings with Talan. Him patiently teaching me how to stand to shoot, then break the gun to insert new cartridges.

'Clay pigeon shooting, Ma,' I said. 'They're not live pigeons. The clue's in the name.' She laughed and things felt good between us. I seized the moment. 'Ma, won't you think again about helping Kit? Maybe not selling the land. I get how you feel about Tregonna. But a mortgage? We've sorted most of the money so it wouldn't be massive.'

But as the words left my mouth, her body stiffened. I should have waited. I wished I could have gathered my words back up and buried them.

Her shoulders rose up and forwards like a BASE jumper about to hurl herself off a cliff.

'Another one,' she said. 'Another one who's only interested in money.' And she swirled round and stalked up the steps into the house, holding the damp material of her dress away from her back with both hands.

I took the pulleys and rope up to the attic. Pa had used a belt and braces system to attach the pulleys to a roof beam. A huge eyebolt screwed into the wood took the weight and a chain slung round the beam provided back-up in case the eyebolt failed. It hadn't failed. But it had come out. The adjustable spanner on the floor beside the window gave a big clue as to how it had been unscrewed. Kit's adjustable spanner, I supposed. Stored up here with the rest of his tools. I ran a finger over the hole where the eyebolt had been. Its mouth was splintered. Someone, I thought, had unscrewed it but left the tip in. Just enough to hold the weight of the ropes and pulleys. They'd waited and watched until I'd come out of the window. Then they'd yanked the bolt and brought the whole lot tumbling down.

The safety chain was missing.

They'd left nothing to chance this time, I thought. No slipping away and trusting that my weight would be enough to pull the bolt free. They'd hung around to make sure. So the lighthouse wasn't a one-off. No, someone had been out there, watching me and waiting for another chance. And they probably still were. Lying low wasn't an option. I'd have to stop them before they had another go.

A text from Rachel Mullins pinged onto my phone. It was Nick Crawford's previous address. Near Plymouth. I was going to Plymouth tomorrow to sell the car and see Grid.

Grid.

How many times had I seen him rig a pulley when we worked together? Watched his hands deftly secure it to a beam and run the rope through it? Countless times.

They call them white nights. The ones where you don't sleep. Is it something to do with summer nights in the Arctic Circle where the sun never sets? Perhaps. But there was nothing white about the October night before my meeting with Grid. It was black, with no stars or moon penetrating the low clouds.

As soon as I started drifting into sleep, the barriers in my brain dissolved and I saw hands on the spanner unscrewing the eyebolt. Then hands undoing the chain. Over and over again and each time the hands were different. Some were familiar although I couldn't remember whose they were. Others were strange to me. I told myself to look up at the faces but, each time I tried, my mind dragged me out of sleep and I came to, sweating and shivery. *Anyone could have done it.* I repeated it like a mantra. The back door was unlocked. It wouldn't have taken long. *It could have been anyone.* It didn't have to be someone who knew about climbing and rigging. It didn't have to be someone like Grid. It could be Nick Crawford. Of course it could. I'd have been visible for miles when I shimmied down the rope into Ma's room. Anybody watching for an opportunity would have seen me.

Eighteen

In the morning, I set off early for Plymouth. Couldn't bear another hour in Tregonna with Ma and Sofija trying to avoid each other. Couldn't bear seeing the desperate expression on Kit's face. It was a large house – a massive house – but we all used the same scruffy kitchen and the same back door.

Besides, it was my last drive in the Aston and I planned to take the long way round, through all the twisty country lanes with their high hedges that broke every now and again to give a tantalising glimpse of the countryside, then over the moors where you could see for miles. But when I drove past the lighthouse, quiet and withdrawn in the morning light, another idea came to me and I stopped the car where the road met the cliff path, and walked down to the ledge where I might have been attacked to see if there was any sign of a struggle – although the storm and the police raising the body from the cove below would have covered over most things...

It was quiet on the ledge and thin clouds let through a soft glimmer of sun that dappled the rocks and grass. Winter mornings in Cornwall were often like this, teasing you with the promise of sunshine, then abruptly piling on heavy layers of cloud.

Nothing seemed out of place. No signs of a fight. I walked back and forth checking the ground from left to right like the police do in TV crime series, feeling ridiculously excited when I found the stub of a rolled cigarette. There were quite a few, in fact: rain-sodden and ground into the grass. I peered over the ledge. It was low tide and the sea had pulled back to reveal nothing. No more bodies, just unmarked sand and rocks, empty of everything except pools and seaweed. It was all as blank as my memory.

I sat on a stone with my back against the cliff and shut my eyes. I tried to remember. Instantly, I became aware of the smells: wet grass overlaid with the rotting tang of seaweed. Nothing else. But nothing ever came when I forced it. Memories only burst upon me when I was thinking of other things. No matter. I opened my eyes. While I'd been sitting, the clouds had thickened, draining the colour from the grass and darkening the stone. I shivered. The ledge felt exposed and I wondered if I'd been sensible coming down here, of all places, on my own. A trickle of fear slid down my neck. I hurried back to the car. A flutter of cloth at the first bend stopped me. Someone was standing there. I looked around for a stick. A stone. Anything. But there was nothing I could use to defend myself. I pressed myself into the cliff, and Kelly walked onto the ledge.

'Kelly!' I wiped my sweaty hands on my jeans. 'I mean, hi. What are you doing here?'

She jumped when I appeared out of the rock and dropped her cigarette.

'Oh Jen.' She bent over and hunted through the grass until she found it. Her hands shook as she lifted it to her mouth and inhaled. 'Shit. You gave me a shock.' Her lips were white and tight round the cigarette and I thought she'd been crying. Her free hand clenched and unclenched the material of the dress she was wearing. She was all in black. Dress, jumper, thick tights and boots. But she always was. Most of the dancers I knew were. As though the grace of their posture and the line of their bodies needed no adornment.

Except Kelly was crumbled and shapeless and pissed off that I was there. In fact, more than pissed off. Like a shabby cat whose fur was still ruffled from the thought of danger, her back was arched and her eyes spat. I'd interrupted her, I thought, in a moment when she'd let all the barriers holding her together go. A private time not meant to be witnessed. I watched her pull the barriers back up and give a sour laugh.

'Tough night,' she said. 'I come down here for a few minutes most mornings after I've finished. It's quiet. Puts a bit of space between me and the night.'

Her hand still gripped her dress. When she saw me looking at it she relaxed and let the crumpled material fall.

'I know,' I said. 'I do that myself. Have a few minutes away from everything. I'll leave you to it.'

'No, no. Stay here. I don't want to drive you away.'

She sat herself down on a rock. As graceful as ever until her knee bent beyond a certain point and she winced and put her hand down to take the weight. I suspected she'd never dance again. Not like she had before, anyway. Whatever she'd done to her knee, it had been catastrophic. I wished she'd tell me because I, of all people, understood what it was like to have the thing you loved most snatched from your life. I understood the jagged hole it left behind.

'You OK? I thought you looked a bit stressed yesterday,' she said.

'I was. A bit.'

'Anything I can do?'

I shook my head. 'Things are tricky at home. But thanks. And you?'

'Not great either. But easier since I started working for Freda. Gives Talan a bit of space to himself in the evenings. The cottage is small.'

'He's very proud of you. He used to talk about you all the time when we were going out.'

'When the two of you were going out,' she said. 'All those years ago. When you were going out and I was still a dancer.'

'Is it –?'

'All over? Dancing? Oh yes. Everything is gone. My life might as well be over.'

Her cigarette was nothing but a stub now. She spat on her fingers, extinguished the last few strands of burning tobacco and threw it into the grass.

'I'm sorry,' I said. She stiffened and I thought how little I would like people being sorry for me but I ploughed on. 'I do get it, Kelly. What it's like, I mean. I don't climb any more. Not since –'

But she cut me off with a slice of her hand and pushed herself up off the rock.

'No, Jen. You don't understand at all. It was your decision to stop. You can climb again. One day, you probably will. I have no choice. Everything has been ripped from me and –' She stopped and gathered all the pain back into herself. 'I'm sorry, but I can't talk about it,' she said and left.

I sold the car. The garage checked it over swiftly and offered me seventy-five thousand for it. They'd probably sell it on for over ninety but Kit needed the money fast, so I only haggled them up to eighty and got them to throw in an ancient Golf, very down-at-heel, but with an engine that still had some life. In fact, after I'd chucked everything from the boot of the Aston into the Golf and driven off, I thought I might have done well. Not that it mattered. I felt too low after my meeting with Kelly to enjoy speeding around the countryside.

I headed off to Little Gidleigh, a village further round the estuary, where Nick had come from according to the address Rachel had texted me. It was a pretty village, high up with views over the estuary. The centre was small, just a pub, a church and a shop that sold a bit of this and a bit of that. It was posh, though, with houses set back from the road behind high hedges and walls and, of course, no street numbers.

I asked at the little shop in the end and bought a chocolate flake, for old times' sake.

'Forty-three, Lower Court Road?' The woman behind the counter asked.

'Yes. It's the only address I've been given and I'm supposed to be picking something up for a friend. I wondered if you knew which house it was.' I was getting good at this investigative stuff.

She put down the pencil she'd been using to write addresses on a pile of copies of the *Plymouth Herald* and thought.

'Can't say I do. Don't you have a name?'

'Aunty Joyce,' I said with a rueful smile. 'That's all she told me. She did say they hadn't lived here long.'

'I don't think anyone's moved into that road recently. You could ask at the Reynolds', though. Mrs Reynolds runs the residents' association. It's the white house at the end, called River View.'

Mrs Reynolds, 'call me Lily', was very friendly. None of the houses had numbers, she told me. They never had. The Parish Council had tried once but the residents put a stop to it. Oh yes. Much nicer with names, didn't I think? The postman knew everybody anyway. Mind you, the courier companies didn't like it much. And as to what would happen to a letter addressed to number forty-three, she didn't know. She supposed it would be returned to sender. Not that anyone wrote these days. It was all virtual, wasn't it? A real pity. And on and on.

When I could get a word in edgeways, I found out what I needed to know. Nick Crawford had lied to Rachel. The address didn't exist. And he'd never lived in Little Gidleigh. Mrs Reynolds knew every family in the street and everything about them. No one who resembled Nick Crawford had ever stayed there. I felt relieved. The case against him was growing.

I got away in the end and pushed the Golf to its limits to get back to Plymouth in time to meet Grid.

The café was not what I'd expected. Stripped wooden floors, round marble-topped tables and bentwood chairs. Very Fifties Paris, with large prints of Leslie Caron and Louis Jourdan and other French film stars of the era. Not a Grid sort of place at all.

I ordered a coffee and watched the clock tick the seconds away. When Grid arrived I understood why he'd chosen this café. There was plenty of space between the tables, and the chairs were easily moved out of the way. I should have sat by the door and saved him having to negotiate a path to the back. Not that you could tell there was a problem. There was a slight hesitation sometimes before he moved his left leg. A sense that something about it had surprised him. That was all.

Of course, I knew straightaway he'd had nothing to do with what had happened to me. He could walk unaided but he couldn't have dragged me up the lighthouse stairs. He'd have needed both hands and all his strength to get himself up. On every level, I'd been stupid to worry he'd been on the lighthouse on Friday night.

He must have seen me looking because, once he'd sat down, he lifted the bottom of his jeans and showed me the sleek, black curves of his prosthetic foot.

'Carbon fibre,' he said. 'With integrated spring technology. Much more dynamic and hardwearing than your puny bone and soft-tissue feet. I'm thinking of having the other one done, too.'

I felt tears prickling the insides of my eyes.

'Don't, Jen,' he said. 'Another coffee?'

I nodded and he went over to the counter and ordered.

If I looked closely, I could see the traces of the last few months. His skin had always been tight over his skull but now there was a thinness to it. A transparency. The rest of him was different, too. His shoulders used to curve, hollowing his chest and they didn't any more. From the waist up he was broader and softer. Maybe it was the result of learning to walk again: using his upper body to drag his legs up and down the parallel bars. Beneath the thick, cable-knitted jumper, the body I remembered wasn't there any longer.

'So what are you up to then?' I said after he'd finished placing the tray of coffee on the table and the look of fierce concentration had left his face.

'This and that. Moved. As you know. Lots of rehab. The clinic here is good. Alan has been talking to me about working at Skyhooks. Plans and prep stuff, for the moment.'

And talking about me, I thought.

'And about me?' I said.

'Some.'

'He sacked me.'

'He told me,' Grid said.

'I don't blame him.'

'It sounded bad, Jen. You OK?'

'I'm not doing stuff any more.'

'You look OK.' He was a liar. I knew how I looked. Thin. Flabby. No muscle tone. 'I mean, you don't look like...'

He meant I wasn't covered in scabs and acne and my nose didn't dribble all the time.

I thought of everything that had happened to me since I'd

last seen Grid in March, and wondered how to tell him. Then I realised I wasn't going to. Just as he wasn't going to tell me about the months in hospital, the struggle to learn to walk again and come to terms with his disability. We'd stopped being able to talk to each other that day in the hospital when he told me they were transferring him to the rehabilitation centre and he'd asked me not to come to see him there, saying he needed time to himself.

'I'm fine, Grid. I've been a bit stupid but, like I said, it's over.'

He started rubbing his fingers and thumbs together.

'Have you stopped smoking?' I asked.

'Uh-huh. You can't smoke here anyway.'

'No, but you used to prepare them for later. Whenever we sat down.'

His fingers stopped.

We sat in silence. His fingers twitched every now and again. *Old habits die hard*, I thought. I looked at my hands and saw they were doing the same, forming and reforming the classic climbing handholds. Pinching, crimping, gripping. I clenched them between my knees.

There was one last thing I needed to know before I could rule out Grid's accident as the cause of the attacks on me.

'How are Vince and Ricky? You said you were in their flat.' I tried to sound casual.

'Good. They're in the States now. Yosemite.'

Yosemite. The rock climber's Mecca. Solid granite carved over aeons by rivers and glaciers into vast cliffs. We'd planned to go together, Grid and I.

Something must have showed in my face. He smiled. Some things hadn't changed. Still the same crack of a smile. Fleeting across his face.

'You should go there, Jen. It's like nowhere else in the world.

If you've got nothing to do, go there now. Climb with Vince and Ricky.'

'I'm not fit.' I said.

'It'd come back quickly.'

Oh, God. I wanted to so badly. Pack a bag. Get a flight. Go. Start on the easy stuff. Grid was right, I'd get fit fast. Once again, I'd feel the cool touch of the granite beneath my fingers and smell its sour, gritty scent. My hands caught the edge of my vision. They were moving through my practice holds again. I shook my head.

'Too much to do. And, anyway, Vince and Ricky. You know. Would they want to climb with me? After…'

'Jen. I told you then and I'll tell you now: you did what you had to do. They know that. No one blames you. It was all of our faults for climbing the stupid tower in the first place.'

'I haven't climbed since.'

'No?'

'No.'

He spread his hand out over the cold marble table-top. His fingers looked as muscled and tight as ever and I wondered if his dreams too were haunted by the feel of the rock on the skin of his hands.

'You must go back to climbing, Jen. You can't stop. It's all wrong.'

He picked up a spoon and tapped it in the space between each of his fingers in turn. Slowly at first then speeding up. It was a game we used to play. See who could be the fastest. The metal against the marble made a noise and the other customers looked over at us. I reached out and put my hand over his, smothering the movement.

'Kit made me promise to stop.'

'What?' He paused while the sense of what I'd said sank in. 'Completely, you mean?'

185

'I guess he thought… No, I know he thinks I can't be trusted. That I won't be able to resist going too far.'

Kit was probably right not to trust me. I wasn't sure I trusted myself.

'I haven't wanted to climb anyway,' I lied.

'Haven't you?' He paused. 'I have. And I will. Somehow.'

Shit. My eyes were prickling. I wouldn't cry. Not now, for fuck's sake.

'Ricky and Vince are definitely in Yosemite?' I asked.

'What?'

'I mean, they told you they were going, but did they?'

'What?'

'Maybe they lied.'

'Like, why would they do that?'

I shrugged.

His eyes raked my face and then he shrugged, too. 'They're blogging about it,' he said. 'Every day. With pictures. Unless you think they're faking it. Difficult, though.'

'What's the blog address?'

His mouth opened on a light gasp of breath. He took my phone and typed in an address and then handed it back to me, his face unmoving as I scrolled through the pictures. There was no doubt. Vince and Ricky were in Yosemite. You couldn't fake the shots of the two of them inching up those vast granite faces towering over the spikes of pine forests. They'd been in the States last Friday, not on top of a lighthouse avenging the reckless stupidity that had cost Grid his foot, his ankle and his climbing dreams. The relief was huge.

I met Grid's gaze after I put the phone down.

'Jen?' he asked.

I told him what had happened on the lighthouse – most of it. I had to. I owed him. And I told him I'd come to suspect someone else had been there.

His face showed little as he listened but I was used to that. Just an occasional flare of amber in his brown eyes when they picked up the beam of the wall light. After I finished he remained silent for a few moments.

'And you're sure,' he said in the end, 'absolutely sure you didn't do this to yourself?'

For answer, I took the rope out of my bag and passed it to him.

'This was what you were hanging by?'

I nodded.

'But you might have used it, Jen, if it was all you had to hand.'

'Look at the knot.'

'Ah. I see. Yes, I understand. A reef knot.'

'I tried to tie one,' I said. 'With the rope in my car. To see if I could. To see if I had. But my fingers don't know how.'

'You still keep a rope in your car? I thought you'd given up climbing.'

'You can use rope for other things.'

'Such as?' He waited for me to answer. 'Tying up runaway horses? Temporary washing line?'

'Shut up.'

We laughed a little.

'Still,' he said. 'At least you know it wasn't one of your climbing friends. None of us would have used that knot. We'd know it wasn't safe.'

The background murmur of chatter and crockery clinking faded behind the ringing in my ears. I swallowed to ease the dryness in my throat. I watched him realise what my silence meant.

'Oh fuck, Jen. You think someone did it on purpose? Someone who knew the knot would fail?' I couldn't look at him then but I felt the weight of understanding land on him. 'Like me, or Vince, or Ricky?' he asked. 'Is that why you wanted to see me? Why you got in touch, out of the blue?'

'Not completely,' I said.

He shut his eyes.

'But when I saw you again, I knew. I knew you'd never have done anything to me. But… before… I thought you might be bitter because I couldn't hold the rope. Couldn't stop you falling. I tried to but…'

I had to lean forward to catch his words as they came.

'I have no hard feelings, Jen. You did what you had to.' I felt him dredge deep inside himself. 'Dealing with what happened. The foot. It's not easy. No way. No fucking way. And if I could go back and change what happened – of course, I would. I have bad days. No, I have crap days, horror days. But I'd never… you know what I mean.'

I nodded.

'And Vince and Ricky?' he said. 'You thought it might be them?'

'Grid, it isn't like you're making it sound. I don't know anything. But I can't sit around being constantly afraid someone might try again. I've got to know what happened.'

'You don't remember anything?'

'It's a blank.'

'But before the blank?'

'I was in the hotel bedroom. Feeling wrung out after the drive.'

He tapped his foot against the iron leg of the table. I tried not to stare at it.

'You should tell the police,' he said.

'What exactly should I tell them?' I bit the inside of my mouth hard. The words had come out wrong. Louder and angrier than I had meant. 'Sorry. But think how it would sound: "Sorry, Officer,

I don't remember anything much but I think someone drugged me, although I am a recovering addict and might have relapsed. Then they hung me over a lighthouse. It might have been for a laugh. Or they might have done it to hurt me. And, by the way, if you look me up in your records, you'll see I have a caution for trespass from climbing dangerous buildings."'

It was his turn to shrug. My mood had reached out and embraced him. His skin had whitened and the knee of his bad leg jerked up and down as though the strain of controlling it had become too much.

I wanted to go. Couldn't bear to watch him force his leg back under control. *This was reality*, I thought. *This was what I'd done to him*.

'I don't think it was anyone I knew, Grid. I think it happened because I saw something I wasn't meant to see. There's lots of stuff going on along the coast. Smuggling, I mean. They use RIBs – rigid inflatable boats. They're powerful and small and they can land in places other boats can't.'

I told Grid my theory and he listened, but I could tell he thought it was far-fetched. His eyes looked beyond me out into the street and suddenly focussed on something.

'Shit,' he said.

I turned.

Someone was picking his way through the tables and chairs towards us. A man. Our age. A biker, I thought, from his battered leather jacket. His black hair was flattened as though he'd not long taken his helmet off. The face was familiar.

'Hey, Grid.' He swung his hand over and clapped Grid's raised one. 'Saw you in here and wanted to come in and say thanks again, man.'

'Mark.' Grid's face was white.

It came back to me. This was Kit's friend, Mark. Mark Vingoe.

Seb's brother, Mark. Dead Seb. *Oh shit, could this get any worse?* I hunted for the right words to say, but there weren't any. There never are.

I wondered how they knew each other. Mark pulled a chair to the table and sat astride it, leaning towards Grid. He'd only given me a quick glance and hadn't recognised me; it was a long time since we'd last met.

'Mark.' I tapped on his shoulder and he swivelled round. 'It's Jen. Kit's sister. I'm up from London for a bit. I just wanted to –'

As I spoke his face distorted. The red, slightly puffy and open-pored skin tightened and wrinkled into lines of fury.

'You!' He paused and Grid reached for his arm.

'Mark,' Grid said. 'Now is not the time –'

But Mark shook Grid's hand and warning words away.

'Jenifry Shaw.' He leaned towards me and his hot breath hit my nose. Sweet mint barely masking the smell of alcohol. 'The wild and wonderful Jenifry Shaw.' Despite the alcohol, his words were sharp and clear. 'That's what he called you. That's what Seb called you.'

I had no idea where this was going but it wasn't good.

'Afraid of nothing.' His voice grew louder as his anger poured out. 'You think you're something else, don't you? You and your famous father and your big house. You think you're so fucking fantastic because you've climbed a few hills.'

He'd lost it. Big time.

Around us was quiet. The other coffee drinkers had fallen silent as Mark started to shout.

Grid took a deep breath and tried again. 'Mark, I know how hard this is for you but now is…'

But his words only provoked Mark.

'And Seb fell for it.' His voice was a burning poker in my ear.

'He fell for all your fucking mystique. Your glamour. Life was too short, you said to him. Too short for wasting. Take risks. Go for it. That's what you told him when he tried to talk to you about how he was. About how things weren't working out like he'd hoped. He was in a bad place and you fed him bullshit. You couldn't just listen. You had to feed him your own personal belief that danger was the stuff of magic. And Seb was always a sucker for magic. So he believed you. He was desperate for something. And he went for it. He said he'd taken a leaf out of your book and that you were right. How he never felt so fucking alive as when he was out leaping over buildings and all that crap.'

And on and on. He spat the words at me and I sat and let them hit me. Piece by piece, they stuck to my skin, oozed through and stole into my brain. I was to blame. I got that first. Seb would never have started free running if he hadn't known me. If I hadn't made him think it was important to take risks. It was all my fault. All of it. Every last bit of it. At one moment, I thought I'd put my head down. Rest it on the table and let the barrage pass over me but I couldn't move.

Eventually it stopped. The words stopped and only the hatred echoed round the café, bounced off the faces of the old French film stars and crackled in my ears. The manager and Grid were standing behind Mark. Arguing. I couldn't hear their words. I was shut off from them as though watching through a small window in an airlock with nothing in it except the noise of Mark's words.

The manager asked him to leave. Grid asked him to leave. And he finally went, shambling to the exit, kicking chairs out of his way, slamming the door.

I drank tea I didn't see arrive and thought how great it was to be with Grid who knew I needed tea.

'You OK?' Grid asked me.

191

I drank more tea and heard the murmur of conversations start up around me.

'You OK?' Grid said again.

I nodded.

'You didn't know?' he asked.

I found my voice. 'That Mark blamed me? No.'

'I thought Kit might have told you.'

'Kit knows?'

'Oh yes.'

I sipped more tea.

'I didn't tell Seb to go free running, Grid.'

'Are you sure?'

I couldn't believe this. Not from Grid.

'I've never told anyone to do anything,' I said.

'Mark's looking for someone to blame. Isn't it what most people do when something dreadful happens?' But his voice lacked conviction and he wouldn't look at me straight on.

'Grid. I would never…'

But now I was not so sure either because the things Mark had said did echo my own beliefs.

Grid reached out and covered my hand. His skin was warm after the cold of the marble.

'Look,' he said, 'I'm not saying you made Seb go parkouring but you should read his blog. It's full of the sort of things you say. You do go on about the joys of free climbing and how important it is to take risks. How most people live lives hedged in with fear and caution. You've been climbing since you were a child so the skills are ingrained in your body and it makes you fearless and daring. Things most of us would like to be. You seem glamorous and exciting. Kit's like that too. And your dad. You make the rest of us feel second-rate. Seb was feeling vulnerable because his life wasn't working out how he'd thought it would. He was going through that moment we all go through when dreams collide with reality. But it's not your fault that he died, Jen. Don't start thinking that.'

'Is that why you stopped me from visiting you?' I heard the sadness in my voice but I didn't care. 'Tell me the truth, Grid.'

'Maybe. You're quite hard to deal with when… when I'm not feeling on top form.'

'Oh shit.'

'Jen, it's just the way you are. So full of life and energy.'

A thought sent a shockwave through my body.

'Grid, you don't think Mark – could he have…? He hates me. You saw that. He loathes everything to do with me. And he's mad with grief. Off his head with it.'

'No, he couldn't.' Grid's voice was curt.

'Oh fuck. You saw him. If we hadn't been in a public place. If you hadn't been with me, I think he might –'

'Mark's angry but he wouldn't hurt you. He'll rant and accuse but that's all. Besides, I was with him on Friday evening.'

'You were with him?'

He nodded.

'But how? I didn't know you knew him, anyway.'

'I don't. I didn't.' He sighed. 'Look, they had a wake for Seb on Friday.'

'I know. Kit and Sofija went.'

'It was by the grave. A bit of a ceremony. Everybody had to remember something about Seb. Kit said it was dire because none of Seb's friends, his close friends, were allowed. Mark wouldn't invite them. Not even his girlfriend. Mark blames them all for not stopping Seb, for not making him see sense. You're not the only one.'

Grid didn't look at me. *I might not be the only one*, I thought, *but I sure as hell am one of the main ones.*

'Afterwards they went to a pub near here,' Grid continued. 'Kit had asked me to meet him there.'

He hesitated.

'Oh shit,' I said. 'Kit borrowed money from you.'

'It's fine.'

'No, it's not.' And it wasn't. Grid had worked for Kit. They got on but he was *my* partner and the thought of Kit tapping him for a few quid made me feel sick.

'It wasn't much. And I didn't mind.'

'How much?'

'It doesn't matter. Listen to me. I met Kit at the pub. There was only Mark, Sofija and him left. Everyone else had gone because Mark was in such a state. Ranting and raving to anyone who'd listen.'

'About me?'

'A bit.'

A lot, I thought. No wonder Kit had been so mad at me when we'd met the next day.

'Kit and Sofija had to go. There was a storm on its way, a big one, and they needed to get back so Kit begged me to see Mark home. Took me hours to drag him out of the pub and then I couldn't get a taxi to take us. It was gone nine by the time we got to his flat and I didn't leave him for quite a while. Once I did, Mark wasn't capable of doing anything but passing out.'

'You're sure. Sure, sure, sure?'

'I'm sure. Kit and Sofija left just before four and Mark wasn't out of my sight after that. It was a long and tedious few hours.'

I'd half risen and my hands were clenched into fists. I made myself sit back down and relax my hands. It wasn't Mark. Mark had been with Grid.

'Anyway,' I said. 'Mark didn't know I was in Cornwall. You saw him just now. He was shocked to see me. I don't think he was faking it. In fact, no one knew I was in Craighston. Not even Kit and Sofija. So I'm right. I've been right all along. Something must have happened while I was out walking on Friday evening.'

Grid nodded. It was clear he'd had enough. Enough of us Hammetts and our problems. I hoped he hadn't lent Kit too much money. We finished our drinks quickly, both desperate to leave. But when he stood and pulled some money from his jeans pocket, he asked me one last question.

'Still got your car?'

'No. It had to go. We needed the money. I've got an old Golf now.'

He fingered the coins in his hand.

'Why?' I asked.

'A volcano-red Aston stands out, that's all. Just thought that anyone who saw it by the hotel would have known you were there. But you'd sold it, so that's OK.'

Nineteen

I can't bear being underground. Something about the tons of rock above me and the buildings with their foundations digging into it. Spurs of concrete as white as knuckles gripping the rock; I hear the ground above grumble and creak with the strain. And I think it will crack and crumble and rain rocks down to bury me.

Grid and I used to climb those tall, tall buildings. Sometimes we climbed with friends of Grid's. Not climbers, really, although they were good. Explorers, they called themselves. Urban explorers. Committed to getting into and photographing or writing about places that are forbidden to the general public. You've probably heard of them and their *Take nothing but photographs, leave nothing but footprints* philosophy, or seen things in the papers about them climbing the Shard or standing on impossibly high cranes in Hong Kong.

Don't be fooled, though, by the guff on their websites about how we're trapped by our everyday existence, forced to walk only the paths the 'powers' want us to, and how urban explorers are striking a blow for freedom on our behalf. Most of them are nutters. Complete nutters, or worse. Sure, they've got a point. Most of humanity is too shit scared of its own shadow to step out of the boring and everyday. But the so-called urban explorers, they're doing it for themselves. Not for us. I mean, you don't need to have a birthday party in the Paris sewers or take photos of your toes on top of a crane with nothing but a thousand feet of space beneath them to make the point about how we're all confined by fears for our safety. It's taking the piss.

But I really liked them.

So we went climbing with them a few times, Grid and I, and it was kind of fun because they'd go anywhere. What they lacked in skill they made up for in sheer bravado.

And then we went pot-holing with them. Urban pot-holing, that is. Down below London. I should have remembered how much I hated being underground and known it would be a disaster. As soon as the clang of the manhole cover rang down into the cramped passages, kicked back into place by the top watchers, panic seized me. Couldn't breathe. Couldn't think. The thump of my heart thudded the blood against my skin so hard I thought it might burst. And everywhere, the smell of damp and soot oozed out of the brick-lined tunnels. I wrapped myself round the ladder, burying my face in my arms, and whimpered.

Grid got me out, muttering words of encouragement with his mouth pressed against my ears and his hands encircling my limbs and helping them to bend and move. As I neared the top, the sense of a shifting mass of earth and rock hanging above and around me receded and I scrambled up the last few rungs unaided and hammered on the cover until the watchers opened it, letting me out into the night with its canopy of dark sky and stars floating up high. Insubstantial. Light.

When Grid left the café, it was like being underground again. Only this time there was no manhole to hammer on and no Grid to show me the way to it. Instead of earth and concrete pressing down on me in the dark, it was the weight of the things I'd done. The weight of the person I was, threatening to suffocate me.

I drove back to Tregonna, pushing my way through the evening traffic, cutting up anyone who gave me a chance, not caring what they thought, not hearing their honks of protest nor feeling their indignant gaze wash over my back. Driving like a mad thing to get ahead of the darkness chasing me.

When I arrived at Tregonna, Kit wasn't there. Sofija was in the back room, ironing and watching *Shaun the Sheep* with Rosa.

'Where's Kit?'

'He's gone to London,' she said. 'Back tomorrow.'

'Not to borrow more money,' I said before I could stop myself.

'No.'

'Just I saw Grid today and Kit borrowed money off him. Do you know how much it was, Sofija? He wouldn't tell me. And we have to pay him back.'

'He said it was a gift.'

'I don't care. We have to pay it back.'

I was furious with Kit.

'I don't know. It was between Kit and Grid. Your father called,' Sofija added and slapped another pillowcase onto the ironing board. 'That's why Kit's gone to London.'

'From South America? Or is he back?'

I hardly cared. The one thing you could say about my father was that he was never there when you needed him. At least my mother was physically present even if her mind was away with the fairies.

'From South America. And Kit threw some stuff in the car and went. No time to explain but he said it was good. Said to tell you that.'

I guessed Pa had come up with some money.

'And Talan called,' she said. 'For you. Wants you to get in touch. He's working today so it might be tricky but he'll be in the mine tomorrow. Not much reception there so if you leave a message, he'll call you back.'

For a moment I couldn't think what she meant and then I remembered Kit telling me Talan was deeply involved in renovating the old mine workings at Cambervale.

I told her I'd call him tomorrow and went upstairs where I hunted online for Seb's blog. The one Grid had mentioned. It was mainly about his writing but also featured posts on his inspirations (both exotic and everyday), his thoughts on the world (on the whole, not good) and a few more personal ones on depression, his love life and free running – including one on why he started.

The Romans understood the link between mind and body; Mens sana in corpore sano. A healthy mind in a healthy body. I've never given it much thought. Until now.

You see, I've taken up free running and it's changed my life. Quite simply, it's set my mind as well as my body free. I feel as though I've returned to the freedom of my childhood when the physical exploring of my world, punctuated with small achievements such as the first time I rode a bike or racing down the path to be first to plunge in the sea, went hand in hand with mental discoveries like reading and understanding the power of words. But somehow, as I became an adult, I stopped pushing myself physically and focussed entirely on the pleasures of the mind. Exercise was a bore. Or dangerous. I might sprain a muscle if I ran too much. Or fall if I tried to climb. Or drown if I swam anywhere other than in the safe confines of a noisy and chlorinated swimming pool. The philosophy of avoiding risk had crept into my soul.

A few setbacks at work, the failure of a pet project I'd spent months on and I became depressed. I stopped writing, gave in to the pressure to become mediocre at work, went out every evening and drank to distance the misery. Another one of life's casualties. How mundane. How mediocre of me.

And then, quite by chance, I discovered free running. A lucky encounter with a few practitioners via an old friend, a wild and wonderful old friend who'd always told me danger was the stuff of magic and most of us were too shit-

scared to live life to the full. So I tried my first climb. Up the front of a three-storey hotel where we were drinking. And I got to the top. Looking back, I've no idea how. But as I sat on the roof and (cliché warning) stared at the stars, despite the pain in my oxygen-starved lungs and my stomach retching from the unaccustomed exertion, I felt more alive than I had for months. Probably years.

Since then, barely an evening has gone by without me taking to the streets with a few free running compatriots. We don't talk, we just do. We challenge ourselves. We take risks. We glory in the pleasure of movement. We leap into the dark trusting only in ourselves to succeed. And it's made me happier. More confident. Readier to take risks in the rest of my life. To fight against mediocrity. To deal with the dull days.

A healthy mind in a healthy body. A happy, stimulated mind in a happy, stimulated body. A free mind in a free body. We were born to run and jump and take risks. Both mentally and physically.

No wonder Mark blamed me. He must have known straightaway who the wild and wonderful friend was. Besides, my words, my stupid, bragging words ran through the blog.

I wished I'd read it while Seb was still alive. While I could still have told him how wonderful he was. And how right he was.

And meant it.

Because, of course, none of it was true. Grid's accident had shown me no risk was worth what had happened to him. *Danger was the stuff of magic.* No it wasn't.

I wondered what words had come to Seb as he'd jumped between those two building and misjudged the distance. If he'd seen how wrong he was as his hands flailed the air on his way down to meet the hard and unforgiving concrete that had smashed his brain into bits.

The air in my bedroom crammed itself full of other thoughts.

The ones I was trying to ignore. I'd reached the end of the line, though. Run out of places to hide. Time to face up to what lay behind Grid's words. I opened the window and leant out into the night and made myself start…

And I started with Grid.

I made myself look at the day he fell.

The early part. When we arrived at the tower having trekked along miles of overgrown paths, stamping on brambles and nettles. Although it was a March day, the weather was mild and I was hot. Sweat trickled down my back and through my hair and I hadn't brought enough water. The others, Grid and Vince and Ricky, looked at the tower and shook their heads. It's too old. Too crumbly. Too dangerous. We can't climb it, they said. And I was furious.

I goaded them. I knew exactly how to do it. How to raise my eyebrows and sigh. When to wonder out-loud exactly what the problem was. And all the rest of the guff. In the end, I said I would climb it on my own. And they could watch.

And so, of course, we climbed together.

And Grid fell.

Because the tower was too old. Too crumbly. Too dangerous.

And some kind of cosmic revenge made me the one who had to decide to cut the rope. To save Vince and Ricky. To save myself.

I forced myself to look at the aftermath. Part of me was sorry for the girl I was. Nothing in her life had prepared her for facing up to what she'd done. What she'd become. She told herself time and time again she'd had to cut the rope. What she couldn't tell herself was that we'd never have been on the tower in the first place if it wasn't for her.

I watched her race into the embrace of drugs and parties, anything to keep the demons away. She didn't climb. She'd

201

promised Kit and the promise made her angry. Instead, she took cocaine and talked about climbing. A lot. All the guff about adventure. About pushing yourself. About breaking boundaries. About fear being the killer. She talked and talked and talked as though the words would fill the cracks splitting her in two.

I don't remember Seb being there. I don't really remember anyone being there. But he must have been. I only remember all the nights melting into one long dark span, shot through with neon letters flashing at club entrances and spotlights changing colour to the thump of music. The glint of mirrors and the glitter of eyes.

I kept very still and stared out of the window into a night whose dark was only shot through by the beam from the lighthouse and answering flashes from the buoys out at sea. The cold and the damp swaddled me and held me tight. Not that I was going to move. I let everything I'd been running from catch me up. I turned and faced her as she raced towards me. It was time to meet the person I'd become because I was going to have to find a way to live with her. And what she'd done.

Twenty

Cambervale had been tidied up since I was last here. The tangle of brambles on the slopes had disappeared and been replaced by rhododendrons and azaleas and a path that wound along the banks of the stream. I stuck to the path for a while, trying to get my bearings. From time to time I came across a tree or part of the bank I remembered but they were like islands in an unknown sea. I'd lost the knowledge that linked them together.

Where was the bloody mine? I'd thought it would all come back to me when I got here but it hadn't. I was heading for the entrance to the lower of the two levels, known rather uninspiringly as 'Number 2 level'. I was sure, though, that it wasn't by the stream so I left the path and clambered up the slope. It was a typical Cornish day: soft, grey and damp. The sun had come out briefly and warmed the air. Fly weather, and they were out in force, buzzing around and irritating me even more than my inability to find the mine. But about halfway up the slope, between the stream at the bottom and the top where the shrubs and trees gave way to open moorland, I came across some of the ruins that pockmarked the valley. These were familiar. Once, a whole section of them had toppled over as we were running down the slope to paddle in the stream. It hit the spongy grass with a thud and we clambered back up to see a pile of stones where there had been none before and a hole in the building as though a giant had taken a bite out of it. I knew where

I was now. The entrance to 'Number 2 level' should be a short distance above me and to my left.

It was silent in the ruins. Utterly silent. No wind to rattle the trees and no birds foraging in the brambles. A chill prickled over my skin. *Shit. Maybe it had been a mistake to come here by myself.*

I thought I knew fear. When I climbed. When I hung over the earth with only the tips of my fingers keeping me out of gravity's claws, tightening every muscle in preparation for a swing to the next hold. Then I knew fear. And like a spice sprinkled over the moment, it enhanced every sensation.

But this fear was different. It was a sucking monster that drained the strength out of my limbs and left me shaking. I was tired, I told myself. Jumpy and wrung out after seeing Grid yesterday. And Mark. That was all. I gritted my teeth, shook the feeling off and ran up the slope to the mine entrance.

Talan was there, sitting on a low wall as if he'd been waiting for me. In his old checked shirt and thick corduroy trousers he looked more like the boy I'd played with than the grave policeman who'd spoken to me at the lighthouse or even the serious young man who had taken me to the cinema and the Friday night disco. He was smoking a tightly rolled cigarette and looked up when he heard my footsteps.

'Jenifry! I thought you'd call. You didn't have to come all the way out here.' His voice was less clipped than before as though he was enjoying the long vowel sounds of his Cornish accent. He smiled and patted the wall next to him. The fright that had driven me up the slope drained away at the sight of him, so solid and reassuring and familiar. *Please God, let him tell me the powder was cocaine.* I hadn't been able to face hearing that it wasn't over the phone. If it was, then I'd tell him about Nick. Leave him to sort it out and go back to London. Away from whoever was trying to kill me. Away from

Ma and Kit and Sofija. Leave Pa to sort out their problems. It was time to grow up anyway. Time to get a job. Time to live sensibly, and I didn't think I could do it here in Cornwall.

If it wasn't cocaine, I didn't know what I was going to do.

And now Talan was in front of me, I couldn't bring myself to ask the fateful question. I sat down beside him.

'Kit told me about the old mine and I came to take a look,' I said.

'You've picked a good time. I was just taking a break.'

'You all alone?'

'Yeah. Most of the others have dropped away. Given up.'

The mine entrance was behind us. I turned and looked. A red metal door opened into a dark hole surrounded by wooden boarding. It looked small. Too small for comfort. I shuddered.

'Still not keen on going underground?'

'No. Sorry.'

'I remember. No guided tour then.'

'Maybe later,' I said. 'But tell me about the mine.'

He took out a tin box, rusted round its edges, and rolled another twig thin cigarette.

'It's been closed since the First World War. Couldn't make a profit out of it any more so they sacked the miners and shut it down. Criminal really, but that's what happened everywhere.'

I nodded. It had been rammed into us at school that the closure of the mines had been the death of many communities in Cornwall. I'd seen the pictures of the displaced miners. Tough little men. Dark and Celtic and not saying very much. Waiting for trains at Redruth and Penzance, arms folded, bags at their feet. Heading off to South Africa and the Americas. Most of them had never been further than St Austell. It must have been exciting for some of them, though, heading off to strange lands.

'Tore the heart out of this place, it did,' Talan said.

I wasn't sure if this was true. There'd been casualties, of course. People had suffered. But many had prospered, sent money back home that had given their families a good life and even funded schools and hospitals. Some had returned, richer in money and experience and bought land or started businesses. But I didn't want to argue with Talan.

He talked at length about the mine. I didn't follow it all but I got the gist. There were two levels. Number 1 level, which was the upper level, was the oldest and linked by a shaft to Number 2 level, the entrance to which was behind us. It gave him an odd feeling, he told me, when he touched the marks on the rock and the joints on the timbers, to think they'd been made by his ancestors.

'All those centuries ago,' I said, but I'd stopped listening. The jitteriness had returned.

'Did you get a chance to test the powder, Talan? Is that why you called?'

'Yup.'

'I don't suppose it was anything, was it?'

'Yup.'

'It wasn't cocaine, then?'

'I mean, yes, it was something. It was cocaine.'

Bells rang a clarion in my head and relief washed through me. *Nick Crawford was the villain.* No need to worry it was someone I knew. No need to wonder if my red Aston had revealed my presence even though it was tucked away in the car park behind the hotel. Time to leave this horrid mess behind me.

'Have you told anyone?' I asked.

'Not yet. I wanted to talk to you first. Listen, Jenifry. It wasn't a lot of cocaine. Are you sure it's nothing to do with your family?

With Sofija or Kit? Or some of their friends? I can forget it, you know. Just have a quiet word with them.'

'No. They've got nothing to do with it. In fact, I didn't even find it at Tregonna. I just said that in case I was wrong. It was somewhere else.'

'Where?'

Talan waited for an answer and I felt his presence become heavy. The boy I'd played with disappeared and Talan the adult, the policeman, took his place.

'The new chap, Nick Crawford,' I said. 'You know who I mean? He was down at the point, at the lighthouse, with Gregory, when I met you.' Talan nodded. He'd turned his face towards me and the cigarette burnt unsmoked in his hand. A trail of grey winding into the air, its harshness softened by the warm, coconut smell of gorse. I took a long breath and let the words out. 'I found it in his house. Hidden in a sideboard he'd made. He's involved in drugs. Deeply involved, I think.'

Talan gave me a patient look and I felt myself being classified again as his inadequate ex-girlfriend who needed a guiding hand to stop her from doing something stupid. Irritation nipped at the edges of my temper.

'He had lots of white powder,' I said.

'In the sideboard?'

'I couldn't really tell, although there was more than I got out. But there was lots of powder in the cupboard and any of it could have…'

As I was speaking, I realised how lame all this sounded.

'Jenifry, it could be anything.'

'But you will investigate him, won't you?'

The relief I'd felt when Talan told me the powder was cocaine was trickling through my fingers.

'I don't think I can,' he said. 'It's only a small amount. I couldn't get a warrant to search his place on the basis of that alone.'

'Can't you just go and take a look?'

'What? Knock on his door and insist on taking samples of all the products he keeps? I'd love to be able to, but there are rules.'

Talan picked up his yellow high-vis jacket and a hard hat with a torch. He was going back into the mine and I was being dismissed.

'Please, Talan. Do something about Nick Crawford. At least look into him.'

He sighed and fiddled with the torch.

'You'll need to make a statement,' he said.

'You mean come down to the police station?'

'That's normally how we do it.'

A wind as cold as if it had come from the depths of the mine behind us had blown the softness of the day away while we were talking. I buried my hands inside the sleeves of my coat but it made no difference. I didn't want to go to the police station. What if I was being watched?

'Do I have to?'

His mouth twitched and I realised I wasn't the first person to complain to him but refuse to commit. I couldn't let it go.

'I mean, of course I will. I'll come down now. With you. If it means you'll take it seriously.'

He still looked unconvinced.

'Please Talan, please look into Nick. I tried to find out about him, you know. No one knows where he came from. He paid Rachel cash for the cottage and the address he gave her was false.'

'Are you sure?'

'Yes, I went there to check. And his website: it's fake. He's pinched the pictures from other websites. I bet he's not even a carpenter really. Probably just buys the stuff and passes it off as his.

Or maybe it's stolen. Because Kit said Nick offered to get him some antiques for Tregonna. On the cheap. But he backed off when Kit told him he wasn't interested. You've got to see how suspicious it all is. Turning up here out of nowhere. With a fake website.'

'He made those doors for Kit. Kit was pleased with them.'

'Have you ever *seen* him actually making anything?'

Talan shook his head.

'He didn't even fit the doors himself. Got someone local to do it for him. And when I visited his workshop, there was no sign of anything being made. It was tidy, very tidy. Too tidy. You know how people who make things are. They always have half-finished stuff lying about, or bits they're going to use to make something else. Nick Crawford's workshop was spartan.'

He looked as if I'd sparked off a complicated set of ideas in his head. I had to get him to do this. 'He's a charmer on the surface and I guess that helps if you're a criminal. But I'm sure he's a villain. Through and through. Like a stick of rock, if you snapped him in two, you'd see it in him.'

'You've been playing private detective?'

'A bit.'

'Well, don't. Crawford could be dangerous.'

He put his helmet and jacket down on the rock between us. For once, I couldn't read him.

'OK. I'll look into him. You don't need to come in and make a statement but you've got to promise me you'll back off, Jenifry. No more haring around asking questions.' He ground his cigarette out on the rock. 'I'm heading back now.'

'I thought you were here for the day?'

'No. I need to talk to some people about what you've told me. Are you in the car park at the bridge?'

'Yup.'

209

'If you hang on a sec while I lock up, I'll give you a lift back to your car.'

'It's OK. I'll walk.'

He jerked his head upwards. A crowd of dark clouds had slipped in from the south with the wind. 'You've got half an hour, tops, before it pours down.'

I thought of rain lashing down on my face and I remembered my earlier fears of being stalked in the valley.

'Maybe a lift is a good idea,' I said.

He picked up his safety gear and headed towards the mine entrance.

'I need to shut the mine. Easiest way is if I go in here and walk up to the top shaft, locking the gates behind me.'

I peered in to the dark hole and felt the hair stretch away from my scalp. Go into the pitch black, I thought. The choking, dust-ridden dark.

'Don't worry. I'm not going to take you down there,' he said.

'Too fucking right you're not.'

He grinned and then his face lit up.

'It's fascinating, though, Jen. There are miles of passages we haven't explored yet. We think there's an older mine deep beneath this one. There's mention of one called Wheal Greet in old documents in the library at St Blazey. It's down there somewhere.' He stepped into the mine and put on his hard hat, switching on its light so the beam illuminated the sides of the tunnel. 'If we could only find it, then we'd get serious funding. At the moment, everyone thinks we're a poxy little scratch on the surface.'

The beam of his hard hat jerked around the cave as he spoke, sending jagged shadows chasing each other across the rock.

'You're mad, Talan Rashleigh.'

He laughed but it was tinged with uneasiness.

'You go ahead up to the top entrance,' he said. 'You can't miss it. I'll meet you there.'

And he disappeared into the dark, slamming the red metal door behind him. Its clang startled the sparrows in the hedges and they flew up with a whir like fluttering flags. Then silence. I was alone. My fears crowded back and I hurried along the path past boulders of granite softened by centuries of rain and wind, with clumps of moss growing in the cracks and spilling out to create strange lines and shapes.

It was growing darker by the minute when I reached the upper entrance, although the threatened rain still hadn't arrived. I wished Talan would hurry up. I was at the top of the slope, close to the moor, and the bushes and trees had petered out. Nowhere to hide except inside the mine. I looked into it. The rock was rough. But the tunnel wasn't dark. Not like the black hole I'd left Talan going down.

I heard voices from above. Coming down the valley from the road where Talan was parked. I flattened my body against the rock face on one side of the mine entrance and peered up through the heather. There were two of them and they looked out of place in the valley. With their white T-shirts, black jeans and leather jackets, they should have been hanging round outside a club, checking for trouble. One of them, the older and balder one, stumbled on a stone beneath the undergrowth and swore.

It was stupid to think they were after me. Paranoid and pathetic. But I couldn't help it.

I took a step into the mine.

It wasn't that bad in there. Further along the passage it was brighter still. I clenched my hands, fixed my eyes on the light beyond and pushed the door closed behind me.

Talan found me, staring up at a tunnel in the roof down which the light came. A shower of soft, grey light falling in a puddle on the floor, catching on the rough edges of the rock as it dropped, dissolving the black into grey. Here and there, a glitter showed where a smear of tin ore had been left behind.

'It doesn't feel like being underground,' I said. 'What is this?' I pointed to the shaft above.

He put the two rubbish sacks he was carrying down and switched off the light on his helmet.

'A raise. A cut down from the surface. This is the original mine. They started off taking tin from the streams above and when it ran out they followed the lodes of ore underground, chipping it out as they went. It's why the raises aren't straight.'

I reached my hands up but the opening was too high. I could feel a faint draught and smell the sweetness of grass through the gritty smell of the rock.

'We're very close to the surface here,' he said. 'Further back, the raises twist and turn a long way through the rock. What are you doing here anyway?'

'Two guys came down from the road and I... All your talk of dangerous men. I didn't like the look of them.'

'Wait here.' He was gone for a while but when he came back he was smiling. 'Their dog's run off. They're trying to find him. Nothing to worry about.'

I tried to smile as well. 'Sorry. Imagination working overtime.'

'But you've got to promise me you'll stop playing private detective, Jenifry.' He picked up the rubbish sacks. 'And don't go telling anyone what you've told me. It might take a while to sort this and if you're right about Crawford, it would be dangerous for you if he and his friends found out you'd shopped them.'

'Don't worry,' I said. 'There's no way I'm going to tell anyone.' The decision I'd made earlier when I met Talan came back to me.

'Anyway,' I said. 'I'm going back to London.'

He looked relieved. 'Good; that way I won't have to worry about what you're up to down here.'

He shut and locked a barred gate, like a cage door, behind us and we walked out. At the entrance he dragged the wooden door closed, securing it with a chain and padlock. I looked around. No sign of the two men.

The threat of rain had receded by the time I got back to my car. My Golf. Talan raised his eyebrows when he saw it but said nothing. I was seriously tempted to tell him then and there about the two attempts on my life.

But I couldn't. Not until I was sure it was Nick and his colleagues. Not while there was still a possibility someone close to me might be involved. This thought ran through my brain constantly, a background hum to everything, occasionally chiming a sharp staccato note when I fell upon some new realisation. Like how it would be easy for Vince and Ricky to fake the 'when' of their blog. Or how Mark and Grid, the two people with cause to hate me most, had given each other an alibi. And I was still haunted by the moment when Nick Crawford had lent me his car, the moment when, fancy umbrella in hand, he'd bowed and gestured towards the open door. I now knew he'd only done it to keep tabs on me but I couldn't forget the grace of the act.

Twenty-One

On the way back from the mine, I stopped at Gregory's cottage. Light shone out of the tiny window buried in the thick stone walls so I was sure he was home. I knocked and shouted his name through the letterbox. Just as I was about to give up, he walked round the outside of the cottage clutching an armful of logs. I took them from him and followed him into a low-ceilinged room that doubled as living room and kitchen. I'd seen bathrooms that were bigger. The hair on my scalp tightened again.

'You all right, Jenifry?' Gregory settled himself into a high-backed wooden chair covered with old rugs and stretched his feet towards a tiny wood burning stove. Everything was as old as he was, and as battered. 'You never did like coming in here.'

'I can cope. Anyway, I want to talk to you.'

'Ay, well put the wood in the basket first.'

I did as I was told and cleared a pile of knitting off a stool, pulled it up to the fire and sat down.

'Careful with that.'

'What are you knitting?'

'Mittens to fit over my gloves.' He spread his bony hands over his knees and looked at them. 'My hands feel the cold. Never used to.'

He seemed much more in the present than he had a few days ago at the lighthouse and I wondered if it was the warmth relaxing him. The stove was small but so was the room.

214

'You come to bring me my tarp back, then?'

I jerked round to look at him and he cackled at the look on my face.

'I might have,' I said.

'Thought so.'

'I might not have, though. Why do you think I've got it?'

'I can put two and two together.'

'And make how many?'

'You always loved going up the lighthouse. Your Pa used to bring you here and he'd sit and chat and Kit would annoy Pip but you'd be away as soon as you could and up them stairs. Then after your Pa upped and went and never came back, I'd find you up there some nights when I went to lock up. Staring out into the dark.'

'Did I? I don't remember.'

'Said it made you feel calm. Thought you might have needed a bit of calm the other night, the way things are at Tregonna.'

'You don't want to believe everything Ma tells you,' I said.

He raised an eyebrow at me.

'Maybe things aren't great. And maybe I like to get away from them all from time to time. But it's a bit much to go from that to thinking I broke down the door, Gregory.'

'Nick Crawford told me he picked you up on the coast road that night wrapped in my tarp and you left bits of blue paint all over his car. So what else was I supposed to think?'

'Nick told you that?'

A faint film of smoke leaked out of the side of the stove door. Gregory kicked it and the smoke disappeared.

'He was worried about you,' he said as he settled back into his chair. 'I told him to leave you be. You'd sort yourself out. Always had. Always would.'

I didn't know what surprised me the most: Gregory's belief that I could sort myself out or Nick telling Gregory that he'd picked me up. It seemed totally wrong.

'I thought Nick might be the one who broke in,' I said.

'Why would he do that? He's got a key.'

'How come he's got a key?'

'I gave him one.'

'What?'

Nick Crawford had a key to the lighthouse.

'Why? Why did you give Nick a key?'

Gregory stared into the fireplace and I watched the flicker of the flames play on his skin. I wondered if he'd got lost in the past and if I'd have to nudge him back to the here and now, but he surprised me again.

'Pip disappeared, you know that?' he said.

'Yes. Sofija told me.'

'He went out one night and never come back. Nick Crawford helped me look for him. Drove me all over the place. The weather was strange that night. The sort that might catch you unawares. Wind from the north and a big, slow swell. Looked calm but it wasn't.' He stopped again. I waited. 'And a couple of nights later, those bodies were washed up. I told Crawford I figured the bodies had gone overboard near the lighthouse. Would have been tricky out at sea that night.'

'You think Pip…'

'The two who drowned weren't sailing the boat. So some of them landed, that's for sure.'

'How do you know?'

'Women, they were.' I started to protest but he overrode me. 'Foreigners. Nick thought Pip might have disturbed the ones who made it to shore. He said he'd keep a look out.'

216

I watched in horror as his face crumpled in on itself. He sniffed and blew his nose on an old hankie. I'd never disliked Nick Crawford more than I did at that point. Taking advantage of an elderly man, grieving for his dog, to gain access to the best surveillance point for miles, was unforgiveable. He'd have been able to see cars on the roads a long way away and coastguard vessels out at sea and warn the boats unloading.

But if he had a key why break the door down? Unless they'd set it up so it looked as though I had? Crap, it was all getting so complicated.

I spoke gently. 'Cup of tea? Shall I make you a cup of tea?'

'Pass me the bottle inside the cupboard behind you. And a glass by the sink. Two, if you like.'

'No thanks.'

He poured himself a half glass. It smelt like rum. Then stretched out to unlace his boots.

'Very smart,' I said. 'They look new. Do you want a hand?'

'I can manage me own boots, Jenifry.'

He was back in control of his emotions now. I tried another question.

'You said "some of them landed". What do you mean?'

'We'd have had a lot more bodies washed up if they'd all drowned.'

So he wasn't talking about drug smugglers.

'Immigrants, illegals, you mean?'

'Ay.'

'Ma said you knew who brought them in.'

'I know some who will bring one or two in. But proper, like. This weren't that. There's talk of others that bring them in close-ish and then dump them into old inflatables. Too many of them. God knows how many of them drown.'

I thought of the pictures on the news. Desperate people fleeing desperate places. Who could blame them? All they wanted was a chance to live without fear of death from violence or starvation. And, of course, there were people out there ready to take advantage of that. Was that what this was all about? Not drugs after all? But what about the cocaine I'd found at Nick's?

A faint snore came from Gregory's chair. I took the glass out of his hands, put it on the grate and went outside to get his tarpaulin. I breathed in the air, its tang of seaweed mixed with the smell of frost rising from the earth, and walked through the gathering dark to the lighthouse door. Someone, presumably Gregory, had nailed a cross piece over the broken planks. Definitely Gregory. No one else would have used a piece of driftwood, soft and crumbling from soaking in the sea.

I leant my head against it and willed myself back to last Friday. If only I could remember, but all that came were flutters of playing with Kit round the lighthouse while Pa and Gregory drank tea.

I tried the handle and the door opened. No one had mended the lock yet.

It was dark and quiet inside as I felt my way up the stairs, gripping the damp, smooth handrail. A flicker of memory. Too fleeting to pin down but enough to catch my breath. Out onto the viewing platform. A line of dark cloud on the horizon. Was this the threatened rain? Another storm brewing? They rolled across the Atlantic regularly at this time of year.

The raucous shouts of seagulls racing inland pierced the clouds and a shockwave of memory broke over me, punching the air out of my body. Friday night collided with the present and I wasn't sure which I was in. In both, seagulls fled the rolling clouds of a storm rushing in over the sea, tension bruised the air and the rough, chisel-edged stone pushed into my hands.

Here and now, only the air surrounded me; in the past, a blow struck my head. I staggered in both the present and the past and heard a great cry of pain swoop up to join the swirling calls of the birds.

So they'd hit me on the head here, on the lighthouse, not at the ledge. Blue flakes in my hair. Blue flakes washing down the plughole along with the blood when I showered. Had they used a stray piece of wood from the lighthouse door to knock me out? That would make sense. There'd been blue specks everywhere on the viewing balcony.

I must have come here on my own then. Broken the door down myself? Thinking the lighthouse was a sanctuary, like I had as a teenager escaping the cold emptiness that was Tregonna without Pa and Kit. Gregory was right. Being high on the lighthouse had always grounded me. Seeing the world below me had made things all right. Maybe I'd managed to run away last Friday night and, drugged-up and off my head, the lighthouse would have seemed the perfect refuge from whatever I was fleeing. Until whoever tried to kill me had crept up after me.

Another flicker of memory.

I'm on the road. I'm rushing up the steep slope where the road leaves the village towards the lighthouse, the tarmac hard beneath my feet. I'm feeling spacey and empty. As though my mind and body are slowly peeling apart from each other. I know I've got to get to the lighthouse. I'm desperate to get to the lighthouse because everything will be all right once I'm there. I know I'll be able to stick myself back together again.

'Humpty Dumpty' ran through my brain.

Humpty Dumpty sat on a wall. A very high wall. And Humpty Dumpty had a great fall. All the king's horses and all the king's men couldn't stick Humpty together again. But Humpty knew if he could only get back up the hill and climb to the top of the wall, it would be all right again.

I hummed the tune but nothing else came back to me. Being on the road out of my mind on roofies made no sense. I'd walked along the coastal path. I knew that because Kelly had seen me. Unless I'd cut through to the road after.

It was cold at the top of the lighthouse. A damp cold that hinted the long-threatened rain would come soon. I needed to think logically. To be cool and calm instead of leaping after random memories that probably weren't real anyway. I'd spent most of my life round here. My brain was stuffed with memories of the place so it was impossible to tell which were from Friday and which were from long ago.

I looked at the wall bordering the viewing platform. How difficult would it have been to hang an unconscious body over the edge? I'd assumed it would have taken a few people but now I wasn't so sure. I took my coat off. Imagined it was a limp body, heavy with unconsciousness. Imagined tying a loop of rope round the body and one of the blocks of stone along the top of the wall. It would have been easy enough to lever the body over the edge and let it hang. I wasn't big and the rough stone of the wall caught and held the rope in place. One person could have done it on their own. No problem. Although one of my boots might well have slipped off as they manhandled me.

But the knowledge didn't help. And the memories were nothing but wisps. Fleeting and insubstantial. I was no closer to learning the truth. Nothing Gregory had told me helped either. Drugs. Immigrants. Nick Crawford telling him he'd helped me back to the hotel. And anyway, I wasn't sure if I could trust

Gregory's observations any more than I could trust my own memories.

Gregory had half woken when I went back with the tarpaulin. He looked surprised to see me, in a grumpy sort of way, but took the tarpaulin with a nod.

'Gregory,' I said. 'The night when the lighthouse was broken into. What do you remember?'

'Already told you.'

'You said a seagull woke you up screaming.'

'Ay.'

'When was that?'

He thought for a bit.

'Must have been around nine. Turned the radio on after that and I seem to remember it was nine.'

I'd thought it was later because he said he'd been sleeping but now I realised he probably dozed the evening away in his chair. I wondered if he ever went to bed.

'And you're sure it was a seagull? Because they cry a lot round the lighthouse and it seems strange it would have woken you.'

He shrugged.

'Might it have been something else?'

'Sounded like a seagull. Screaming.'

But it could have been a human scream, I thought. *It could have been me.*

I concentrated on what I knew. I'd got to the hotel around four-thirty. I'd had to park up, check in and take my stuff to my room. I reckoned I'd been out of the hotel by quarter past five. Maybe a bit earlier because Kelly had seen me around six and to walk that far along the coastal path in forty-five minutes was going some.

Next sighting was around seven, back in Craighston in the rain. If that had been me; I was beginning to think it wasn't.

221

After that, nothing until a cry had woken Gregory around nine.

'Do you remember anything else?' I asked Gregory. He looked blank. 'What about earlier? Before the storm.'

'Kit stopped by because of the storm coming. He wanted to check I was going to be all right. I had a bit of a flood last time. He offered to take me back to Tregonna for the night.'

Kit and Sofija must have been on their way back from Seb's wake.

'We had a cup of tea. He told me what your Pa was up to. But he didn't stay long because he had to go and pick up Rosa.'

'Where was Sofija?'

'Kit said she had something to do in the village.' He started to lever himself out of his chair. 'I'll maybe have a cup of tea.'

'Sit down, I'll put the kettle on.'

'You'll have one too?'

'I ought to get back to Tregonna. But, Gregory, be careful of Nick Crawford. I think there's more to him than meets the eye. And not good stuff.'

I sensed he wasn't listening. I put the kettle on and stared at the hooks above Gregory's sink and the strange mixture of things that hung from them: old rags, a pair of long-nosed pliers, a tea strainer, a carrier bag full of kindling and a collection of postcards balanced above. All showing lighthouses from different parts of the country.

'The night of the storm,' I said. 'Did you go outside?'

Gregory nodded. 'When the seagulls woke me. Put on my waterproof and had a quick look round. Just in case.'

If he'd gone up onto the lighthouse, I wondered, what would he have seen? It was probably a good thing he hadn't.

'Make a pot,' he said when the water boiled. I did as I was told and put the pot and a mug on the grate with a carton of milk nearby, where he could reach it all without standing.

'He's all right, you know,' Gregory said as I opened the front door to go. 'That Nick Crawford.'

I thought about trying to persuade Gregory otherwise but it wasn't worth it. Anyway, Talan was on the case and, with luck, Nick Crawford wouldn't be around for much longer.

'He likes you.' Gregory laughed to himself. 'That old Hammett magic. Always works.'

It was dark when I got back to Tregonna and I knew Kit was home because the first thing I heard was his voice. Sharp with anger but muffled so his words were indistinct. He was in the kitchen and the door was closed. Correction. The kitchen door was locked. *What the hell was going on?* I banged my fists against the wood.

Silence.

I hammered again and shouted, 'It's Jen. Open the door.'

Silence, then the sound of the key turning in the lock, and Sofija pulled it open. Kit stood by the sink and Ma sat, head in her hands, coat slung on the table next to three empty bottles of wine and a fourth that was half full. Clearly Sofija had drunk some of it: she looked close to the point of collapse and leaned into the wall for support, her face loose and her mouth sagging.

'What's going on?'

'Ask her.' Kit flung his arm in Ma's direction. The force of it wrecked his balance and for a moment I thought he was going to fall. Kit was drunk, too.

Ma lifted her head from the table and looked at me steadily. I didn't think she was drunk. She didn't speak. She didn't need to because Kit started.

'I've been to see Pa's solicitors,' he said. 'In London. Pa told me to. He phoned the other night on a satellite phone. He said his solicitors would sort something out for me. Told me they'd explain it all.' He used his hands to lever himself round to face me. 'Tregonna belongs to Pa.'

'What?'

'Tregonna. The house. The land. Everything. He owns it.'

'Not…?' I turned to Ma but she put her head back down in her hands.

'No. She's never owned it. He was the one who bought it. It was his money plus a mortgage. Which he's still paying off, by the way.'

'But the divorce. Didn't Ma get it in the divorce? I thought she'd got it when they split up.' Actually, I'd never thought about it. Ma and Tregonna went together. Inseparable in my mind. Tregonna was her home, her past, her life.

'They're not divorced. They were never married.'

I tried to take it in. *Never married*. Yes, it made sense. Ma wouldn't have cared, free spirit and anti-Establishment as she was. No wonder there'd been no wedding pictures in her chest when I'd searched her room – or divorce papers.

There'd been an unwritten agreement between the two of them, Kit told me, that Ma could stay in Tregonna after they split. Pa would carry on paying the mortgage but Ma would have to pay for everything else or she could sell up and they'd divide the money. She'd chosen to stay. No surprise there.

But when Kit wrote about his problems, Pa realised he could sort them out. The land over the road was as much his as the rest of the house. On paper. In the eyes of the law. Besides, his solicitor had told Kit, he'd agreed Ma could stay in the house; he'd never said anything about the land.

A thought came to me.

'So we're…'

'Illegitimate. Bastards. Yes.'

I laughed. It was funny. But no one else thought so. And my

laughter stirred Kit back to anger. He staggered over to the table and leaned over Ma.

'And you never mentioned it. When I asked you about selling the land, you never told us it wasn't up to you. You let us go mad with worry instead.'

I knew he was drunk but the venom in his voice and on his face was too much. I grabbed his arm.

'That's enough, Kit,' I said. And to Ma, 'He's drunk.'

She went to stand and push her chair back in one movement but misjudged it and sent the chair scuttling over the tiled floor until it hit the wall and stopped there, leaning against it at a crazy angle. It was enough to stop Kit but as he went over to get the chair, Ma slipped out of the room.

'Come back!' Sofija shouted. 'Don't run away again.'

'Is that why you locked the door?' I asked her.

'Of course. She slips away. She always slips away. But this time I stopped her. Kit had things to say.' Her voice was low again and her words slow with the effort of speaking through the alcohol.

'You locked her in?' I said to Kit.

'No. Yes. But it was only for a minute. She didn't want to listen.'

Sofija muttered something in Bulgarian and slid down the wall onto the floor.

'Go to bed, Sofija,' I said. 'I'll tidy up.'

She stopped muttering and seemed surprised to see me. As if she'd thought she was alone, muttering her private thoughts into the night. I helped her up, took her upstairs and pushed her into their bedroom.

What a mess. What a shitty, horrible mess. Kit and Sofija's anger had left my nerves jangling. I fancied a spliff, just a small one, and I wondered if Ma was doing exactly that.

She was in her room, sitting by the window and looking out

into the night. It must be a Hammett thing, I thought, staring into the dark when your life is falling apart. And when she turned her face to me, I saw I was right. Tears ran down her cheeks. I had never seen her cry before, not when she broke her ankle tripping over a rabbit hole on the moor and lay there for hours before Pa found her, nor during the years after Pa left when she and I were alone together and she was trying to make everything all right. She never wept. I should have gone in and put my arms round her but it felt impossible. There was something essentially untouchable at the heart of her. Something I'd never understood.

'Ma,' I said from the door. 'Ma. Are you OK?'

She flicked the tears away with the backs of her hands.

'Can I put the light on?' I asked.

'No.'

'Don't sit in the dark.'

'I like the dark.'

'They're drunk, you know. And the stress of it all has been too much.'

'I don't think so, Jenifry.' Her voice was perfectly calm. Tears ran down her cheeks but her breathing was quiet. 'They hate me. Sofija hates me. Kit –'

'Kit is angry. But he's angry with everyone.' Somehow Kit felt we'd all let him down. Ma by not helping him. Me with my stupid risk-taking. That's why he'd been so angry when he made me promise to give up climbing. How strange. The old Kit would have put his arm round me and given me a hug.

'He'll get over it,' I said, but I wasn't sure he would. I wasn't sure there was a way back for him.

'I don't think so.' Ma stood up and pushed the window open. A chilly breath of air rushed in. 'I don't think I can stay here.'

'Ma, give it time. We can sort it out.'

'No. I've lost. I've failed. I should never have asked Kit for help. He's destroyed Tregonna, bit by bit. Killed its spirit. I kept on hoping he'd see that and leave some part of it free. And then, when it started getting difficult for him, I hoped he'd give up and walk away. That's what Kit always does. When something doesn't work out his way. When he gets bored with something. But she wouldn't let him.'

'You mean Sofija?'

'It was a bad day when Kit met her.'

'Ma. You're being...'

'You don't see it, do you? She told Kit he had to see it through. Told him he couldn't give up. She'll do anything to get Tregonna from me. Anything. So you be careful not to get in the way of what she wants.'

I can't deal with Ma when she goes all dramatic. It sets my teeth on edge. So I muttered something and left. Time, I thought: they all needed a bit of time to recover, and for a lot of alcohol to leave their systems.

Downstairs Kit was slumped on the kitchen table, fast asleep, his head lolling on his arms and a small snore escaping with each breath. I removed the debris from their meal, stacked the dishes into the sink and sat down opposite him. In some ways he was as stubborn as Ma. Trying to get either of them to do something they didn't want was like building a sandcastle from the fine, white sand at the top of the cove where the tide never reaches. The tighter you held it, the faster it sifted away through your fingers.

Our family was crap at communicating, anyway.

So many things unsaid.

The front door slammed. I went to look but when I opened it there was no one there. I ran upstairs. Ma was not in her room. I checked the rest of the house. No sign of her. *Shit*. She'd gone out.

She'd said she couldn't stay but I hadn't thought she meant she'd leave straightaway. I stood on the steps outside the front door and called for her until the cold drove me indoors.

Kit was still asleep on the kitchen table and he wasn't too happy about being shaken awake.

'Fuck off, Jen. Your hands are freezing.'

'Come on, Kit. I need your help.'

'Leave me alone. I've got an early start tomorrow.'

'You're asleep on the kitchen table.'

'Am I?' He lifted his head and rotated it like an owl. 'Oh yes,' he said and put his head back down on his arms.

He was right: my hands were freezing. I grabbed a coat from the hooks outside the back door and put it on, burying my hands in opposing sleeves like we used to do when we were children.

'Ma's gone out without her coat.' I said.

Kit lifted his head again and gazed at me as though trying to make sense of what I'd said. There were red marks on his face where it had rested on the table and his eyes were bleary and unfocussed.

'Ma's gone out,' I said again. 'She hasn't got a coat. I guess she couldn't face coming in here to get it.'

Kit shut his eyes. 'What did she say?'

'Nothing. I didn't see her leave. Just heard the door slam.'

'She's got other coats. In her room.' He stood up and stretched his arms above his head. The bones in his back cracked as he reached for the ceiling. 'I'm going to bed.'

'But we need to find her.'

'I'm going to bed, Jen. I've got to be up early tomorrow.'

'It's freezing out there.'

'She'll stomp around in the woods for a bit. Hug a few trees and then come in. You know what she's like. She wants you to go looking for her.'

He gave the table a quick wipe and flung the cloth back into the sink.

'She was really upset, Kit.'

'So she should be.'

'What's the problem between her and Sofija?'

'The same as between me and her. Money. And now, her lies.'

'There's more to it. She's very angry with Sofija.'

'Christ,' he said. 'Now is hardly the time...' He sighed heavily and sat down again. 'When I first realised how desperate things were, Sofija wanted me to get some kind of written agreement from Ma.'

'And Ma said no?'

'Not exactly. You know how she is. Impossible to pin down. Always changing the subject or picking up on some minor bit of it. Or saying we were family so we didn't need to put things on paper. Finally Sofija lost it and asked her to at least make a will in our favour. And yours, of course.'

'Does Ma have a will? I mean with solicitors and stuff?' It seemed improbable. She'd be more likely to arrange for some of her madder friends to burn Tregonna down around her dead body as a sacrificial funeral pyre.

'I don't have a clue. I don't think so, judging by her reaction. She went mad. Accused Sofija of wanting her dead. Anyway, now I know she hasn't got anything to leave.' He paused as a new idea occurred to him. 'Maybe that was why she was so furious when Sofija suggested it: because Tregonna wasn't hers to leave.' He considered that thought for a moment. 'Are you really going to go looking for her?'

'Yes.'

He stretched again, uncurling his body vertebra by vertebra. 'OK. I'll help.'

I looked at him, so tall in the dingy room, and suddenly I wasn't so sure. His words jangled in my head. He'd spoken about Ma making a will. A *will*. Something about this had poked awake a flurry of unease. But why?

'You won't be much help, the state you're in.' I said. 'I'll be better on my own.'

'Sure?'

'Sure.'

'It's going to rain,' he said.

My thoughts came together and a frisson of fear chilled my skin. I didn't want to go out into the dark with Kit. Oh, God! How had I not seen it before?

All the talk about Ma's will.

I'd written a will when I bought my flat. The solicitor had told me I should. Just a simple one. Everything to Kit. All my worldly wealth: my car, the money in my accounts and my flat. Especially my flat. Free and clear, the debt paid off by the life insurance I'd had to take out as a condition of the mortgage.

I'd told Kit and Sofija. I was sure I had. Had all the fuss over Ma's will reminded them?

Kit was watching me with a puzzled look on his face. I forced a smile.

'I'm going to bed, Jen,' he said. 'Pa's solicitors have given me a letter for the bank that'll get them off my back and I want to go down there first thing.' He headed for the door but turned at the last minute. 'You know, I thought tonight would be a celebration. Problems finally solved.'

For a moment I was tempted to go to bed, too. Lock the door behind me and ram a couple of chairs against it. It had been a hellish few days but tonight was the shittiest moment by far. Except I knew I wouldn't sleep. I'd lie in bed and think about Kit and Sofija's rage with Ma and the way their financial difficulties had driven them to the edge of reason so that stress ate the flesh from Sofija's bones and Kit thought nothing of cadging money from my ex-boyfriend. Sleep would be impossible. I'd think about Sofija wanting me to clean the windows at Tregonna. I'd think about the look in her eyes when she held Rosa to her. She'd do almost anything for her daughter. I'd think about how much Kit had changed.

Stop. No more. I was mad. Paranoid. But I could no more stop my brain from chasing down dark pathways than I could stop breathing.

Friday afternoon, Sofija and Kit had come back from Seb's wake with Mark's words condemning me ringing in their ears. They'd left Plymouth around four, according to Grid. They'd have arrived at Craighston about the same time as me. Had they seen my car then? Or had they seen me on the road and followed me? Who knew? But they, of all people, would have guessed straightaway that the appearance of a red Aston meant I'd arrived. After all, they were the ones who'd asked me to come down in the first place.

And then what?

Kit had gone up to see Gregory and invited him to stay the night at Tregonna. Was it kindness or was it a desire to get him away from the lighthouse? Sofija wasn't with him. Had she gone to the hotel to find out what I was doing there? Had she been the person talking to Vivian in the room behind reception?

And then they'd got lucky. I'd left the hotel for a walk.

And after that...

I couldn't bear to think any more.

So I pulled an old hat and scarf off the hooks by the back door and unbolted it. My mother was wandering about in the freezing night, possibly upset and definitely not sensibly dressed. I'd go and

231

look for her because anything was better than staying in Tregonna with suspicions running through my head and Kit and Sofija in the room below mine.

Twenty-Two

Ma wasn't in the woods. I was sure because I'd been over every square metre with a strong torch. Even the bit in the middle where the brambles are fierce. She wasn't in the gardens either and she hadn't crept round the house to the lawns at the front. Nor was she in any of the sheds, outhouses, stables and so on that lie like drunken tramps around the east side of the house, some still standing but wobbly, the rest collapsed and offering shelter only to spiders, mice and the occasional bird – none of whom were pleased to be roused by the beam of my torch.

By the time I'd finished looking, I was tired, scratched, grubby and festooned with spider webs. *Brambles 5, Jen 0.* And my ankle hurt where a loose stone on a step into the tool shed had leapt up and whacked me.

And did I mention I was furious? Fucking boiling with rage. I'd stopped peering through the cracks of opening doors ready to whirl round and run. Instead, I kicked doors open. Stamped on plants in my way. I was mad at all of them. Furious with Kit and Sofija for making me suspect them. Furious with Ma for swanning off into the night rather than standing up for herself. The heat of rage made me feel better. But then anything was better than thinking about what might have happened after I headed out of the hotel on Friday night.

Clearly, Ma had left Tregonna. I slammed myself into the Golf and set off to try to find her. I knew I was doing what she wanted me to do and that was even more annoying. She was probably sitting in front of a fire in a friend's house, sipping a herbal tea and 'being zen' about the whole situation.

But the wind was rising, bringing in an edge of ice and the smell of a rainstorm from over the sea. So, tempting as it was, I couldn't leave her out there. I jabbed my foot on the accelerator and let the night rush past. The speed calmed my mood, at least a bit. Eventually, I slowed to a crawl and began the tedious business of trying to find her, scouring the roads and getting out from time to time to call her name.

By the time I reached the village, I knew it was hopeless. Even Ma in a huff couldn't have walked this far. I was just driving for the sake of doing something. The long-awaited rain finally arrived. I got out one last time, shouted for her and then, chucking my sodden coat into the boot, gave up.

On the way back to Tregonna, the rain became one continuous slap of water against the windscreen. The wipers could hardly cope and I slowed right down, gripping the road with my eyes, trying not to lose sight of the white lines in the centre. So I was barely aware of what made me screech to a halt, sending great plumes of water over the grass at the side as my tyres slid across the tarmac.

I'd seen someone… a white face looking back at me, streaked to a blur by the wipers. The sight had bypassed my conscious mind and spoken straight to my feet.

Ma?

I looked in the mirror.

A figure ran towards the car, towards the passenger door. It wasn't Ma. Too tall. My hand reached out automatically and pressed the central locking. The clunk reassured me.

But the figure didn't stop. It kept on running. Past the door.

Past the car. Into the headlights. Feet hitting the ground too fast for its body. Staggering and swaying. Like a tightrope walker struggling to balance.

Not Ma. A man.

I slid the car into gear and eased forward. The runner's speed increased. His head whipped from side to side, as though looking for a way off the road but the cliffs fell away after the grassy strip on one side and high rocks loomed on the other. He slipped in the mud and fell, saving himself with one hand, then forced himself back up and stood bent double, his ribs heaving for breath and visible through the jacket plastered against his back.

I stopped the car a few paces behind him and waited.

He straightened his back and turned to face me.

Nick Crawford.

For a moment I thought I was hallucinating.

But it was unmistakably Nick. Even through the jumble of water and wiper on my windscreen I knew it was him. Details registered. Blood was trickling down his face as fast as the deluge could wash it away. His left eye was puffy and closing to a slit as if he'd been in a fight. He strode forward and raised his right arm.

Some stupid instinct made me cower back in the seat and raise my hands as though to ward off a blow. I even whimpered. Then I remembered how hard it had been for me to see him inside the car, last Friday night, in the rain, with the headlights dazzling me. He wouldn't recognise this car. So I turned the headlights off and put the inside lights on instead, wondering if I was making a huge mistake.

I couldn't see his face now. I could barely see his shape.

Nothing happened. No more crashes on the outside of the car. No rock smashed the windscreen. And when I turned the headlights back on, he was still standing in the same place but looking behind me and beyond the car. Then he snapped his body round and started running again. When I glanced in the mirror, I saw the jagged beams of torches coming down the hill onto the road and I knew where I was. Nick's cottage was a couple of hundred metres up above and the torches were on the steep path that connected his road with the coast road.

I looked at Nick. He waved his right arm at me, his hand a blur of white at the end, telling me to go. Then he turned and ran again. His legs pounded the ground, his right arm bent and jerked like a piston thrusting him forward but his left arm dangled by his side and every so often unbalanced him, so he staggered and lost ground as he fought to stay upright. He wasn't going to get away from the dark figures with torches chasing him. They were almost down the hill now.

Something inside me settled as though it had been waiting, edgy and stressy, feet skittering from side to side, for this moment. I knew what I was going to do. Part of my brain screamed at me to be sensible and get the fuck out of there but I couldn't leave Nick battered and bleeding and running desperately down the road. Not now I was full of doubts about his guilt. Not while suspicions of Kit and Sofija crowded my head. Not if Nick's loan of his car to me on Friday had truly been an act of kindness. A few brief seconds of fight in my head and then I felt the adrenalin fizz through my blood and clear all the crap clogging up my head. I drove forward, pulled up beside Nick, reached over and pushed the passenger door open.

He didn't stop. Kept on running. I yanked the door shut, followed him and pulled up again a few yards in front of him and slid the passenger window down. This time he came to a stumbling halt and screamed at me.

'Get the fuck out of here.'

He turned and ran off again and I shouted, 'No, get in the car.'

And then I got out and slammed my door shut. The noise stopped him.

'Get in the car,' I yelled.

A horde of doubts raced through my mind. *What the fuck was I doing? I must be completely off my head.* But underneath, I knew this was right. Like the moments when the route up a rock face suddenly becomes clear and I know exactly which series of holds to use and which ledges and cracks will link to get me to the top. The glorious feeling when I don't think, I just act.

Nick waited until the last minute, though. Until I could smell the danger emanating from his pursuers and hear their sweaty panting, their pounding steps. Just as I thought it was going to be too late, he wrenched the passenger door open and thrust his body into the seat. I leapt in after him.

'Now drive,' he said. 'Drive anywhere as fast as you can,' and he pulled the rear-view mirror towards him. 'Fucking drive, Jen.'

'They're not going to catch you now,' I said as I shot off. 'A few men on foot!'

'They've got cars. They're on the road down.' A sharp intake of breath. 'Shit!'

I glanced over at his face, lit up by the reflection of headlights in my mirror.

'Is it the police?'

'What?'

'Are the police after you?'

'That is not the police behind us. And believe me, Jen, you don't want them to catch us up and prove me right.'

His words were stripped of all emotion and that, more than anything else, more than the blood and bruises marking his face and the injured arm he clutched to his side, made me concentrate on driving as fast as I dared. I drove like I'd never driven before. Life narrowed down to keeping the car on the road, throwing it round corners and staring through sheets of water, fighting to see beyond the dazzle of my reflected headlights.

Nick was a presence on the outer edges of my awareness. A rhythm of snatched breaths and rustles as he alternated between looking ahead and turning to gaze at the lights behind us as though it was not enough to see them in the mirror.

I didn't look in the side mirror. I didn't need to. The headlights of the car chasing us were a constant glare and flared on the periphery of my vision every time we turned a corner. Each time brighter and closer.

'I'm heading for St Austell,' I said in a staccato burst. 'There'll be people and cars there. We'll be safer.' He said nothing but looked behind again. 'Won't we?' I asked.

'Have you got a phone?'

'In my coat. But it's in the boot.'

He swore.

'They'll have one,' he said.

'So?'

'They'll get someone to head you off before you get to St Austell.'

I gritted my teeth and clenched the steering wheel tighter. The coast road was deserted. It would be easy to trap us.

I snatched the next turning off. A little lane lined with high hedgerows that went straight up into the back country and through a couple of little hamlets. I knew families in both but there wouldn't be time to rouse them before we were caught.

I gained a few seconds because they overshot the turning but I knew it wouldn't be long before they reversed and followed us. My eyes raked the sides of the road ahead, looking for another turning. Somewhere to screech into and hide while we were out of view. But there was nothing and a few minutes later I heard Nick mutter something under his breath as the headlights reappeared in my side mirrors.

'Haven't *you* got a phone?' I asked.

'They took it off me. First thing they did.'

The rain rattled on the car roof. A thousand things I wanted to know stormed my head but Nick's voice, hot and sharp, sliced through them all.

'Don't slow down,' he said.

I pushed my foot down until the accelerator would go no further. But as the hedgerows flashed by, interspersed with sudden openings and tantalising glimpses of dark-windowed houses wrapped around their sleeping occupants, the car behind seemed chained to mine. It never dropped back and if I lost concentration for a moment, the lights crept up on me, two cold eyes of a beast waiting to pounce.

The back of the Golf skidded as I wrenched the wheel round the first of the bends which marked the beginning of the climb up to the moors. The road was no longer lined with high hedgerows but had a forest of young oaks on either side. Their trunks and naked branches flashed in the light as I passed. The road was a snake, coiling and uncoiling in front of me, and the water on the road hissed as my tyres washed it out of the way. I bit my lip, tasted blood and put my foot down again. Somehow, I had to get every last bit of power out of the Golf. I no longer bothered to change gear much but drove until the engine screeched in agony.

I flicked a glance into the side mirrors again. The gap between us was growing.

'I think they're giving up,' I said, hearing hope make my voice husky.

'Where does this road go?' Nick's voice was harsh.

'Over the moors and joins the main road to Bodmin.'

'Any turn-offs between now and then?'

I let the familiar route unroll in my mind.

'Only one. There's a fork at a village called –'

He bit me off. 'And after the fork?'

'Nothing. No turning until it reaches the main road.'

'And if you take the other road at the fork?'

'The same. It takes you to the main road too. But past a couple of farms.'

Too late, I understood. Once I'd chosen which road to take at the fork, we'd be trapped. All they had to do was send another car down the road from the other end and we'd be caught between them. They must have other cars driving around out there, waiting for a call. I saw them in my mind like a circle of hawks hovering over the moor, their shadows terrifying the little creatures caught in the open. My foot faltered on the accelerator and the car slowed.

'Keep driving,' Nick said. 'As fast as you can. What's the road like between here and the moors?'

'Bendy until we get out onto the moor and then it's straight and flat. All they have to do is follow us to the top, then wait and watch which way we go. There's no cover up there at all.'

'Can we get off the road?' he asked. 'You said the moor was flat.'

'You used to be able to. But they stopped it. Quad bikes doing too much damage. Now the sides are hedged or fenced or ditched.'

Little explosions of fear dislodged my concentration and I felt dampness prickle the palms of my hands. A rabbit ran across the road, a flash of grey through the pouring rain, and I braked and swerved to avoid it. My tyres squealed as I fought to keep the car on the road. The movement flung Nick sideways and he cried out as his body smashed into the side of the car.

240

The shock cleared my brain. There's always a way up the rock. You just have to find it. Something came to me. Something that might work. I raced through it in my mind, seeing what had to happen. Then I floored the car and felt it pick up speed again.

'I have an idea,' I said. 'No time to explain, but get ready.'

A white flash of skin as he turned to look at me, but all he said was 'OK.'

I liked that about him. So much. No questions. No fuss.

Another glance in the mirror. The gap between us and the men behind had stretched. They were sure they had us. Easier for them to keep an eye on us from further back. It suited me fine. I'd never driven like this before, with a reckless disregard of every safety precaution. Just me and the car and the road. Judging within a hair's breadth how fast I could go and still keep the three of us together.

We shot over the top of the hill and onto the moor. We were out of their view for a few seconds while they drove the last hundred metres up through the forest. High hedgerows lined most of the road we were on until just after the crucial fork. I blessed them and cut the headlights. We were invisible now.

The two roads after the fork were open and unhedged. They rose away from the junction and climbed over the moor. If the men had any sense, they'd wait at the top behind us and watch to see which road we took, call ahead and snap the trap shut. But they might not. They might follow us all the way.

I lifted my foot off the accelerator a little. This was the tricky part. I needed to keep far enough in front so they wouldn't catch up with us but go slowly enough to turn off when the time came. And all without using the brakes. A sudden flare of red would give us away. I blinked my eyes, holding them shut each time for as long as I dared, forcing them to adjust to the dark. My feet screamed at me to brake. I ignored them. Nick was a statue beside me. He knew, I thought, this was the moment.

It was round the next corner. Even in the dark, with rain distorting the windscreen, with no lights, and the hedge blurring the road, I was sure. Or was I? Don't overthink it, I told myself. Breathe and go for it. I took my foot right off the accelerator. Still too fucking fast. *Shit, shit, shit.* I fought my foot, stopping it from stabbing the brake. *Too fast*, my senses howled. There'd be no time to check the planks were there. The bend approached. I crunched the gearstick into second. Felt the car judder. *Don't stall. Don't fucking stall.* The end of the hedge flashed past. The road was open to the moor except for the ditch deep in the verge. The familiar landmarks slipped past. The car slowed. And I dragged the wheels to the right, mounted the verge and went down. And down. And down. And just as I was sure we were going into the ditch, I felt the wheels hit the wooden planks Jory Treeve put down every year to get his tractor onto the moors during the bad weather, when he needed to check his sheep and didn't want to go the long way round.

My speed made the planks bounce wildly and I fought to keep the car straight. The front wheels hit the bank on the other side with a thump and the car stalled. *Fuck.* Jory's tractor had big wheels with a thick grip. Mine were tiny and smooth. My hands shook as I turned the ignition key, expecting the lights of our pursuers' car to round the corner any moment. The engine fired.

'Put your foot down and get into second as fast as you can,' Nick said. His voice was icy calm.

The wheels gripped and took the front of the car up onto the bank and into the field. As soon as the back wheels were clear, I dragged the car round to the right and tore back the way we'd come, splattering the windows with gobbets of grass and mud, until the hedge hid us from the road. Too fucking fast again. A dry-stone wall raced towards us. I watched it. Helpless. Didn't dare brake. We smashed into it and, once again, the car stalled.

Twenty-Three

A moment of nothingness. Not long. Seconds, maybe. I wasn't even sure if I'd lost consciousness. There was a break, though. A sense of *before* and *after*, as if shock washed through my body and shut it down. I moved my arms and legs. They all worked and nothing hurt. Much. Rain drummed on the car roof.

Nick was beside me. Quiet and still.

Get out of the car, I thought. *The men are still out there*. I clawed at my seat belt and reached for the door.

'Wait.' Nick was awake and moving. Pain had mangled him into a jumble of limbs and hands.

'Got to get out.'

'Lights,' he said. He tried to form other words, gave up and said, 'Lights' again. I reached out for the door.

'No.' His voice was sharp. *With pain? With… what?*

And then his meaning hit me and I snatched my hand away from the door. I had so nearly blown it. Outside the dark dripped with water. Each droplet waiting to reflect a stray beam of light. And the interior light in my car was bright. A beacon for the watchers who must now be waiting on the top ridge, eyes fixed on the darkness in front of them like hungry raptors. I stretched my hand up slowly to the switch and turned it off. Beside me, Nick sighed and slowly uncurled. I wondered how badly he'd been hurt.

244

'We have to get out of the car,' I said.

'I know. But quietly.'

I opened the door and the steady tumble of the rain blotted everything else out. I shook out my arms. The shock of the smash and the aches from driving were disappearing. My shins and toes were sore but I moved freely. Nick got out of the car. He seemed OK. A bit of a stagger as he stood but he walked round the back of the car to me without too much difficulty.

The Golf was totalled. It didn't matter, though. We weren't going to be using it again and we'd ended up in a place where the hedge was super thick. No headlights would penetrate and reflect back a giveaway glint.

Nick's hand pushed my shoulder.

'Get down,' he whispered.

Through the noise of the rain came the sound of a car. I slammed my body down, knocking the breath out of my lungs. Nick followed. It must have been agony for him but he didn't even grunt. The car swept by, its lights poking through the bottom of the hedge where the leaves were thin. It passed and disappeared.

'Was it them?'

'Who else?'

'It wasn't going very fast,' I said. 'I think they know they've lost us.'

I ran to the planks over the ditch. They were too much of a giveaway and I started heaving them up the bank but it was impossible. They were heavy and embedded in the soft muddy earth. My feet slipped from under me and I fell. Nick came up behind me.

'I need to get rid of the planks. They'll work out where we left the road.'

He tried to help me up with one hand but it was no good. 'Listen for the car,' I shouted through the rain. He nodded and drops of water flew off the end of his hair.

'Did you say your phone was in the back of the car?'

'Shit, yes.'

How could I have forgotten?

'I told him the code and even in the dark, I swear I caught the quick flash of his smile as he went back to the car. I kicked at the planks until they slid sideways through the wet earth and jumped up and down on them until most of their length was under the muddy water in the ditch, scanning the road for any sign of the car coming back. It wouldn't be long. As soon as they reached the fork, they'd realise we'd gone off the road and come back to look for us.

Nick came back, talking to someone on my phone and clutching my coat. The rain was lighter now and a faint wind had got up. It curled round my legs and chilled my skin through jeans heavy with mud and water. If we didn't get moving soon we'd be in trouble.

I clambered out of the ditch and Nick broke off his conversation.

'Where are we exactly?' he asked.

'Opposite the entrance to Typridl Farm, but we can't wait here. We'll take the path through the woods on the ridge and follow it down to Garswell village.'

He repeated what I said and then swore and looked at the phone. No signal. It was always patchy up on the moor.

The rain stopped and the wind was shifting the clouds above us. I shivered. He handed me my coat.

'Put it on.'

'You need it more than I do.'

'I can't get it over my arm.'

It wasn't going to be easy getting him down the path to Garswell. It was steep in places and you needed both hands to steady you. We didn't have a choice, though, not unless we went over the moor, and if the clouds lifted like I thought they were going to, the moon would poke through and we'd be two vertical sticks on miles of flat land. I looked at him. His arm must have been in agony but he was in control of himself. We'd manage.

'The Garswell path? Is it the best way?'

Every bit of me shrieked we should be moving, not talking about it.

'Once we're on the path they'll never catch up with us,' I said. 'Otherwise, we walk on the road – obviously stupid. Or go out onto the moor, where there's nowhere to hide. No-brainer, isn't it? So can we get a move on?'

'Which way over the moor?'

I exploded.

'Listen. There's nowhere to hide on the moor. What part of that don't you understand? We haven't got time to get far enough away. You're not exactly in a state to be challenging Usain Bolt, are you?'

My rage passed over him without settling. He thought for a few seconds and then spoke.

'OK,' he said. 'You're going down the Garswell path but on your own. I'm going to take my chances on the moor.'

His words made perfect sense. They were after him. Not me. This wasn't my affair and here was my chance to escape, except my feet stayed stubbornly fixed to the mud and my brain hunted for reasons why I shouldn't leave.

'Go on, Jen.' His voice was cool. No hint of emotion. No trace of doubt. 'You've given me a chance. I'd never have got away from them if you hadn't picked me up.'

He held his hand out. Not to me. He held it out as if ushering me towards the path. The gesture reminded me of the first time we met, when he opened the door of his car and offered it to me. And suddenly it was all too much. Too confusing. The contradictions in him. My own tangled feelings.

'Come with me,' I said.

'No.'

'Look, I know exactly what you are, Nick Crawford. And what you and your thug friends do. I found the coke in your sideboard. You're a crook. But I don't think you're as bad as your friends and you won't get away from them over the moors.'

His hand wavered and he took a step towards me. Then he froze. Like a dog we'd had, a pointer, when it caught sight of a bird and every muscle in its body twanged and vibrated with the alert. I heard it too. A car.

We dived behind the hedge and onto the ground.

The road was visible through the bottom of the hedge and I saw the headlights coming. But slowly – so, so slowly. I sensed the gaze of the men inside, piercing the dark like searchlights. They'd worked out where they'd lost us. Not hard to do. And now they were coming back to see where our car had left the road. I held my breath as they passed the place where the planks had bridged the ditch but they didn't stop, didn't even hesitate. There was more than one car, though. *Fuck*. Three other vehicles in convoy. I mouthed curses into the grass. They were big four-wheel drive brutes, capable of driving over the moorland at speed.

A long, slow moment while they passed. Nick raised his head and risked a look. Then he dragged his legs beneath his body and pushed himself up. He slipped round the side of the hedge, as quiet as a shadow.

'They've stopped further up,' he whispered when he came back, his breath warm on my ear. 'I think some of them are getting out.'

'Fuck. The path to Garswell starts there.'

He pointed onto the moor. I shook my head.

'We can't stay here, Jen.'

Torch beams cut the dark, far up but on our side of the hedge. They were coming back on foot as well as by car. And on both sides of the hedge. But with torches. Idiots. A seed of an idea took hold.

'Come on,' I said.

I spent precious seconds rummaging in the boot of my car, my coat rammed over the interior light, and pulled out my rucksack and rope. We ran onto the moor, crouched over and staying close to the dry-stone wall until we were a few hundred metres from the road. Then I turned and headed towards the coast, using the scrubby bushes and rocks as cover until we reached the trees lining the ridge. No cries came from the hunters. No shouts of discovery. That's the problem with torches. They light up everything in their beam but they blind you to everything outside it. They'd find the car, though, and guess we were out on the moor.

'Careful,' I said as Nick's feet skidded through damp leaves. 'There's a sheer drop the other side of the trees. Follow the path along the ridge.'

And then, because I was cold and crampy from running bent double, I raced down the path, jumping and bouncing over the tree roots and rocks. I ran and ran without caring if Nick was keeping up, feeling the tightness in my chest relax and my lungs pump air into my body. The clouds had thinned and a watery moonlight cast the trees' shadows over the path but it was bright enough to see where I was going. It felt glorious.

After a while, I made myself stop and think. I forced myself to go over all the details of my plan, to be sure it was going to work. Kit would have been proud of me. Except I wasn't going to think about Kit and his meticulous planning right now.

Nick stumbled down the path, his steps uneven and his breathing rough. The moon caught his face full-on as he came near. It was set in grim lines, a black and white sketch of someone forcing himself to keep going. He stopped when he saw me and took a few shuddering breaths, then laughed and ran the fingers of his good hand through his hair to fling the wetness away. He smiled at me.

'Where to now, boss?'

'About a mile from here we'll disappear. But we need to go fast. They'll get the cars onto the moor.'

'Disappear?'

'You'll see.'

We ran on. This time I kept with him. Ready to push him on. But it wasn't necessary. He ran with his right hand clutching his left arm and if he'd gone any faster he would have fallen over.

The trees thinned until we came out of the woods and onto the bare ridge that was the south-western boundary of the moor. The land dropped vertically down into a valley which curled back to the coast road. It was the last place on the moor they'd look for us, but they'd come here eventually.

When we got to the highest point, I stopped and pulled the rucksack off my back.

'Here?'

'Yup.'

'We must be visible for miles.'

'Then keep down.'

The moon was low in the sky and its cloudy light threw long shadows after the tussocks of reedy grass and the stray bushes of sloes and thorns scattered across the ground. Nick looked drained. His lips were the same grey as his face and dark stains were spreading from his beaten eye over the bridge of his nose.

I emptied the rucksack and prayed everything would still be there. I hadn't checked it in a long time. Not since the day of Grid's fall. Doubt drained my confidence. *Was I leading us into more danger?*

'What is it?' Nick's voice was quiet but insistent. 'Are you missing something?'

'No. It's all here.'

He crawled over from where he'd lain down and looked.

'Rope,' he said. 'A harness and some other things whose names I don't know, but I'd say you were planning to climb down the rock.'

He picked up a karabiner and clicked it open and shut a few times.

'Very clever. You're very, very clever, Ms Jenifry Shaw. But I would have expected nothing less.'

'I don't see another way off the moor, do you?'

I was speaking to myself as much as to him.

'You know it better than I do.'

There was no other way off. They had four vehicles, maybe more, three of which could comb the moor. So, yes, I could see no other way. And if I got it right, they'd never know where we'd gone. I started preparing the kit.

Nick rolled over and lay on his back and watched me coil the rope and prepare the belay. My hands worked automatically as I went through all the steps of my plan. Nick still lay in the heather. His ribcage slowed. He said nothing and after a while his silence worried me.

'Maybe they'll give up,' I said.

'I don't think so.'

So he was still conscious.

'What have you done to fall out with them?'

There was a short pause before he answered. 'I really don't know.'

I passed him the harness. 'Put this on.'

The moonlight was a blessing and a curse. It made rigging the belay far easier but it would light me up like a beacon of white fire against the sky when I lowered him down.

'Phone?' he said.

I looked at it.

'Still no signal.'

I tied the rope round the rock we'd always used as an anchor and checked everything. All ready.

'Put the harness on.'

'I can't climb.'

'You don't need to. I'm going to lower you. That's the reason for all this stuff.'

'I'm too heavy.'

'I don't take your weight. The rope round the rock does. I just pay the rope out through the belay.'

I showed him how the belay controlled the speed of the rope passing through the device.

'It's easy,' I said.

'And you?'

'I'll climb down.'

There was a pause while he considered what I'd said and I felt the old, familiar rush of impatience. We didn't have time for this. The men would be on the moor already. Coming after us. Nick was sharp, though – I'll give him that. He went straight to the flaw in the plan.

'They'll find the ropes and come down after us.'

Or what would have been the flaw if it hadn't been *my* plan.

I laughed. And suddenly my impatience drained away. This was a place of safety for me. There was no need to rush. The flatness and emptiness of the moor worked both ways. They could see me for miles and I could see them. And no matter how quickly they crossed the distance between us, I'd be away before they got close. I laughed again.

He hauled himself upright, grabbing a handful of tall grass. 'Or,' he went on. 'They'll cut the rope when you're halfway down. We'd be better keeping going. They've got a lot of moor to search.'

'They've got locals with them, I'm sure. People who're used to herding the sheep up here. They know how to find missing animals. Which is exactly what we are. This is our only chance.'

His hands fingered the metal pieces of the harness while he scoured the horizon. He was not, I thought, a man used to trusting. I gave the knots a final tug and checked the rope would uncoil freely.

Everything was ready.

And there was no sign of our pursuers. Not yet.

'They won't find the ropes,' I said. 'And they won't cut them when I'm halfway down.'

He went to interrupt me but I spoke over him. Hissed in his face. Suddenly pissed off at his doubts. At his silences. At the questions I hadn't asked and he hadn't answered.

'Listen. I don't need the fucking ropes to get down this rock face. I've been climbing it since I was a child. I know it like I know how to tie my shoelaces. Because, guess what? I'm an ace rock climber. An absolute magician.' And then because some tiny bit of me wanted to be sure. 'How did you think I escaped when you left me dangling off the lighthouse?'

He froze.

What did it mean? Did he know what I was talking about?

I staggered to my feet and went to the anchor rock. I put my arms round it, leant my cheek against its wet roughness, breathing heavily.

He came up behind me and put a hand on my shoulder. I didn't want to look round. I didn't want to see the answers in his face.

'They're coming,' he said.

I turned, but he was in shadow.

'There are headlights on the horizon. All round us. You were right.'

I whirled round. Soft flashes shone against the sky, sudden glimmerings, still far away but closing in.

'I've put the harness on,' he said. 'But I don't know if I've done it right.'

I checked.

'It's fine.'

'So. You're going to lower me down, chuck the ropes and stuff after me and then come down yourself.' I nodded. 'And you can do that? Lower me and get down without ropes?' I nodded again. 'OK. Then we're going to do it. With one change.'

He had something in his hand. A knife. My knife. The one from my climbing kit. I stared at it, wondering if I should be afraid. I dug my heels into the soft earth and flexed my knees. I could outrun him and outfight him, too. With his broken arm. I could be over the edge and out of here before he could draw breath. But he held it out to me.

'Take it,' he said. 'And put it in your pocket. Lower me down. But if they come, you cut the ropes, chuck everything over the edge and then come down yourself. Don't leave it too late either. The moment you hear or see anything, you cut the ropes. I won't go down until you promise.'

I was empty. Everything had spilled out of me.

'Promise.' His voice was insistent.

I nodded.

'I need you to say it.'

'I promise.'

It meant nothing. It was just words and I'd have said anything to make him do what I wanted.

I clipped the rope to his harness and checked the length on auto pilot. The edge overhung slightly which made it easier for him to descend without banging against the side. After that, it fell sheer for a hundred feet or so before narrowing down into a steep-sided valley, the bottom of which was lined with bushes and small trees.

'Climb over,' I said.

I watched him hesitate. Going over the edge is the scariest part. Especially the first time. Especially with only one working arm. His hand clutched the trunk of a small elder tree as he went over and he still grasped it as I prepared to lower him.

'You'll have to let go,' I said.

His fist whitened.

I flicked a glance behind me. The headlights were closer.

'Nick…'

'I guess I'll have to trust you, then.'

He smiled.

'One thing,' he said rapidly. 'I don't know anything about what happened to you on the lighthouse. The first time I met you was on the coast road. I only go up the lighthouse when I have to. Don't like heights, you see. Never been able to bear them.'

And with that he let go of the tree and pushed himself off.

I lowered him quickly. It's frightening but over sooner. And we didn't have time to waste. When the mark I'd put on the rope appeared, I slowed its speed and peered over the edge. It was impossible to see where he was. I'd have to let him go the rest of the way gently.

I heard the Land Rover before I saw it. The sound of its engine revving tore the silence apart. Stuck in a muddy dip, I guessed and whipped a glance behind me. Its headlights jerked up and down in the distance. I lowered Nick as quickly as I dared. The rope ran a little faster.

How far away from the bottom was he? Not much? But even a short fall can damage. Or kill.

I remembered my promise: to cut the rope as soon as I saw or heard anything.

But while the Land Rover was stuck in the mud, I was safe. I angled myself so the anchor rock hid me but so I could still see the car's lights in the distance.

Time slowed. The Land Rover's beams sliced the horizon and the rope inched out of my belay. The sky pressed down on me like the top half of a dark blue, grey-streaky mussel shell, closing slowly to snap me shut in a trap.

Doors slammed and men shouted. I peered round the stone. They were getting out to push the Land Rover through the mud. It would be free any second.

I took the knife out of my pocket. It glinted, heavy and cold in my hand. I closed my fist around it and remembered.

Remembered the crumbling tower, remembered clinging to the window sill with my knees and the rope holding Grid dragging me over the edge, remembered my hands grabbing this knife and shaking as they prised it open. It took me longer than you'd think to cut the rope holding Grid. You'd think it was a quick slash and then… job done. But it wasn't. It took me nine passes of the blade to drop Grid to the ground. Nine times of deciding I had no choice. Nine times of feeling the rope jerk an infinitesimal fraction of an inch longer and realising Grid, dangling down below, must know exactly what I was doing.

But now, on the top of the cliff, with the rope holding Nick slowly running through the belay, I swung my arm in a great arc, as perfect as a rainbow, and threw the knife into the dark.

A promise broken. Two promises broken. The one I'd made to Nick and the one I'd made to Kit. But I didn't give a fuck. I was tired of promises. It was time for me to make up my own mind about what I would and wouldn't do. I'd never cut Nick's rope. Even if the chasers arrived, I'd get him down. Nothing else was possible. I knew I could and it mattered more to me than being caught myself.

The noise of revving started again and shouting came from the direction of the Land Rover. At the same time, the rope carrying Nick slackened and dropped on my foot. He'd reached the bottom. I tore the ropes loose from the anchor rock, grabbed everything, raced to the cliff and threw it all over.

With a great roar, the Land Rover came free; its headlights gave a final bounce and the beast was loose on the moor again. More doors slammed and the car moved towards me – but they were too late. Out of view behind the rock, I dropped onto the ground, scrabbled to the cliff and lowered myself over the edge.

They'd never know we'd been there.

Twenty-Four

For one kick-heart moment, I thought I'd forgotten the way down. My fingers clung paralysed to the first ledge as I heard the Land Rover coming closer. Heard it stop. It wouldn't take them long to come to the edge. To look over and see me hanging a couple of feet from the top. Easy enough to lean down and grab me. Easy enough to reach down and kick me loose.

I forced myself to push the panic away. With my eyes shut I let my body feel the rock. I knew this climb. It was fixed in the memory of my muscles from the countless times Pa had made Kit and me climb up and down the face. Every bit of me thanked him for making us downclimb it instead of rapping down on ropes. As the panic receded, my left foot moved automatically towards the ledge that was the first foothold and my hands reached down to find the crack that took you down the first few metres.

I climbed down to a wide ledge and took a moment to catch my breath and calm the blood beating through my body. I couldn't see Nick below. I swung off the ledge and carried on down. My hands and feet remembered the way before my head did and I let them lead.

I missed my climbing shoes but I didn't miss the ropes. In fact, it was easier without them. There was nothing to push out of the way and nothing to weigh me down. It was just me and the rock.

And about a third of the way down, the magic came back and took me by surprise.

I'd always loved the physical stuff. The feel of the different rocks. Sandstone with its rough, grainy surface giving my feet and hands grip. Granite, with its smooth-edged cracks, and limestone, full of pockets for fingers and toes and fossils of little dead things that once lived underwater and caught my eye as I climbed. And the more I climbed, the more the magic took me over and the rock came alive.

Sometimes, it's kind, pushing knobs into my hand and narrowing cracks to the perfect width. Other times, it is moody. It dangles ledges a few millimetres out of my reach and slips an overhang between me and the next hold. It pushes me to the outside edge of my strength, makes me cling with three fingers lacerating on a knife-like edge and leap towards an untested flake.

It's my partner, my enemy, my lover, my friend.

That night, it was an old friend, a childhood friend, visited after a long absence but as familiar as the taste of the fruit gums I used to buy from the village shop on a Saturday morning. Everything fell away from me but the pleasure of its feel. I was nothing but eyes and ears, and nerve endings where my skin touched the rock. I forgot the men up on the moor, the fear that Kit or Sofija had tried to kill me, my grief over Grid and Seb and lost myself in the simplicity of the moment. Perform or fall. Not that I was worried or frightened. All I needed was to concentrate on the purity of each move, and that came easily.

I hadn't wanted coke for a couple of days. Not since the night I found it at Nick's. And I sensed I might be free from its grasp forever so long as I could keep on climbing. All the craziness, all the drug-fuelled highs had been a reaction to the awfulness of what had happened to Grid. I'd have done better to go climbing straightaway. Alone. Given myself time to face up to what I'd done and work out how I'd let the thrill of danger take me over. Climbing was about so much more than that. It was a part of me. It made me who I was. And nothing else came close.

'Not bad,' Nick said when I jumped down the last few feet and landed in the soft earth and leaf mould at the base of the face. I gasped; I'd forgotten he was waiting at the bottom.

'Shh,' I said. 'They're nearby.'

He'd hidden my climbing gear behind a bush. I'd come back for it another day.

'Did they see you?' His eyes raked the line of the edge above.

'No,' I said. 'But they'll work it out eventually.'

I pointed down the valley. The sooner we were away from the moor the better. 'We need to go down there. Are you OK to do that?'

'Where does it go to?'

'The coast road.'

'Phone?' he said.

I shook my head. 'No signal until we get to the road.'

'Can I check?'

I handed it to him without a word. His hair had dried in tight curls tangled round bits of twig and grass, and bruises and blood showed black on his face.

'Let's get going.' The sharpness of his voice startled me. 'They must have rope in one of those cars and if they work out we've climbed down here, they'll come after us.'

We stumbled along the bottom of the ravine. A slash in the moors, whittled away over thousands of years by a stream or a small river that had dried up or gone underground, it was covered in stones washed down from the sides by rain. Moss and weed had grown on the stones and they were slippery. I led and Nick followed, putting his feet where I put mine and grabbing my outstretched arm in places where he needed help to lever himself up and over. He was always right behind me, forcing the pace, waiting for me to move my feet so he could step where they'd been. The only time he stopped was to hold the phone up and check it for signal.

We didn't speak. Which was fine by me. Despite the fear that the men might be behind us, the magic of the climb still flowed through my blood. I didn't tell him I'd broken my promise and chucked the knife. Too late, I realised how reckless that was. Fingers crossed we wouldn't need it later.

After a while, the pace took its toll. Nick started to slip on nearly every rock. I slowed a little.

'Keep going.' His voice was grim.

All my doubts about him crowded back.

'You need a rest. Take a break. We'll be faster after that. Anyway, I'm not going any further until you give me some answers. I'm not moving, Nick,' I said. 'Not until I know what's going on.' I wondered if he'd leave me. The same thought seemed to come to him and he peered ahead into the moon-shadowed gully.

'You're a stubborn...' he said. 'We really don't have time for this.'

'I don't care. Who are those men after us? What have you done?'

A wave of an emotion I couldn't read crossed his face, but then I could never tell what he was thinking. As if aware of my scrutiny, he flashed me a smile then bent his head again so the moon hit his hair and left his face dark. Afterwards, when I wasn't so tired, I'd think about all this. Work out why I found him so attractive. Even now, I wanted to move closer to him. Close enough to see into the shadows where the moonlight missed his face.

He swore and muttered something to himself. It was my turn to wait and a sick, breathless feeling flooded my body.

'What do you think I am?' he said.

'I don't know,' I said. 'I really don't know.'

'A criminal?'

'Probably.'

'Yet you helped me.'

I shrugged. If he couldn't see the symmetry between tonight and last Friday night, I wasn't going to explain.

'I'm a police officer,' he said.

I laughed. Couldn't help myself.

'I am,' he said. 'Why are you laughing?'

'You don't strike me as being the policeman type.'

'Maybe that's why I'm good at my job. I don't strike people as the policeman type.'

I thought about it. Something unknown ran through him, like a hidden vein of knife-sharp quartz. I'd always sensed it.

And like a pattern of dominoes falling in a ripple, changing colour as they tumbled, everything about him looked completely different. The fake website, the cocaine hidden in his workshop, the sleazy propositions he'd made to Kit, they were all a lure.

'Ah. Undercover, I suppose.'

'Exactly,' he said. 'And the people I'm after, they've got a cargo coming in tonight. And if we're quick, we might be able to catch them.'

He turned to move off but something held me back. Some vestige of doubt clung to me and rooted my feet to the ground. Then I thought of men running down the ravine after us and cars speeding round to head us off on the coast road and my feet started to move. He let me go first but flung a last few words at me before stepping in behind.

'It's not drugs, by the way,' he said. 'It's people. They're the cargo.'

I clambered over moss-covered rocks, grabbing at stumpy hawthorn trees to stop my feet from slipping, my head full of vivid images. A cargo of people: migrants clinging to the sides of boats; children sitting in makeshift tents with only a square of cardboard between them and the mud; faces, endless lines of faces, all sharing the same hollow look of despair. I thought of Ma trying to get her friend out of Libya. My feet faltered and I stumbled, tripped and fell.

Nick was by me in a flash, holding out his good arm. I shook my head and levered myself up.

My phone bleeped. We had signal.

I looked at the text. A string of question marks. And passed the phone to him.

I gathered some things from his rapid speech. Firstly, he was definitely a police officer. The conversation left no doubt. Secondly, there was something major going on tonight. *A delivery*, he called it. *A large one*, he thought. He didn't know where or exactly when but he was desperate for it to be intercepted because he was coming in. So this was last-chance saloon. It was all over. His cover had failed. He didn't know how. They'd turned up at his cottage this evening. Knocked him about a bit and locked him in the workshop, ready for someone else to come and deal with him. After the delivery. But he had a key hidden in the workshop and had escaped.

That was all he said. Nothing about me. Nothing about the chase through the narrow lanes or the crash. He told them there were men looking for him on the moor and on the coast road, but that was all. I couldn't follow the rest. Just questions from the other end, and Nick's answers were terse. When the call was over, he sat with his head leaning on his good arm for a moment.

'What will happen to them?' I asked. 'To the people in your delivery? If you get them.'

His eyes didn't leave my face but their focus shifted.

'*If* we get them,' he replied. 'It's not looking very likely.'

Images of people fleeing war, or torture, or poverty flowed through my head. The whole undercover thing seemed a massive amount of work to catch a few refugees.

'But what will happen? Will they get sent back to wherever they came from?'

'Perhaps. I don't really know.'

'No. You only catch them.'

Something in my tone of voice startled him and his focus returned to my face.

'These people? Who do you think they are?'

'Just people. Caught up in something beyond their control and trying to escape it.'

'You're right. And you're wrong.'

There was a long silence. He looked down at the ground. Bent over and picked up a stone, cleared the moss and mud off it and threw it out into the night. It landed below us and clattered against unseen rocks.

'Let's hope no one was watching from above,' I said.

'We should head down,' he replied.

'No,' I said, firmly. I knew he hadn't told me everything. 'I'm right and wrong about what?'

Another silence.

'I might as well tell you,' he sighed, 'you know so much already. They *are* refugees. Not necessarily legal ones but they're looking for refuge. They think they've found it, too. They think they're coming to safety. And they all have great plans. Work, of course.

They want to work. Most of them owe money to the traffickers and many of them have families they need to support back where they came from. And they *are* going to work. Hard work. Rotten work. Long, long hours. Work no one else wants to do.'

He picked up another stone and made as though to throw it again, then thought better of it.

'But they'll never see a penny from any of it,' he continued, 'because they belong to the gangs who've brought them in. Who've cherry-picked them because they're strong or good-looking. They'll be sold on to other gangs. They're slaves.'

'Slaves.' Of course. I'd seen stuff on the news about modern slavery. 'But they come in here? In Cornwall?'

'They come in everywhere. Refugees come in everywhere. It's hard to tell the difference because it's only when they arrive they become slaves. They're forced into sex work, or domestic work. Some end up in the fields. Some end up in cannabis factories. They're stuck. Too frightened to tell anyone because they're here illegally. And, after a while, too abused to try to escape. I know who brings them in but I'm not after them. I'm after the men who distribute them round the country. There's a network of traffickers and gang-masters in the UK and if I'd got in with them, we could identify many of the slavery operations in this country. That was my job. That was why I was sent here.

'We know when deliveries are due but we haven't caught them landing even when we kept a lookout on the lighthouse after Gregory gave me a key. There are too many places and they always come in where we're not watching and disappear as soon as they land. Twenty or thirty people at a time. We think they're hidden somewhere and then shipped out later in small groups. All across the country. And it's the network organising this we want to penetrate.'

He picked at the moss on the rock beneath his hand.

'And I was so close,' he said. 'So close. I've spent months trying to get in with them and I'd finally been asked if I'd run some people up to Manchester in a few days. No questions. Well paid. Finally, after all these months.' He stood up. 'Nothing anyone can do. Sometimes it works out like that. Come on. They said they'd pick me up on the road.'

The last few hundred yards of the gully were narrow and dark but the ground was flat and grassy. We walked side by side. Nick was a solid black figure against the streaky shadows of the bushes, changing shape as his body moved. His confession seemed to have unlocked him and he talked about the months he'd spent in Cornwall.

They'd chosen carpentry as a profession because a bespoke furniture business delivering all over the UK would be useful to the men they'd been after. Plus, he'd had some wood-working experience, although anything really difficult was made elsewhere and sent on to him. He'd spent months doing nothing but working with wood, while putting his story out. Nick Crawford's story.

Nick Crawford was a self-contained man with some lurking bitterness and a sense that he didn't think the world had treated him fairly. There was a history there but he wasn't going to shout about it. He was a lure and the kind of people he was designed to attract didn't like mouthy types.

After a few minutes, I stopped looking at him and just listened. As the sides of the narrow gully slowly lowered and opened out I felt, for the first time, as though there was no barrier between his thoughts and words. He talked about how he got himself in with the men he was after. A slow process but one he'd been through many times before. A gradual descent through layers of criminality. A bit of handling stolen stuff. A bit of drug dealing.

And so on, until he became known and trusted as a useful contact.

And then he stopped his tale. Nick Crawford had made contact with the men he was luring and that, the tone of his voice said, was all I needed to know.

'I shouldn't be talking to you about any of it really,' he said. 'But it's been a weird night. Like a time out of normal life.'

'Normal life. Do you have one?'

'Yup.'

'What is it? Where is it?'

'That really is something I can't talk about.'

I thought he was going to say something more but he turned and walked on. He'd got his second wind and I was the one stumbling now. My energy had drained away and been replaced by a heavy pool of depression. Nick was right. This had felt like a time out of normal life. A time away from the problems I was going to have to resolve.

I stopped when we reached the place where the ravine opened out and became a wide valley descending to the coast and the road. The sea stretched out before us, calm, the waves mere ripples running over its smooth surface and reflecting back the moon. The sky was still veiled with a thin layer of cloud so there were no stars. Only the moon was strong enough to penetrate and even its edges were blurred.

I sat down, suddenly realising how tired I was.

Nick sat, too.

'Where are we? I think I recognise this but…'

'The coast road's at the bottom of this field. Round the corner there's a place called Poltallack: bunch of cottages and a little teashop. It has a big sign advertising cream teas so, depending which way your friends are coming from, we'll be a hundred yards before or after it.'

He sighed.

'We'll wait here,' he said. 'We can see the cars coming before they see us. Can you call someone to come and get you?'

Kit. In the past I'd have called Kit. But I couldn't call him. Not while…

'I know some people who live behind the teashop.' I said. 'I can go there.'

'Sure?'

'Yep.'

'You could come with me but it'd be easier for you not to. You'll end up stuck at the station for hours and there'll be a lot of questions about your involvement.'

'I'll be fine.'

He asked for my phone, called and told them where to pick him up and afterwards we sat on separate boulders in uneasy silence. He turned to look at me a few times and cleared his throat like he was going to say something. It had been a long night, I thought, and although the news he was on the side of the angels was good, so good, it meant all my worst suspicions might be true.

'Why did you let me have your car?' I asked. 'The night we met?'

'I thought you'd come in from the sea. You were wet through and carrying nothing but a tarp.'

'You thought I was one of your refugees?'

'You behaved like one. Speechless with terror. And when I realised you weren't, I couldn't just drive off and leave you.' He cleared his throat. 'What had happened to you? You said something about the lighthouse. Was that it?'

'Yup, but it doesn't matter now.'

A cold trickle of water dripped from my hair and ran down my neck. I kicked a few stones.

'Thank you,' he said suddenly and I laughed. 'I mean it. I'd be dead if you hadn't stopped to pick me up. And dead if you hadn't got us off the moor.'

I didn't reply.

'You're quite something,' he went on. 'And I wish you'd tell me what happened to you on the lighthouse.' I pulled a few blades of grass up and looked at them. 'Because whatever it was, I had nothing to do with it.'

'OK,' I said. 'So what were you doing on the coast road? On a night like that?'

'Going to check Gregory was all right. Last time we had a bad storm he had water in the cottage. It's slowly falling apart around him. I went the next morning instead when I met you again.'

It made sense.

So I told him the whole saga from arriving in the hotel to the moment he stopped his car in the storm. He was quiet while I spoke, only interrupting once at the beginning, when I told him about the moment I came to from the drugs.

'Hanging from the...'

'Yes.'

The dark made it easier to talk calmly. It was a blanket around me protecting me from the awfulness of it all, making it seem as though it had happened to someone else or was only a strange and unreal story. Sitting still made me cold so I got up and strode around and slapped my arms around me as I finished the tale while Nick's eyes tracked the horizon. I had the sense of his brain pulling my story apart and reassembling it behind his unfocussed gaze.

'There you go,' I said in the end.

'It wasn't the traffickers. I'm sure of it,' he said slowly. I tried to speak but he cut me off. 'Listen. Listen to me for a while. You think you came across them bringing cargo in?' I nodded. 'But there wasn't anything going on that night. Definitely not. The weather was shocking. Everyone knew the storm was coming. Besides, they'd never get rid of you in such an idiotic way. If they'd wanted to kill you, you'd be dead. They'd shoot you. Cut your throat. Run you over several times. Or simply smash your head in. And then dispose of your body so no one would know. It's not hard.'

'You would know, wouldn't you?' My voice soared above his list of killing methods like the shriek of the seagulls wheeling round the fishing boats. 'What if they wanted to make it look like an accident? A climbing accident? With drugs?'

'They'd have thrown you off, maybe frayed a bit of rope and dropped it after you,' he said. 'Not left you hanging. It smacks of the amateur, Jen. Someone with no experience. Someone acting on the spur of the moment.'

I'd seen Nick play a lot of roles. From the saviour in the storm to the player jousting words with me. But this Nick, serious, professional, was a new one.

'It was personal, too,' he continued. 'I'm sure of it and I'm sorry, Jen, because it means it was probably someone who knows you.' He paused as though he thought I might say something.

But I couldn't speak. *Someone who knew me.* Nick's words were one confirmation too many of what I was now sure was the truth.

The silence between us became a buzzing in my ears, like the flapping of thousands of distant wings and the sense the air was turning inside out. A cloud of birds. A murmuration of starlings, I think they call it.

Nick waited a while longer then carried on speaking.

'But, for what it's worth, I think whoever it was couldn't quite bring themselves to do it. They planned to throw you off the top but when it came to it, they couldn't and they left you a way out.'

The birds inside my head wheeled and banked violently because I didn't think this was true. Nick, with his fear of heights, hadn't spent time gazing over the top of the lighthouse at the ground far below like I had.

'And one other thing,' he continued. 'You said you were slipped something like Rohypnol.'

'Yup.'

'I think you're right. I guess you know Rohypnol blurs your memory of the time before you take it.'

I nodded.

'But not to the extent you think it does. Your memory loss starts at the hotel. You should be thinking who could have spiked something you ate or drank there. That's where you need to look – the hotel, and who knew you were there.'

'But I went straight out. The woman who runs the hotel told me. I was OK then.'

'Rohypnol takes a while to work completely. Half an hour. Maybe less.'

Was he right? I thought he was.

And then I remembered something. Maybe because I was with Nick. I remembered hunting for his keys in my hotel room while Vivian waited at the door. I'd found them behind an empty cup and saucer. On the table by the door. Had Vivian regretted her dour welcome and brought me a cup of tea? It wouldn't have taken a moment to slip something in it. Not for someone chatting to Vivian in the room behind reception while she made the tea. Someone like Sofija. Who'd popped in to see Vivian. To apologise for the cheque bouncing, maybe. But really, to check I was there.

Nick's voice went on but it felt as though he was talking to someone else. Another Jen, standing next to me and taking his words in while my thoughts reeled.

'Someone who knew you well, I'd say.' Nick's voice was a relentless drum beating against my ears. 'Who knew your history of climbing dangerous things. Who thought, if you were found at the base of the lighthouse, the police would think it was a mad scheme gone wrong. And that you'd taken the drugs found in your body for pleasure.'

'Enough! That's enough!' I shouted into the night, disturbing a few sheep who got to their feet and thundered about aimlessly until the momentum of their fright ran down and they settled back to sleep.

I wondered if there was a tinge of light towards the east but when I looked at my watch it was still too early for a winter's dawn.

Headlights appeared round the bend on the road below.

'Is it them? I mean, the police?' I asked and my phone bleeped at the same time.

'Yes.'

Neither of us moved.

'I won't see you again, will I?' I said.

The question came out before I thought about it.

'No. Are you sure you'll be OK?'

'Yes.' It came out sharper than I intended. 'I'm only going round the corner. I'll be fine.'

'Like I said, it would be easier if I went down alone.'

'I get it. No worries.'

He stood up and came close to me. He smelled of damp wool and mud mixed with something sharp and green. I wanted to cry.

'Thank you,' he said. 'I should say much more but there isn't time. So thank you will have to do.'

His face was close to mine and I breathed in the scent of him. He wasn't tall, Nick Crawford, but he was the right height for me. The car stopped on the road and he spoke rapidly.

'Next week,' he said. 'I'll be back in the place where I grew up. I call it home, although I only get back there from time to time. A little village where everybody knows me. It's where my grandparents lived and where my mother was brought up. I'll stay in their old house. And most evenings, around nine o'clock, I'll go down to the little bar off the central square. A funny little place, with a ceiling carved out of cork. Quite intricate and fabulous. Anyway, when I'm there next week, I'll think of you. You'll be hard to forget. I'll have a drink and toast you. Jenifry the valiant.'

His lips touched my forehead.

'Goodbye, Jen.'

'Goodbye, Nick.'

A silent black Mercedes picked him up. He hauled himself into the back and, as it moved off, I thought I saw the flash of a white face through the rear window, as if he'd turned to look back at me.

I walked down the slope and sat on the dry-stone wall that kept the sheep from the road. I needed a bit of space before I walked into Poltallack. If I hadn't been so cold, I'd have curled up by the side of the road and slept.

Instead, I thought about Kit and Sofija and the desperate straits they'd got themselves into. I thought about the fraying rope at the lighthouse. I thought about how my body would have fallen outside Gregory's window. Nick was wrong. No one had had second thoughts about killing me. I hadn't been left a way out. It had all been a timing device. A way of letting the perpetrators disappear before I fell and disturbed Gregory. I thought about Kit and the precision of his planning and Sofija wanting me to clean the windows at Tregonna…

The stones of the wall were hard and I was damp, cold, tired and sad. If what I suspected was true, the danger was over. Pa had come to the rescue not only of Kit and Sofija, but of me, too. I couldn't think about it any more now. I stood up and stamped my feet up and down to get some warmth back into them.

Now, I was going to sit in front of a wood stove until my clothes steamed and drink five cups of tea with sugar in a kitchen I'd always found homely. While Nick and his colleagues rounded up the criminals, I was going to eat toast with lots of butter with Kelly and Talan who lived round the corner. And maybe even laugh with them when I told Talan that he'd been investigating an undercover police officer.

Twenty-Five

It was only a couple of hundred yards to Talan and Kelly's cottage, one of a cluster of small stone houses huddled along a tiny inlet. They'd been built for fishermen around two hundred years ago and crammed into the limited space so bits of one rested on top of another and it was hard to see where each house began and ended. Even if they were out, I knew where Talan kept the spare key. Or where he used to. He might have moved it but I didn't think so. People like Talan didn't change, that was what was so comfortable about them. He wouldn't mind, either, if I let myself in and made myself at home. I walked faster, the longing to feel heat on my skin overpowering every other thought.

Talan opened the door. He was dressed and not long in. Muddy boots lay on their side in the tiny porch and the legs of his tracksuit were spattered with wet earth. His eyes widened when he saw me. I looked down. I was covered in half-dried mud but he ushered me in straightaway, down the narrow corridor and into the back kitchen.

I hadn't been here in years but it hadn't changed much since his mother used to sit me on the table to bathe my scratches and grazes after a fall. The fridge and dishwasher were new but the cupboards and surfaces were the same scratched blue painted wood. I crossed to the old range and stretched my hands over its top. The heat, rising through my fingers, felt solid and graspable.

I felt my body give a huge sigh. Even the acrid smell of burning coke biting my nostrils was familiar and comforting.

Talan's hand reached past me and took the kettle.

'Tea?'

'Please.'

The clink of a spoon against china and the slosh of water. It was great to do nothing. My mind was empty of everything except the glorious touch of warmth on my skin. I leaned my head over the range and shut my eyes.

'Are you falling asleep?'

'I might be.'

He dragged a wooden armchair over to the range and I fell into it. A mug of tea arrived. It wasn't very hot but I gulped it down.

'Another cup, Talan, please.'

He busied himself with the teabags and the kettle. My eyes started to shut again. I felt relaxed for the first time for days. No, weeks. Maybe months.

'Toast,' I said. 'Is there any chance of toast?'

'What have you been doing, Jen?'

I was too tired to lie.

'Racing round the countryside, chased by a gang of criminals. With butter. And marmalade. If you've got any.'

'So it was you,' he said slowly.

'What do you mean?'

He was silent and, when I looked round, his eyes were fixed on the teabag he was squeezing into my mug.

'I don't understand,' I said. 'How do you know about it? Did someone call the police?'

My thoughts tried to grip and form a chain, but my brain was too soft and slippery. I put my head into my hands and tried to press the tiredness away. When I looked up, Talan was stirring the tea and closing the cupboard door.

'Talan?'

'It was you with Crawford.' he said. 'You who picked him up on the road.'

I nodded and took the second cup of tea. The local police must have been informed when Nick had rung his boss to say he was coming in.

'But why? Why didn't you leave well alone?'

'I happened to be driving by when he came out onto the road. I couldn't…'

I thought back to the strangeness of the meeting. Nick running through the rain and the dark. Mindlessly. Desperately. Hopelessly. Away from the men who'd beaten him.

'He's a police officer – like you, Talan. But undercover. Here in Craighston. Who'd have thought it! Apparently we're the centre of a huge people-trafficking operation. I'm probably not supposed to tell anyone because the police, Nick's lot, I mean, they're trying to pick them all up now but of course I can tell *you*.'

'You can tell me,' he said and patted my hand. I took a gulp of tea, hoping its familiar taste would clear my brain. 'Drink your tea. Relax for a moment, and then you can tell me everything.'

He went into the front room. *I was safe*, I thought. It was a wonderful feeling. I let my tiredness run free. Swallowed my tea. Drained the cup dry. Looked around for somewhere to put it before it fell out of my hands. I made one last effort and pushed myself up and put the cup in the sink. A cork board on the wall caught my eye. It was covered with scraps of paper with phone numbers written on them, scribbled reminders of appointments and photos. The old ones, their corners bent, were half hidden under the more recent stuff: a clipping from a newspaper about the open day at the mine and flyers from nearby takeaways. I wondered if I'd find a photo of me and Talan together if I excavated far enough. There was a programme from Kelly's first performance in London and a clipping from the local paper when she came on tour to Plymouth, numerous photos of her dancing and a few of her with friends.

And beneath a flyer for a window-cleaner – a strip of photos from a booth. The kind of booth supermarkets used to have for taking passport photos that you now only see at wedding receptions and parties. Four snaps of two people kissing against a psychedelic background of swirling pinks and greens. My legs gave way and I grabbed the sink. All my ideas about Friday night shot up into the air; when they fluttered back down to land, they had a completely different shape.

Talan's voice slipped through the door in snatches. He was on the phone, trying to speak quietly, but his words were staccato and carrying. I caught Nick's name, and then *escaped*. *Picked up*. Pause. *Not safe*. Pause. *No, she's here*. Pause. *OK*. Pause. *OK*.

I made myself stand up.

Who was he talking to?

Something wasn't safe. I wanted to know what it was.

I staggered into the little front room, furnished with an old-fashioned, wooden-armed sofa and chairs with antimacassars on their tops. Talan was still on the phone, putting his boots back on with the other hand. He didn't see me.

'You've got to hurry,' he said and his voice was panicked. 'Get them off the road before –' Whoever was on the other end interrupted him and he listened, doing his boot laces up with the phone clenched between chin and shoulder. 'I'll sort that,' he said. 'I'll dump her and then come over to you. No. Give it a couple of minutes and she'll be out for the count.'

I wondered who 'she' was. The one who'd be out for the count in a few minutes. My legs felt as though they were made of rubber and I grabbed the door frame to stop myself falling. Talan heard me.

'I'll have to go. Speak later.'

I understood then that it was me who would soon be out for the count. The floppiness wasn't merely tiredness. He'd put something in my tea. If I didn't get out, something very bad was going to happen.

'Kelly,' I gasped.

'She's not here. She's working.'

Of course she was. She was at Freda's.

The sofa between us protected me but the strength was seeping from my body. I needed to be quick. A brass fire set squatted on the hearth. I lunged as though to go for the door but, as he moved to cut me off, turned and reached for the poker. Reached and stumbled. My legs no longer did what I wanted. I reached again and half fell against a chair. He was on me in a moment, his weight pinning me down, his breath hot and savoury on my face.

'You stupid bint. Why couldn't you leave it alone? It was all under control. Crawford would have disappeared and no one would have been any wiser.'

My hand touched the cold metal of the poker and with a last effort of will, I lifted it ready to smash it into his head. But my grasp was loose and it fell through my hand and clattered onto the floor, banging his forehead as it went. He grabbed my arms and pinned them to my waist.

'It was *you*, you know, who gave him away,' he said. 'Your precious Mr Crawford. All the things you said about his website and address being fake. Made me wonder. Made me check up on him. Wasn't hard to work it out.'

His face, red and puckered like an old balloon that had lost most of its air, wavered in the steam filling the room. He needed to turn the kettle off. I tried to tell him. Except it wasn't steam, it was his voice filling the room and drowning my vision. He was sorry. He kept on saying it. What he was doing was for my own good. He'd take me somewhere safe. Until he could think what to do.

I fought to hold onto his words but they melted into each other and slipped away. I tumbled a long way down into nothingness but gravity was gentle, cradling me as I floated. Talan's voice reached me, faint and thin. I couldn't quite make it out but I thought he was saying, 'You'll be mine. You'll be mine.'

Twenty-Six

Consciousness returned. Slowly, but not smoothly. In fits and starts. I knew where I was early on, as my brain made sense of Talan's last words. I was in the mine. The fear took a while to return, though. There were long moments of dreamy peace that I wanted to cuddle into; then little nudges to my brain to wake up. When the last dregs of the sedative wore off, panic hit me. I flung my arms out wide into solid rock all around me. I was buried in the dark. I was a tiny kernel surrounded by layer after layer of pitch-black, flint-hard rock. My hands battered it, looking for a way out as it encircled me, pulling tighter and tighter. I screamed until the effort of it hurt my lungs and made me gasp for breath. And then I screwed myself into a tight ball, desperate to avoid the rough knuckles of the rock poking into my body.

I dredged through my memories for all the calming words I'd ever heard and told myself the rock wasn't closing round me. Told myself I could breathe. In the end, the words worked. The trembling stopped. I unfolded and welcomed the air flowing into my lungs. And opened my eyes.

It wasn't utterly black.

I breathed.

I was at the dark end of a passage. A small, narrow hole of a passage. However, silvery remnants of tin ore gleamed along the edges of the rock. Daylight was getting in somewhere. *Follow the light*. I took a deep breath and crawled towards it until the passage grew wider, with enough space for me to stand and stretch my arms.

Pain woke in my body. I felt my legs. They were sore but only bruised. My hands ran over a rectangular shape in my pocket.

My phone. Talan hadn't checked my pockets. I pulled it out, praying it would have some battery left. It did. But no signal. Of course not. I was buried deep underground. *Fuck. Fuck. Fuck.*

But I had missed calls and two texts. All from Kit. They must have arrived while I was unconscious but still above ground.

The first: *WTF? It's 7 and U not back. Ma is. Told U. Call me.*

The second, longer and less irritable: *Call me, please. Your phone is switched off. Ma is packing! Won't talk to me. Have you gone to London? Call me. Please.*

After that, nothing. I wondered what was going on at Tregonna, but only briefly. There were other, more urgent things to think about.

Talan was involved with the traffickers. Nothing else made sense. Nick had said they needed local people. How much better if one of those locals was a police officer, able to tip them off whenever the police were getting close? No wonder Nick and his colleagues never found the places where the boats landed.

Shit! I'd told Talan about Nick; I was the one who'd given him away with my talk about fake websites and falsified addresses. He was safe now, though. Thank God I'd stopped my car and picked him up. He'd be dead otherwise and it would have been my fault.

Why hadn't Talan killed me? I guessed he couldn't face it. He'd left me here instead. *For someone else to deal with? Or just to die in the dark?* I slithered down the wall and sat, willing myself to stay calm. Someone would look for me. Eventually. They'd come across the car, smashed on the moor, and think I'd wandered off. There'd be a hunt but no one would be surprised when they couldn't find me. The moor was littered with old mine workings. Sheep disappeared every year. One day, I guessed, Talan would take my body and drop it down an old shaft. And that would be that.

My phone was no use as a phone but OK as a torch. I checked the time. A few minutes after nine. I hadn't been out for as long as I'd thought. Maybe, just maybe, Talan had missed something. I pushed myself up. *Time to explore.* Anything was better than sitting in the black and imagining my flesh darkening and drying on my bones. Ahead the passage split in two. The right-hand side led to light and the left to a dark entrance into a cave of sorts. With a door. An open door. Thick and wooden, with a square hole with bars to look through and a lock. The door wasn't old; neither was the lock. Someone wanted to keep something very safe. I went inside.

Torn mattresses and grubby sleeping bags, stubs of candles and old crates lay on the floor along with empty food packets and plastic bottles, discarded clothing and, worst of all, items that must have been treasured by someone once. A cutting from a newspaper in a script I didn't recognise, soft and worn, splitting where it had been folded. A photo of two men standing in the shade of a tree, the blue of the sky and the bareness of the field around them revealing it had been taken somewhere foreign and hot. The elder had his arm over the younger one's shoulder. Father and son?

A pungent smell rose from a bucket in the far corner. I pulled my T-shirt over my nose. I didn't need to look. I knew what it was.

And I knew what the cave was used for. Obvious, really. Nick had said the slaves disappeared as soon as they landed and they'd never found any trace of them on the roads out of Cornwall. That would be because they didn't leave Cornwall immediately. Maybe not for days, or even weeks. No. Instead, men, women and, I realised upon picking up a small crocheted blanket and a plastic bag of Lego, children were kept here in the mine until it was safe to move them.

The prison cave was a storage facility. And if I needed confirmation that the people who stayed here did so against their will, it was present in the large coil of rope just outside the door, with a pile of shorter lengths already cut. A point must come when even the most trusting of passengers realised their transporters meant them no good.

I left the dark, cramped prison cave and walked into the light. The passage opened into a round pool of space: a stope, teardrop-shaped, with smooth walls gleaming in the dim grey light coming through a hole in the roof three metres or so above me. A raise, I remembered Talan calling it, axed out by the early miners following a vein of tin down from the moor. I must be in the old part of the mine, I realised. The part nearest the surface.

I stood underneath the raise and breathed. I couldn't see the sky because the tunnel twisted out of view a short way up and probably turned a few more times before reaching the moor but the light and the nearness of the outdoors made me feel better.

Two passages ran off the stope. Three, if you counted the one high above me. There was the one I'd come from which was the smallest and darkest and, at a right angle to it, a far larger passage blocked by bars. Someone had drilled great bolts into the rock to hold them in place. The middle section formed a door with a chain wound round it and fastened with a padlock. I smacked the bars with my hands and shoved the door with my body but it stood firm. *This must be the way out.* I was sure it led to the upper entrance, the one I'd gone a short way down while waiting for Talan. I remembered him locking the doors behind him and wondered how many lay between me and daylight. I slammed my hands against the bars again, this time in hopeless frustration. I wasn't going to get out and no one was going to rescue me. No one was even looking for me. Not yet. Maybe later on today someone would start to wonder where I was. Kit would call again. And my phone wouldn't ring because the fucking thing was useless all these metres below the surface. It was nothing but an expensive torch, already starting to fade.

Unless... Unless I could climb out. The shaft above me led upwards. To the surface. Hope fluttered its wings in my chest. The shaft was narrow but I could squeeze through. The problem was getting up to it. It punched through the roof of the stope high above me and the walls were smooth, with little in the way of holds. I paced around under it, stroking the rock, willing my hands to find cracks and ridges my eyes couldn't see in the dim light but they slid unhindered over the surface.

The most uneven and most climbable bit of wall was in the darkest corner. Water seeped in from somewhere above and, oozing down over years, had coated the rock with a marble-like deposit, rounding the protrusions and filling the cracks I would need to climb. But it was the best surface by far. I thought I could drive myself up the first few feet by sheer momentum then hope that somewhere up there in the dark shadow, out of reach of my hands and eyes, the rock would roughen its face and let me climb.

I lost count of the number of times I tried. Running and leaping up the rock, arms flailing for a grip until gravity unpeeled me and flung me back down. It became automatic. *Fall to ground. Stand up. Pace back. Run at rock and up.* Once, my fingers grazed the bottom of a ledge and I tried again and again to propel my body far enough up to grab it. Enough to pull myself further up and grasp it with my other hand.

I got tired. And thirsty. I ran a finger over the wetness on the rock. It smelt bitter and, when I licked my finger, the taste was harsh.

Time to stop hurling myself blindly at the rock. In my last few tries, I'd not made it as high as before, as if my body knew it wasn't going to succeed and was conserving its energy.

Then I swore at my own idiocy.

I went back to the prison cave and dragged a pile of crates through. Piling them up under the hole, I stood back to look. From the top, if they didn't topple, I could reach the tunnel.

A flicker of movement caught my eye. A pale gleam in the midst of the black through the other side of the bars. It resolved into a face. A silent figure, dressed in black, watching me. My skin crackled. It was Kelly. We stared at each other. A long silence, full of thoughts clattering around inside my head.

Another noise rattled down the mine from behind her. The sound of chains falling to the ground and voices, staccato and hard-edged. Kelly slipped back into the dark and disappeared. I had no time to think what her presence might mean. I had to disappear, too. Fast.

I clambered up the crates and balanced on the top. The noises down the passage grew closer. I kicked down with my feet and leaped into the void, thrusting my body towards the raise. My hands outstretched to grab. They hit the rock inside the opening and scrabbled. My right hand grasped a ledge, solid and flat, but my left found only a sharp edge. I had no choice. I crimped my fingers hard over it, seized the last scrap of momentum and hauled my body up. The sharp edge sliced into my flesh and I clenched my mouth shut over the gasp of pain. It was enough. My body moved far enough into the raise for my knees to meet the rock and wedge me tight. I squirmed up until my feet rested on the first ledge. I was clear of the stope.

I looked down. The pile of crates had collapsed with the force of my kick and looked like random discards. No one would guess what they'd been used for. Anyway, with my body crammed in the shaft, it was dark in the stope. I'd have to keep still because every movement threw changing shadows onto the ground below. I heard the key unlock the chain on the bars and the grind of the door opening. The noise of trudging feet and murmuring interspersed with shouts rose up the shaft. Torchlight bounced around beneath me. I peered down through the gap between the rock and my legs. The talk became louder and I realised it wasn't English. This must be the delivery Nick had talked about. Coming to be stored in a hiding place he had been so close to discovering until I gave him away.

Louder voices pierced the chatter. They shouted orders. *Move along. Down here. Keep going.* The tops of heads came into sight. The traffickers were out of view, leaning against the walls of the stope, their torches picking out odd details of the figures traipsing through. A hand clutching the damp T-shirt of the person in front. The grey, curly hair of an older man limping with his head bent over and fixed on the uneven floor. The scarfed head of a woman stabbing panicked glances around her and clutching a blanket to her chest. One of the few to stand upright. The muttering faded as they moved towards the prison cave and then grew again. They clearly didn't want to go in, and who could blame them? Some must have tried to resist because a couple of sickening slaps echoed out, the thwacks made by something hard hitting flesh. Then quiet.

Then voices right beneath me.

'How much longer?' A Cornish voice.

'Just waiting for water.'

'They gonna be here a long time, then?'

'All a bit of a mess.'

Two men. One local. The other with his sharp, nasal twang came from elsewhere. London, I suspected. Their voices were clear against the background noise. I dared not look down.

'How we gonna get home? If there's police all over.'

'PC Plod's with them. He'll call Fred and tell him which way to avoid them.'

'Christ.'

'You can wait it out here if you'd rather.'

'No, thanks.'

Relief surged through my body. They had no plans to stay in the mine. My muscles were crying out with the effort of keeping still and my fingers were agony where the rock had pierced the flesh.

'What's Plod done with the girl?'

'She's in here somewhere.'

They were talking about me and Talan.

'Want to go and find her?'

'No, ta. Let Plod deal with her. The little passages give me the horrors.'

A narrow line of something wet glinted as it ran down the rough surface of the shaft beside me.

'What'll they do to her?'

'Don't know.'

My eyes traced the trickle of liquid back up. It was coming from my left hand. Blood from the gashes in my fingers, mingling with the water on the rock and running down.

'Maybe chuck her where we threw that dog.'

They laughed.

I followed the line of blood down with my eyes, keeping my head rigid. *Fuck!* It was inches away from the bottom edge of the raise. I moved my head, a millimetre at a time, until I could see directly beneath me. A bald head, faintly freckled, gleamed below in the cave. In a few seconds, the blood would fall and splash onto it. I pictured it. A blob of red staining his skin. He'd feel it. Reach up his hand to wipe it, see its colour and realise what it was. And then he'd look up.

I heard footsteps. A box dragged across the ground. More murmuring.

But Baldy didn't move. And all the time the blood ran further and further down the rock. Every part of me shrieked that I should climb. Onwards and upwards. While I still could. My muscles were nearing the end. Tremors had started under the skin of my forearms. But all I could do was watch the blood trickle and wait for the moment of discovery.

There was a moment of silence and the blood fell.

A woman's voice rang out in protest. Baldy moved. A couple of inches. But enough for the blood to hit the shoulder of his coat. It sat on the surface for a few seconds and then seeped into the fibres. Quietly, calmly, discreetly.

And with the same lack of fuss, the men departed, slamming and locking as they left. I counted three doors as well as the one blocking the exit to the stope, each bang and clatter quieter than the one before as they moved further towards the open air, until it was silent. No noise from the people locked in the prison cave. Or none that I could hear. Only a faint and flickering light from the passage leading to their cave gave their presence away. Maybe they were too shocked to speak. Or maybe they were seizing the chance to rest despite the squalor of their surroundings.

I moved.

A shiver of shadows on the ground below.

Nothing happened. No one came.

Beneath my feet there was a dark hole with four locked doors between it and the outside, while above me the raise wriggled its way towards the light, promising daylight and air at the end of its twists and bends. No brainer. It was time to climb.

The first part was a tight fit. Anyone larger would have got stuck. And then the raise widened and finally there was space and air around me. The light from above was stronger although the top was still out of sight behind the rock, which now curved to the left. Sweat ran down my face, as though it had stored itself beneath my skin until a moment of safety. It didn't matter. Up here, the air moved and snatched the dampness off my skin.

And it was lovely climbing. The stone was gloriously ragged where the old miners had chipped out every vestige of ore. There was no need to hunt and feel for the next hold. Hope sped my hands and feet. Adrenalin blocked the pain in my hand. The raise would carry me up into the light and onto the moor. Soon, I'd feel the breeze rustling the rough grass and hear the scratchy chirps of warblers and buntings mingling with the tremulous song of the skylark. Soon, I'd be under the vast cloudy arc of sky punctuated only by the occasional swirling of a gull swept inland or a buzzard hovering on the wind.

I turned the last corner and a jagged disc of light blinded me. *I'd done it. I'd escaped.* The day was reaching down the raise to welcome me. I tore up the last few metres, thinking of nothing but freedom, until my hand, stretching above, smashed into something smooth. I screwed my eyes up against the light and looked. An iron grille was concreted into the rock a few feet below the surface. Only a few feet below the surface. Something to stop the sheep tumbling into the mine. *Something that trapped me in this fucking hell-hole.*

I shook the bars, wrenched at them, scrabbled at the concrete gripping them tight, but it was useless. A few flakes of rust floated down, colouring the air with their distinctive, bloody smell. Nothing else budged. And then I screamed. And wailed and begged. Tears washed through the sticky residue of sweat and dirt on my face.

I was trapped. There was no way out.

Then I remembered my phone. I was close to the surface but the signal on the moor was patchy and unreliable. *Oh God*, I thought, *let me be lucky.* My fingers shook as I eased the phone out of my pocket with my injured hand while my good one clutched the bars above. It had signal. One bar.

The iron grille above seemed to thin and let freedom pour down the tunnel to meet me. *Please. Let me have a life.* Years and years of it. Bad times. Good times. I didn't care. I wanted it all.

Who should I call? Not the police. Not with Talan monitoring everything.

Kit. Of course. I could call Kit. Now I knew he wasn't my would-be killer. I hadn't had time to think about the photos I'd seen on the cork board in Talan's kitchen. I'd been too busy surviving, but I understood what they meant now.

Kit's phone went straight to voicemail.

I left a message.

It was a shaking, weeping cry for help. Disorganised. Disordered. But the key bits were there. *Danger. Mine. Shut in. Tell the police. But don't tell Talan. Not a joke. Come and get me. Please come and get me. And above all, don't tell Talan.*

But the phone was very quiet. My voice didn't echo in my ears. And when I looked at it, feet and knees digging into the rock to support my body and right hand gripping the iron grille above, I saw it was dead. No battery. Fucking thing. Shouldn't have used it as a torch.

My feet slipped. The muscles were weakening. I let the phone go and gripped the iron bars with both hands, ignoring the warning stab from the left one. *When had the phone cut out? Before I'd left the message? Before I'd told Kit not to tell Talan? Both would be disastrous.* I shuddered and the muscles in my arms warned me not to push them too far. My hands slid round the iron. It pinched the fleshy parts of my right hand with a cold burn and dug into the cuts on my left.

But I was safe here. No one would be able to get up into the shaft. It had been hard enough for me. I needed to stay up here until Kit came. Except my left hand hurt more than I could bear and the muscles in my arms were insisting I let go. I wedged my feet and knees back against the sides and let them take the strain.

I got thirsty and wished it would rain. Then I prayed for rope. Remembered the rope outside the prison cave and cursed myself. I needed something to tie me to the bars. To give my juddering arms and legs a chance to rest. I gripped for a last few seconds with every bit of me: knees, feet and hips forced into the rock and hands clinging up above. Until my muscles failed. And as I slid down the crumpled surface of the tunnel, my body catching against its knobs and edges, I felt nothing but relief that I was no longer trying to hold on.

Twenty-Seven

I tumbled down the shaft like Alice falling down the rabbit hole. The knobs and ridges of the narrow end above the stope slowed my fall and I landed gently on the floor.

When I looked up, there was no white rabbit disappearing down a dark passage. Instead, Kelly looked at me through the bars. The white face I'd seen before, floating in the dark, had been real. It was, I realised, the same face that had stared through the windscreen at me last Friday night when I woke from my sleep in Nick's car. I felt very tired. I'd got it all so wrong.

A male voice called out from the prison cave. Quavering but piercing, he sounded like someone waking from a dream. Someone muttered a response and then all was silent again.

Kelly stared at me. I stared back. Her gaze, so empty of emotion, hid… *what?* Despite my exhaustion, fear churned my stomach and my brain stuttered into action.

Was she involved in the trafficking? I didn't think so.

Had she guessed I knew what she'd done? I wasn't sure.

Could I get her to help me? It was worth a try. If I could only get outside into the air, I could run away. From the mine. From the men who might come back at any moment.

From Kelly.

I said the first thing that came to mind.

'Kelly! Thank God. We need to get out of here. It's dangerous.'

293

She clutched the bars and leaned her head against them. The gap between was only wide enough for one eye and a bar cut her blank face in half. She looked like the cover of a horror story.

'You must have seen all those people come in,' I babbled on. 'They're shut in a cave down there. It's people smuggling. We need to get out before the traffickers come back.'

She said nothing but looked at me as though she couldn't follow what I was saying. As though her mind was miles away. I didn't think this was going to work.

'Kelly?' Fear and longing soaked my voice. But that was only natural. Of course I'd be afraid.

'I can't let you out.' She sounded puzzled. Maybe she didn't have the keys.

'Go and get help then. Find Kit. He'll know what to do.'

She half turned towards the tunnel to the exit and, for a moment, I thought she might actually get Kit. But then she stopped and whirled back to me with a dancer's spin, full of poise and grace, until the weakness in her injured knee knocked her off-balance. Her body jack-knifed and she swore a stream of wild words that rose into the dark and echoed along the passages.

'I'll never let you out,' she screamed.

And I never for a moment doubted her.

The muscles in my legs trembled again, warning me they'd give way soon. I arranged the heap of broken crates into a precarious seat and lowered myself onto it, trying to work out what she meant to do.

'I saw Talan,' she hissed. 'This morning. Putting you in his boot. When I came back from Freda's. I knew he'd take you here.'

She didn't ask me why Talan had locked me up. I guessed she must have known what he was up to. I didn't think she cared. All the things that mattered had been torn from her. If she hadn't tried to kill me twice, I'd have felt sorry for her.

I gathered my thoughts. *She must have keys. How else would she have got here? But did she have the key to the barred door between us?* The thought of her unlocking it in her half-mad state frightened me. But why? I'd fight her if she did. I'd fight her and I'd win because I was desperate, too and, although I was sore and battered, I had a knee I could trust.

Kelly was still my best hope of getting out. My only hope unless Kit had got my message. Above all, I didn't want her to leave me here to die, killed by the traffickers or from starvation as I hid in the dark passages.

Time to talk. I asked the first question that came to me.

'Where did you get the roofies, Kelly?'

'Plymouth. For Freda.' she said.

She didn't seem surprised I knew.

'Freda?'

'To keep her quiet. At night.'

No wonder Freda had told the Mullins she slept better when Kelly was there.

'You were at the hotel when I arrived, weren't you? In the room behind reception? And when Vivian made me a cup of tea, you put in the roofies. That was how you did it, wasn't it?'

'They owed me money for some cleaning I did. I was waiting for the cheque in the office when you drove in. Vivian made me hang around while she checked you in even though she knew I had to get to Freda's. And after, when she came back and told me you wanted a kettle, I said I'd make you a cup of tea while she wrote my cheque. And I put in the roofies. Clever, wasn't it?'

Her voice was as devoid of colour as her face. We could have been talking about a complicated episode of some TV crime series

– but she was still here and, while she was, I might get her to open the door. 'But then you left,' I said. 'Why was that?'

'I was due at Freda's. Couldn't be late.'

'Of course not.'

'The family check on me. But you know that, Jenifry. Why are you asking these stupid questions?'

'I'm trying to work out what happened. I don't remember, you see.'

'That's what Rohypnol does to you. It stops you remembering and calms you down.'

'So you went to Freda's and… I suppose you drugged her, too.'

'Course.'

I stretched my legs out in front of me. The trembling had stopped. They'd be sore tomorrow and covered with bruises but nothing was damaged.

I'd worked the rest of it out. I'd left the hotel and gone for a walk. Maybe to shake the cravings for cocaine out of my body. Or because I wanted the feeling of fresh air against my skin. Or because the roofies were making me feel weird and I wanted to get out of the small hotel room. I didn't think I'd walked along the cliff path. Kelly had lied about that to confuse me. I'd walked up the road towards the lighthouse. It was the way I walked home from school every day and the road was steep as it left the village, exactly what you'd fancy after a day in the car. A quick, hard walk to the lighthouse. No time for anything longer. Not before night fell.

And I'd broken into the lighthouse. Maybe the roofies had started to space me out and it had seemed like a place of refuge or the rain had started and I'd only wanted shelter.

I kneaded my thigh muscles and wondered what had gone on in Kelly's head during the cagey conversations we'd had since. She must have realised very early on that the roofies had worked and I remembered nothing.

'Once Freda was asleep, I went back to the hotel for you,' she said. 'But you'd vanished. I looked everywhere.'

The old chap leaving the pub had told Talan about a strange woman in the village. It must have been Kelly.

'It started to rain but I still couldn't find you.'

Her calmness was cracking and her voice jagged, rousing the prisoners. One of them cried out. Others hushed him.

I didn't want her to tell me the next bit. How she'd got to the lighthouse and seen its broken door swinging open in the storm. How she'd picked up a bit of its wood and crept up the steps, smashed it into my head and hung me over the edge.

'It doesn't matter now, Kelly,' I said.

'It doesn't matter! How can you say that? How dare you say that! It might not fucking matter to you but he was everything to me. Seb –'

Her wail spiralled out of control. For a moment, I thought she was going to lose it but she clamped her arms round her body and dragged her grief back inside. The cave was silent. They must have heard Kelly's cry. Were they listening as intently as I was, desperately trying to work out what was going on?

The photos of Kelly and Seb on the board in Talan's kitchen. Four moments in time, separated by a few seconds, showing how close they were. You could see it in the way they looked at each other and the way they smiled and the way they kissed. Seb and Kelly. As soon as I'd seen the photos I'd known. Seb and Kelly. Kelly was the girlfriend Seb's family blamed for his accident. She was the lover Mark had barred from Seb's wake.

And I wasn't surprised. It made perfect sense. They were both passionate, creative people. They came from the same background.

It must have been recent, though, because I'd have known if it wasn't. Wouldn't I?

'I didn't know,' I said to her.

'You didn't know.' She spat the words at me. 'How could you not know? Don't worry, I'll tell you. Because you're so fucking full of yourself you don't notice anyone else. You don't listen to anybody else. I couldn't believe it when I saw you at the hotel. Getting out of your flashy car. Stretching your arms up to the sky and yawning. Looking around like you fucking owned the place. And I knew you must have come down for the wake Mark was organising. For Seb's wake. His mother didn't want me at the funeral and Mark wouldn't let me come to the wake. They both said it was my fault. That I should have stopped Seb. But *you*... Mark asked *you* to come...'

Her words came out of her mouth in fragments as broken as my memories and, somehow, as meaningless. Already, it felt a long time ago. And not real. Only now was real, with Kelly bending and rummaging in a bag at her feet. And standing back up with a key in her hand. *Oh, God. This was my chance.*

'You've got the key to this door?'

'Yeah, I've got all the keys. Talan came back and put his uniform on and went out again, so I took the keys and came here.'

She kicked the bag and it jangled with the harsh clink of metal on metal.

'Talan won't do it,' she said. 'He doesn't have the guts. So I'm going to finish what I started on the lighthouse. I was going to throw you over, except you screamed when I hit you and Gregory came out. I hid behind the wall so he couldn't see me. And he couldn't hear you moaning and jabbering about flying. You were out of it but still you wouldn't stop babbling about flying. So I thought I'd give you a chance to see what flying was like. Flying and falling. Like Seb. And I hoped you'd wake up to feel the air racing upwards past you and know you were falling. Know you were going to smash into the ground. Except you'd have landed outside Gregory's window and woken him. I needed time to get away. So I hung you over, frayed the rope and left. I slipped back later but you'd disappeared. You'd fucking disappeared. You'd got away. Like you always do.'

She thrust the key into the padlock. It clattered as she fought to keep her anger under control. I kept my mouth shut, flexing my muscles, preparing to attack when she came through the door.

'Seb. My Seb. He thought you were wonderful. Always going on about you. How fearless you were.' She paused and bowed her head over the padlock for a moment and then raised it and threw her last words at me. 'What a fucking inspiration you were to him.'

There was no point in talking to her but I couldn't help it.

'Kelly. I never meant to encourage Seb to go free running. I was off my head. All that time. I…' The padlock sprang apart and the chain rattled to the ground. Her face was wild with anger. My moment was coming but I mustn't rush it. *Wait*, I told myself. *Wait till she's closer.* I tensed, ready to leap and shove and kick when she burst in. She didn't. Instead, she bent down, reached inside her bag and pulled out a long, dark object.

It was a gun. A twelve-bore shotgun.

Fuck.

Waves of alarm shot along my nerves as she took up the shooting stance. The one Talan had drilled into me on those damp expeditions. Feet shoulder-width apart, one slightly forward, knees bent.

I didn't wait to see how carefully Kelly aimed or how she squeezed the trigger. I leaped for the narrow passageway to the prison cave and rolled inside it. A shot whizzed past my feet as I landed outside the door to the cell. Displaced air rushed down the passage and then the noise blasted everything else from my head. It shattered against the rock and reverberated down the passage. A splintering smash followed by a cry before another shot crashed into the echo of the first. More cries rose from the cell next to me.

Two shots. She'd fired twice. After two shots she'd have to reload. For a moment, we were on equal terms. Only a moment, though, because as soon as she'd reloaded, she'd come after me. She'd do what she should have done in the first place and only fire when she had me trapped with nowhere to go.

I had one chance. Rush out now and fight her. But I couldn't. My body still shook with the dying echoes of the shot and all I could force it to do was peer round the edge of the passage into the stope. She wasn't there. I moved further round and looked out beyond the bars. Still nothing.

A movement on the ground. I was looking too high.

She was a black figure sprawled on the floor of the rock, only visible now because she'd lifted her head. I knew what had happened. She'd taken her time over the first shot, prepared herself, but the second, fired in rage at seeing me leap to safety, had knocked her back and she'd fallen.

We locked eyes. She grabbed the gun and staggered up, slamming her back against the door so that her weight held it tight shut. She broke the gun open and fumbled at the spent cartridges. I had seconds before she reloaded. I stumbled back into the passage, scrabbled on the floor and found the rope I'd seen earlier, grabbed it near the centre and folded it in two. The familiar feel of the nylon was smooth against my skin. I forced myself back out into the stope. Kelly was still fumbling with the gun, her back turned to me.

I poked the loop through and round the outside bar of the door and its frame, threaded the ends of the rope through the loop and pulled as tight as I could, as quickly as I could, so it would hold the door firmly shut. My eyes were tied to the rope. Hers were fixed on the gun. The noise of the barrel clicking shut warned me time was up. As she turned I fled back into the passage, round the corner and out of her sight, my hands gripping the rope ends like a shark's jaw locked into its prey.

She was shut out. Without the ends she couldn't undo the loop holding the door closed. I felt her tug, tentative at first, then a fierce yank that jerked my arms forward while my hands held tight.

Opposite my hiding place, a face rose from the bottom of the barred hole in the prison cave door. They shot me a quick glance through deep brown eyes, then ducked. Someone said a few curt words and the eyes arrived again and then the face of a youngish man with a moustache straggling over his mouth and deep hollows below his cheekbones. He started to speak. I shook my head. Not now. I needed to listen. The man raised his hand, made the shape of a gun and mimed firing it. I jerked my head towards the outside. Towards Kelly. Towards the rope. Trying to tell him I was not the one with the gun. That the rope was all that was protecting us. He nodded, threw a few guttural words over his shoulder, provoking a babble of replies and disappeared.

I waited. Did Kelly have a knife? *Please God don't let her have a knife.*

The minutes went on forever. Until I heard her swear. The clink of the chain wound back round the door, the padlock snapping shut, footsteps fading. The door further down the passage slammed behind her.

She'd gone but how long before she came back with a knife or a saw to cut the rope?

Inside the prison cave, a tight mass of bodies huddled as far from the door as they could, the fluttering flame of a candle casting glimmers of light over their faces. Little details imprinted themselves on my eyes as I looked for the man with the moustache. In one corner, a young woman held an older one tight against her shoulder with hands splayed out as though to protect every bit of her head. At the front, a man with curly grey hair squatted, holding one of the filthy mattresses in front of his little group. Helping him was the man with the moustache.

'Please,' I called. 'Please, I need to talk to you.' He didn't move. I tried again. 'The woman with the gun has gone but she'll come back. Please. I need your help.'

Two hands stretched out from behind him, pushed him out of the way and a woman emerged from the shadows. Tall and upright, she left the frightened huddle, picked up the candle and came towards the door. A headscarf shadowed her features until she was close and raised the candle. Its light flattened her jutting cheekbones and leached the colour from her face. She was an older woman with the shut-in look of the very exhausted but behind the stretched skin of her jaw, her teeth were clenched.

Did she speak English?

'The gun,' I said. 'The woman with the gun.' I mimed the gun.

'Eisha,' she said.

Eisha? She didn't speak English. She hadn't understood.

'I am Eisha.' She turned and beckoned to someone in the mass behind. A gangly lad emerged from the shadows and came to join her. 'He is Farid.' No expression broke the rigid lines of the youngster's face. Eisha put an arm round his shoulders.

'We are from Afghanistan.' She spoke quickly now, nudging Farid until he took the candle she thrust into his hands as she rummaged in a bag round her waist.

'I am a nurse. I have papers.'

There was no time for this.

302

'I'm Jen. Jenifry. My name is Jenifry.' The words tumbled out in an ungainly muddle. 'I need –'

'We worked with your army.'

'Please. Later. I will help you later. I am a prisoner, too. I don't have keys. The gun. You heard the gun. She will come back and kill me.'

'Where are we?'

'A tin mine. An old tin mine.'

She looked confused.

'In Cornwall.' I said urgently.

'Cornwall?'

'In England.'

For the first time Farid's face changed. England meant something to him. He turned to tell the others. Voices rose in response.

'Please,' I shouted over them. 'Please, Eisha. Farid. All of you. I will help you. I promise. But first we must stop the woman with the gun. Then we will escape before the men who shut you in come back.'

I'd have said anything to get them to help but I meant this promise. Underneath the roiling waves of fear that Kelly would return before I could explain what I needed them to do, I was angry as fuck. Horrified. How could anyone treat people like this?

'Tell me,' Eisha said. 'Tell me and I will translate for the others.'

I explained as quickly and simply as I could, all the time clenching the rope tight in my hands. The man with the moustache and the grey-haired man who had held the mattress came forward as Eisha translated and asked her questions in a language I couldn't identify.

In the end, they nodded. I thought they'd understood. Farid reached out for the rope and I passed it through the hole in the door and went back into the stope, only checking to see they'd pulled it tight.

I scrambled up into the raise again, taking care to upend the tower of crates with a last kick and wedged myself once more in the passage above the stope. Every bit of my body protested. Every cut and bruise screamed that enough was enough.

Kelly was gone a long time. It was probably only minutes but it was longer than I'd dared to expect. Long enough to hope that Kit had got my message and the cavalry might arrive. Long enough to fear my muscles might grow tired and slip. To fear Eisha might not have understood properly or that the men might not do exactly as she'd said. The waiting was unbearable. Ideas dropped like heavy stones into my mind and broke my concentration. I might never see the sun again. Might never leave this hole buried underground. Everything depended on Eisha and Farid and the others. I wished I'd asked them all their names. It would be good to know whose hands held my future. *Focus*, I told myself. *Listen for Kelly.* But my mind wandered, wondering where they'd come from. How they'd ended up in here. My hand slipped, damp with sweat and blood. *How much longer could I hold on? How much longer would she be?* Already I could feel the adrenalin oozing away. Stabs from my muscles warned me they were near the end. *Think of something else.* I thought of Eisha. Travelling alone with the teenage Farid. Maybe her work with the army had put her in danger when they pulled out so she'd had no choice but to flee, leaving everything behind. They'd all lost everything except maybe some hope that the future could be different. It wouldn't be unless we got out. *Keep holding on.* Their escape was as much in my hands as mine was in theirs. Our life stories ran intertwined through this narrow gap in time and none of us knew what lay the other side.

The clatter of the big door down the passage as it was unlocked jerked me back to the present. Kelly made no effort to be quiet, kicking the bars still held tight shut by the loop of rope when she reached the entrance to the stope. Her bag jangled as she threw it to the ground. I sensed her rage. It pulsated through the dead air. A beam of light stabbed the dark. She'd got a torch. A head torch, I thought, as the sound of the chain tumbling to the floor rang out. Her hands were free.

Then came the noise of sawing. I gripped the rock tighter, despite the pain from the cuts in my fingers. Kelly had found a hacksaw somewhere. I peered down. The rope, stretched round the corner, trembled with the force of her wild, jagged cuts. Eisha started to shriek. Joined swiftly by bellowing male voices. *Make a noise,* I'd said, *as much as you can, as soon as she starts cutting the rope.* And they did me proud, hammering the door with fists and throwing empty cans and stones through the hole in the cell door, to bounce off the rock and clatter into the stope. But it was their screams that made the most noise. The cries torn from their depths echoed round the mine. Even I, who knew the plan, shivered. Kelly faltered when the noise began. The rope stopped vibrating for a few seconds then she carried on sawing as though deaf to the cacophony around her.

The rope slashed from side to side despite the hands holding it tight. Nothing could resist the sharp teeth of the saw. A few seconds later it fell to the ground. She'd cut through the last strand and now nothing prevented her from entering the stope. The prisoners' screams masked the sound of the barred door opening. I waited though, thanking the gods that Kelly had worn a torch because I could see from the stillness of its light that she wasn't moving. Maybe she'd paused at the threshold, letting herself anticipate the moment when she'd hunt me down through the little passages, blasting holes in my body when I ran out of places to hide.

But my moment was coming. The most dangerous moment.

The moment when my timing had to be perfect. The beam of light jolted. She moved into the stope and the prisoners' screams and the terror flowing through my body became pure fuel, ignited, and roared through my blood.

At the last moment, I thought she sensed me above her. Or that the movement as I tensed my body, ready to push down, sent a warning breeze to disturb the hair on the top of her head. She began to look up, suddenly understanding that I wasn't at the end of the rope but she was too late.

I burst out of the dark hole above her head and knocked her flying. The gun scuttled into the dark. I tensed, ready for her next move, but she lay motionless at my feet, a black shadow in the dimness. Instinct told me to stamp on her knee, kick her, punch her face, but something about her stillness stopped me. She shifted, a slight curl of her body round itself, and moaned. My assault had knocked the rage out of her, flattened her and left her quivering like an empty bag rustling in the wind. I thought she was weeping. The violence and anger seeped away until only the cries of the refugees echoing round the mine were a reminder of what had gone before. Her mouth opened. I thought she was speaking but I couldn't hear her.

I knew it was stupid but I knelt and put my ear to her mouth.

'My knee,' she said. 'My knee. My knee.'

I picked up the shotgun, gleaming gently in the light from the raise, broke it open and removed the cartridges; then I went back to Kelly and forced her body against the bars at the entrance to the stope. She shrieked. I thought about tying her up but I couldn't bring myself to prise her hands from her knee. Even between her fingers the joint looked all wrong. She wasn't going anywhere. It was over. But I felt no joy, not even relief, just a grey sadness that things had ended the way they had.

I picked up Kelly's bag, with all the keys rattling and clinking at the bottom and went to let the refugees out. Their cries stopped as they saw me. Farid, still clutching the end of the rope, smiled. My fingers hurt too much to unlock the door so I posted the keys through the bars and let Eisha try while I leaned against the rock and bit my lips shut to stop me shouting at her to hurry up. The traffickers could come back at any moment. We weren't safe yet.

When we emerged into a Cornish afternoon, the air sweet with moisture and the only sound the rush of the river swollen by storms far down in the valley, the man with the moustache knelt on the ground and dug his fingers into the peaty earth, dragging up great handfuls and rubbing and smelling it.

Even here, we weren't safe. I hurried them away. Up the valley. Away from the main roads. Until we were far away from the mine. I stopped in a clearing, half hidden among the scraggly oak trees, and sat.

The man with the moustache came over and sat by me. I shook his soil-covered hand and said thank you. Asked him his name. He was Hassan. From Syria. A farmer. The older man who'd held the mattress was Jamal, also from Syria. He'd had a shop. He introduced me to his wife, Fatima, who stood under a tree and gazed at the grey sky through its naked branches, reaching out every now and then to touch its bark. I understood. If it hadn't been for the pain in my fingers, I might well have started stroking leaves and tree bark myself.

I stood up and tried to ask them all their names and where they'd come from. Most told me. Some smiled and repeated my name back to me. But a few slipped away before I could get to them and gradually the others followed. Eisha and Farid were the last. I didn't notice them go but they must have because when the cavalry finally arrived, I was all alone.

Twenty-Eight

A few days later, another boatload of refugees was rescued in the Mediterranean. I watched it on TV. They huddled together, damp and fearful, their worn out clothing hanging in shreds. It was like seeing someone's story backwards: Eisha and Farid had lived the same experience. Fear had sent them on the same terrible journey. They must have faced the same hardship and felt the same despair, along with Hassan and Jamal and Fatima, all of them. The relief I'd seen on their faces in the quiet valley outside the mine as they'd wandered round in the sweetness of the open air stayed with me.

If only it had lasted.

In between the news, I watched the daytime soaps and chat shows, swallowed antibiotics to combat the infection in my fingers, and dozed. From time to time, I'd wake to find I was watching cartoons with Rosa sitting next to me. From time to time, the police would come to visit.

They'd arrived at the mine with Kit. He'd got my message as he left a long meeting with the bank in Plymouth, gone straight to the nearest police station and told them what I'd said, then left and come to the mine himself. The police had made the necessary connections and by the time he arrived, a posse of armed police had already found the mine empty except for Kelly and were making their way up the valley. They found me and went on to pick up the refugees, one by one. Their freedom was short-lived.

I lied from the start, concocting a story that omitted all mention of Nick. I told them I'd been looking for Ma and gone to Talan's house to ask for help, interrupting him and some others in the middle of organising the transport of the slaves to the mine. They'd seized me and locked me in the mine. I'd hidden in the shaft above the stope and overpowered Kelly when she came. Kit confirmed the first part. Talan wasn't around to confirm or deny the second part and Kelly refused to speak to anyone.

For a while, the police came regularly to ask if I'd remembered anything else and to show me photos of possible villains. Gradually their interviews tailed off and when they picked Talan up in France, they stopped coming.

I thought about going back to London, to the flat I no longer needed to sell, but I didn't. I stopped watching TV and I went for longer and longer walks. I found a park with swings and took Rosa every day while Kit and Sofija oversaw the final work on Tregonna. We started to talk in the evenings and Sofija helped me find a lawyer to fight for Eisha and Farid and the others to stay in the country.

The infection in my fingers went and the cuts healed. I walked past Nick's cottage and peered in through the windows. It was empty. I wondered if he'd emptied it or if there was a police department devoted to clearing up after undercover officers. I asked Rachel where he'd gone and she said family commitments had called him away urgently. She wasn't bothered as he'd paid up to the end of the tenancy.

A few weeks later, around the time when my fingers were finally healed, the police came again. They were going to charge Kelly with attempted murder. They knew she'd fired the gun. They'd swabbed her fingers and found the residue. And Kelly was going to plead guilty.

It should have been the closing of the circle she'd opened when she tried to kill me on the lighthouse. But it was a circle within a bigger circle. One that my passion for risk had begun, that had swept Grid and Seb up into its arc. It had swept up Kelly, too. And it didn't feel finished.

I should have been happy but I wasn't. I was stuck.

I forced myself to go back to the mine, hoping that I might undo some strands of the web holding me tight to Tregonna and Cornwall. I didn't go in. The entrances were shut and locked, with remnants of police tape blowing in the breeze. I hoped it would stay closed.

Then I went onto the moors and retraced my mad escape with Nick. I climbed down into the gully and collected my equipment, then sat at the bottom and thought for a long time. Mainly about climbing, which was somehow also about myself. Afterwards, I followed the path down to the sea where I'd said goodbye to Nick.

Something in me hadn't thought the goodbye was final. I'd thought he'd get in touch. It might be forbidden, against all regulations and so on, but the Nick Crawford I'd run across the moors with wouldn't have cared about that. I felt there was something between us. A connection. Something worth exploring. But he must have felt differently.

It was a long walk and I was starving when I got back to Tregonna. I made myself a stack of sandwiches – peanut butter, crisp lettuce and a dab of marmite on granary bread – and ate the lot, sitting at the kitchen table and tracing the lines and dents that pockmarked its surface with my fingers. I could feel every ridge and hollow. The doctor had stitched the cuts on my hand

and only narrow seams of scar tissue showed where they had been. I was rubbing Ma's herbal oils and creams into them and I knew that with time, they'd fade into nothing. The nerves and skin had healed but climbing down the ridge again had shown me how weak the muscles had become.

I went to the door between the kitchen and the hall, reached up and planted my fingers on the top of the frame. It was covered with greasy dust but I didn't care. I pulled myself up and hung using the front three fingers of both hands. *Breathe*, I thought. *Breathe and count ten seconds.* Except I couldn't. Five was the most I could do before my fingers screamed with pain. Still, it wasn't bad. I ran through a series of exercises using my fingers to support my weight in different crimps and holds.

Kit opened the door and ran into my hanging body. I crumpled to the floor. Kit laughed, then creased his eyes and looked at my hands.

'How are they?'

'They're good. Or bad. Months of not exercising, you know. But the strength will come back.'

'Go carefully.'

'When I start climbing again, you mean.' It wasn't a question.

He nodded.

'I will be careful.'

We smiled at each other.

'I might have to clean that door frame though,' I said.

He reached under the sink and threw me a cloth.

'About time you earned your keep.'

'Knock it off the money you owe me.' I threw the cloth back at him.

The stress and worry had rolled off him since Pa had ridden to his rescue. It had, I thought, mended something in him that

311

had been broken for a while. He was back to being the brother I remembered. Well, almost.

'About the money,' he said. 'The sale of the land will complete in a couple of weeks. And then I'll pay you back.'

'There's no need, Kit.'

'No, listen. I want to tell you what's happening. The debts will be paid off first, including the money I owe you, and Tregonna will be finished. There'll be some left over. Pa wanted to give it to Ma but she's refused.'

'She's been in touch?'

'Her solicitors wrote to his.'

Ma had come back to Tregonna and packed the morning I'd got out of the mine. By the time Kit and I had returned from the police station, she'd left again. We'd had nothing but a postcard from her since, saying she was fine and not coming back. That was all.

'You keep the money, Kit. It'll help you get the centre started.'

'I'm not sure if we're going to do it.'

I looked at him rinsing the cloth in the sink.

'Pa's giving me some money. He wants you to have the same. The rest he's put aside in case Ma changes her mind. I'm going to take the money because it'll buy me time. After everything that's happened, I'm not sure I want to stay here. It was a dream I had but maybe it should have stayed a dream. Sofija thinks I should stick with it. She says I don't see things through and maybe she's right, but I'm still not sure if running Tregonna is what I want to do.'

He got up and paced around the kitchen restlessly, fiddling with things, lining up the pots on the shelf above the sink. I took pity on him and changed the subject.

'Where have you been?' I asked.

'Just at Gregory's.'

'How is he?'

'Quiet. Missing Ma, I think, and cut up about Pip, although he doesn't say much. We told him Pip was dead before they threw him down the shaft. We're going to bury his ashes. Will you come? Gregory would like to see you.'

'Of course.'

I went to Seb's grave where I tried to find the words to tell him how I felt but he'd been the one with magic in his tongue and all I could dredge up was *I'm sorry, truly sorry.*

I packed the rest of Ma's stuff up to wait until she sent for it and using account details from an old bank statement, I sent her ten thousand pounds from the money Kit had paid me back. In the box for the payment reference, I wrote *For your friend's voyage, XXX.* I figured no one but Ma and a computer would read it.

So that was that. I'd been everywhere except the lighthouse. I knew I should go back there but I couldn't. Mainly because I no longer wanted to remember what had happened between me and Kelly. Funny really. After all that time desperately chasing after memories that floated in the far corners of my mind and burst as soon as I reached out for them.

In the end, I had to go. Kit got Pip's ashes back from the crematorium and I could think of no reason to let him and Sofija take them to Gregory without me. We went on a watercolour sort of day. The kind that Ma had painted for a while, using so much water the colours ran into each other and lost definition. There was no wind. Everything was still and a light mist coated the sky, the sea, the cliffs and the grass. Even the white of the lighthouse seemed dulled and I walked past it without a flicker of emotion.

'We've brought you Pip's ashes,' Kit said when Gregory came out of his cottage. He held out the plain cardboard box that had seemed more appropriate than the undertaker's range of cardboard tubes decorated with flowers and birds. Pip was a plain sort of dog. Gregory didn't take the box.

'Do you want us to bury them for you?' This was Sofija. 'Kit's got a spade in the car.'

Gregory looked doubtful.

'We could throw them into the sea.' I said.

Gregory looked even more doubtful.

'Yer ma would know best.'

This was true. Ma would have come up with some mad scheme and justified it with an overlay of mythology, then carried us all along with her enthusiasm. I realised I missed her.

'She'd have told you to give him back to the earth, Gregory,' I said. 'What's in the box is nothing but the remnants of his body. His spirit is already running along his favourite paths. This is only our way of saying goodbye to him.'

I felt a bit of a fool saying all that but I did sort of believe it. Kit squeezed my arm and I felt less stupid.

'We should let him go in his favourite place,' Sofija said. 'Where would you say that was, Gregory?'

Gregory thought for an age. 'He went everywhere.'

'Well, maybe we should all take a bit and…' Sofija looked at us both for support as a breeze rippled in from the sea. She laughed. 'There you go. The wind will help.'

'He liked the lighthouse, Pip did. Often came up with me.'

'Perfect! We'll let his ashes go up there.'

I trudged up after the others but once I came out onto the viewing platform, I was surprisingly fine. The lighthouse had been there for too long and seen too many violent storms to retain anything of that Friday night when Kelly tried to kill me. The wind and rain scoured every corner clean of moss, spider webs and memories. It was just bricks and cement and a fabulous view.

Afterwards, I went back to Gregory's cottage while Kit and Sofija locked the new door. I put the kettle on and found myself staring once again at the strange collection of things hanging from the row of hooks above his sink; things most people would have thrown away. I reached up for a spare mug and dislodged one of the postcards of lighthouses. It fluttered to the ground and Gregory caught it.

'That reminds me. This came for you,' he said. He rummaged among the pile of local newspapers by his chair and held out a postcard to me.

On the front was a picture of the inside of a bar. Old-fashioned. Wood and raffia bar stools and brick walls hung with glazed plates and bowls. But it was the ceiling that caught my eye. It was golden-brown like freshly baked bread and as intricate as layers of lace on a wedding dress. The description on the front said simply *The Cork Bar at Alajar* and when I looked at the back, the print said the same and added the information that Alajar was in Andalusia. There were only four other words – handwritten. Not many, even for a postcard, although the angular writing filled the space. *Wish you were here*, it said. *Wish you were here.*

There was no address so it must have been delivered by hand or sent in an envelope. I went to ask Gregory but stopped. There was a reason for all this secrecy. Nick's safety depended on it. No one must know who he really was.

Why had he sent it? I thought I knew. I thought it was an invitation and the thought made me smile inside. I wondered if I was going to accept it.

Acknowledgements

I started writing *On The Edge* before I really knew how to write a book and came close to giving up several times as I slowly acquired the necessary skills to create something that a reader might enjoy. However, two things kept me going. First, there was something about Jen and her exploits that wouldn't let me abandon the book and, second, the help of so many people.

Huge thanks to all my writer friends who have encouraged and supported me over the years, who have picked me up and dried my tears during the difficult times, who have rejoiced with me when I've had good news, who have been ever willing to help with research, who have beta-read and offered wise and tactful advice. I couldn't have done it without you all: William Angelo, Shell Bromley, Thea Burgess, Sandra Davies, Philippa East, Fiona Erskine, Martin Gilbert, Karen Ginnane, Katherine Hetzel, Jules Ironside, Arabella Murray, Janette Owen, Matthew Willis, Lorraine Wilson and all the other wonderful writers who hang out at the Den of Writers (https://www.denofwriters.com). Big thank you to Alex Cotter for holding my hand during the worst of my stressful moments.

I was lucky enough to meet Debi Alper and Emma Darwin via their Self-Editing Course early on in my writing adventure. I will always be grateful for their eye-opening course which, besides knocking a lot of writing fundamentals into my head, also introduced me to the fabulous resource for writers that is Emma's blog, *The Itch of Writing.* A massive thank you to Debi Alper for her editing, her guidance and her wisdom but mainly for being a very special person.

Thank you to my publisher Verve Books, not only for plucking me out of the slush pile and for loving *On The Edge* but also for being unfailingly supportive as I navigate my voyage to publication. Thank you Claire Watts, Lisa Gooding, Paru Rai and the rest of the team. A particular thank you to Jenna Gordon for making my day back in October 2020 and for understanding *On The Edge* so well. Thank you to Jennie for your insightful editorial suggestions, to Elsa for the glorious cover and to Hollie McDevitt for her enthusiasm and expertise with the marketing of *On The Edge.* Hopefully I might get to meet you all in real life soon!

Thank you to Jon Garside of The British Mountaineering Council for reading the climbing sections of *On The Edge* and correcting my mistakes. Any remaining errors are entirely my own fault.

A big thank you to all my friends and family for your love and support. Thank you Rosina, Tara, Dorcas, Jonathan, Madeleine and Stephen for reading *On The Edge* and being so encouraging. Thank you to Oliver for helping me with everything technical. And thank you to my mum, Cilla, for getting me started in the first place. I only wish you had been along for the ride. I know you would have loved it.

A very, very special thank you to my sister, Nikki, who has read every single word I've written (and some of them more than once) and found something positive to say about everything. I couldn't have done it without you.

Finally to my husband, Alex. There are times in everybody's life when they need a hero. I'm lucky enough to have one around all the time.

Author's Note

Although many of the places in *On The Edge* exist in real life, readers who are familiar with the area around St Austell and Fowey will have noticed that many of them don't. They are instead amalgamations of places I have visited and loved in Cornwall that insisted on being included.

A LETTER FROM JANE

Dear Reader,

On The Edge is my debut novel and all the time I was writing I imagined you, the reader, sitting in your kitchen, or on a train, or maybe curled up in bed on a Sunday morning with a cup of tea while it poured down outside, engrossed in Jen's story. I loved writing the book and if you have had half as much pleasure from reading it then my job is done.

On The Edge is the first in the Jen Shaw series. The second is due out in autumn 2022. If you'd like to be the first to know the exact date and have a sneak preview of Jen's next adventure, then sign up to my Newsletter at **jane-jesmond.com/contact**. There'll also be news of special offers, details of events and other exclusive content as well as interviews with other writers.

And finally, I'd love to know what you thought of *On The Edge*. Seriously, your opinion matters much more to me than any reviewer's. Please let me know. I'm on Twitter **@AuthorJJesmond**, on Facebook as **Jane Jesmond Author** or you can send me an email at **JaneJesmond@ gmail.com**. If you enjoyed *On The Edge*, please tell your friends and, if you have time, leave a review or a rating on Amazon, Goodreads or Bookbub. It makes a big difference.

Best wishes and thank you,

Jane

To be the first to hear about new books and exclusive deals from Verve Books, sign up to our newsletters:

vervebooks.co.uk/signup

VERVE
BOOKS